PATCHING TIME

KATHLEEN CURTIN

Published by Kathleen Curtin
spleodrach
Email: kurtin@orange.fr
Twitter: Kathleen curtin@kitybern
Facebook: Patching Time-Kathleen Curtin

Copyright © Kathleen Curtin
All rights reserved. No part of this book may be reproduced, scanned, or distributed in any printed or electronic form without permission except in the case of brief quotations embodied in critical articles and reviews.
Editors: Ellen M. Curtin and Majella Flynn
Photo © Archangel, Shutter stock
Design: www.emmagraves.co.uk
Formatter: Yvonne Betancourt - www.ebook-format.com

ISBN: 979-10-96434-00-8
ISBN: 979-10-96434-01-5

Acknowledgements

A bucket of thank yous to a special person, Aileen, my sister, whose invaluable advice, artistic flair and endless encouragement has made my work better. Thanks also to your husband Bruce for his assistance on many fronts.

Majella, your stalwart loyalty and investment of time and skills in my projects are without equal. I am forever indebted to you and your husband Paul.

There is a warm place in my heart for exceptional friends who have grounded and heartened me in countless ways: Eilis O'Mahony, Joan Cahill, Breda Crowley, Mary and Ian Stoyle, Mary and Dan Kelleher, Kevin and Anne Long, Tim Flynn, Maggie and Philip Mohally, Eddy and Triona Fitzgerald - and all your children, spouses and partners who contributed their time and energy.

I am deeply appreciative of the continued support of some great people; Christele Autin, Carmela Barloy, Sylvie Brunet, Christine Lemorvan, Ines Martins, Agnes Quelin.

Go raimh maith agat Monsieur Mauduit for your engagement and motivation.

Thanks Madame Lecorvec, the ever patient ear.

I am very grateful to Raymond at UCC Geography Department for making invaluable links.

A salute to Professor William Smyth for being a gifted teacher and inspiring a love of research and curiosity about people and place.

The tips and sincere interest of students and enthusiasts have helped enormously: Anita, Annie, Beatrice, Catherine, Christine V., Edouard, Elaine, Isabelle, Karen, Kristel F., Madeleine, Maura, Marieline, Muriel, Marie-Pierre, Norma, Sandrine M., Sylvie M.

To family and cousins, near and far, MERCI!

To all the readers and book people: every story of mine that you have ever bought, read, or spoken about has given me great pleasure and makes it all worthwhile.

This book is dedicated to Huguette Jarrosson.
Huguette, a few words are small recompense for your unfailing guidance and wisdom through the years. Your courage will forever inspire and your light always shine brightly - there is nobody quite like you.

History is personal to each and every one of us, lending many colours to the truth. Thus, while the past echoes all around casting light and shadow, we are imperfect conductors of its music. What counts is true love, boundless and ageless, helping us stitch it all together to make up happier sounds – patching time and making it rhyme.

Kinsale, County Cork, June 4th

A gloved hand stifled Lily's scream to a helpless yelp. A knife blade flashed before her eyes and the cool metal pressed against her throat.

"Now, you listen carefully, Lily Casey," a deep voice growled in her ear. "I've already warned you, but you just don't seem to get it. So I'm telling you for the last time – keep your nose out of things. Do you understand?"

Lily was paralysed, only aware of the sound of the man's voice and the strong smell of sweat from his body.

"Do you understand?" he repeated.

She nodded.

"Because if you don't, your daughter will pay the price with her life, and that's a promise," he turned the knife and caressed her neck with the tip.

She nodded again, fiercely.

"Good," he sneered and shoved her away from him.

Lily fell over a chair and brought it clattering to the ground. Her right knee struck the tiled floor. For several seconds, she stayed immobile – then a door banged and she scrambled to her feet painfully, keeping a hand to her chest.

The place had fallen silent – he had gone. Her legs were still wobbly and barely held her upright in the middle of the small utility room, surrounded by mops, brooms and cleaning products.

"Oh my God, oh my God," she wept out loud. Genie was in danger – what would she do? Lily held her head, rocking it from side to side. This was awful, it couldn't be happening to her.

She tried to steady her nerves, but failed as shock waves kept rising. Her daughter was alone and at risk. 'I have to get home and make sure Genie is safe,' Lily threw off the blue overalls and put on her jacket. She then hurried, limping slightly, into the reception hall.

The mirrored walls showed off different shapes and forms shifting in the dim lighting. Every shadow made her jump. 'Get me out of here, quick,' Lily buttoned up her light rain jacket, her trembling fingers clumsily completing what should have been a simple task. A light flickered and she turned sharply only to stumble and trip over her laces. It took several efforts to retie them. Straightening, Lily looked towards the security lodge. Ryan's warehouse offices changed security men all the time; every month there seemed to be different faces. But Johnny was friendlier and had been working there a couple of months. Where had he been when she'd been held at knife-point? Shouldn't Johnny have seen or heard something?

"Ah, Johnny?" Lily called to him.

A small blocky man sitting behind the security desk put down the *Classic Cars* magazine he had been poring over, "Are you off, Lily?"

"I am, but – amm – thought I heard some noise in the storage room area. Is there somebody else on duty with you?"

Johnny laughed, "You're only messing with me. There's nobody here but the two of us and I don't believe in ghosts. Though in this dark building, I wouldn't blame anyone for imagining things."

"What about the late worker?"

"Who are you talking about?"

"A small, slightly built fellow – works on the third floor at some sort of administrative job. He's there at all hours."

Johnny screwed up his face, "Can't say who he is. What's his name?"

"I don't know, but he wears a grey suit."

"There are a lot of grey suits on the administrative floor."

Lily had noticed the grey-suited man because he usually worked long after the others had gone home. She had often heard him walking in the corridor; his tipped shoes made a distinctive sound. There was something odd about him – he mixed with nobody and his office was bare apart from his computer and phone. It might be that he was up to no good and behind some of the bad business that she'd got tangled up in? He could have been the man with the knife.

"Lily, are you alright?" Johnny got off his swivel chair and leaned over the desk towards her.

Lily took off her glasses and cleaned them. Inquiring further was too chancy and would only give her more trouble. Whoever had put the knife to her throat might be listening. "Can't see a thing, it's hard to keep them clean. Good night so, Johnny."

"Good night, Lily. You'll need your umbrella in this awful weather, it's like the middle of winter," Johnny pressed a button to open the gates and took up his magazine again.

Once out on the street, Lily ran as fast as she could down Pier Road. It was foggy and a heavy mist was falling. The lapping water and flapping of sails did nothing to reassure her; anybody might be waiting to pounce from one of those moored boats or yachts. Every rattling flag pole made her hop with fright and quicken her step.

It had all started a few months before because of interfering to help Martin and Margaret, her colleagues on the morning shift. They had both sunk themselves in debt with a nasty, illegal money lender. Everyone knew Séan Mullane was in that business, but he'd been ill and keeping a low profile. Martin and Margaret had been desperate and had borrowed from an outsider. Word had it that the competing lender came from Cork City and was cutting into Mullane's territory. He was known by the nickname The Bishop. However, no sooner had she gotten involved to sort it out than the names of other lending victims started cropping up, and that's when it had seemed a good idea to encourage them to report the financial scamming problem to the management. Nobody had the courage to report the scam – and in the end, Lily had told the management herself. Because none of her co-workers had been willing to come forward with information due to intimidation, management did not take Lily's report seriously and the investigation had gone no further. However, since Lily reported to management a few weeks earlier, a threatening note had turned up under a duster in her cleaning trolley. She immediately went to the Gardaí to report the note. The Gardaí calmed Lily down and assured her that they were investigating. But when they asked her for the actual blackmail note, she was unable to produce it. It had vanished from her bag. How silly and foolish that had made her look in the Garda Síochana station.

There was no point in going back to the Gardaí, Lily thought, as they wouldn't believe her or do anything. Why should they take her word for it? It wasn't worth risking her daughter's life by reporting it. Anyway, she'd been told that apparently there were thousands of illegal money lending agents operating all over Cork City and County and the Gardaí hadn't the resources to deal with the racketeering.

Lily pushed the red wooden door of number 26. That was another thing – it wasn't safe living in a place where the main door was often unlocked. Residents were so careless – everyone and anyone could come in.

"Genie," Lily called as she took the steps of the stairs two at a time. "Genie," she reached the fourth floor flat, fumbled with the key in the lock and flung open the door.

Her daughter was standing by the window, but didn't turn around.

"Genie, are you okay?" Lily dropped her bag and went to her.

"I'm fine," Genie's eyes were puffed.

"Genie, were you crying?"

"I lost my football, that's all."

Lily let her breath out; her twelve-year-old daughter was always losing or misplacing things, and labelling her name on garments and football gear had become the usual practice. They had even put her name on the football itself with a special marker designed for that purpose.

"Don't worry, if it was in the school yard it might turn up again."

Genie didn't answer and kept her hands in her pockets.

An uneasy thought came to Lily. Some of the school children played in Ryan's warehouse yard, and although it was off bounds with KEEP OUT signs everywhere, some local teenagers ignored the signage. "Genie – did you lose it in Ryan's yard?"

"I just went to practise my shots," Genie blurted out. "But I didn't stay because there was a fight in one of the sheds – a man was doing something to a woman. I was afraid and ran away. I lost the ball climbing over the wall."

"Did you recognise any of them?"

Genie shook her head, "But I saw the man's face."

Lily grasped her daughter's arm, "Listen, Genie, I will go back to the yard to find the ball. You stay here. Keep the door locked and don't open it to anyone."

Lily hated frightening Genie more than necessary, but they couldn't take any chances. She ran along the quays and only slowed down on reaching Ryan's yard. The large iron gates were open and the sound of commotion filled the yard. There was an ambulance, Garda cars, and a large crowd had gathered. Lily recognised Peter Hartnett, the father of a girl in Genie's class.

"Peter, what's going on?"

Peter rubbed his forehead, "Terrible, they found a woman's body."

The blood drained from Lily, "Who was it?"

"Somebody said her name was Mary Sheehan —" Peter stopped, "oh, I'm sorry — do you know her?"

Lily swallowed, "Not very well."

"I heard she may have overdosed. Lily, are you alright?"

But Lily was already running for the gate, "I have to go, Peter — have to go."

She'd only spoken to Mary a few times. The woman had been new to the cleaning team and had worked on a different shift. And now Mary was dead. Genie had seen a man doing something to a woman in one of the yard sheds, Lily thought. Mary's death was no overdose, but criminal homicide, and Genie's life may too be in danger.

Lily didn't stop until she came to the building entrance. The door was slightly open and she banged it firmly after her. She climbed the stairs huffing and puffing this time and rested at the top to catch her breath.

"Oh my God!" Lily screamed as she saw the Primero ball outside the apartment door. Lily turned the white leather football around — 'GENIE CASEY' was printed in bold black ink. Somebody had circled the name several times with a red marker. She took her handkerchief, spat on it, and tried to rub off the red circles. It was an ordinary marker and wiped off easily enough. Lily decided right then and there — they couldn't stay in Kinsale anymore. She would have to explain the gravity of the situation to Genie, enough for her to understand, and at the same time filter some of the details to avoid terrifying her young daughter. But where would they go to?

Late supper was a solemn and silent affair. Neither of them had an appetite for the tomato and tuna salad. They washed up quickly afterwards. Then Lily went to stand beside her daughter who was gazing out at the harbour. The quay was illuminated and lights glimmered on the water. Lily knew Genie was sad and angry about her decision to move again. They'd been happy in Kinsale, but that was over.

'*Go home, Lily, you have to go home.*'

"What was that, Genie, did you say something?"

"No, Mum."

Lily wiped her damp hands on the front of her skirt. '*Go home, Lily, go to Killdoe – Killdoe –*' there was that voice again. It sounded like Granda. She put her palms together and for the first time in years said a little prayer.

1

Kent Station, Cork City, August 24th

"What time is it, Genie, are we late?"

"Don't know."

Lily swung around towards her daughter. Oh what was the use? Genie would be like that for the whole trip and being narky back wasn't going to help. Lily gulped in some air, making a valiant effort at doing a running entrance through the station doors, and although out of breath and laden down with luggage, made it in double quick time.

Lily dropped her load, "Watch the bags, Genie, while I get our tickets. And will you put the football away, this is no place to be bouncing it."

Her daughter slouched on the first bench and rested her feet on the ball. Lily frowned; she hadn't had the heart to tell Genie to leave the football behind in Kinsale.

She made her way to the ticket office, grateful that there wasn't any queue. But there were always unexpected hitches like that when travelling and it was better to leave nothing to chance. Still, the station was very quiet; there was just a handful of people and all of them appeared to be taking their time on this lazy afternoon. She walked past the automatic ticket distributors; one of these days, she might ask Genie to show her how to use them.

"Could I have two singles for Tralee, please?"

A young woman inside the office mumbled the price.

A small fortune, Lily said to herself, opening her purse. "Is the train going at five past two on time?"

It was difficult to catch the woman's words through the glass window, but Lily understood 'yes'.

Being suspicious of this single piece of information and distrustful of timetable panels, she looked around her for further assurance. The Station Master stood nearby with his arms folded.

"Is the Tralee train on time, sir?"

He looked at her, took off his cap and scratched his head. She wasn't sure if it were the formality of her question or its nature that caused such deep reflection.

"There's a thirty minute delay, madam, 'twill be going soon from platform two."

Huh, just as she'd suspected, there would be no train at five past two. "Why so – why is it late, sir? Is there a problem?"

He put his cap back on again, "Oh, it's hardly late at all. There is no problem, nothing to be worried about. You'll be there in time enough. Tralee, is it? We'll have you there in plenty time. Don't forget, you change trains at Mallow. It's the train coming down from Dublin that's late and the one leaving Mallow must wait for those passengers on the Dublin train."

Lily didn't lose time trying to make sense of his explanation, "But we have a bus to catch after in Tralee, sir."

"Oh, the bus will wait, madam, it has to wait for the passengers from the Dublin train. No need to worry," he patted her shoulder.

That old feeling came back, bringing with it words she'd often heard growing up: 'be happy with your lot – take it or leave it, but that's all you're getting.'

That's when she felt the urge to stock up her collection of sweets and to drink horrible tea out of a paper cup. Her daughter was holding her own bag of treats that had been stashed away earlier in the day. Lily planked herself down on the bench beside her. She wasn't at ease and couldn't help feeling that someone was watching them. Although there was no evidence to support her feeling, it didn't stop her from being aware of her surroundings. A slight twitch of Genie's lips was enough to make Lily stiffen and move into high alert mode.

Her feet tapped impatiently; the damp day and coldness of the station seeped through Lily's bones. She regretted being out of sorts today. Usually there was nothing more enjoyable for her than watching people, and there was no better place to do it than at a station. It was fascinating looking on at unknown lives, trying to guess who this one and that one was and wondering about their story.

If she'd been put under the spotlight a few short weeks before, her reply would have been simple: 'I'm Lily Casey and I'm just a cleaning lady. I work for Euro Cleaners, outsourced to Dawson Services, and in turn outsourced to Blarney & Lee. So today, I'm not sure who pays me really, but I get the money. I'm not certain either if Euro means the currency or the continent itself. On their brochure, it says 'Euro Cleaners: at your service – for a day – for a night.' It's their way of saying that it is a 24-hour deal. They'll clean anything you want, wherever you want and whenever you want. That's why sometimes I work days and sometimes nights. Indeed, that's why you can find me at all hours in schools, hairdressers, or on office and factory floors. That's me, Lily Casey.'

She shook her head – that was Lily. The same story had been given to so many people that she'd convinced herself it was true; never mind if it wasn't the total truth or if she juggled the facts a little. However, cleaning was the last thing on her mind right now – this time Lily Casey was outsourcing herself. She was in a hurry, a big hurry out of Kinsale and out of Cork, and when her hand started dipping compulsively into the bag of fruit pastilles in her cardigan pocket, Lily knew she was under a lot of pressure. There was no point in blaming her compulsion on the sugar's addictive nature or the deadly additives flavouring the jellies. The truth was: Lily was in fear of her life.

She cursed the trouble that had sent her packing out of Kinsale. Trouble had nosed its way into her world a few times before. It had come when she had found out she was pregnant with Genie, but despite the sighing of the girl slumped beside her, she wouldn't change that bag of trouble for all the riches on the earth. As soon as the father was out of her life, Genie was hardly any trouble at all. Now unfortunately, there was that terrible incident in Kinsale.

Just then, Lily saw a lady walk elegantly into the station. The lady appeared rich, but not overly so, and exuded an ease and confidence. She was wearing a small, smart red cap, like something a horse rider might have. The red handkerchief peeping out of her off-white jacket pocket matched it. Her slacks were navy and without a wrinkle. She looked tall, but Lily saw that a pair of leather high-heeled navy shoes with white tips added to that effect. The lady wore pearl earrings and a simple wedding band. This was a lady, thought Lily, who wasn't so easily labelled or who fit readily into a traditional box. The lady addressed the Station Master. Lily kept her ear open and realised she asked about the Tralee train and the Station Master had given the same spiel about the Dublin train. Lily could tell by the look on the elegant lady's face that she was confused by and none the wiser from the Station Master's response.

The lady turned right, left, and then to her, "Excuse me, madam."

Lily looked up guardedly, "Yes?" The last thing she wanted right now was to be dragged into a discussion with someone. This wasn't the time to attract attention or to make any attachments, however fleeting.

"Can you tell me if I have missed the train to T R A L E E," the words were spoken loudly and articulated clearly. Her English was good, but Lily had a sharp ear and had picked out the French accent immediately.

"No, you've missed nothing. Don't worry, you've buckets of time," Lily reassured.

"Buckets?" the lady looked at her watch, looked at the station clock, then looked at the departures panel and back again to her watch.

"That's right," Lily said, helpfully, "the train is late – we're all late."

"Except me apparently," the lady smiled, "I am lucky, a stranger's luck."

"That you are, though, I'm inclined to think that we make our own luck."

"Perhaps." The lady seemed to study them closely then. Her eyes twinkled at Genie, "We certainly do."

Lily smiled broadly, feeling a little pride as the words were meant as a compliment – and for a moment, forgot her personal plight.

The lady sat down, making a diplomatic choice: near enough for conversation and far enough for privacy.

At last, Lily thought, as a little sunlight came through the windows, cheering up the station. It relaxed her and like a cat she stretched her face towards it.

It didn't last. Lily opened her eyes and could see through the sliding glass doors that the cloudy sky was filling up for more rain. A tall woman in a black coat, shaking a black umbrella, walked through, wheeling a large, black bulky suitcase after her. There was something vaguely familiar about the tall woman, but Lily couldn't recall where or when their paths had crossed.

Lily continued sizing up and evaluating the French lady. During their brief conversation, she had detected the undertones of an impediment in the lady's speech; it was very slight and might come from the effort of speaking in a foreign language. But everything about her, from the stylishness of her clothes to the refinement of her movements, spelt a successful life. She and Lily were worlds apart. Lily didn't envy people like that, but admired them though. She had nothing to boast about herself and certainly wasn't proud, knowing it wasn't bravery that was bringing her to Killdoe. She had avoided home long enough, but was returning, even if there was nobody left of her family. Everyone had their own time, and for some reason she and Genie were destined to go back to their ancestral roots.

It was hardly a giant leap from Kinsale to Killdoe, but Lily had no love for her birthplace and only had this 'sinking feeling' in the pit of her stomach when she was going home. She'd been bustled on crowded undergrounds, hassled on the London Tube, felt lost when scurrying across desolate industrial landscapes in foreign lands, but never felt heavy in her heart like she did now and always in the past when going home.

It was important to think of her daughter; they couldn't go back that easily to London or even Dublin. Genie would be starting secondary school and better off in a smaller locale. But Lily Casey knew in her heart that moving home wasn't a choice made out of free will, as it was a last resort for Genie and herself. Killdoe would be her fortress – her instincts told her that in the circumstances it was the best option even if not the first choice.

That severe woman in the black coat came into her view again. Lily shuddered – once they got to the flat in Killdoe, she would relax. It was just the stress of Kinsale that was playing on her nerves and making her paranoid. She took deep breaths, hoping to settle her mind.

****

When the old train rolled up to the platform in Mallow Station, Genie let out a loud groan.

Lily led her gloomy daughter into another carriage. She felt for Genie; it was bad enough having to change trains. "Get a table, Genie."

Genie dropped her bag at the first table.

"It's handy to have a table," Lily said, "we'll be an hour and a half on this train and we might as well make ourselves as comfortable as we can."

"God," Genie whined, "an hour and a half, that long! What are the stations, Mum?"

Lily knew them by heart and rattled them off: "---- Banteer ---- Rathmore ---- Killarney ---- Farranfore ---- Tralee."

Lily scrabbled around in Genie's bag for another packet of Tayto's cheese and onion; something to keep her quiet. The paperback was a page turner but it was hard work today for her to concentrate.

Genie had a newspaper and Lily observed that she went to the back page first to the sports news; her girl was mad on sport. Genie turned the pages and fiddled around with her MP3 player. Lily had tried to ensure that her daughter lacked for nothing and provided her with the latest gadgets all girls her age had.

Lily caught the woman in black staring at them and her disquiet grew. She moved closer to Genie, giving her a little hug, "We won't be long more now."

Her daughter shied away from her arms. There was indeed something familiar about that woman in black. On her feet was a pair of low round-toed, laced shoes. Then the name came to her – Sheila O'Connell. The woman was what one might call a 'good' person. Those sorts of people were always considered to be pillars of the community in Killdoe.

Her daughter shifted to pull out another newspaper from her bag, using table, window and anything possible to lean against. Lily refrained from telling her to sit up straight. Lily studied Genie's slightly angled head and held her breath. It was amazing how genes came through. For a second her face reminded her of Nana; there was something in the jaw line and the tilt of Genie's nose. Genie's eyes, of course, were like her late father's – dark and fiery. When Genie lifted her shoulders, it was also her father's genes coming out. Yet the girl had never known him. He'd been there somewhere when she was a baby and out of her life after that. Fortunately, her daughter's personality would be of her own making and carved in her way. Lily felt a wrench deep inside; if anything happened to her girl, she could never live either. Her hand reached out instinctively to finger a strand of Genie's wavy black hair. She had done her best not to alarm her about what happened in Kinsale, assuring her that once they got to

Killdoe everything would be all right. But her daughter was such a silent one sometimes that it was hard to know what was turning in her mind.

Something else had attracted Genie's attention. Was that a wink? Had the French lady with the red cap just winked at Genie? There was something appealing and warm about this French lady. To a young girl like Genie, such a lady must appear classy and interesting.

2

Henrietta sat serenely, reading a book, but inside was struggling and willing her body to relax, suppressing a feeling of panic that kept rising and resounding in her ears. There was something about the rhythm of the train and the chu-chu-chu pounding in her head that ushered in unwelcome memories. Flashes of the past tumbled in, knocking at her mind: the evening shadows, the tread of boots on a cobbled yard, and chairs scraping on a stone floor. She focused hard on the book, holding it tightly as her knuckles stiffened and whitened. It was a fight to regain control, but by biding her time, the panic attack finally passed and the tide of years gone by washed back. Her grip loosened again, she took a handkerchief from her bag and dried her hands. The blue veins were more prominent and her skin was creased with heavy cross stitching, sewing the years together and basting the colours of eight decades. Her life was printed on every crevice and wrinkle – backstitching the lines, from sallow old age to the callow innocence of her childhood in Normandy, France.

Her attention was drawn to the mother and daughter. The mother's clothes were frumpy; there was no other way to describe them. A shapeless plaid skirt and long navy cardigan were the perfect combination for someone who didn't care or didn't want to care about her appearance. But there was cleverness in those eyes and lots of energy in a healthy body which was well hidden under layers of old-fashioned clothing. Henrietta had spent her life in fashion and was trained to see beyond the trimmings of clothes. Something was not okay with the mother; though pretending to read, Henrietta could tell, she was like a frightened goose, trusting nobody and ready to run.

Henrietta returned to the pages of her own book, the corners of her mouth curving into a smile. The daughter was eleven or twelve – growing up time, but such a serious face. She remembered the responsibilities of another girl, though younger, whose young shoulders had borne a lot. No two lives were comparable; it depended on the bearer. Whether strong or weak, life's challenges and experience would break and mould.

She eased her left foot a little out of the shoe bringing relief to the bump that was hurting her. It would have been wiser to wear something less dressy. The bunions had deformed the leather. All her footwear carried that trade mark; the hard clogs of her wartime childhood had branded her.

Her gaze moved to the window and she was hypnotised by the scenes whizzing by. The patchwork of fields shaded in greens and golds, together with snatches of motley wildflowers, trees and shrubs, soothed her mind.

"Next stop Rathmore Station," the train conductor announced through the loud speakers.

As the train approached the station, Henrietta observed majestic purple mountains on the distant horizon.

Although the train only delayed a few minutes at Rathmore Station, the scenery through the window was already changing, growing murkier under the heavy mist that had begun to fall. The landscape appeared bleaker and greyer, but somehow, to Henrietta, the ashen and lead hues made it even more haunting and mysterious. Sedated by the movement, Henrietta's mind drifted once more to another time and place. For much of her life, many painful memories had been successfully pushed aside. But the older she got the more often they came, and for some inexplicable reason, journeying to Ireland triggered them. It was hard to resist the pulses and recollections of one particular day in her childhood. Before her was the coffee-stained cover of an old prayer book. There was a crushed flower crumpled inside its fading pages, and the stench of horse sweat filled the stables. A man's wicked, twisted visage appeared and a gun shot rang out, followed by the helpless cry of her sister. Her own tears flowed and the sound of the soldier's boots still echoed in her ears. "Francoise – Francoise, if only I could see you again, I would ask you so many things. But most of all, I would wish to see your smile," Henrietta whispered to herself.

A movement disturbed Henrietta. There was a shock as an electricity current bolted through her body, jerking her out of the trance. She sought out the source and found it. The woman in black, two seats down, appeared completely still, but Henrietta knew the vibes had come from her. Henrietta's eyes fell on the crucifix; she had grown up with religious symbols, but this one was unsettling. The woman wearing it was severely dressed, with not one hint of another colour in her black outfit. Perhaps she was a nun. The cross was made of heavy wood and metal and Christ crucified stuck out between the dark lapels of the half open coat. The woman's hair was short and raven. She too was reading from what seemed to be a small booklet. From time to time, her eyes lifted and took in the whole carriage. They were cold eyes and when they glided briefly over mother and child, they held distain.

It shook Henrietta because the distain turned to something else — a glint of hate flashed from the silver of her cross. She had left her mark.

****

They walked down the platform at Tralee Station. Henrietta found herself automatically relaxing in the languid atmosphere of the station. Here, nobody seemed to be in a hurry; it was such a contrast to the speed and stress of a city like Paris. Henrietta fell in line with the mother and daughter, aware that the mother would have preferred distance from her. But they all appeared to be going in the same direction and nobody wanted to be rude.

"Are we all getting the bus so? Are you going to Listowel, madam?" the mother asked.

"I am going farther than Listowel, I am going to Killdoe."

"Well, well, my daughter, Genie, and I are going to Killdoe too. In fact, I'm from near there — I'm settling back after a few years away. I grew up in a place called Malt Hill about five miles outside the town of Killdoe."

"I see," the mother was talking, but at the same time turning around like a weather-vane. Henrietta volunteered more information to put her at ease, "My husband and I love Ireland. We have bought a cottage in Killdoe for short stays and we visit regularly to supervise the renovations. Travelling this way suits me because I do not like driving long distances."

"That's understandable, madam."

"Please – Henrietta."

"Yes – Henrietta – it's a bit of a bother getting up and down the country by train and bus. But if you aren't used to long drives, then it's the surest and safest way."

"That's right – amm – "

"Lily, Lily Casey."

"And we get there in the end, Lily. I had to go through Cork City, had an appointment with someone there."

"Do you know Cork well?"

"No, but unfortunately I might have to get to know it better." Seeing the other woman at a loss for words, Henrietta raised an eyebrow at the daughter, Genie. She pulled a lock of the girl's long hair, teasingly, "Pretty hair – pretty girl."

Genie's eyes widened.

"You do not drive yourself, Lily?"

"I do, or did, but a car is an expense. I've got friends in places here and there and have never been stuck for a ride. Sheamie will help me."

"Sheamie?"

"Sheamie Fitzgerald."

"Indeed. Is he a friend of yours?"

"You could say that."

"Ah –"

"Oh there's the bus," Lily hurried ahead. "We mustn't dally."

"NO. I'll manage," the voice was loud and hard. The woman in black was determined to bring her black suitcase on the bus.

"Missus, that case is too big to take on board. Let me carry it for you and put it in the storage bin with the others?" the driver tried once again to take the large suitcase.

"NO – I said I will manage it myself. It can go in the front," the woman began mounting the steps.

The driver shrugged, "As you wish, missus."

"There must be bars of gold in her precious case," Lily commented, "he was only trying to be kind."

The engine grumbled with growing assertiveness as the bus pulled away. Henrietta took out a packet of sweets and offered one to Lily, "Travelling does not agree with me either."

"I'll pass, thank you. If I put that in on top of the rest, it won't sit well."

Henrietta held the bag towards Genie, "They are called 'Papillons' in France. See how the soft wings of the paper flutter," she blew on it. The shiny ends danced in the breeze of her breath, while her fingers ran through the shimmering tinsel. It was just paper, but it seemed magical.

Genie reached for one.

"Can you imagine the fluttering of butterfly wings?" Henrietta asked.

Genie nodded and took it fully in her hand; then un-wrapped the chocolate and placed it in her mouth.

"How does it taste?"

"Good, thank you," Genie put the paper in her pocket.

How easily one could make contact; offering a sweet to a stranger was so old-fashioned, but very effective. By the time the bus had clocked up a few more kilometres, they had become quite acquainted and Genie had chatted away about moving and her old home in Kinsale. Henrietta did not miss the sigh suppressed by her mother and felt sorry for making her more anxious. It had not been her intention to do so, but Lily Casey knew Sheamie Fitzgerald and it might be useful to learn more about him and his friends in Killdoe.

The bus passed through a crossroads and Henrietta was struck by an expression of sorrow that passed over Lily's face.

Henrietta sensed it stirred something deep inside Lily and asked, "Is that crossroads near your home?"

"Yes, it's near Malt Hill."

"Is it a long time since you were back?"

"A while."

"It must bring back memories?"

"It does. I remember an old man standing at that crossroads. His son worked in Killarney. At around six every evening, the man would wait with his dog, Monday to Friday, waiting for his son to come home. Then, the father and son would milk the cows together. One evening, he waited as usual, but nobody came. The sun went down, and Master and dog continued to wait. The cows started bellowing in the fields and still the pair didn't budge. In the end, someone brought the awful news to him. Everyone said that the boy was a terror for speeding. The son wasn't ever coming back. For a long time after that, the old man kept up his daily vigil at the crossroads. When the man died, they say that the dog would sit there. That's what they say anyway –" Lily stopped.

"It is a sad story. It could be about love and loss and how to carry on."

There was a catch in Lily's voice, "It is a lonesome story and I'm telling it all wrong."

Henrietta reached across the aisle and squeezed her hand, "Was it someone you knew?"

"That's right," Lily blew her nose.

"Someone close to you?"

Lily nodded and looked away.

Lily was going home. It must revive a lot of memories and make it hard to look out the window without seeing it all: every field, every bush, and every bend of the winding road. 'Oh,' thought Henrietta, 'I know, I know. How long is it since you had the courage to go home, Henrietta Morney? Too long – much too long.'

Henrietta heard a hoarse cough in the seat behind them and caught a glimpse of a cross swinging. A hand shifted to pull the lapels of a black coat closer together.

3

The bus driver pulled up in Killdoe Square.

Sheila O'Connell was first off, hoisting her black suitcase with her. Henrietta took her time while Lily and Genie picked out their luggage. It was then the footsteps caught Lily's attention. It was a sound made by shoes with tipped heels. The streets of Killdoe were quiet except for the clip – clip – clip. There was something about the familiar sound of that tidy walk that reminded Lily of the late evening worker on the administrative floor of Ryan's Headquarters in Kinsale. Lily kept her head down, studying the bags, only lifting her eyes again when the steps faded.

Lily flipped and flapped her skirt and looked hard; it was possible to discern the back of a grey suit catching up with the O'Connell woman. She flapped her skirt again and straightened her cardigan, knowing full well that her clothes were rumpled. "We won't make a ceremony about parting," Lily's voice squeaked.

"No, Lily. Killdoe is a small place and we will certainly meet up soon," Henrietta shook hands with them solemnly and went on her way.

That's for sure, Lily thought, probably everyday if they chose.

They trundled their luggage down Main Street, shuffling and waddling. Lily looked back and saw that Henrietta had taken the opposite direction towards Fitzgerald's Hotel.

After a few minutes, Lily paused and rested one of her bags. Genie copied her. Lily thought that her daughter wanted to take her hand but would fight it because she was supposed to be a big girl now. So Lily took her daughter's hand instead, "Genie, you're taking your first walk in Killdoe and it's probably all strange to you. You look at those houses and shop windows and they mean nothing to you. One day, I hope they will and that you'll stand on this street, look up and down and say, 'This is home'. For this will be your home from now on."

Genie made a face.

Lily pointed at a window, "That house there is empty. In my day, it was a wonderful confectionary and sweet shop. As children, when we came into town from Malt Hill for the groceries, we raced to that place first. We ruined our teeth on toffee and chewy bars that we bought there – but the taste was heavenly."

Genie shifted from one foot to the other and examined her football.

Lily tried to picture the vacant shop as her daughter might and saw a sad, dreary window, dressed in faded curtains. There was nothing inside apart from an empty shelf display where once there had been biscuit jars and other confectionery.

"Mum, it's depressing."

"But somebody might open up a shop there again."

"Yeah, a mobile phone store would be useful."

Lily snapped out of her wistful mood. Genie was right; although it wasn't good to get negative, she had to admit that there was something cheerless about the place. The window was like the face of a dowdy, crabby woman who wanted to be left alone in her old days. The town was dying and had lost out to bigger, busier places. It seemed so much smaller to her now. Everything had shrunk: the street, shops and houses. Lily took up her bag again and walked on.

Her daughter's head lifted as they passed a line of motorbikes in front of a place called The Sapphire. That must be the spot to be; there was a poster on the window advertising the night club part. A couple of leather-jacketed boys were loafing outside. Lily and Genie looked away, not wanting to catch any eye, yet aware that the boys were following the procession of mother and daughter going down the street.

At the corner of Abbey Street they passed a betting office – Fitzgerald's Turf Accountants – when Sheamie Fitzgerald had bought into the bookie business, he'd made his fortune.

Finally, they stood outside a three-storey building dominated by the supermarket sign LONDIS. Despite the franchise name, locals still called it Mack's after the family who owned it.

"This is it now, Genie, this is 21 Abbey Street. This is where we'll be living. We're sharing the building with the supermarket. Isn't that something, you couldn't find handier? There's a post office attached too — imagine that!"

"Can we go inside, Mum, I'm tired."

Lily sensed eyes on them, but on surveying the street noticed nobody. There seemed to be nothing out of the ordinary, just a few cars and a fellow smoking at a door. Abbey Street was very calm. Church bells rang from the top of the town signalling some mass or ceremony. She put a protective hand on her daughter's shoulder, "It's been a long day." Lily gave one last glance behind her and thought somebody had been peeping out one of the windows across the street. There had been the quick shifting of a shadow behind the curtains. It was probably nothing, just curious neighbours.

Lily slotted the key in the door of their new home, a simple flat, pleased that it turned easily. They stepped inside, looking around curiously. Sheamie was a man of his word; the boxes had been arranged in tidy piles. He would have been very happy to do that, to show that as a person of influence he could grant favours. She needed this one badly and wasn't in a position to refuse, but had made it clear that Lily Casey didn't want special handouts and charity from him and had insisted on paying for services.

The flat was clean, large enough for two, and within her budget. It was adequately furnished; a dark brown leather suite of furniture and a round glass table were the main features of the living room which opened into a small kitchen. The kitchen was well equipped; its units and counter were covered with a fake oak veneer. The two bedrooms were almost identical, with small beds and chip-wood wardrobes which had inbuilt dressing tables. Each bedroom also had a bedside locker. The floor covering was intended to imitate parquet and was brightened here and there with orange and green mats. The curtains were equally colourful and light in texture. It wasn't all easy on the eye, Lily concluded, but it felt homely.

Things could be worse. Life paths moved in strange ways and Lily Casey's had brought her back to Killdoe. But looking across at Genie standing with that forlorn expression by the window, she was no longer sure of her decision.

Genie flopped down on a chair, a pout on her face.

'Oh, daughter, daughter,' thought Lily, 'you came from here, you are a part of here and have roots here.' The best thing she could do for her girl was to anchor her. Genie had to know that there was a place where she belonged and where her mother had come from.

****

Lily couldn't sleep. The tossing and turning in the next room told her all that was needed to know about Genie's night. She rolled out of bed and went to the kitchen to make a hot chocolate. It took less than a minute for Genie to make an appearance.

"Can't you sleep, Genie?"

"No, it's the walls."

"The walls?"

"Yes, they're all around me. It's like being in a box. When I look out the back there are walls, and out the front – more walls. There's no sea, I'll suffocate here. From the flat in Kinsale, we were able to see boats on the bay and watch the lights on the water."

"But this flat is bigger."

"It might be bigger, but it smells of paint."

"Oh, that smell will go. Here, drink some hot chocolate and then we'll both get a good night's sleep," Lily handed a steaming mug to Genie.

"Are you afraid, Mum?"

"Damn!" the chocolate splashed and nearly scalded her. She went to the sink and ran cold water over her finger. "Of course I'm not afraid. What would I have to be afraid of? I'm as strong as a horse," Lily raised her arm as if to show off muscle.

Genie laughed, "I remember the time you fought off a pick-pocket."

That laugh brought relief, "And I'll fight one again if I have to."

Genie put a hand to her mouth and yawned.

"Now off to bed with you and no listening to music."

Genie didn't argue and disappeared back into her room.

Lily bit her lip, if her daughter only knew how terrified her mother really was. If she could only be sure that what had happened in Kinsale was behind them. It was impossible to forget about the blackmail note, the knife to her neck, and Mary's body in Ryan's yard. The article in the *Evening Echo* newspaper was printed in her mind:

-BODY OF WOMAN FOUND IN RYAN'S WAREHOUSE YARD-

Thinking about it made her sick. However, there hadn't been any further information printed in newspapers, except to say that the death was being investigated.

She'd checked the papers every day since.

Lily stole into her daughter's bedroom and was happy to hear her steady breathing. Genie had left something lying on the turned back quilt. It was her little box of personal treasures. Her girl hoarded objects that brought her solace when feeling lost or lonely. It was no surprise that Genie was confused and anxious with all the running and moving.

Lily took the box to replace it on the bedside locker. Some things had fallen out. There was a photograph; the faces of a kindly old couple looked back at her. Granda was there, looking distinguished in a smart suit and hat. Nana stood beside him, white haired and dressed in her best Sunday coat. Her grandmother, whom Genie had been called after, had been a very courageous woman. She wouldn't mind having Nana's courage right now. There was something else on the floor. It looked like the sweet wrapper Henrietta had given Genie on the bus. Lily picked it up and blew on it as she'd seen Henrietta do and wished for better days.

Despite pumping up the pillows, her own bed wasn't more inviting the second time round. There were too many emotions and memories of her growing up. It was like being back in the old farmhouse on Malt Hill and hearing the arguments between her parents over and across the table – and seeing her brother, Frank, standing by his new car. Lily closed her mind to the memory. It was useless – she scrambled back out of bed, padded across the room and pulled aside a curtain. Genie was right – there was nothing to see there, only a back yard full of wooden pallets and empty milk crates. Lily heard a rattling sound – something was moving out there.

Lily opened the window to the damp air. There was a choking noise followed by panting and yelping – it was just a dog. Genie had been pestering her about getting a pet, but that was out of the question with back to school just round the corner. Besides, a small flat was no place for a dog.

Still restless, Lily wandered to the front window of the living room and looked out idly onto Abbey Street. She tried to occupy her mind by going over plans for the next day. It would be good to show Genie round some of the town and take her to meet the principal at St. Mary's Secondary School. She would drop into the Business Park too and sort out her own cleaning work.

A woman and a dog under the street lamp caught her eye. They disappeared into O'Connell's shop. She had noted the sign on the shop front earlier. It read – THE TREASURE CHEST. It wasn't very original, but appropriate. The shop had been there for as long as she could remember. Years earlier it had been a hardware store, but Sheila O'Connell had changed the business. There had just been the two sisters, Sheila and Bernie. Both had joined the Poor Clare order of nuns, but Sheila left a few years after entering because of poor health. The rumour at the time was of a mental breakdown. There was an old graveyard behind her shop, off Abbey Lane. They would go there one day to visit the ancestral graves, although that would hardly be exciting to Genie. It was impossible to ignore the ache in her daughter, but easy to understand. Killdoe couldn't be more different to Kinsale. Even if the people and faces were the usual fare, nothing was quite the same. While Killdoe was barely an hour and a quarter's drive from the Atlantic Ocean, it was an inland market town, shaped by farmers, cows and agricultural business; it reeked of it. Genie knew best the smells and sounds of the sea port; one couldn't catch the whiff of fish and fishermen here. Who wouldn't miss the narrow cobbled streets and medieval air of Kinsale? Killdoe didn't have the yachts, the jazz and the pungent garlic in the air. Killdoe town would be humdrum to a young girl, lacking that Mediterranean feel and touch of 'glam'. People went to Kinsale for the party life, to give a boost to their weekend; they wanted to go there. Nobody really came to Killdoe expressly, other than locals. The rest were simply passing through, driving on to more dynamic places.

Shadows shifted and moved inside The Treasure Chest shop window. Somebody seemed to be carrying something like a box. Lily craned her neck and wondered about the man in the grey suit, who he was and what he was doing in Killdoe. She had to stop this paranoia and connecting one thing to another. He was probably just here on business, making a short stop off on his way somewhere else. Then again, he'd been waiting for the

O'Connell woman who got off the bus and could be staying with her. If that were the case, he was right across the street. He might even be related to the O'Connells. On the other hand, he could be booked into Sheamie Fitzgerald's hotel where Henrietta was. Lily forced herself to be calm and logical. Whatever reason had brought that man to town, it had nothing to do with her. Lily Casey was just a cleaning lady and didn't have anything to do with other people's affairs. She'd learnt her lesson and intended to keep it that way.

Lily gave another quick sconce, following the row of houses to the street corner. There was nothing unusual going on. It would be easier to calm down in the action of day time, she thought. The paranoia took root at night when her mind gave in to all sorts of imaginings.

4

Henrietta walked northwards towards the outskirts of the town, and as she followed the streets was hit by the tang of stale beer through open bar doors. From her different visits, she had surmised that there seemed to be more pubs in Killdoe than any other business. Some of the names over the premises were becoming very familiar to her: Foley, Daly, McCarthy, O'Connor, Healy… She was beginning to appreciate also some of the nicknames given to people that helped to distinguish individuals and different families of the same name. The nicknames were drawn from many sources, including ancestors, trades, skills… She'd heard of John Danny Bill O'Connor, Patrick James Hartnett, the Fiddler, the Mason…

Apart from Fitzgerald's Hotel, Killdoe was almost bereft of restaurants. There was the chip shop and two humble coffee shops, and of course what they called pub grub. She especially liked the old-fashioned look of many houses with their unusual encrusted plaster decoration and contrasting loud colours: yellow, pink, lilac, blue…

A church bell resounded, its peals rolling off the steeple like a tree shedding leaves. Henrietta looked at her watch – maybe it was a funeral. She pictured again the cross and the eyes of the woman in black. Was that woman a religious fanatic? In the past, she had seen such faces of revenge. Henrietta Morney knew all about it. She'd seen the shaven heads of women and heard the shouts of 'traitor'. Though only a child, it remained burned into her memory, as it had been on their heads. 'Shame, shame…' And the shame was for whom? Were the crimes after the war less than what went before? They had created divisions that cut so deeply. She had watched lives and characters felled with mighty axes of betrayal and then split asunder. Families, friends and neighbours had been torn apart. Hate and misunderstanding had followed, generation after generation. Perhaps time did eventually find its way and bring justice to all, in the end. Age brought its problems, but she would not like to relive those days of her childhood and World War II, when German occupation and liberation by the Allies had changed their lives forever.

Her thoughts returned to Lily and her daughter; the eyes of the woman with the cross came between them. How powerless we were to understand the arbitrary meetings of people, or to comprehend the true reality and where our natures took us. Henrietta had lived it; she had seen how the abnormal and slightly mad could attract and how that pull succeeded better than the so-called normal in impacting others. It seeped into their consciousness. Surely that was part of the past and of another world, and Killdoe was a long way from those darker periods? Yet there was no mistaking the evil intention of that woman with the cross – the mother and child were in danger. But they were strangers to her. Her own strength was running out fast; there was no time for new people, new lives and new problems.

Henrietta followed Main Street which turned into the main road out of town. She passed school gates, a business park and a line of silver birch trees. It was a small town with a population of a little over two and a half thousand. While there was some ribbon development evident in the houses built along the roads leading from the town, one was quickly in the countryside. It had given Henrietta quite a headache at the beginning trying to make sense of how natives identified places and how old civil and religious administrative boundaries were central to that. Locals talked about being from Killdoe Parish, an area which extended well beyond the town, rather than identifying with the administrative district of North Kerry. On top, they also used townland and place names that harked back to ancient times. The unofficial address of her cottage was: The Forge, Sméar-dhubh, Upper Killdoe, County Kerry; but in reality the official address should simply have the owner's name followed by: Killdoe North East, County

Kerry. Fortunately so far, Henrietta noted that whichever address people used, all postage arrived safely to the cottage.

Henrietta breathed in the fresh air with satisfaction. On her trips since spring, she had come to love the changing flora of the hedgerows. She had seen them overgrown with lush grass and smothered in brambles and a tree called the whitethorn because of its white blossoms. From late spring, some parts of the roadside were invaded by rich golden-yellow gorse with an enticing coconut aroma that tempted Henrietta to touch and smell it, but it was prickly and thorny. However, she had taken time to cup and sniff some of the wildflowers, managing to identify a few: primrose, buttercup, daisy… Henrietta was especially fond of a shrub which had a host of purple tubular-shaped flowers, with white speckles. One of the workers in the hotel told her that some locals called it the Fairy Thimble and others the Fox Glove. She took delight in imagining little fairies seated on the thickets and sewing merrily with purple thimbles on their fingers, and foxes sporting purple gloves on their paws.

Henrietta took a narrow lane up a small hill, called Sméar-dhubh because of the wealth of blackberry bushes growing there, and in less than ten minutes was at the cottage gate. There stood the cottage, known locally as The Old Forge, in grey cut stone; a narrow pathway ran at either side linking up with an unfinished back garden. On her first visit it had seemed dirty and tumbledown and she'd had many doubts about buying it. Then, little things about the place began to appeal to her. There was the dark oak front door and the cosiness of the attic. The little nooks and corners, the large windows downstairs, the way the light flooded through, and other irregularities made it a nightmare to renovate, but a treasure to discover. The small, iron gate rattled after her.

She turned a big, heavy key – the door creaked slightly, resisting. It was too stiff; the carpenter would have to plane it down a little more. It was nice to walk across the wooden floor-boarding and breathe in the aroma of wax and pine coming from the sanded and polished planks. There was something lovely and refreshing about that perfume. This had been the kitchen in the past. She had paid stonemasons to restore and preserve the large fireplace and chimney, keeping the flag stones in front and the wooden oak beams overhead.

Everything else was new. Yet, behind all that newness, the past was pushing through. It was even stronger this time; there was something in the smell of the place which made Henrietta inhale the years.

"Oh, what is that?" Henrietta spoke out loud as a strange feeling came over her and at the same time an impenetrable mist veiled the room. The mist gradually cleared and some images emerged through the haze. It was possible to make out a bright fire and several people sitting in front of it. They were speaking in accents she had difficulty understanding. Above the others, one eerie voice twined its way round the old chimney and called out '– *Jenny – Jenny – Jenny*'. Henrietta could smell the smoke coming from the burning sod and the odour of drying sweat off the damp clothes that hung from the beams. Someone was singing; it was the sweet, sad lilting voice of a young woman. The poignancy of the singing plucked tears from her heart.

Henrietta had to sit down for a moment; her body and mind were weary, making her vulnerable to such lapses. That vision had not been too different from what she had lived, growing up on the Normandy farm. It was of another time – of past lives and the people who had lived in the cottage. It did not frighten Henrietta; she'd experienced visions like that before.

Suddenly the fog thickened once more and the room started spinning around her. Henrietta put her hands to her eyes to try to stop the sensation. But the ghostly voices came again, more forcefully. Henrietta could not help tuning into the sounds.

A pale silhouette of a young woman with long dark hair appeared. Several voices were shouting at the woman. This time, the words were discernable: '*Shame on you, Jenny – Shame – Shame –*'

Almost immediately, the same words resonated in French: 'Honté – Honté – Francoise Morney –'

No, Henrietta thought, I do not want to hear that; I will not be pulled back to my childhood. My sister, Francoise, is dead, has been dead since I was a girl. The past is over. Whatever memories lingered around the cottage and for whatever reason, they had nothing to do with Francoise and less to do with her past.

But she had seen them and could not help wondering who Jenny was and what her crime had been. Why was her ghost lingering around the place? Had she died here – was that it? Did Francoise's ghost also hang around where their Normandy farm had been? Did she haunt the forests?

"Enough of that," Henrietta slapped her cheeks lightly. "Wake up,

Henrietta, wake up." Dazed, she rubbed her eyes to clear the vision. It was better to keep busy and high time to check the work that had been done by the tradesmen since her last visit. She got up, took her note pad and began making a list. There were still lots of finishing touches to be added and corrections to be made. A tour of the cottage gave her plenty to note down. Her critical eye fell on a glitch in the tiling around the bath; that was not good enough, and was added to her list for the workmen.

Henrietta had been drawn to buying a house in Ireland against her better judgement. She had not wanted the responsibility of a new place, thinking herself too old to start renovating another residence. However, she had given in to her husband and son. Jean's argument about the practicabilities of an airport just over an hour away had been convincing. He had insisted that their son would need to use a midway house during his frequent business trips to Ireland. Deep down, Henrietta did not really believe that Thibault would use it for long; her son was too pampered, and so was her husband, for that matter. Granted, they all liked County Kerry and Killdoe was small and quiet. More importantly, the bottom line was good and they would not lose financially on it. Henrietta knew what it was to have nothing and to build from nothing. She hated waste. That had been a hard learned lesson from her simple, rural upbringing.

The transaction had been an honest one; Sheamie Fitzgerald, the auctioneer, had not cheated on that deal. The other business deal had her worried, though. How had he managed to coax Jean and Thibault into that business venture with a racehorse? Could Sheamie Fitzgerald be trusted? Would it be a good idea to talk to Lily and find out more about him? Probably not – it was a small town and people would gossip. It would be wiser to wait for Mr. Curran, the private detective she had hired in Cork, to carry out his inquiry and hope that his investigation produced nothing negative. She'd been prompted to seek the detective's services after her old friend, Frederic, who had some experience with horses, had pointed out to her that some pedigree references on the identification documents were dubious.

Whatever happened, it would be impossible at this stage to leave the cottage unfinished. Fortunately, most of the remaining work was outdoors. The cottage itself was already quite homely and it would be a good idea to come here every day and begin making the curtains. By her calculation, everything should be finished by early next year.

Henrietta closed the heavy door and locked it. Standing back, she tried to view the cottage objectively. It was looking good; today it had nothing to hide and looked straight back at her, holding its own. Her shoes sank into the soft earth – the same could not be said of the garden. Gardening was not her strong point; she would have to speak to the gardener, Jack Riordan, and get him to explain what was already growing and how they would landscape it. It did not even have a proper lawn yet. Jack had called it a cabbage plot; it was a narrow rectangular piece of ground that lost shape at the bottom. It was big enough for a few apple trees, a couple of rowan trees, and a kitchen garden if one wished. There might be room for flower beds and a stretch of green that would allow children some running space. The perimeter wall and fence would also need reinforcing.

Looking beyond into the distance, the green hills around Killdoe were indeed pretty. The beauty of the region grew on one. But Killdoe was not anything like her place of birth; it was the wrong period, wrong language and wrong culture. Yet so many little details here and there made her remember. It was her age perhaps and the grey skyline. The view was mild and gentle, and the soft hills peeping up from the distance were unspectacular, but soothing. The little town and countryside ebbed in and out together, telling a story of gradual acceptance and of give and take.

It was so near the sea and yet so far. The town was humming quietly, almost to itself. Beneath the calm of ordinariness were flats and sharps as the music of both tears and laughter vibrated. She understood that like every place Killdoe was built on ages of hurt and pain. In all of that, there were strains of happiness and willingness to do better. A marching tune sounded – her head reeled under a blazing sky, erupting hills and a sunset of blood. Henrietta blinked – Killdoe was a long way from the Normandy beaches and Deliverance Day of 1944 when the Allies liberated France. It was just the lights coming up and the town's people beginning their preparations for the evening.

It was time to return to the hotel. She took the footpath that bordered the cottage to avoid getting more mud on her shoes.

"Mon Dieu!" What was that? One of the garden shed windows was broken. How had that happened? Henrietta picked up a fragment of glass; it was worse than she had thought. And who had covered the kitchen window sill with branches of palm? Was that ash that had been rubbed onto one of the glass panes? It smelt unusual, like incense. There was something else smeared on the gable wall; it appeared to be some form of writing created with the same ash. What were they trying to do, to protect or to curse? Was it just the foolish games of children, or the misguided deed of a rival?

Henrietta wrote the words down on a piece of paper – 'D'anam don diabhal' – then got a brush from the shed and swept everything off. She had no time for such nonsense and refused to give in to rage.

The walk back into town abated her anger and enabled her to think more logically. Not ready yet to go to the hotel, Henrietta stood in the middle of Main Street, hesitating before finally giving into temptation. It was curiosity that took her for a stroll down Abbey Street; Lily had mentioned about having a flat over the supermarket and post office. Although herself a stranger, Henrietta had a feeling that Lily and her daughter were even more lost and lonely. She thought about going into the supermarket to get something small, changed her mind and crossed to the shop called The Treasure Chest. Why not get a souvenir or something there? But it was late and from the outside it was not clear if the shop were open or closed.

The door was slightly ajar. Feeling somewhat like a naughty school girl, Henrietta went inside. The only light came from a dimly lit corner at the far end; the shop was clearly not open for business. Somebody was mumbling; a woman had her back to her and seemed quite occupied with removing books from a case. What was that language being muttered? It sounded like what had been spoken in her vision.

"Go mbeannaí Dia, is naofa Thú." One by one, the woman removed some books from a suitcase and sprinkled the covers with water, before placing them reverently in a box. Was she blessing the books with holy water? What odd behaviour.

"Moladh go deo le Dia," the woman touched the cross that hung around her neck.

It was the woman she had seen on the train and bus – the woman whose eyes had been filled with hate. Henrietta was afraid to move; it was awkward witnessing something so private and personal. She watched as the woman took a volume in her hand and examined it. Henrietta squinted and could see that there was gold leaf tooling on the spine and it was beautifully bound. It looked like a Bible. The title was large and bold – *AN*

BÍOBLA NAOFA.

"Thank you, Pádraig Óg," the woman whispered, "you will come for them when you can and these sacred books, some of which hold relics, will find good homes. Nobody knows how devoted you are, Pádraig Óg. You are a true soldier of Christ."

I should not be here, Henrietta thought, and moved backwards to the door.

The muttering continued, "I will help you in your mission. It is my duty to protect all that is sacred, for I am the keeper of the place."

Henrietta was almost at the threshold when the woman raised her voice and went towards a door farther back in the shop. Something was scratching and whining at the other side.

"What is it Faelen?" A key turned and a bolt was pulled, "To heel, boy. Down, Faelen, down. We are not alone, we have a lodger upstairs, so you must behave."

Henrietta escaped. The sky had grown very dark and thundery, but it was more comforting than the sombre atmosphere in that dusty shop. She took out a handkerchief and sneezed. It was fortunate to have escaped unnoticed; that dog was a Wolfhound breed and could have taken a big bite out of her.

Henrietta read the face of her watch under the street lamp. There was other business to attend to, and her appointment with Sheamie Fitzgerald was one she intended to keep.

****

"The Old Forge is coming on fine. You've done a great job with that cottage, Mrs. Bontemps."

"Thank you, Monsieur Fitzgerald."

"I mean it, it was a terrible eyesore."

"It still amazes me that nobody else was interested."

"Oh, there was interest, but you – you –"

"I paid more. Is that what you want to say?"

"Not only, I knew you would do it up and turn it into a lovely dwelling. It's funny, but I could see you in it from the beginning, it suits you."

"Does it? What about Jean and Thibault?"

"Well now," Sheamie fiddled with his pen, "I don't know, but it's definitely you. I never thought when I met your husband and son at the Listowel Races last September that it would lead to The Old Forge."

"Neither did I." Henrietta looked around his office; it was a very simple room, functional without frills. There was a plain desk and chairs, computer and filing cabinet; his black leather chair was the only luxury. Maybe he was what he appeared to be – a small town business man. "You are keen on horses?"

"Oh, it's just a side interest," Sheamie shuffled some papers.

"We are sitting over your betting office."

He cleared his throat, "We are indeed, but that doesn't make me an expert."

"Please, Monsieur Fitzgerald, my husband told me."

"In that case, he'll have told you that it's a chance in a million," Sheamie rubbed his chin.

"A chance, perhaps, to lose a million." She should have known better than to leave that part of the business to Jean, but after all these years Henrietta had not learnt and never would.

"Look, I didn't mention it because I didn't want to mix it up with The Old Forge deal. It's a separate thing. Your husband and son were as enthusiastic as I was, and it was really fifty-fifty as to who wanted it more."

"I am not holding you responsible. But you did buy a horse called Golden Girl, and for some reason Jean and Thibault bought it with you."

"We're not alone. There's a third stakeholder and he's the real expert."

"So I gather," Henrietta said, "and he's supposed to be based in Cork. You know him very well, I presume?"

"The references are good," Sheamie tapped a pile of files with his pen.

"I have the papers, but they are short on detail. I want you to give me all the documents and much more precise information. Here is a list," Henrietta handed Sheamie a single sheet of paper.

"Oh right, that's no problem, I'll get my accountant on to it." He skimmed down the page and smiled, "No worries."

She could not really blame him. But buying a racehorse – what would they think of next? She loved Jean, doted on Thibault, but money came too easily to them, and it disappeared just as easily. Sheamie Fitzgerald was hardly responsible for their foolishness. He was a successful business man and surely would not invest in something if it were not fool-proof. That should reassure her, but unfortunately did not.

"That is one of my reasons for coming to see you, Monsieur –"

"Sheamie will do. I know you like to keep things on a formal footing, but –"

"Okay then, Sheamie, and you may call me Henrietta."

"It's about time. So, you were saying, Henrietta – is there something else, some other business?"

"Yes," she was not sure about telling him, but damage had been done and it needed to be said. "Somebody broke the garden shed window."

"What! When?"

"I noticed it this evening. Is that usual to happen in Killdoe?"

"It most certainly is not. Did you report it?"

"Yes I did and the window is being replaced right now."

"That's terrible – we can't put up with that! Do you want me to get on to the Gardaí again?"

"No, Sheamie, we will wait. It may have been one of the stonemasons when they were working on the garden wall. It might have been an accident."

"It had better be so, but they should admit to it and pay for any damage."

"I cannot prove anything," she stood up.

"I'm sorry Henrietta, that's an awful welcome." Sheamie walked her to the door, "I'll make inquiries of my own. I hope it isn't going to make you change your mind about Killdoe. But as you say, maybe it was an accident."

"Probably. Do you mind my asking who the other interested party for the cottage was?"

"Not at all. It was Sheila O'Connell of The Treasure Chest shop."

"You would not have preferred a local to have it?"

"Oh no, it was fair competition. We're open-minded here in Killdoe and we can't live in the past. Her purchase offer didn't match yours. Besides, she wouldn't have done anything to restore the place and would have left it derelict. Look at her ramshackle of a shop that brings down the property value of the street. It's completely out of date. Your renovations have given that part of Killdoe a welcome face-lift."

"I am glad you think so. Do you speak – what do you call it – Gaelic – Irish – Sheamie?"

"Useless at it, I was never good at speaking Irish. Are you planning to take it up?"

"No, but a little dictionary of phrases might be nice."

"There's one at the hotel reception desk. We keep it for tourists and you're welcome to have it," Sheamie shook her hand.

Henrietta had heard enough; for now nothing more need be said. The words had been written in another language, evidently Irish – 'D'anam don diabhal'. She did not know what they meant, but imagined nothing good, given the other evidence of vandalism at The Old Forge.

5

"Lily, Lily!" He practically lifted her off the ground in a bear-like hug, "you haven't changed a bit."

Her cheeks were hot, "Put me down, Sheamie."

He set her down on her feet again.

She stood back and took a good look at him. They'd both changed, of course they had. Although they had met briefly at the funerals, it was like seeing him for the first time. Sheamie had aged; his sandy hair was greying and receding. The pouch was more pronounced, all squeezed into a fine suit. He'd always been dapper in his dress and that was still the same. Although quite a tall man, his rounded appearance took from his height. But the charm was there as ever and the energetic fervour and intelligence highlighted by his slate blue eyes.

Sheamie still had that way of making her feel good, even if she didn't believe a word of his compliments. He'd given her a few days to settle in, but Lily had known that sooner or later, he'd pounce.

"You should have rung me," Sheamie reprimanded, "I'd have driven you or picked you up from the station. God damn it, Lily, I'd have gone to Kinsale for you."

And he would have too.

He smiled, "Forever guarding your independence. But you found things in order, as you requested?"

She smiled back, "It was more than that."

Lily hadn't wanted any special gifts from him and was paying her own way. But Sheamie had waivered the usual deposits. When they'd spoken on the phone, he'd been offended by her insistence on wanting to make a down payment.

"Lily," he'd said, "I trust you. Are you questioning that?"

She'd felt mean then and had given in to him.

Sheamie took her arm firmly and looked at her, "Is everything all right, Lily? It was a quick decision, you might be regretting it. There's nothing wrong, is there?"

He was wily – hadn't lost any of that. "Nothing's wrong, Sheamie. It was time for a change. An opportunity came up and that's all."

Sheamie Fitzgerald was the real all-round business man. As well as being an auctioneer, owning the betting office and hotel, he had a fish and chip shop and pub. He'd come up in the world and called all the shots now. The joviality was maybe sometimes too forced and too political and it had become his mask; yet, underneath everything, Lily felt that her old friend was grounded and still remembered where he came from.

"And how is Genie taking the change? Will she be able to settle down here?"

"It will take time. She's just gone in there to O'Connell's – been dying to go in and examine the curios since we arrived." Sheamie asking about Genie touched her more than anything else he could have said or done.

"Lily, listen, there's no need for you to stay with that cleaning company. I can sort something better out for you."

What an aggravating man. Her voice dropped in temperature, "I might be just a cleaning lady, but cleaning pleases me fine. I'm paid well enough."

"But Lily –"

"Sheamie, is it me cleaning or the company that's bothering you?"

Sheamie adjusted his tie, "Which company is it anyway?"

"You should know – you own the Business Park."

"I own the grounds. Look, Lily, let me –"

"Sheamie!"

Seeing his mistake, he put an arm around her shoulder, "Oh, Lily, you have to forgive me, I can't help being awkward."

"Let it go, Sheamie. We're too set in our ways, but we won't let trifles come between us."

"Right, agreed. Now, you'll do me the honour, at least, of having a cup of tea with me."

"Oh, if you insist," Lily tried not to be begrudging. "I'll just run in and see what's keeping Genie," daughters were handy excuses sometimes.

Lily had been as curious as her daughter about the shop. It was easy to understand why it might draw in children; it was so old-fashioned that it would be way out and weird to the young. It reminded her of a chocolate house from a fairytale; fudge and smarties in the front, and all dark and dusty at the back. After walking past the beach balls, wind spinners and the ice-cream machine, it got more interesting. There seemed to be endless plastic containers of loose sweets, chocolate chunks and dolly mixtures. There was more chewing gum on display under glass counters here than in any shop in Cork. There were pieces of every shape and flavour: long, oblong, round, lemon, blackcurrant, cherry, cola, and at least twenty varieties of orange. That would make anyone's mouth water. She'd never seen chocolate soldiers for sale anywhere else; Sheila O'Connell must make them herself. What was in that enormous jar? It was sherbet powder; there were several jars. That was clever; one could mix and fill their own bag and choose whatever lollypop they wished to dip into it.

Lily kept walking – where had Genie gone to? The shop was longer than she'd remembered. The next part was bursting with cheap curios and ornaments: snow globes, magic boxes and loads of imitation Barbie dolls. Now that was strange, Lily thought – more soldiers – there must be hundreds of plastic soldiers. She looked closely at some that had been set out on a large table. They had different coloured uniforms and were apparently staged in battle.

Lily coughed, it smelt musty and it got darker as one went along. She almost knocked over a pile of comics: Jackie's, Beano's... Now those brought back memories. There were mountains of books: Mills and Boon, Barbara Cartland... Magazines such as *The Messenger, St. Martin's, Ireland's Eye* and *Ireland's Own* were plentiful. There were stacks and stacks, winding back and piled up.

"Genie," she called, "Genie, where are you?"

"Here," Genie replied faintly.

Lily reached the end of a line of bouncing balls. Was that the last row of shelves? There seemed to be something else at the very back where

Genie's voice had come from.

"Genie, come on, I want to introduce you to Sheamie. What are you doing there?"

"Nothing, Mum," Genie was standing in front of a strange door; it was shiny black and at the centre, a large cross was painted in gold. Hanging from the door handle was a sign clearly marked PRIVATE.

"Are you looking for something or just looking?" the hoarse words were uttered from the opposite corner.

Lily took Genie's hand; it was difficult to make out the woman's face in the dusty air, but she seemed to be doing something with bags.

"Just looking, thank you," Lily said. "You have a very interesting shop. It must do good business."

"I do alright," Sheila O'Connell sniffed, "a lot of people come in just looking and they often buy."

Lily could well imagine it; this was the place the drunken father would end up, full of guilt and remorse, cramming his hands with gadgets to take home to his family. It was exactly how Genie's father would have tried to make amends. "I suppose you get a lot of school children?"

"Ha, indeed, spoilt rotten all of them."

Something about her raspy tone began to irritate Lily. "I'm sure they're not all spoilt," she wasn't going to have Genie categorised as much. Her daughter seemed to have completely lost her tongue and was practically gaping at Sheila O'Connell.

"Oh they have plenty computers and gadgets, but they'll come in here again and again. Some of them can hardly write or spell and they'll try to steal fancy stationery – pampered brats that should be severely punished. Parents have no control any more over their children."

Lily held her tongue with some difficulty. Sheila O'Connell was filling a lucky bag with items: chewing gum, a pen, a chocolate soldier and a yo-yo. There was a lot of money to be made from such things. It was the promise of surprise over content.

Genie had started to wander between shelves again. "Come on, Genie, Sheamie is waiting," Lily took out her purse.

Genie came away with two football magazines, a red bouncing ball, eight chewing gums in a small paper bag and a yellow plastic pen.

Lily was surprised to see the shake in Sheila O'Connell's hands as she fingered the money.

"You might know us," Lily tried to be friendlier, "we're new to Killdoe, but I originally came from here."

"Oh, I know who you are, Lily Casey." Sheila O'Connell's eyes flared, "Such a pity."

"What do you mean?" Lily snapped the purse clasp loudly.

"The Caseys had a fine farm out on Malt Hill one time, and today Lily Casey is renting a small flat over Mack's supermarket," Sheila O'Connell cackled and slammed the drawer of the cash register.

"There are more important things in life than land ownership. Come on, Genie, let's go," she didn't spare Sheila O'Connell another backwards glance.

Lily and Genie blinked several times to adjust their eyes to the daylight. Sheamie was talking on his mobile.

"Sorry, sorry," Lily said, "we're holding you up."

He finished his conversation quickly, "Not at all, don't worry about it. Time goes at a different pace in Killdoe."

"That it does," Lily threw a sour glance at the shop.

Genie was looking up shyly at Sheamie and Lily introduced them.

The girl's hands stayed by her side and her mouth seemed to be glued shut.

"I'm delighted to meet you." Sheamie took one of Genie's hands and shook it warmly, "I've been hearing great things about you. But any daughter of Lily Casey's couldn't be any different."

"Are we going to get a cup of tea in your hotel or not?" Lily asked.

"Well of course," Sheamie encompassed both mother and daughter under each of his arms and escorted them across the street.

Henrietta walked gracefully out from the hotel entrance into the bar, "How nice to see friendly faces."

"Come on over and have a cup of tea with us, Henrietta," Sheamie called.

Of course, Lily thought, he would know the French lady and would have made it his business to do so. He owned half the town anyway, so it was natural he would be abreast of what was happening. Why hadn't Henrietta mentioned her acquaintance with Sheamie on the bus? She'd encouraged Lily to blab, but had never let on about having already met

Sheamie Fitzgerald. And there was Genie looking at Henrietta in adulation. Without her cap and with her hair dyed dark blond and styled in a pixie crop, Henrietta managed to look both feminine and strong. Those sky blue eyes gave off an open and naive air, but didn't miss a beat. Lily brushed off some fluff or crumbs. Much thought hadn't gone into her clothes or appearance for a long time, at least not until spotting Genie's look, comparing her to Henrietta. Well, Lily Casey couldn't match up to the elegance of 'Haute Couture' Henrietta, so her daughter would just have to accept her as she was.

The hotel was quiet, except for a few after-lunch customers droning around the bar, while others watched the racing on television. Over the years, Sheamie had done a lot of work to the premises. It offered a good meal and a good pint at a good price. Although distracted, Lily took everything in. People often thought that she never noticed a lot, they just saw her as someone with her head in a book or behind a cleaning trolley. But Lily Casey noticed many things. She noticed that Henrietta was wary of Sheamie; her manner was polite, but distant. It struck Lily because Sheamie usually put people at ease. Sheamie wasn't himself; his forced jollity was a sure sign of his nervousness. There was something going on there. Damn it anyway, why couldn't people be simple?

She barely stopped herself from swearing on catching sight of the grey-suited man reflected off the mirror behind the bar. What was that fellow up to? It was difficult to say precisely – he didn't fit in here, no more than he had in Kinsale. He was a salt and pepper-haired, pasty-faced man, with long bony fingers. He was probably no older than his mid-thirties, though he would have passed for mid-fifties – and looked like he had been born that way – old. He sat at the corner table finishing his lunch, his back to them. Lily ground her teeth. Why would a guy like that transfer to a place like Killdoe? Maybe he was here to do the same as in the last place, whatever that was exactly. It was the tipped heels that stuck in her memory. It was like he was following her.

It was better to focus on other things. Here she was sitting in Sheamie's hotel in Killdoe. Life was full of magnets pulling people where they didn't want to go. There was one thing sure and certain: knowledge was dangerous.

Lily brought herself back to the discussion around her and heard Henrietta say something about having been a dressmaker in her younger days.

Dressmaker, my foot – that didn't tie in – a high-powered designer in top society more like it.

Henrietta caught her eye, "With a needle and thread, one can go anywhere in life and open the doors of prince and pauper."

"I don't doubt it." Lily wondered how Henrietta had managed to pick up the undercurrent of her thoughts, "And with a mop and a bucket, you can get into most places, at least through the back door."

"I believe you," Henrietta said, "and I have been down that road also."

They both laughed, and Sheamie's glower couldn't dampen it. But Lily's laughter fizzled out quickly on seeing the man in grey turn to look in their direction. She drew her chair closer to Genie's.

Henrietta frowned and was about to say something, but instead asked Lily a question that took her mind off the man. "What is the name of the area again that you come from?"

"Malt Hill," Sheamie spoke up before Lily had a chance, "It's a fine place and there's no finer view to be found in these parts. It went back generations in Lily's family. There's also a great forest to get lost in, there."

"That about describes Malt Hill," Lily affirmed. "It got its name because behind that hill is a long sweeping valley with some fine, rich land."

That seemed to get Genie's attention. Lily had been filling her daughter in on bits and pieces of her past and wanted her to be proud of who she was and where her ancestors had come from. She had often told her daughter the story of how Nana had saved the life of an English soldier left for dead in the forest. She had hidden him in a secret den there and nursed him back to health, using old cures to do it. But the English were considered to be worse than the devil himself back in those days, around 1922, and when the community found out, they condemned Nana. Even the priest cursed her from the altar. Nana had borne it all courageously and Granda had always stood by her. He said it wasn't Christian to let a man die. Granda had stopped going to mass because of how the priest behaved. Later Granda married Nana and it was a real love match. Nana had many miscarriages as was common given the poor medical conditions; yet some people had still believed that it was bad luck drawn on her for saving the English soldier. But her grandparents' love had held strong through it all.

Genie had asked why the farm was no longer in the family.

Lily usually kept the specifics vague telling her that it was a long story, but basically there was no one in her family to take it up and it had been sold to a cousin, Ben Casey. That cousin didn't have much mind for farming and had sold it off again piece by piece. Thank God, Nana and Granda weren't there to see that happen.

"Why didn't you take it, Mum, you were there?" Genie had asked her once.

"Oh, back then it wasn't usual for a woman to inherit land and become a farmer. My parents were very traditional and believed that to keep the family name on the land it was better to pass it on to a boy."

Lily didn't like to dwell on those details, but always tried to impress one point on her daughter that she had learned from Nana and Granda: "You are responsible for your own honour and nobody can take that from you. It doesn't matter what your mother was or your father was or anybody else, you are in charge of your own good and bad deeds."

But since their arrival in Killdoe, Genie had been asking when they were going to visit Malt Hill and Lily had been running out of excuses for putting it off. She just wasn't ready to face going there or to grapple with the memories that still hurt.

****

Lily stood outside the open doors of the large assembly hall and tried not to be too obvious about it. Genie would be mortified to know of her presence. It just hadn't felt right letting Genie begin her first day at St. Mary's Secondary School totally alone. There were talks about amalgamating St. Mary's with the boys' school in two years. That was probably a good idea, but somewhere Lily was glad that the change was not for now.

There was her Genie, standing in the very same hall where she'd stood herself as a girl. How well her daughter looked in uniform: crispy white blouse under a navy pinafore and cardigan. Genie had made a fuss about hating it, comparing it to a penguin suit. Not having worn anything close to a dress for the last two years, it was a change for her.

"Excuse me," somebody rushed past, almost colliding with Lily. "Sorry, sorry, I'm late."

Sister Xavier had been explaining the rules from a rostrum at the top; she paused as the girl came running in. Lily watched the tinted top of a bobbing head make her way inside.

"Miss Hartigan – Branly Hartigan – where is your uniform?"

"It's coming tomorrow, Sister, my mam was late ordering it."

The other girls started sniggering.

"Make sure it is," Sister Xavier continued her speech about rules, hard work and respect.

Lily gave one last glance to where Genie stood and saw that the late arrival had picked a spot right next to her. Then she slipped away down the shiny tiled corridor, hoping her girl would get more out of school than she had. Times were different and young people needed to do well in their studies to get on in adult life. Exams and degrees weren't everything, but it would make it a lot easier if Genie had a leaning in that direction.

Lily stood on Main Street, there was an hour to spare before going to work and lots to do, but she had no mind to do anything. It was awful to be in a constant state of nerves, "Genie will be safe – no harm can come to her there –"

Lily heard a chuckle and looked up, "Oh sorry, Henrietta, didn't see you. I was talking to myself – it's a bad habit I have."

"Think nothing of it, I do it too. In fact I was doing it for most of the past hour during my walk by the River Keale."

Henrietta was dressed in a casual brown pair of trousers, matching cream pullover, beige suede jacket and soft brown walking shoes. Lily didn't know much about designer brands and labels, but was willing to bet that Henrietta's whole outfit was designer made. She yanked at her own dark grey off-the-rack jacket and straightened her below knee length navy skirt.

Lily would gladly have continued walking, but Henrietta asked her questions about her work. That made Lily gabble more and let out the fact that she had an hour to kill before starting her shift at the Business Park. She explained to Henrietta that in future she would also be on the earlier shifts, but Blarney & Lee had given her some leniency so she could settle in to Killdoe.

Henrietta hesitated, "Do you have time for a cup of coffee, or tea?"

"Well, I –"

"A quick one – we are practically at the hotel entrance," Henrietta smiled.

Lily poured in a good dollop of milk and stirred her tea hard; her spoon made a loud clinking noise, more audible in the empty bar. She took a big sip and looked around. There was no sign of Sheamie or of anyone in a grey suit. The tea might do her good after all.

Henrietta snapped a sugar cube in two and dropped it in her coffee, "Your daughter will be just fine and will fit in very well here."

"That's kind of you to say."

"I am not saying it to be kind. I have seen your daughter – Genie is a very bright girl."

"She's not slow," Lily pulled herself up in the chair.

"And neither is her mother."

"Well now," Lily took another mouthful of tea.

"Have you taken her to her ancestral home? I am sure when Genie gets to know that farm you were talking about on Malt Hill she will even have a better sense of place."

Lily was sorry for ever mentioning it, "Sure we've hardly unpacked yet. I must give her time to get used to school and the town and –"

"I was thinking it might be nice to walk out to Malt Hill, or even go by bicycle. You said it was only about five miles. People have told me there are lovely views and that the forest is a good place to ramble."

"It's alright, but there are better walks closer to the sea. There's Ballybunion and Brandon to begin with."

"You must have lots of memories from Malt Hill with so much of your family history there. Sheamie said it goes back many generations?"

"It did – it's no longer in the family." Lily drank her tea faster – would Henrietta ever stop going on about Malt Hill.

"So your grandparents would have remembered the Irish Civil War. My husband likes history and often reads it to me. I've been learning a lot about that period."

"I was never a great one for history. There were some stories handed down, but I don't remember all of them. When you get it second hand, it isn't the same. You never know what's true or not."

Henrietta gazed beyond her, "Even if you live it, you never know what is true or not."

Now that was insensitive of her; she should have realised that Henrietta would have grown up during the Second World War. But it was easy to believe that Henrietta was younger.

"I must be off," Lily put her spoon back in the saucer.

"I do not want to delay you. Lily – would you like to visit the cottage one day to see what we have done?"

Lily took her cup again and drained the last drop out of it, "I – I would – I'm sure you have done great work there."

"Certainly hope so and you will tell me. We had a few hic-cups, but it is coming along.

"Hic-cups?"

"A broken shed window for one, and some damage to a wall also. But Sheamie is looking into it."

Her 'Sorry' seemed inadequate and Lily could see from Henrietta's overly bright eyes that the vandalism had affected her. Under the spotlights of the bar, she appeared frailer; some of her allure had faded and spidery lines showed up more on her skin. Lily felt a softening towards her and assured Henrietta that Sheamie Fitzgerald wouldn't let her down. Having said it, she regretted giving such guarantees. He'd always been kind with her, but what did she know of how Sheamie had been conducting business down the years. Then Henrietta mentioned casually that her husband and son had bought a racehorse together with Sheamie. That sounded mad and risky to Lily.

"Is it a good horse?"

"I hope so," Henrietta finished her coffee and tapped her on the shoulder, "Do not put off coming to the cottage."

"I won't," Lily gathered up her bag and re-adjusted her jacket. She admired Henrietta's shoes.

Henrietta laughed and explained that her feet had a lot of bumps and lumps and regretted she couldn't tailor make them like her clothes.

Lily looked closely at Henrietta's jacket, "You made that?"

"I did and it took a lot of work. As the body gets older, the more work it takes. It is probably the last time I will go to that much trouble."

"Whatever trouble you went to, I can tell you it was worth it – it is a beautiful jacket."

****

Locals called it Killdoe Business Park or simply the Business Park, although the official name was North Kerry Business Park. The companies established there were all about technology and research; in contrast, Ryan's had been a string of warehouses and import/export companies. She had been fortunate that Blarney & Lee had branches in Kerry and had been willing to transfer her. Lily's work wasn't so different to Kinsale in that most of her time was spent pushing trolleys down administrative floors. Maybe that explained why at every dark corner she kept expecting someone to jump out at her with a knife. That was why it was hard to enter the utility area in the basement, where all the cleaning products and appliances were kept, without checking ten times that there was nobody following her or hiding in there. It was time to end her anxiety, and also, in the coming weeks, to stop turning up at the school gates to meet Genie in the evenings.

But at least that afternoon before starting work, there had been a genuine excuse for meeting her daughter. Giving Genie her own set of keys to the flat had been the right thing to do.

"How're you, Lily?" a small woman with a head of blond curls greeted her cheerfully. "You're on the third floor and I'm on the second."

"That's okay with me, Maura." It was difficult not to like her colleague. Despite her best efforts of not getting too close to the staff, Lily had found it impossible to resist Maura's banter. There were of course slews of questions that she was skilled at diverting. Maura also freely shared details of her own life and had been telling her how hard it was to run the household since her husband was laid off. Lily had inquired about the late comer to the school assembly and was told that the girl was definitely one of the Hartigans who lived in Ash Road Council Estate. They were called the 'Blow-in Hartigans' because they had no ancestral roots in Killdoe. Lily had nothing against people from estates, but there was often trouble in those places and that reminded her of why she'd run from Kinsale.

Maura pressed the lift button, "Oh, by the way, dearie, someone was asking about you earlier."

"Who, was it Sheamie Fitzgerald?"

"No, it wasn't Sheamie, though he's been in here several times. We've never seen him more often since you arrived."

Lily didn't comment and was certainly not going to encourage any rumours like that, "Who was he so?"

"A boss of sorts. He was from our own crowd, Blarney & Lee, and he only wanted to know your shift. He's new and I didn't recognise him. He was wearing a grey suit and that means boss to me. Lily, watch out!"

"Damn, I didn't see that box." Lily tried to bring her trolley under control, "Sorry, Maura."

"Careful with that trolley, dearie," Maura tittered. "Did you tell me you were thinking of getting a car? I wouldn't advise it if you're driving is anything like your trolley skills." Maura wheeled hers away with a fancy manoeuvre, demonstrating how a vehicle should be handled.

Lily tried to stop shaking and looked down the long corridor of offices, not liking it one bit; working late evenings wasn't going to be much fun.

She dried her hands on a cloth and took out her mobile phone, "Genie, did you find the dinner?"

The cranky reply told her that she was mollycoddling too much. But her daughter was safe and sound; that's what she needed to know.

6

Henrietta swung a small plastic shopping bag from her hand. It would not be a good idea to keep too many things at the cottage until it was properly lived in, but one should have a few provisions, especially to make a cup of tea or coffee. She did not know what had possessed her to invite Lily Casey; it had been an instinctive, spontaneous gesture. Something drew her to Lily; maybe it was need for company. Talking on the phone to Jean was all very well, but it was nice also to exchange with people from Killdoe.

There was Lily's daughter, kicking a ball off a wall. The Business Park grounds were a good place to practise football, but the poor girl was all alone. Her mother must know she played there.

Henrietta stepped in on the footpath to avoid a car which was being driven close to the kerb. She thought that the driver was stopping to ask for directions, instead the car was parked a little farther along the road. Nobody got out, but the window slid down and cigarette smoke drifted out.

She watched for a while as Genie took the ball and blazed it against the wall, striking it again and again and again, before pulling up short to rub her leg. Then she grabbed the ball and hit it with her fist several times. Henrietta's heart went out to her. She went into the yard and was about to round a truck just next to where Genie was playing when suddenly somebody called out –

"You'll burst the ball, so you will."

A girl with highlighted hair and tight jeans was sitting with folded arms on a wall. Genie seemed to recognise her. They were probably in the same class, although the other girl was much smaller and without the blond highlights might be mistaken for a child.

The girl jumped off the wall and offered a cigarette to Genie.

Oh dear, smoking – that was not good. Henrietta hesitated to show herself or to stay out of sight; eavesdropping had become quite a habit of hers since coming to Killdoe. She stayed hidden, but had a good view from the side mirror of the truck.

"Where are you from?" The girl put the packet back in a brightly coloured bag.

"I'm from Kinsale, mostly," Genie said.

"That's in Cork, isn't it? I'm from Ash Road Estate myself."

"Where exactly?"

The girl waved her cigarette, "At the very end of this road. The family live there – and yours?"

"We're over the supermarket and the post office on Abbey Street. There's just my mother and myself, I have no brothers and sisters."

"I have too many."

"I have no father."

"I have several," the girl took a sophisticated pull from her cigarette and contemplated the smoke as it rose upwards.

"Why did they call you Branly?" Genie asked.

"They didn't, I made it up myself," the girl said proudly. "When I was in primary school, the nuns said I was a manly brat. Some of the other girls kept repeating it. I was fed up of my nickname, so I put it together and it stuck to me."

Genie asked why she had missed school the day before. Branly jigged from one foot to the other and bragged that her absence had been due to drinking vodka and puking her guts up. Apparently the underage Branly also knew how to enter The Sapphire nightclub and offered to get Genie in too.

It was when Branly lit up a second cigarette and dropped the lighter that Henrietta noticed her bandaged hand; it looked to be a serious injury.

When Genie questioned her about it, her voice dropped to a whisper.

Henrietta had heard enough and ducked discretely away, back onto the street.

The soft purring of a car engine made her turn around. It dawned on her that the driver had been watching the girls too. It might be a security man for the Business Park because the car was not driven very far. The driver made a U-turn and drove through the main gates of the park. Henrietta put a hand to her tummy not liking the uneasy queasy feeling.

****

Henrietta did a little dusting around the cottage, though she knew it was pointless until the contract work was finished. She opened several windows, noting that it still felt strange not to have any shutters. She would soon change that; instructions had been given to the woodworker. Shutters would give more protection especially as the cottage was likely to be vacant for long periods.

"Shush, quiet," a whisper came from outside.

Henrietta listened – somebody was up to mischief.

"Maybe she isn't here," another whisper.

"Knock and see."

"No, you knock."

"We'll both knock."

"Ok."

Before anyone knocked, Henrietta had opened the door and stood looking at the two girls, "What is it? What is that?"

Genie was holding something wrapped in a newspaper.

"Madame," began the girl with highlighted hair that Henrietta recognised as Branly, "we have 'un oiseau' to bury in your 'jardin'."

"You want to make a cemetery for a bird here?"

"Yes," Genie said, "it's a small one – a Thrush. We found it on the lane outside your gate."

Branly giggled.

"Hmm," Henrietta's response was drowned out by several motorbikes thundering up the lane.

Branly looked after them in awe, "Cool, they're friends of mine."

"Is that so?"

"What will we do with the bird?" Genie asked.

Henrietta decided that they were being mostly sincere, "Go ahead and bury it then. There are spades and shovels around the back."

They went about the task with some dedication. When finished, they looked down, "Now it's a graveyard," Genie said.

"Funny things, graveyards," Branly leaned on the shovel.

"Why do you say that?" Henrietta rubbed a smudge of soil from the girl's cheek.

"Sheila O'Connell said you can get to know a lot about yourself by going to graveyards."

Henrietta considered her point, "Maybe you can get to know a lot about yourself without going. I imagine, she meant about families – you can read names and dates, and guess who was rich or poor from where they are buried and the type of tombstone. It tells you something about the history of a place. It is a spiritual and cultural statement."

Both girls were looking at her with big eyes.

"It's the ultimate sacrifice, isn't it?" Branly's face had become grave.

"What is?" Henrietta felt herself break out in a cold sweat.

"Death."

"It is hardly a sacrifice, Branly, it is natural – at least it should be."

"Not always – it depends, according to Sheila O'Connell." Branly swung her shovel and looked mysterious – "Sheila has special powers."

"That is nonsense," Henrietta gave a backward flick of her hand.

The girls chattered on and Henrietta struggled to follow because of their accents. She only managed to pick up words like *secret doors* and *special powers*. They certainly had over-active imaginations.

"That is enough, girls," Henrietta interrupted their chatter.

Branly laid the shovel against the garden shed.

"What will happen to the bird now?" Genie asked.

"It will become part of nature," Henrietta explained.

Branly sniffled and wiped her nose with a tattered paper hanky, "It has gone to the other side. Some people are able to get in contact with the other side."

"Who is telling you things like that?" Henrietta was sure this time of having understood that comment clearly.

Branly shrugged.

"I'd like to hear from Nana," Genie blurted out, "Nana might know what to do –" She clapped her hand over her mouth.

"About what?" Henrietta asked.

Instead of answering, Genie digressed telling them how her great-grandmother from Malt Hill had saved an English soldier during the Irish War of Independence?"

"Wow," Branly took out her packet of cigarettes.

Henrietta instructed her to put them back in her pocket. She told Genie that her great-grandmother must indeed have been very courageous and inquired if she were buried in a local cemetery.

Genie informed them that her mother had told her that her Nana and Granda were in the old graveyard.

Branly called it 'Sheila O'Connell's graveyard', saying that Sheila knew all about people's ancestors.

Henrietta was beginning to hate hearing that woman's name, but asked about the entrance to the old graveyard, making a mental decision to check out this Sheila woman for real. Branly went into a wandering explanation while squinting at her phone. One entrance was through The Treasure Chest and the other was from River Road; Sheila O'Connell had keys to both.

That girl needed glasses, Henrietta thought, and did seem to have hurt her hand badly – but the bandage had not been put on very well.

There was silence for a moment. Henrietta pondered as she massaged the stiffness from her fingers; she was beginning to understand and make one more connection about what was going on. What choice was there except to hope her hunch was wrong, "Do you want to come in?"

The two girls smiled and trotted around the house and in the front door.

There was wheezing from the lane where a large wolfhound stood with its owner. Henrietta's eyes met with a stony, hard stare from Sheila O'Connell which for a split second blinded her. Then she drew herself up and stayed on the doorstep, willing the evil away. Nobody was going to threaten her like that, not on her property; this place was hers. She closed the door with a resounding bang.

Henrietta decided to lay down a few ground rules.

"I will not have idle hands and want you doing something. It is not about working for me, it is about learning. You cannot sew, but I can teach you a few basics. And I want you to use those phones to tell your parents where you are."

"But –" Branly pulled a face, "but – what will we use sewing for?"

"You might be surprised. You can start by undoing the stitches in this," a jacket was thrust into Branly's hands, followed by a pair of scissors. "And this," another jacket arrived in Genie's hands.

"But this isn't for the house," Genie was quick to spot a loophole.

"No," Henrietta said, "but it is the way to start learning. What you have are jackets I bought and which need alterations."

"Why did you buy them if they weren't right?" Genie asked.

"Because they had potential. I am old and do not have the time or energy to start making things from scratch anymore as I did in my younger days."

The girls looked at the garments and listened in astonishment as Henrietta explained that the sleeves would have to come off and the lining would have to be taken out.

"What's the point?" Genie continued to protest, "Wouldn't it be easier to make it all from the very beginning?"

"That is how it is," Henrietta wasn't to be argued with.

"It seems like ass-ways work to me," Branly whinged, "and for what – a jacket is just a jacket after all?"

"Watch your language," Henrietta warned. "If you want to stay, that is what you will do. But nobody is forcing you to stay."

Their curiosity was too strong and both girls pulled up a stool. They sat side by side at the large wooden table and began to attack the job. Henrietta explained that the material that was spread over most of the table was to make curtains.

"I have never seen someone make curtains," Genie said. "Mum and I never put up any real curtains on our windows, not big and heavy curtains like those ones."

"You can watch and learn, and maybe one day put up curtains like these."

Henrietta had set up the temporary work table near the open fireplace. It was perfect for sewing and working on some of the interior trimmings for the cottage. She watched the girls with their heads bent over the pieces of material, toiling seriously at picking and sewing, their faces fixed in concentration. Branly looked up briefly and smiled.

That smile – it came back to her like yesterday. It was impossible to forget the last time her sister, Francoise, had smiled. As a child, she used to sit sewing with her mother and sister by an open fire. Francoise sewed beautifully and had shown her how to fix buttons on her coat. She would never forget her darling sister.

Suddenly, Henrietta heard a far-off humming sound that gradually grew louder and turned into singing; she was sure the sweet notes came from the silvery voice of the ghost called Jenny. She looked to where the singing appeared to be coming from and could see the faint image of Jenny. The ghostly vision of the young woman seemed agitated and overly excited – and kept pointing at the girls. The girls continued sewing oblivious to the vision. Henrietta replaced her glasses and the image melted away.

"Damn it, I pricked myself with the needle!" Genie swore.

Henrietta came fully out of her trance and looked at Genie severely, "Take your time and channel your energy."

"She talks funny," Henrietta overheard, as Branly nudged Genie.

"It was your idea to come here," Genie stabbed the material with her scissors.

"Quiet! Concentrate, girls," Henrietta had become the school mistress. She repositioned her spectacles on the tip of her nose. Her hands worked automatically drawing on the experience of years and professionalism. She sewed at even speed, moving ahead, surely – although her fingers were not as strong or as steady as they used to be.

It was so easy to read the personalities of the girls from the way they approached the work. Branly's pair of hands showed plenty capacity; her movements were deft and neat. She was a fast learner with an instinctive mind, but wavering a little too much on the edge, not sure whether to apply herself fully or not.

Genie's hands were clumsy and impatient, fighting the fabric like a challenge, determined to reach the end one way or another; definitely not cut out for the business.

Not someone to remain silent for long, Branly soon started asking many questions about Paris and why Henrietta had come to Killdoe.

"Sheila O'Connell said that there is nothing in Killdoe for a foreigner like you."

Henrietta controlled her irritation, "That bandage on your hand needs changing. Come here, I have got a first aid kit and will do it for you."

"No, I'll change it when I get home," Branly picked at the stitches more enthusiastically.

"Hmm, make sure you do."

There was something in Branly's look that reminded her so much of her sister, Francoise. What could a Normandy girl who had lived during the Second World War have in common with Branly Hartigan? Watching Branly thread a needle brought back memories of her sister sewing that fateful day – the thread wrapped round her finger.

"Where are you hanging them?" Genie asked.

"Sorry?"

"Are you hanging them in a bedroom?"

"Yes." Henrietta smoothed out her material, dissatisfied with the result. She was capable of better.

It wasn't long before the girls insisted on seeing the rest of the house. Henrietta showed them round with the care and attention one might give to future buyers. She pointed to where the tiling had to be redone and regretted the bad workmanship that cut corners. Branly agreed wisely that workers didn't do anything right if one wasn't standing over them.

Henrietta tried to impart the importance of proportion and balance which was one of the reasons her husband had helped her draft the plans, working for hours to gain millimetres. They had looked for days to find the correct sized washbasin; anything larger would have shrunk the bathroom. Everybody had told them that furniture and fixtures were standard, but if one accepted what was standard, one would end up with standard.

"What's wrong with standard?" Genie asked.

"Standard makes you lose ground and space, centimetres and centimetres of it. The beauty is getting the harmony right, from the windows to the stairway, to the taps of the kitchen sink. It is marvellous to experience the difference when you finally get to live in the place. We will put a mirror here and you will see that the room will appear larger."

Both girls wanted to know if the cottage would have a name or a number.

Henrietta recalled again the face of Sheila O'Connell and thought of the discoloured patch on the gable wall; it had taken a lot of work to wash it off. 'D'anam don diabhal' had translated as, 'Your soul to the devil'. The message was clear. "It will keep the name locals use, The Old Forge."

By the time the girls were ready to leave a pact had been made: if they were willing to do some chores in the cottage, Henrietta would give them sewing tips and help with their French.

She assisted them with their coats.

Branly pulled a face at her reflection in the hall mirror.

Genie stood beside her, "Stop admiring yourself, Branly."

It was an instance, no more than a split second, but Henrietta saw and understood; one light was burning brightly and the other flickering out. Maybe it was age and being an outsider that made it so glaringly obvious.

"Goodbye then," Henrietta held out her hand, "business partners."

Branly flinched as she shook hers.

"Ma pauvre, your hand is hurting you. What exactly happened to it?"

"Nothing, an accident cutting carrots."

"She's awkward," Genie explained.

"Come back inside and let me put something on it."

"No, it's fine."

"I insist, no arguing."

It was a deep wound on her palm, "Branly, that could get infected!"

Branly looked away while Henrietta removed the plaster.

Henrietta could see that the girl was close to tears and said no more. She dressed the wound neatly, "Okay, that is better. Will you promise me to show your mother the cut and ask her to take you to the doctor?"

"I'll show her," Branly promised.

Henrietta would not normally have followed the girls down the street, but she sensed something was really wrong. She watched them say goodbye and go in separate directions and then continued to follow Branly. It did not take great detective skills to work out where the girl was headed.

Henrietta walked past The Treasure Chest, hesitated, came back and entered. There was nobody in sight, but this time the sign clearly said

OPEN. She walked down the long aisle, stopping to browse through a display stand of Ordinance Survey Road Maps. The air was heavy and gloomy. At the end of the aisle, a cross loomed at her from a black background – that was the strange door the girls had spoken of.

"Yes?"

Henrietta was startled to turn around and find herself face to face with Sheila O'Connell. A shiver ran through her under the other's cold stare. She took a step back, "I would like to buy this map of North Kerry please."

"That will be €5.20," Sheila O'Connell took the map, walked to the counter, and put it in a paper bag.

Henrietta paid for it and looked around, "I was wondering if Branly was here?"

"This is not her home."

"I know, but I saw her come in."

"Is there something else?

"No."

"Then good evening, madam."

Henrietta knew Branly was in that shop somewhere, maybe in the part behind that door. Why would Sheila O'Connell deny it and pretend otherwise? Dusk was falling and the bleak sky was dousing the town with a grimy mist. There was light on in the Caseys' flat over the supermarket; it might be useful to talk to Lily and find out her thoughts about the owner of The Treasure Chest.

Henrietta returned to the hotel. A few people were seated in the bar; a waitress was wiping some tables and a middle-aged couple checking out at the reception desk.

Sheamie was in the lobby examining what looked like defective lighting with a workman. "Henrietta, no more trouble at The Old Forge, I hope?"

"Nothing new, everything seems to be fine."

"Good, good."

"Sheamie, do you have those papers?"

"The papers – oh yes–yes. The accountant was off today, but you'll have them tomorrow or the day after. We've got beautiful fresh trout on the menu this evening; you should try it, it's delicious."

"I will, Sheamie."

"Ah, if you'll excuse me," he went to greet a grim grey-suited man who had just entered. Henrietta had seen the same man having lunch in the hotel and she remembered that something about his presence made Lily nervous.

"Mrs. Bontemps," the receptionist called her, "you have a message."

"Thank you," Henrietta took the envelope and went to her room. On reading the note, her heart sank. It had been too much to hope that the detective would find nothing questionable in the deal, but unfortunately everything was not above board. She always had doubts about going into business with that third party in Cork, and about the risk of buying Golden Girl in the way they did with Sheamie Fitzgerald. It looked like her doubts were well founded.

Henrietta dialled the number of the detective agency, "Hello, this is Mrs. Bontemps – yes – tell me all."

7

Lily noticed that her work colleague, Maura, had been unusually quiet since the beginning of their cleaning shift at the Business Park that morning. Maybe it was something she had said to offend her. Lily was still pondering over the situation an hour later when Maura beckoned her to come to the drinks dispenser.

Lily put the brakes on her trolley and waited expectantly.

Maura gave several glances up and down the corridor and pulled her own trolley closer.

"What is it?" Lily asked.

Maura wrung her hands anxiously, seeming to deliberate over whether or not to share her trouble. "Lily, I'm not right in myself."

"Is it your health?"

"No, it isn't that." Maura cast her eyes all around once again and lowered her voice, "I'm trusting you because I think you're a woman who doesn't talk."

"I know when to guard my tongue, I can guarantee you that."

"Lily, it's like this – I told you that Joe's out of a job and things are tight, very tight. Well, a while back we were really short. There were the bills, school books were costly, and everything had to be paid at once – we needed money and needed it fast. Somebody told Joe where he could borrow some.”

“Oh no, Maura, you didn’t go to a money lender?” Lily drew back as if someone had slapped her.

“Joe did behind my back. He rues the day, but at the time we were desperate. The thing is, the deadline for payment is Friday and we haven’t the money together. Now, you know the all of it,” Maura twisted a cloth in her hands.

“Who is the lender, tell me, Maura?” Lily’s head was pounding.

“Joe won’t tell me because he’s afraid for me and the children. He never sees the lender’s face through the car window. It must be that – what do they call it – opaque glass and he only opens it a slit. It’s all envelope exchanges.”

Lily pressed again for a name, but Maura swore she didn’t know it. She had gathered that he was new to the scene and not a local. Word had gotten round that his interest rates were lower. He preferred to meet in Tralee or in Limerick and if he turned up closer to home, it was to increase pressure for payment.

There was no point in insisting, thought Lily, it would be just like Kinsale, all hush hush. “How much do you owe?”

Maura whispered into Lily’s ear.

“Two thousand!”

“Shush.”

Lily pulled off a rubber glove, “We’ll go to the bank right this minute – it’s the only way.”

“But how, they’ll never give us that?” Maura asked, alarmed.

“Sheamie might help.”

Maura panicked, “No, Lily, don’t say a word to Sheamie or to anyone, or the fellow will turn nasty on Joe. I’m afraid, Lily.”

Lily felt Maura’s desperation. Her heart thumped in her chest; she hated that dreaded feeling. Why was this happening to her? It was the same money racket scheme as before. But she couldn’t see Maura stuck, “I have some money put aside Maura, I’ll sort you out. You can pay me back when you’re able.”

“Oh, Lily,” Maura choked on tears, “I don’t know how to thank you.”

“You’ll thank me by not doing it again. If you’re short of a penny, come directly to me. There are better solutions than borrowing from those gangsters.”

Maura dried her eyes, "Lily, I could kiss you."

"Well don't."

But Maura fell on Lily and buried her in a hug.

"There, there," Lily comforted, "I'll mention to Sheamie that Joe's looking for work. There's no harm in doing that, is there?"

"No Lily, you're marvellous," Maura hugged her again.

"Off with you now. I'll call into the bank before closing and arrange the withdrawal for you," Lily patted her on the back.

Maura practically danced on to a new line of desks with a lighter whish of the duster.

Lily felt heavier in herself; this job brought nothing but trials and tribulations. Was bailing them out the right thing – had Maura's husband learnt his lesson?

Lily entered the next office – and reversed at great speed. 'Bloody hell, it was him!' In front of the computer was her man in his grey suit. First he turned up in the town and right across the street from her – now, he was in her work place. She wanted to take flight off down the corridor, but couldn't. There was nothing for it but to go in and get on with her task. 'Calm down,' Lily told herself, 'just walk in and act normal.' She nudged the trolley through the doorway.

The man raised his head for a second and his "Hello" was barely audible.

He was either a really good actor or genuinely didn't know her. Was it possible he didn't remember her?

Lily held her breath and did the necessary, making short work of it, before withdrawing again. She just caught his whispered "Thank you."

That fellow had given no indication whatsoever of recognising her. It was a temporary office for workers on the move. He could be some sort of financial man; those people often transferred from place to place. Then again, he might have overheard her talking with Maura; he was so quiet they wouldn't have noticed him. He could even be dealing in dirty money. He might be the money lender himself in disguise – a killer! She hadn't seen the face of the man who had threatened her. The voice wasn't the same, but voices could easily be distorted.

Lily rolled her trolley to the lift and went back down to the basement. It was very quiet down there and she suddenly felt hot and feverish. Putting a shaking hand to her neck, Lily could still feel where the point of the knife had lain. It had been more than a criminal threat – she'd sensed evil that night in Kinsale. It was the evil that terrified her.

"I'm off, Lily." Maura ran a brush quickly through her hair, "I have to hurry, I'm running late. You don't want to hear it, but I'll say it anyway, thanks again."

"Don't mention it, Maura."

"You've taken ten years off my life."

Lily put on her coat – ten years had been added to her own.

Lily took out her phone, in two minds about using it – finally putting it away. If she checked on Genie again, the girl would never forgive her.

She flashed her badge through the gates.

"Good afternoon," Lily addressed the security man.

He didn't reply.

Well he was a grumpy fellow, and rude into the bargain. All she ever saw of him was his back. Much good security was when they spent their time looking at screens. As far as she could tell, that fellow spent his time playing games instead of doing his security detail. There was no work quality these days.

✳✳✳✳✳✳✳✳✳✳✳✳✳✳✳✳✳✳✳✳✳✳✳✳✳✳

"Curtains!" Lily exclaimed, "You want to hang curtains? Aren't there curtains already up in your room?" This was something Henrietta had put in Genie's head. Lily hadn't been too pleased to learn that Genie and Branly Hartigan had turned up at The Old Forge and that it was becoming a daily occurrence.

"They aren't proper ones." Genie pulled at the fibre, "The material's threadbare. I'll make them, Henrietta promised to help."

Lily thought quickly – it would be no harm either to have decent, thick material for the front windows and stop others from looking in. "Alright then, new curtains it is."

"I'm going across for chewing gum."

Lily shook her head. That shop – Genie had an excuse to go in there several times a day. It was a pity that the owner was so strange.

The ritual of making tea helped Lily to focus. Nothing was going according to plan, not that she had a plan. That's what she'd better start doing, making plans.

"Jesus, what was that!" Lily put her hand to her heart – something had hit the window pane. On turning, she saw a cat staring sedately from the balcony. From time to time, a little miaow formed on its mouth. The creature must belong next door or next door again. That being said, cats belonged to whomever they chose.

Her daughter's returning footsteps sounded on the stairs. Genie came in empty handed and looking more secretive than usual. Lily was about to inquire about her purchase, but the cat took over – and from Genie's face, Lily knew it was a lost battle.

"Oh, just let it in, Genie, open the window."

Lily couldn't resist either; some impulses were just stronger than her. And so, a new member was added to the household.

Food and milk were served and then the cat took the inevitable direction – leaping onto her lap. "Well, have you got a name for her yet?"

Genie didn't hesitate, "Messy."

"I suppose it's as good as any other and it is a mess of colours, ginger, white and specks of black. That's settled then, Messy."

The cat looked up and made a little purring sound. Lily stroked its head and the purring increased. It was a friendly, affectionate little creature and they'd manage with it. If an owner turned up, they'd deal with that too. It wasn't the most pressing thing on her mind.

She went to look at the curtains again. Damn, Sheila O'Connell was at her door staring up at them. The grey-suited man passed in the shop door, briefcase in hand, and a few seconds later, came back out and now they were both looking up. The sooner the new curtains were hung the better.

****

Lily thought over it for a few days and in the end decided to inquire about the man in the grey suit. But she wasn't going to start by asking questions up in the Business Park or going through Maura as a source; it was best to keep work out of it. Sheamie was the one to ask, he'd surely know. Men were less suspicious about such queries.

Lily had tried first at the betting office and then at the hotel. She finally caught up with him near The Sapphire, resting against the door of his sleek black Mercedes, smoking a cigar and talking to Paul Brady, the club owner.

When he started evading her questions like a boxer on the defensive, she'd second thoughts about Sheamie taking her queries in his stride.

"What fellow in a grey suit?" Sheamie stubbed out his cigar.

"The one I saw having lunch in your hotel several times."

"Oh, him, he's ah – just a sort of tax auditor. You must have seen him up at the offices."

Lily watched Sheamie closely, "I figured that much out."

"His name is Michael McGrath. The man is just passing through, only doing his job. I don't know much more about him, he's barely an acquaintance."

It was exactly why she understood that her Sheamie knew an awful lot more than he pretended. There was that high awkward laugh and that shifty glance away. Was she gullible in believing that Sheamie would have climbed to the top the honest way?

Lily tried to wriggle more information, "He's staying over O'Connell's shop."

"So I heard."

"What's he inspecting?"

"Did I say he was inspecting? He's only having a look at – amm, businesses here and there. It's a routine check."

"You have your hand in so many things, Sheamie – it must be hard keeping up with it all."

He leaned his head back a little, "No worries, Lily, no worries at all."

"I suppose you have property in Cork too?"

"Ah – I've a few small interests there."

"Where exactly?"

"They're scattered around. Lily, don't be worrying on my behalf, I know what I'm doing."

Oh, worried was what he was; she could see it. But he wasn't going to tell her anything. Then again, why should he? They'd been close many years before, but a lot of water had passed under the bridge since then.

"What about this racehorse – Henrietta was telling me that you have shares in a horse?"

"Did she tell you that?"

"She did, and I don't think she was too happy about it."

"Ah – that's just a little sideline. That's how we first met. I got friendly at the Listowel Races with her husband and son. One thing led to another and the Bontemps ended up getting The Old Forge. Golden Girl is a good horse."

"Golden Girl," Lily made a face.

"Golden Girl is a bit of fun for all of us."

"Fun or not, it's a risky business. The Bontemps are very rich and know what they are doing."

Sheamie looked insulted, "Lily, where's your faith in me, I never take risks that I can't afford."

"That's how it starts and then people get into debt. They spend their lives on credit, and end up going to money lenders."

"Money lenders! I hope you haven't fallen into that trap."

"What do you take me for?"

"Now, Lily."

"Anyway, it's your own business if you want to buy a horse."

Sheamie put an arm around her shoulders, "You know me too well, Lily. Are you giving my offer consideration?" he reminded Lily of one of his job proposals.

If Sheamie Fitzgerald thought she was falling for that diversion, he had another thing coming to him. But she'd let on nothing and play it for a while. "I am – I'm doing that."

Satisfied, he let her off, "Can I offer you a lift somewhere?"

"No thanks, a walk will do me good," she rapped the car bonnet and watched him drive away.

Lily looked around her, not knowing what to do with her frustration. Michael McGrath, indeed – wasn't that a fine name for a shadow of a man. Why couldn't people be simple? The worst of it was that she still had something for Sheamie; those old feelings hadn't died. It had been easy when she was away from the place, but in Killdoe, she saw or heard about him every day – damn it anyway.

$$8$$

The knocks were loud and persistent; Henrietta was glad that The Old Forge door bell was still disconnected. She took one look at the girls, "What on earth! You can't possibly sew with all those wires hanging out of your ears and pockets. Take them off, nobody can concentrate with those."

Henrietta had nothing against young people being tuned into electronic sounds once in a while, but wished they learned to tune into nature and life around them. She was too old and out of step with the modern times. Humans had all sorts of technology to make the world seem smaller and yet the distance was never greater and time never more meaningless. What had been won in one way with technology had been wiped out by the loss of human warmth and closeness. The eyes and ears became less discerning and receptive to the sights and sounds of their surrounds: a humming bee, a frail note from a song bird, or the crunch of ice under foot.

Fortunately, thought Henrietta, nothing is really lost. Physical work was good to remind us. We needed just to touch and feel skin, stone, wood and earth. The prick of a thorn hurt and the softness of a kiss healed. When one sewed, scrubbed or brushed, it slowed one down. Taking time saved time. Her views were old-fashioned, but in years to come, they might find their place again.

Sewing was physical, but Henrietta was not sure that the girls would become addicts. They were sure to tire of something that did not promise an instantaneous result.

How reluctant their fingers were, it certainly was hard work today. Half an hour later, they started fidgeting. She decided to go easy on them, they needed only small bouts, prescribed just in the right amounts.

"Are you hungry, girls, I am making coffee and there are some biscuits in the cupboard?"

"We ate at the chipper," Branly said.

"Because Branly is after Mikie in the motorbike gang," Genie made a cross-eyed expression.

"And Genie fancies Peter, the leader."

Genie jabbed Branly with her needle, "He's gross."

"Ouch," Branly giggled, "his family are English and they came to Killdoe a few years ago. I love his accent."

I must be really out of touch, Henrietta thought; was twelve not too young to be talking about boyfriends?

Then Branly was up and folding her sewing away, "We have to go, come on, Genie."

"What's the hurry?" Henrietta asked.

Branly took out a crumpled piece of paper from her pocket, "Sheila O'Connell gave this to us. If we want our wishes to come true, we must repeat it ten times in the morning, afternoon and night in different places. I think if we do it a few times in the church, it might be a stronger hit."

"Isn't ten times a lot?" Henrietta reached for her reading glasses.

"Well," Branly said, looking at the small print in puzzlement, "it's supposed to be three times. But if you're wishing for something to happen, you have to really wish it."

Henrietta took the scrap of paper and read it out loud.

'Most holy Apostle, St. Jude, faithful servant and friend of Jesus, the Church honours and invokes you universally, as the Patron Saint of difficult cases, of things most despaired of – pray for me, I am so helpless and alone –

Intercede with God for me that he bring visible and speedy help where help is almost despaired of. Come to my assistance ------'

"It is a chain letter – you should throw it away. Why do you not just make up a prayer of your own? You can wish for something without that ceremony. But it is not enough to wish something or dream, you must also act on it. You have to work towards things to make them happen."

"Praying is hard enough," Branly took the paper back and balled it into her pocket. "I think if I had one of Sheila's Bibles, it would have more power."

"Does Sheila O'Connell sell Bibles?" Henrietta asked, recalling the books she had seen Sheila putting into a box.

"She's not selling them, they're too sacred. She keeps them in a special place."

"They're just books," Genie said.

"Spiritual books," Henrietta said, "but the power is in you."

Branly's eyes opened wide.

Henrietta put an envelope in each child's hand and a pleased look flashed across two pale faces.

"Spend it and enjoy it," Henrietta advised. She was glad to notice that Branly's hand looked better.

"Au revoir," Genie made a poor effort at a French accent.

"It's – salut," Henrietta corrected.

"Salut," they both chorused.

Henrietta watched until they disappeared from view. Was it all innocence and ignorance, or should she be paying closer attention? Things entered people's minds in different ways. The girls had received the same paper, but each had taken a different message from it. Branly was the weak link, more susceptible and open to suggestion. Genie was stubborn and harder to control. But the girls' friendship was very binding and if Branly got into trouble, Genie would try to protect her. It might not be a bad idea to visit Sheila O'Connell again. There was probably nothing left to see of the old abbey, but it was a good excuse to go back to The Treasure Chest and try to figure out its owner.

✳✳✳✳✳✳✳✳✳✳✳✳✳✳✳✳✳✳✳✳✳✳✳✳✳✳✳

"Hello," Henrietta called out on entering The Treasure Chest.

"Yes?" Sheila O'Connell was rearranging some second-hand books.

"Oh, what interesting titles." Henrietta picked out a couple and read them, *The Life of a Blacksmith – Patrick-James McCarthy*, and *Saint Ita's Holy Well*. Are they both about Killdoe's past?"

"They are," Sheila O'Connell took them from her hand, "but they have been promised to someone and are not for sale."

"I will take this one about making jam then, *Grandmother's Jam Making Recipes*," Henrietta refused to be put off her mission. She checked the price and went directly to the counter, shaking out some coins from her purse, "I think I have the exact change."

Sheila O'Connell picked the coins up one by one and dropped them into the till.

Henrietta was reminded of her large hands; up close, her strength was more striking. Where was her dog – the pair made a formidable team? "If you do not mind, I would like to visit the cemetery?"

Sheila O'Connell stared at her, "The Abbey Graveyard?"

"Yes, but it is not necessary to come with me, I just need the key."

"River Road is the official entrance."

"In that case," Henrietta said, "I will ask for a key at the church."

"There is no need, you can come through here this time." Sheila O'Connell drew her lips into a thin line, felt in the pocket of her black skirt and produced a key. She put a closed sign on the shop door. "Follow me."

They went to the back of the shop until they were in front of the black door with the gold cross.

"Wait," I have to put Faelen on a leash. Sheila O'Connell disappeared behind the door for several minutes and returned with her wolfhound.

"This way."

Henrietta obeyed, keeping a safe distance from the wolfhound; its mouth dribbled and it smelt strongly.

They went down a very poorly lit, long corridor and came to a second door. The air stank of burning oil coming from some lamps which were set on shallow ledges. Sheila O'Connell pulled back three heavy bolts and led her through to a narrow stone stairs.

Henrietta's palms grew damp; she did not do well in small spaces and kept her hand on the wall going down the steps. At the bottom they faced another door.

Sheila attached the dog's leash to an iron ring on the wall and commanded, "Sit, Faelen." She then unlocked the door and pointed at Henrietta, "Enter."

Henrietta walked through, "It is too dark – I need light, please."

Slowly the room brightened up as Sheila O'Connell drew back heavy mauve curtains that were draping two large stained glass windows.

Henrietta looked around her; it was like the inside of a small chapel. There were four long wooden pews and candles everywhere; though not lit, they had burnt down to different lengths. The air was stuffy with melted wax and incense. "What is this place?" her shoes clicked on the floor tiles.

"This is a house of prayer."

There were holy pictures and statues everywhere: The Virgin Mary, Saint Joseph, The Sacred Heart…

"Is that the original altar?"

"It is." Sheila O'Connell knelt and bowed her head in front of the white and black marble, "Guide me Lord to do your will."

Henrietta stood uncomfortably; she did not want to kneel or pay homage to anyone. This was the sanctuary of a woman who appeared too extreme in her faith.

Sheila O'Connell touched the altar, "This has always been a place of prayer. The abbey has almost disappeared, but the most sacred parts have been saved." She blessed herself and stood up, "We are honoured to be standing on the tiled floor where the feet of the monks imprinted their faith."

Some of the multi-shaded blue tiling was indeed old, but other parts were newer.

"The tiles I am standing on are ancient." Sheila O'Connell bent down and caressed one. Then she raised her head to the blue and white ceiling, "God looks down from above."

"Where are the abbey ruins and the cemetery?" Henrietta shivered, all that blue chilled her to the bone.

Sheila went to the stained glass window and extended her hands, "It is here before you, what's left of the O'Connell heritage. I can walk it blindfolded. I know every grave and tombstone – I know the dates, the names and their histories. God has trusted my family with those souls." She blessed herself again and moved slowly, lighting candle after candle with a taper, murmuring, "Bless you, bless you…"

There was something out of kilter in the woman's explanation. Henrietta felt the blessing like suffocating heat, but breathed more easily at the window from where the ruins were visible and beyond the beginning of the cemetery.

"Is this place used by Killdoe parish?" The other woman appeared to have forgotten her.

"It is a holy place reserved for special purposes."

"Have Genie Casey and Branly Hartigan visited here?"

Sheila O'Connell's eyes darkened, "Those girls are spoilt. Young ladies like that need protection. Branly Hartigan is weak. What can you expect with foreign blood in her? She's already taken the bad path of her English mother. Genie Casey will be no better than her and just like all her ancestors – land grabbers and traitors."

"That is a harsh judgement."

"It is God's judgement. You are an outsider here and know nothing of our past."

Sheila opened a door that led outside, "When you are leaving, please do so through the River Road gate. I will have it opened for you."

"Thank you, Mrs. O'Connell."

The door banged behind her.

It was a relief to be outdoors and away from the so-called guardian of the abbey heritage. Finally it was the presence of Sheila O'Connell rather than the prayer room that bothered her more. Having a place to pray near where the abbey had once stood was not unusual. The pictures, candles and altar were not out of the ordinary either. It was quite a plain place. But what troubled her was how it might appear in the mind of a needy twelve-year-old or younger; Branly could have been coming here for several years. A susceptible, impressionable child would be very marked by such things, especially if guided by a twisted mind. Sheila did not seem to have much love for Lily Casey either; those scathing remarks about Lily's family left her in no doubt about that. There must have been some bad blood between the families in the past.

It was difficult to see what the abbey would have been like from the ruins. Only the bottom of two walls remained. Henrietta continued down the sloping cemetery. Although it was quite small and probably contained no more than five hundred gravestones, it looked like all headstones and tombs had been packed together. It went back to Early Medieval times, so there were probably graves superimposed on one another. She had read in a pamphlet at the hotel that the abbey was originally built in the twelfth century by the Cistercian Order.

There was no clear path; she had to weave round old headstones and watch her footing on the rough, stony ground. If there had been any original planned layout, it was no longer evident. It was delineated by a high wall covered in ivy and creepers, while other sections had wild hedging and birch. The grass was thick between the tombs, but not too high. Clearly, it was tended to a few times in the year.

Some inscriptions were faded, others covered in moss, and more were well pruned. Henrietta searched for her glasses and then changed her mind; the sky was moody and it wasn't a good idea to stay out for long or she would end up among the dead herself. It might be an idea to come back another day and maybe bring Lily or even the girls and learn more.

She stumbled on a rough patch of ground and put her hand on a headstone to regain her balance. A few rays of sunlight broke through the clouds forcing her eyes shut for an instant. Another cemetery appeared in her mind; it was situated in a Normandy village. In a corner of the cemetery stood a tombstone, abandoned, dirty, and the grave over-run with weeds and briars. It was quiet there too, even quieter than Killdoe; the cows bellowed in the surrounding fields. She did not want to read the gravestones in her vision because one was missing – that of her sister, Francoise, who had not been laid to rest with her own people. If Henrietta's mind were allowed to travel, it would roam away from that cemetery, not very far, towards a forest until it found a lonely unmarked stone slab. She opened her eyes and wiped a tear that had escaped, 'You can come to a foreign cemetery, Henrietta Morney, and spend time walking among strangers, and you have not looked after your own.'

She peered at the inscription of the headstone beside her – 'DANIEL CASEY and his loving wife JENNY CASEY (nee McCarthy)'. Could they be Lily's people? Jenny – wasn't that the name that kept echoing in The Old Forge?

A gate clanged. Sheila O'Connell hadn't waited for her to ring, but had opened the River Road gate. The signal was clear, 'Time for you to leave'. Henrietta could not see very clearly, though the long strides and the wolfhound were distinctive. Sheila was not alone and was in discussion with someone in a dark car. A tall man got out and opened the door; Mistress and dog got in. Henrietta put her glasses on her nose, but too late; they had gone. In future she would not bother that woman for a key and would get a key at the church and enter by River Road gate, it was a lot easier.

9

Lily switched on the lights in the utility room and looked at the shift board. She then picked out a small key from her bunch and opened a locker. She liked the familiar ritual of putting on the overalls, knotting a scarf around her head and pulling on a pair of rubber gloves. Lily filled the bucket with water, added detergent and loaded everything she needed onto the trolley, and then went to fetch a selection of mops and cloths.

Getting only two hours' sleep made her feel drained of energy. It was difficult to forget Genie's blood-curdling scream that had brought her out of bed. She'd tripped over Messy in the living room, running to the bedroom. Her daughter had been sitting up in the bed, still asleep but mumbling garbled words. She seemed to be telling Branly to return something and then started crying about her football. Lily had taken Genie in her arms to reassure her that it was just a bad dream and remained with her until she fell back to sleep again. That, however, had ended Lily's sleep. The rest of her night had been spent trying to push out images of knives, blackmail notes and raspy threatening voices.

"Dearie, how are you?" Maura ran in, parked her trolley beside her and also began systematically preparing her materials.

"I'm grand, Maura, and yourself?"

"Busy, but not complaining."

"That's the way when you have a family."

"Now you've said it; you can't keep up with them half the time. Amm – dearie," Maura lowered her voice and Lily drew a patient breath.

"It isn't for me to be putting my nose in your business, but I will anyway. You've been good to me and I'll never forget it, not for as long as I live. That's why I'm concerned for your girl – she's around a lot with young Hartigan and –"

"Maura –"

"I'm just saying that you shouldn't let her too far out of your sight. I'm fond of Branly myself – she's a nice girl, but easily led, and you never know what company they might fall into."

"I appreciate the advice, Maura; growing up isn't easy, but trust is important and Genie might be a positive influence on Branly."

"Maybe so," Maura made little effort to hide her disbelief in Lily's take on the situation. She had important information to pass on and intended to warn Lily. Her list was long: the girls were often seen in the chipper where the motorbike gangs loitered, Branly was spotted several times in The Sapphire and on the back of Mikie Horan's bike. Mike was airy, but nothing compared to the far more dangerous English boy, Peter Sykes, who was the leader of a motorbike gang. The gang was meddling in drugs. The Sapphire had a bad reputation for drugs but apparently Malt Hill Forest, where a lot of bikers hung out, was rumoured to be a hive of drug activity.

"Why don't the Gardaí do something?" Lily wanted to kick the trolley.

"The Gardaí, huh," Maura waved her hand, "they can't keep up with them. Believe me, the only solution is to have nothing to do with Sykes and his likes."

"But why isn't Branly's mother controlling her?" Lily switched off the light and they swung their trolleys out of the utility room and down the basement corridor.

"A drink problem. It's very sad, but that family is growing up by itself."

Maura turned and shouted down the corridor, "Evening to you."

A tall man strode out of the security lodge. "Evening," he replied gruffly.

"What's his name?" Lily steered her trolley into the lift.

"I'm ashamed to say that I don't know him – he's not a regular. Well, we better get started," Maura got out on the first floor.

Lily pressed the button for the fourth floor, then took out her phone and checked in on Genie.

Genie's cryptic text about being home from football practice was little comfort. Suppose her daughter was lying to her and wasn't at home at all? How was she to know that Genie wasn't gone off somewhere with Branly? Was she right to trust her?

Lily squeezed out her mop. She'd have to pay closer attention; what Maura had told her couldn't be ignored. Branly had already been on one sleep-over with Genie. Lily remembered Genie saying that Branly had no place to keep her possessions safe, that her brothers often got into her things and ruined them. Come to think about it, the last time Branly had been to the flat, her jacket had been very bulky and fully zipped up; no doubt sneaking some treasures in. Lily couldn't really forbid Genie from keeping them in her room; sharing is what girlfriends normally did at this age. It was hard juggling Genie's safety without curbing her freedom.

That the girls were still going to Henrietta's cottage surprised Lily; the odds were that they would have given up going there by now and that the novelty would have worn off. Genie could be telling Henrietta all sorts of things. Maybe it would be a good idea to inquire about the curtains that Genie was to make. It made her feel better having decided that.

Lily went on tip toe to the next office. It was stupid, but until she understood what McGrath was up to, it was impossible to treat his office like the others. There was no reply to her timid knock. She tried the door – huh, locked. How were cleaners supposed to clean it if it was locked? He would have to clean it himself. She pushed her trolley on, glad to leave it behind her.

✳✳✳✳✳✳✳✳✳✳✳✳✳✳✳✳✳✳✳✳✳✳✳✳✳✳✳✳✳

Lily waited in the hotel lounge. She had picked a seat with a view into the dining area where the tables were being prepared for dinner.

Henrietta came towards her in an elegant fuchsia dress and black high heels; her necklace and earrings sparkled. "Lily?" Her eyes were anxious, "Is something the matter?"

"Oh no, no," Lily drew her navy coat over her shabby worn-out skirt. "I'm sorry for disturbing you, I just wanted to talk to you about the curtains

Genie will be making. But I can see that you're dressed to go out," Lily made a move to leave.

Henrietta put a hand on her arm and sat next to her, "Lily, don't go. I will tell you everything you need to know about the curtains. I was expecting you to visit the cottage – otherwise I would have told you more, sooner. You want to get the material, do you not?"

"Yes, that's it."

"Have you and Genie picked out a colour?"

"I was thinking brown and cream."

"Good choice. I already got Genie to take the measurements, but you might just double check them. As soon as you have bought the material, I will show her what to do. We can use my work table and the sewing machine at the cottage. Is that okay?"

"Yes, yes. I might go up to the cottage then to see the machine and things."

"Absolutely, I would love it."

"Thanks. I'm holding you up, I can see that."

"Lily, please stay. My husband, Jean, is joining me for the weekend and is on his way from Shannon Airport. He will not be here for at least another half an hour."

"That's nice to have him come," Lily calculated to stay five minutes and to be well gone before Henrietta's husband got there.

"Now that you are here, I would like to ask you about something," Henrietta said.

"Is it about Sheamie?"

Henrietta's well plucked brows knitted together, "No, that was not what I wanted to ask you. I was in the Abbey Graveyard this week. I had to go through The Treasure Chest to access it – Sheila O'Connell is a difficult woman."

"You can say that again," Lily was happy to move on to the subject of Sheila O'Connell. "She's as odd as two left shoes."

"'As two left shoes', I like that expression. Is the woman dangerous – are the girls safe with her?"

Lily put a second hand to her cup and placed it carefully on the saucer – dreading another warning about the girls, "Sheila O'Connell is contrary and unpleasant, but I have not heard anyone say more than that. The girls come and go to The Treasure Chest for sweets and treats, that's all. Is there something I should know?"

Henrietta touched a diamond earring briefly as if it were hurting her – shook her head and asked Lily about the part of her family buried in the cemetery, before bringing the conversation back to Malt Hill. But Lily wasn't going to be led there. Henrietta touched one of her earrings again, "You know, Lily, I grew up during World War II and there are a lot of things I would like to forgot about that period of my life. I'm no example, I have not visited my home place in Normandy for more than sixty-five years. Going back can be hard, but we all must do it eventually."

"Sixty-five years! What age were you when you left your home?"

"I was fourteen."

So young, Lily thought; Henrietta hadn't been much older than Genie. "Those times must have been very hard."

"They were. But I must think of my son, Thibault – that is why I am determined about going back to where I came from and putting all those memories to rest. I need to heal myself and let go."

"Do you have grandchildren?"

Henrietta smiled, "I would like to. My son was a late starter, one of those bachelors who took his time. He is almost forty and just got married last year."

"Better to be late than sorry – I never married myself."

"You are a strong woman, Lily."

Lily stood up, "I don't know about that." A tall silver-haired gentleman had passed through the hotel lobby; she'd enough to think about for one day, without meeting Henrietta's other half.

10

Henrietta waited at the traffic lights on Main Street. For a small town, Killdoe surprisingly got clogged up with heavy traffic. Her joints were aching today; the damp Irish weather stiffened her bones. She had decided to go to Killdoe Public Library on Bridge Street to research a little first on her own about The Old Forge and Killdoe's past. The street also had a court house, funeral parlour and two banks, but didn't host many retail shops.

Henrietta liked libraries and this one was bright and airy. The carpet was soft and the rainbow colours cheerful. The quietness of learning and knowledge rose to meet her. The librarian smiled gently, her face was placid and kind.

"I am just looking," Henrietta responded to her inquiring eye, "but I may need your help later on."

"You go right ahead," the librarian smiled again.

Henrietta walked past the computers and ran her fingers across a keyboard. She used to play the piano and could produce beautiful sounds from its ivory keys. She was not afraid of change and modern things and understood the value and marvel of progress. But when you wrapped that cloth around your body, stood in the natural light and spun forward the years, you appreciated the feel of a needle in your hand. You thanked your stars for the skill to transform the material to fit your body exactly in both size and style.

Her skin was hardened at the finger tips from working material. Francoise was her first sewing mistress and it had been a joy. However, at fourteen, it had not been a pleasure. She didn't have fond memories of the time spent straining her eyes in the low light of Parisian workshops, back rooms and basements. The rotary cutters, shears, stitching awls and rhythm of spinning held no magic, and the repetitive sound of wheels turning and turning was not a welcome music. It had just been long hard nights of work and holding back the tears until she could no longer see to sew. Those had been hard earned centimes grafted from the velvet and silk taffels, suede and corded strips that toppled down around her. But the Normandy teenager had learned how to spin fabric into gold and was grateful for her talent as a designer.

Henrietta looked through some books; it was a pleasant treat to spend time idly browsing. She had heard Lily say that the devil made work for idle hands. It was an old, familiar expression she'd heard umpteen times; her mother, or any of the older wise women of her Normandy village would have said the same, decades before. Lily, she observed, had the new and the old all mixed inside.

The door opened suddenly and an icy draught lanced the mild atmosphere.

Oh, yes, Henrietta thought, the devil makes work for idle hands.

Sheila O'Connell went directly to a row of shelves, picked out a volume and returned to one of the tables.

Henrietta took the same path to the history section, selected a book on French history from the shelf and flicked through the pages. It was her life, had been her life – *World War II 1939-1945 – Life Under German Occupation*. The story of the historian seemed far away. The so-called evidence was arranged chronologically. It was all in there, laid out neatly in words and lines, chapters and footnotes, and hundreds of references to prove every fact.

It was only the veneer; the truth was forever shifting and real life had gone on differently. Her family, like others, had scraped together and stored what they could in case of need, never knowing what would happen from one moment to the next. Every move had been surveyed and the child, Henrietta, had learned to control her feelings. They'd had a sort of freedom; a bird hopping along the ground with its wings clipped has a sort of freedom also, but no liberty at all. 'Go bird, you are free, free to jump away. But you cannot fly. You cannot be free when your heart and mind are possessed.'

It was impossible to hold back the thoughts that brushed off the cobwebs from her memories or to forget the steel cages closing in around the hearts of people. What had come after the war had brought more shackles. In her mind's eye they all stood before her; girls lined up, bending to the order of terror – and her own voice, the voice of a stammering child and the face of her sister in despair. She had seen that despair again in Branly's eyes and looked once more towards Sheila O'Connell, reading the anger around her. 'Why, oh why,' she thought, 'what have the girls ever done to you?'

Henrietta left the library and walked on, looking in from one window to the next. The butcher was preparing beef to roast. He strung and tightened the cord netting around the meat. It was dropped in a bag and the customer left the shop carrying a prime piece ready for the oven. During the war, they had never known what they would eat and never felt full. The hunger had stayed with her so much so that even after eating, that gnawing emptiness was there.

A warm, forceful wind blew her down the street from the butcher's shop. The rain sprinkled her face lightly. It was lovely – the perfect antidote to invigorate and lift. There was no need to hide from some types of weather. And there was Lily, a soul sister, coming up the street, occasionally carried sideways by the wind.

"Henrietta," Lily called to her, "you should cover yourself up in this weather."

"The same goes."

Lily laughed, "True enough, but there's something about a day like this that brings out the child in me."

"We must never lose the child."

"No, indeed." Lily paused, "I hope Genie and Branly aren't too much of a bother."

"No trouble, Lily, it is a pleasure. I carry on working, they help me when they can, and we are all learning."

"I notice," Lily said, "that it fits in with my own routine and cleaning shifts."

"That is completely accidental, nothing planned, it just happens."

"I know, it's just amazing how magnets fly around."

"I agree, people and places do seem to attract each other. By the way, I really like your earrings, and is that not a new bag – how lovely?"

"Oh, just a few accessories." Lily put a hand to her face, "The wind makes my skin raw and it gets red – I must get moisturising cream for it."

Henrietta raised the collar of her beige Cashmere coat and rearranged her red scarf. Her boots were solid, but the heels gave her height advantage.

"Each time I meet you," Lily said, "you have beautiful outfits."

"But you have seen this coat before. I have just learned a way of wearing and adjusting scarves that changes the look."

Lily drew closer, "Henrietta, I was wondering – oh, never mind, it will keep."

Henrietta didn't let her off, "Why don't you come up to the cottage? I have a few things to check there and you will be able to see the curtains that Genie has almost finished?"

"Well – I don't know."

"You promised."

"I did and I will visit, but I have an errand to run and a meeting with a garage fellow about a car. I'll call later in the week."

Henrietta walked Sméar-dhubh Lane towards The Old Forge enjoying the autumn landscape. The assortment of russets and yellow-browns could never be captured on canvas or in photographs; it was a privilege reserved for the naked eye. Henrietta thought about Lily and did understand why she was loath to visit The Old Forge. Lily had a lot of settling in to do, between coping with her job, raising Genie and re-learning to fit into a place she had come from. But there was something else shadowing her; Lily had not lost that look of a frightened animal, ready to run for cover.

There was someone at the cottage? Voices came from round the back. Henrietta turned the gable of the cottage and found Branly praying over the bird grave, and Genie standing nearby. Branly's face was tear-stained and her eyes wild. Henrietta detected a faint smell of alcohol from her breath.

"What makes you sad?" Henrietta asked Branly.

"I was thinking about death and my father. He is buried in Limerick and there is nobody to pray over his grave and I hate my mother."

"Hate is a hard word, Branly."

"All my people are bad and I have the same badness inside me. That's why I don't fit in," Branly picked at her painted nails.

Henrietta tilted Branly's chin, "Who has been telling you this? Are you still reading those chain prayers?"

"No. I have found something more powerful – the Holy Bible."

"Shush," Genie nudged Branly and kicked her football.

Henrietta took her keys, "Come inside."

She sat them at the kitchen counter near the stove and made three hot chocolates. She waited until they had taken several sips, "Branly, have you been drinking alcohol?"

Genie bounced her ball.

Branly looked into her cup.

Henrietta put some biscuits on a tray; it was not a good approach to interrogate the girls and make them cower like this. She patted Genie's football, "You really do like the game, don't you?"

Branly spoke up, "Genie's brilliant at football, but football got her into a lot of trouble in Kinsale."

Henrietta saw Genie's foot tap Branly's ankle.

Branly kicked back, "I'm not going to tell."

"Loyalty is important," Henrietta took Branly's arm, "Can I see how the wound is healing?"

"No," Branly jerked it away and slid off the stool pulling Genie with her; "it's fine – we have to go."

"We have a lot of homework," Genie added.

Henrietta rinsed the mugs; young girls and their secrets. Branly had drunk something alcoholic – that was certain. She knew it was cowardly to think that way, but it was best to leave these things for Genie's mother to manage; Lily was better placed to interfere in Branly's life.

She went back into the garden – it must have seen better days. The privet hedging camouflaging some of the fencing and bare apple trees were the only decorations on a coarse lawn. Jack Riordan had asked her if she wanted to plant some flowers and shrubs.

"Plant nothing," Henrietta had replied, "I want to see what grows up naturally and what generations before me planted."

She stood by the bird grave. In truth, what could someone like her, who was passing through Killdoe, plant? One planted with the hope of seeing it flower and flourish in the future.

11

Lily put her arms on her hips, well, what would you know; there was Sheamie in deep conversation with Michael McGrath. What was he doing in the Business Park grounds at this early hour of the day? It was only half past seven. That was hardly the behaviour of someone who didn't know 'the what, the where, and the why'. She pulled her trolley closer to the window to have a better view. Casual as you like, McGrath had slithered out – and 'lo and behold' who should be outside to meet him at the gate, but her bold Sheamie. It had been a full ten minutes and they were still in the car, discussing. The question was – would she take him on or string it out? She decided to string it for a while longer.

"Psst, Lily, what are you doing?" Maura called to her.

"Only looking out."

Maura stood next to her, "There isn't a lot to be looking at, just a few cars."

"I was more daydreaming than looking, but I was taking in the cars too."

"Are you still thinking of getting one?"

"I'm not thinking, Maura, it's time to get one, a good second-hand one."

"You can ask Sheamie Fitz', can't you?" Maura cocked an eye.

"Are you finished on this floor?"

"Almost, dearie," Maura pushed on laboriously.

Lily wished Maura would push faster as an idea had just come to her. She armed herself with a cloth and stepped inside McGrath's office; she might come across something, one never knew. The computer screen was flashing on standby and everything was squeaky clean. He was so meticulous that one wouldn't learn much from his desk.

Then her eye fell on an old newspaper. She picked it up and immediately a highlighted title caught her attention.

`'- BODY OF WOMAN FOUND IN RYAN'S WAREHOUSE YARD -`
`Last night in Kinsale the body of Mary Sheehan----'`

Oh, she knew it by heart. Lily dropped the paper as if burnt by it. Why was he carrying a newspaper five months out of date with him? Her suspicions were right; there was nothing accidental about his arrival in Killdoe.

Lily left the Business Park late morning not knowing whether to turn right or left. In the end, she took the road to The Old Forge.

Henrietta was standing at the door, "Welcome to my humble cottage, Lily; the curtains are ready."

That was strange; it was like she'd been expecting her.

Lily examined the beautifully sewn and lined curtains. "They're perfect, Henrietta."

"We are pleased with them. Genie was planning to take them home tomorrow, so you will have to pretend surprise."

Lily walked to the stony-grey old chimney. Though it had been restored, she could tell the original stone work was intact and the flue still went all the way to the ceiling. The flag stones showed fine workmanship and the central hearth was very deeply set. The whole cottage was tastefully done. Henrietta had managed to keep the rustic feel, from the original oak beam ceilings to the floor boarding that had been polished darker to harmonise with the beams. The kitchen had the same balance of old and new and was equipped with all the modern day conveniences. There was a Stanley stove that looked period, but was high quality. A customised wooden counter had been added to complete the kitchen units.

"You will need help to clean this place; I can help you wash and polish."

"You will not be my cleaner, Lily. But I would love your assistance with some measurements I need to make. This way I can enjoy your company too."

"Then let's get going." Action and doing suited Lily very well.

Lily stood on a step ladder at the living room window. Pins and needles tingled up and down her back. She saw Sheila O'Connell striding swiftly along the lane, the big hound loping after her. Every time she looked, Sheila was there. That woman of God was everywhere, spreading her 'holier than thou' ideas.

The measuring tape was tugged from Lily's hand.

"Sorry, Henrietta, I wasn't paying attention."

"It's Sheila O'Connell, is it not?"

"Yes, I remember when Sheila O'Connell got under my skin first." Lily reflected, "It was many years ago, so long it seems like a dream. It was around the same time that I got the notion of travelling in my head. It was a fine day, early in the summer, and I was just standing on the footpath looking at a grocer's shop window. I sensed a presence behind me, I didn't turn around but knew who was there and listened – " Lily stopped, "You'll think I'm crazy, but do you believe in voices, I mean sensing people who have passed away and feeling that they are talking to you – you hear them, even smell them, it's like they are there with you?"

"I do not think you are crazy," Henrietta said, "I fully believe that there is a whole other world we know little about."

"Do you?" Lily turned the measuring tape in her hand, "I don't know what to think myself, but I recognised the voice, and it was Granda. He had passed away a few years before, but I swear it was his voice.

"'That woman is evil,' he said, 'she's in there planting bad seeds. Sheila O'Connell is evil, but camouflages her evil in good deeds. Sheila wants to return to a time she thinks was glorious and it's her life's mission to make amends for the past. In fact, she's just making up her own version of the past. For her, our family fought on the wrong side.'"

"Were your family on the wrong side?" Henrietta asked.

"I wondered about that. It didn't mean much to me then, still doesn't."

"And what did the voice really mean?"

Lily waved her hand, "Oh, any number of things. It could be switching religions for a bit of bread during The Famine. It might have been taking the wrong side during the Irish Civil War, as if there was a right side. Or it might have been Nana's deed."

"Genie has spoken about that."

"Has she? Nana had to face a lot of hate for saving the English soldier during the Irish War of Independence. But Granda defended her to his death."

"Oops!" Henrietta dropped the tape, "I have butter fingers; we will have to do that again. What you tell me reminds me of my own mother and her courage in World War II. We are living in different times, but still fighting the same battles."

"That we are. The warning voice of Granda has often come to me. The strangest thing was hearing his voice for the first time – now, I know it's him. In that grocer's, all sorts of misfortune struck the family. They say that their ancestors had taken the shop wrongly during The Famine, causing the original owners to be evicted. It was a question of who paid the highest rent. The original owners were from Sheila O'Connell's mother's side, the Mulcahys. Who knows the real truth? But from that day, I've avoided her sort of 'good people'."

Henrietta pencilled numbers in her notebook. "I will do that measurement again to double check."

"Certainly," Lily obliged. "There's a lot of anger and hurt festering under the surface with people. They say we have to know the past, learn from it and then let go of it."

"Yes, it's only natural. But going back to the past to make a selection from poor reservoirs of memory and forcing it into the present is not," Henrietta wound up the tape.

"Some people love to drag up the dregs," Lily walked around admiring the work. Henrietta was a surprising lady, gifted and practical all in one. Lily had seen Henrietta's husband for herself at a distance and heard from many about the wealthy French man who had stayed in the hotel. Maura also reported details of a big chauffeured car. It was then she'd understood the other world of Henrietta and the strength of the woman. Not everybody could live in different social spheres and be totally at ease in all of them.

Henrietta wanted to learn more about the history of The Old Forge and Lily obliged by telling her what she knew. The cottage originally did not only have a forge, it was also a meeting point in times of rebellion and where many conspiracies were plotted. The Irish rebels met secretly in the cottage when they were fighting the Royal Irish Constabulary (RIC) and Black and Tans during the War of Independence and plotted an ambush that killed twenty British soldiers. The Royal Irish Constabulary represented official Crown forces and the Black and Tans were recruits from Britain and known for their cruelty. They got the name because of the black and tan colour of their uniform.

"There really is a lot of history in The Old Forge," Henrietta marvelled.

"You know, Henrietta, my grandmother was born here too."

"Why, Lily, you never said –"

"Nana's name was Jenny McCarthy; the family was known as the Blacksmith McCarthys. She grew up here, then married Daniel Casey and lived the rest of her life on Malt Hill. I don't have all the history from those times, just bits and pieces. You seem to know a bit about Irish history."

"I have been learning. I believe I saw your grandparents' headstone in the cemetery."

"Did you indeed?" Lily folded up the ladder, "It's hard to believe that this is where Nana grew up and it's difficult to imagine when this was a working forge. There are some books about Killdoe's past in the library on Bridge Street."

Henrietta coiled the tape measure round her fingers, "I have been there and will go back. Genie likes history and talks a great deal about Malt Hill."

Lily realised that Genie was telling Henrietta a lot.

"I have to take her there one of these days."

"Yes." Henrietta seemed to be studying the windows again, "Has Sheamie spoken to you recently?"

"Why?"

"Just wondering. You and Sheamie are close?"

Lily was silent.

"I am sorry, I am prying and it is not my business."

"That's all in the past." Lily got busy fixing her cardigan, "Isn't there always something – first there's Kinsale and now Sheamie."

"Did you have many friends in Kinsale?"

"I was beginning to get to know some people well – and – in the end, I decided it was best for Genie to come to Killdoe."

"You did not want to leave Kinsale?"

"Not exactly."

"Why did you leave?"

"For Genie – and – and a lot of reasons."

"Lily – did you not want to speak to me about something else that's bothering you from Kinsale and that is still haunting you here? I am a good listener and a total outsider."

Lily drew back – it was tempting. "Did you say 'haunting'?" She laughed, "All this talk about Granda. No – I didn't have anything in particular to say to you. But now that I think of it I did want to mention that it'll be Genie's birthday soon. I hesitated between a computer and a bicycle and finally decided on the bicycle."

Henrietta followed Lily's wandering change of theme, "She will love it."

Lily sat down.

"Lily, can I offer you something to drink?

"No thanks, I'm fine." Lily got up, paced, sat on a stool, got up and paced again – "Henrietta, if you overheard something that you weren't supposed to, something that was people's own business, what would you do?"

"I would leave them to their own business."

"If what you heard might be vaguely related to something more serious."

"Then, I would be very careful. I would probably tell an outsider, someone objective, to see what was coming from my imagination or what was real."

"I did that. I reported it, but to no avail."

"Are you talking about a crime here?"

"Yes and no, I don't know."

"You are not making much sense, Lily. Tell me in plain English."

Lily took a deep breath, "I overheard a lot of stories about money lending and drugs in the offices where I cleaned. Then one day, a cleaner in the same place was found dead from a drug overdose. I didn't know her well but never noticed she had a drug problem."

"Once is enough."

"True – and –"

"And?"

"Ah, there was another incident. That's why I got out of there as fast as I could."

"Of your own accord?" Henrietta asked.

"Sort of."

"You left Kinsale just for that, but what were you afraid of?"

Lily pulled at her cardigan. It couldn't be explained without revealing all. She was back to square one, lying.

"I'm not very brave and frighten easily, Henrietta; if complication comes my way I'm gone."

"What exactly was this other incident, Lily?"

Lily glanced at Henrietta, unsure, "It was not just the incident – oh I don't know – I would have ignored the trouble if it weren't for what came after."

"Lily?" Henrietta fixed her with a stern eye, "It is too big for you."

"What is – this cardigan?" Lily began closing the buttons.

"Lily – you –"

"Is that the time, Henrietta," Lily made a pretence at looking at her watch. "I must be off. I have a few errands to run, but I'm sure we'll be talking about it again."

12

Henrietta took her sewing bag to the lazy armchair in the living room. Her body was less willing today – her fingers were leaden and the needle felt heavy.

Her eyes flickered shut and the old cottage rocked her to its rhythm. Sleepless nights were catching up with her. The needle fell from her hands and the material slipped to the floor.

Many memories from Normandy passed through her mind, churning out images of her stolen youth and scenes that no child should ever experience.

One image prevailed:

......Her mother and sister sit on stools in the cowshed – heads slightly angled, enamel buckets held in place between their knees as they milk the cows. As their hands pulse up and down, creamy milk squirts and splashes into the buckets. Occasionally the cows shift from hoof to hoof and swish their tails.

A little girl skips out through the open door trying to catch the morning light. Suddenly there is an explosion and the little girl runs back, only to see the cowshed wall collapse –

"Not my mother and sister!" she cries.

Dust settles from the rubble on one side. On the other side, her mother pauses. Seeing her daughters are okay, she draws her lips together and continues milking. Her calmness stills the cows.

"Henrietta," Francoise runs to comfort her.

"Francoise, keep milking," orders her mother. "Henrietta, go back to the house, go back. The work has to be done and the cows must be milked – we need the milk. Do you understand, Henrietta, we need the milk?"……

Henrietta woke with a start and rubbed her eyes. Her watch showed that she had slept for over an hour. She went outside; a breath of fresh garden air might help revive her. The evening sounds were soothing compared to the noise ringing in her ears. She was stunned for a moment by the exquisite orange and pink sky as the sun set. No illumination could recreate the beauty of natural light. Nature got its dimmers and brighteners just right and the silent arrival of dusk was perfection. Henrietta walked towards the little bird grave. The cooing pigeons and chattering magpies were loud this evening. She remembered first becoming aware of that chorus as a child. It had reached inside her, a deep physical pain, hurting, as she felt the agony of knowing that someone she'd loved so dearly had passed away.

The memory overwhelmed her and another thread loosened taking her back to a very sad day:

……An eight-year-old Henrietta is chatting with her mother and sister in the Normandy farmhouse. The clock on the village church strikes midday. They are sitting down to lunch when Beau, their dog, starts barking in the yard. Her mother gets up from the table and walks slowly to open the door. A tall man wearing a long dark coat is standing there. Her mother invites him in and pulls up a chair for him; the legs of the chair scrape across the stone floor. Reluctantly, the man sits; his face is very grave as he takes a letter from his pocket and hands it to her mother. He tells her that her husband has been shot dead. Henrietta doesn't hear any more and races out the door to the fields where she crawls into a ditch and balls herself up. She stays there for hours until the wood pigeons sing in the night and the magpies' chattering fades.

Her sister finally comes, "We were calling you. Papa is in heaven now, Henrietta, but we have each other. Papa will watch over us."……

Henrietta brought her mind back to the present, standing in The Old Forge garden. She could never forget that day the news came of her father's death. It was in the arms of Francoise she wept. Her mother didn't cry in front of her; she never saw her mother cry. Duty came first and that meant her mother had to continue managing the farm alone. The war meant that millions of widows and grieving mothers had to manage alone.

At eight years, everything was confusing to Henrietta and little was explained in those times. It took her many years to make sense of what had really happened. The signing of the second Armistice Compiègne on June 22nd 1939 had resulted in the division of France whereby Germany occupied north and west, Italy controlled a small southeastern zone, and the zone libre was governed by the Vichy government led by Marshal Pétain. This remained so until liberation by the Allies in June 1944.

Her father had died fighting in the French Resistance. Henrietta realised later that her mother's silence was the only way to protect the family. Resisters were not heroes for everybody back then. Nobody knew anymore who was a friend or enemy. The explosion of the cowshed had been carried out by locals who believed her father's role in the Resistance was bringing trouble to the village. They feared the Germans' reaction and so preferred to bend to the rules of the invader.

The Germans took over and seized what they needed from the farms to provide their soldiers with food and provisions. They took the horses, chopped the wood and opened the barrels of cider. It was like living in a foreign land. She no longer recognised the smells, the voices, the eyes – and her father was gone. How much more her older sister, Francoise, must have understood and suffered. Worse was to come. But as a child, Henrietta had been lost and terrified, her voice had become a stammer and the truth had perished. The enemy had changed sides and the wrong man had died. There had been many heads shaved and shamed. The family had been punished – ostracised for years. But her sister had paid the full price.

The shouts of angry villagers came into Henrietta's mind, "Francoise Morney – HONTE – TRAITRE – TRAITRE – '

Henrietta blocked her ears as if that could stop the voices, but they got louder. They had never returned like that before, not so many and so torturous. She had to let those memories out – she had suppressed them all her life. It was something about the children, Lily, Sheila O'Connell and The Old Forge; everything was mixed up and had snared her. Henrietta would have no peace until she confronted those memories.

The Old Forge was soaked in the past; every stone spoke to her of anger, hurt and dishonour. Lily was right; rebellions had been plotted here, but hearts had been broken too.

The voices of its ghosts reverberated off the walls of the cottage:
'– *Jenny McCarthy – SHAME ON YOU – TRAITOR – TRAITOR –*'
Henrietta heard the name again and again, *'Jenny – Jenny –*'

"I know who you are now, you are the blacksmith's daughter," Henrietta spoke out loud.

'Jenny – Jenny –'

"I hear your name. Why are they shouting at you? Why are you calling out to me?" Henrietta listened as her own words echoed back to her.

Then she recalled a different set of words – 'The Caseys were nothing more than land grabbers and traitors'. Sheila O'Connell would have her own answers and personal history from her ancestors. Henrietta felt Sheila's anger – she was steeped in hate because of things that had happened to her family in the past.

Why did the spirits want to tell Henrietta Bontemps? She was an old woman, lacking the energy necessary to counter that kind of hate. Was there something in her childhood experiences that should help her understand the ghost, Jenny, and why she appeared to be a target of hate?

****

Branly's lip-gloss shone and her face sparkled with glitter. Branly, Henrietta thought, you paint your face so brightly, yet the shadows creep around you and your eyes grow duller.

They sat at the work table in the kitchen of The Old Forge. Henrietta had promised them just an hour of sewing and a trip to Tralee afterwards in the Volvo she had rented for a couple of days. But Branly had little concentration for sewing today and had been doodling on tracing paper.

"What are you doing with the tailor's chalk, Branly? It is made for drawing lines and patterns on material, not for sketching whatever takes your fancy."

"I'm drawing a bird – a thrush. After, I'm going to draw a cage around it."

Henrietta stood over her to look at it, "It is quite good. I wonder if it is better to draw the bird first or the cage?"

"If the cage is done second, it means the bird was free first and it will be very sad to have the cage put on top of it," Genie summed up for her friend. "Branly – is it sad?"

"I'm not sure." Branly fiddled with the chalk, "If I draw the cage first, how do I paint in the bird?"

Henrietta took another piece of chalk and added a bar to the cage, "An old painter in Paris once told me this fable about how to attract the most beautiful bird into your cage – a bird that will not only look beautiful, but sing beautifully too."

"How do you do that?" Branly put down her chalk.

"Yes, tell us," Genie needed no encouragement to put aside her sewing.

Henrietta waved her hands like a conductor, "You must firstly gather all your things together – take your paint brush, canvas and get your tubes of paint. Then, select and mix some colours on your palate. Dip your brush and with delicate strokes draw only some of the cage bars. Next, you must take your canvas to the forest. Shade in the light and the colours – paint the brightest sprigs and flowers inside."

Henrietta paused – "And here comes the difficult part. You must wait. You may have to wait one hour or several hours, maybe all morning, maybe all day, and maybe several days. But you must wait. Do not make or utter a sound – stay silent and wait. Eventually your perseverance will pay off. The little bird will come and choose your cage. It will skip closer and closer, fly away and come back again. It will play that game for a long time and you must continue to wait… And one day – voila! It will fly in and perch inside. Quickly – take your brush and paint the remaining bars in completely. Then with a final dab, paint in the cage door, but making sure to leave it wide open."

"That doesn't make sense," Genie said.

"It's a metaphor. Think about it, Genie, the best way to keep someone is to give them the freedom of choice."

"I heard that some birds don't want to fly away even when the cage doors are opened," Branly looked to Henrietta for explanation.

"That is different and I cannot say why, except that it is probably fear of change. We paint ourselves into imaginary cages all our lives. But, perhaps, we all need our cages for reassurance."

"Now I get it," Genie mused, examining her needle – "there's a sort of cage around me and I cannot find the open door."

"What makes you say that?" Henrietta asked.

"Her secret," Branly said.

"Yes," Genie admitted, "I'm locked in a secret."

"Do you want to tell me?"

"No."

"We all have secrets. They lock us in and we keep them locked inside," Branly whispered.

Oh, we do, we do, Henrietta thought.

✳✳✳✳✳✳✳✳✳✳✳✳✳✳✳✳✳✳✳✳✳✳✳✳✳✳✳✳✳

Henrietta drove slowly. It was not a long journey to Tralee; if they got there a few minutes sooner or later, what difference was it going to make to anyone? She smiled, realising she was beginning to think like Lily. Genie's serious face and her talk of secrets had been worrying her, but the air was easier since getting into the car and the girls' non-stop nattering was pleasant to hear. Shopping was their one and only aim in Tralee and it seemed reasonable to give the girls an hour on their own while tending to her business in Hanlon's Hardware Store.

Henrietta hurried to Denny Street Shopping Mall.

The security man stood close to both girls and held up two bottles of pink nail varnish in his hand, "Are you responsible for these girls?"

"Yes, they are under my charge – what happened?"

"It was just for the laugh," Branly said.

Genie hung her head and Henrietta regretted leaving them unsupervised.

The security man led them to the Garda Síochana Station on New Street. Branly and Genie were made sit on a bench while Henrietta went to the main desk and answered several questions. A Garda registered everything on his computer, before finally printing a document for her signature. It was then explained to the girls in very serious tones that they were lucky; this time there would be no charges filed, but the next time would be different.

Henrietta rang Lily and in clipped sentences told her about the arrest. She appreciated Lily's controlled reply.

The girls followed her obediently from the Garda Station; the town had lost its attraction for all of them.

"We will eat," Henrietta kept her tone neutral and took them into the first fast food restaurant.

"What would you like?" she asked them.

They both shook their heads.

"Do not be silly, you must eat something. I will order chips and…?"

"Chicken nuggets," Genie eventually volunteered.

They ate a little and Branly was inclined to talk again, "You saved us."

Henrietta dismissed the words, not feeling able to enter a discussion right then. Her anger surprised her. She did not shout or accuse, but before talking to the girls wanted to be in command of her emotions. Her own coffee was untouched. Where had that feeling of hurt come from? It was all so stupid; Branly had been given pocket money and had no need to steal the nail varnish.

She had been forced to steal herself in the past. She and her family had stolen blankets and coats from the German soldiers and had cheated in whatever way they could to get food. When penniless in Paris, she had taken things. It had been for survival – to eat and to put some shoes on her feet.

The girls had done it while under her responsibility, and that was what hurt, that lack of concern and respect for her authority. Teenagers just acted in ways that could be very unpredictable; she'd forgotten how impulsive they were.

A tiny voice piped up, "You saved us from prison," Genie was looking at her with those large eyes.

"I did not save you. You are minors and they were not going to send you there. I followed the law – one does not negotiate things like that."

Genie shoved her chips around the tray, "We're sorry that we put you to a lot of trouble."

Henrietta just inclined her head and looked at Branly. The girl was busy working out her story, deciding how to put it across. When it came, it was well crafted.

"I'm sorrier than anyone." Branly pulled out her purse, "I'd the money for the bottles of nail varnish – it was just for the fun of it, I didn't even want them. Genie wasn't involved at all and didn't know what I was going to do. It's all my fault – I'm just bad inside and out and always getting people in trouble. You can punish me in whatever way you want."

Henrietta studied the face, so transparent, clambering for attention. The girls had let her down, but her resolve was weakening. She was beginning to see how it had happened and appreciated that Genie had not tried to defend her passive part or evade responsibility. Although probably an innocent bystander, Genie was taking equal blame with Branly. It was good too that Branly had come out honestly with the facts, even if playing the tragic heroine was over the top and so typical for Branly. Henrietta's eyes softened, forgiveness came naturally. But she was not putting anything into words just then; that would be too easy, too soon.

Something hit against the back of Henrietta's chair. A man was trying to squeeze in to sit at the table behind her. He then began to rudely speak on his mobile phone about nothing that seemed very pressing; all she understood were the words football and trouble.

"Genie?"

Genie raced to the door – Branly rushed after her.

Henrietta got up, brushing slightly against her neighbour, "Sorry, excuse me."

The man did not turn or acknowledge her and remained glued to his phone.

She called out, "Genie, come back – where are you running to?"

She followed and could see that Genie had not gone far and was bent over double, vomiting into the street gutter.

She found some handkerchiefs, "Genie! Come back to the chip shop – we can use the toilets there to clean up."

"NO!"

"Genie wants to go home," Branly said.

Henrietta parked on Abbey Street and glanced in the rear view mirror. Genie's face was absolutely miserable and Branly was already elsewhere, gone off to her imaginative world.

"Genie, I rang your mother earlier and she is at home waiting for you. Branly, I could not reach your mother, so we are going to drive to Ash Road Estate and go directly to your home now."

Genie whispered something to Branly and got out, but remained standing on the pavement, hands by her side.

Henrietta let the window down, "Goodbye, Genie."

Branly had that look of desperation again, "If my mother didn't answer the phone, then she's not at home, Henrietta. If you have to report something, can't you come out tomorrow, or I'll send her to the hotel to you?"

"No, Branly, these things must be done today. We will locate your mother – that is all."

"My mother's not well today," Branly started crying.

Henrietta felt mean; it was not the petty theft that was bothering Branly, it was somebody going to her home and finding her mother possibly inebriated. 'I cannot humiliate her,' Henrietta thought and slowed down the car. She would have to think about this one and talk to Lily first.

"Come with me to the hotel then, we will try ringing your mother and getting her to meet us there."

13

It was October 23rd and Lily had put Genie's birthday card on the breakfast table. Genie didn't want a party or any fuss for her thirteenth birthday. However, Lily was determined that the terrible day in Tralee be put behind them. The sermons had been meted out and it was time to move on. Genie had been pale and shocked. Branly had talked regret; however, Lily wasn't sure that the gravity of the act had sunk in. Branly's mother had been on a drinking binge that day and in no condition to understand anything. So Lily had taken it upon herself to lecture both girls. It was bad enough, but getting Henrietta caught up in the whole thing was worse again. In the end, Lily's message to the girls was very simple – "Your chance is gone now, you've used it up. Your names are marked down and you can't rub them out. If you do something like that again, you'll have a label – labels stick for life."

Genie went for the cereal box not noticing the gifts or the card.

Oh, that girl, thought Lily. "Go on, open the packages, they're for no one else but you."

Genie finally began to open them. There was a pair of football boots from Henrietta and a Liverpool jersey from Branly.

"Thanks Mum. I'll go and thank Henrietta just after breakfast."

"You do that. Will you fetch me the newspaper from the armchair over there?"

"What – what is that?" Genie pointed to the sofa – Messy's head popped out of a red helmet.

Lily laughed; she hadn't counted on Messy's participation. "What do you think it is?"

Genie removed Messy and took the helmet in her hand.

"Not all treasures are outside the front window, Genie."

When that brought no reaction, Lily went to the back window.

At last, Genie got the hint and followed her. Lily threw it open wide, "Look down there." Next to the empty cardboard boxes and milk crates stood a silver and red bicycle.

A large grin spread across Genie's face, "Is it mine, really mine?"

"Go down and check, there might be a name on it." Lily was pleased with her success – bull's eye.

"Thanks Mum. I'll be the fastest racer on the planet – Genie Casey – Champion Cyclist," Lily was on the receiving end of a big hug and kiss.

"Go and see it," she urged impatiently, not wanting to appear too emotional, knowing how it made Genie cringe. However, it had been a long time since she'd had that unrestrained show of tenderness. Genie doled out her gestures of affection sparingly, but each one Lily remembered and cherished as glimmers of sunshine on a rainy day. Her belief was that the bicycle would be better than the computer at this stage. She just couldn't come around to considering a computer as a birthday present. A bicycle was special.

Genie made it into the supermarket yard in seconds. Lily watched with delight as she mounted the Raleigh bike. In the old days, there had been a bicycle shop in Killdoe. However, that had long since closed down and Lily had bought the bicycle in Tralee. The young salesman had been very helpful, although his sophisticated vocabulary with words like 'lightweight graphite' and 'hybrid with tyres of medium thread' hadn't been easy to grasp. But as soon as the Raleigh brand appeared before her eyes, she'd felt at home. She had settled for a red and silver hybrid Raleigh with twenty-one gears and suitable for different terrains. It had cost her the best part of eight hundred euros with the helmet thrown in.

Lily hadn't bought it immediately, not before seeking Sheamie's advice.

He'd endorsed her choice and had insisted on transporting it for her. She couldn't be stubborn about that, though for a horrible moment thought that Sheamie had been about to offer to pay for it too. Fortunately he'd understood that it wouldn't have won any points with her.

She'd been dishing out a lot of money lately; with a car coming soon, it was high time to watch her spending. But Sheamie had eased the way for many things, saving her time, money and trouble; and thankfully Maura had been paying back the loan.

Lily made sure that Maura heard nothing about the shop lifting. However, that didn't stop rumours about Branly's mother. According to Maura, Lena Hartigan was living it up with a new boyfriend. There were stories of spending sprees, drinking and carousing, and speculation that the source of all this money was linked to a money lender. Lily could have broken the handle of her mop in two when Maura told her that; again a money lender. How was Branly to mature in that sort of household?

There was a screech of brakes. What was happening down below? Why had Genie stopped circling the yard? She had one foot on the ground and was listening to someone. Damn, it was impossible to see who it was. The way Genie was looking up it must be a tall person. It might be Peter Sykes, he was tall enough. If it was Peter Sykes, wouldn't she have heard his bike – those engines were deafening? She leaned out the window; Genie hadn't put a proper jacket on and it was very cold. But Lily didn't have to call because her daughter had abandoned the bicycle and was running back towards the building. Lily rushed out to meet her, but Genie had already almost reached the landing.

"It's him, it's him," she panted – "he said to tell you that if either of us open our mouths, we're for it."

Lily's throat was so dry that it hurt to speak, "Did you see his face?"

Genie shook her head, "He's disguised differently each time. This time he had a beard, black hair and glasses, but in Tralee he was blond."

"Tralee!"

"There was a man in the take away; his back was turned, but when he spoke into his phone about a girl's football causing a lot of trouble, I knew it was him."

She gripped her daughter's arm, "Why didn't you tell me?"

Tears welled up in Genie's eyes, "I didn't want to upset you more – My bike, I forgot to put it in the shed."

Lily swallowed hard, "I'll go down and see to it."

"But Mum, will we have to move again?"

"No, we are not moving. We have done nothing wrong. I'll handle it, Genie, leave it to me. Now, put on the kettle while I go downstairs."

Lily waited until the door was closed behind her before giving into the trembles. He wasn't going to leave them be. She went into the supermarket yard. Extending from the storage and delivery section was a small car park where about a dozen cars were parked. Her eye fell on a big black Mercedes that appeared empty. Hadn't Maura said that the money lender had a big black car? Then so did Sheamie and many others. She wheeled Genie's bicycle, locked it in the little shed that went with the flat and then walked through the car park onto Abbey Street.

"Lily, hello," Henrietta almost bumped into her.

"Henrietta! Were you going into the supermarket?"

"No, I am coming back from my walk."

"You have more courage than I have," Lily wasn't in any mood for talking; besides Henrietta must think her strange after the discussion they'd had about hearing her grandfather's voice and leaving Kinsale in a hurry.

'Swish, swish, swish' – Sheila O'Connell was sweeping dust off the footpath in front of her shop. How convenient to have to do it just now, Lily thought. A man holding a box stood inside the shop door, but the interior was too dark to see what he looked like.

"Good morning, Mrs. O'Connell," Henrietta saluted.

Sheila O'Connell gave one big massive sweep with her long arms, turned and went inside, banging the blue door hard. The CLOSED sign was put back up.

I used to like blue, Lily thought, but the front of that shop had at least three shades of blue and it seemed cold and harsh.

"Sheila O'Connell is certainly not friendly," Henrietta stamped her boots on the frosty ground.

"Don't talk to me about her," Lily turned to go.

"Lily, I do not want to take up your time, but I have a favour to ask you."

"Me?"

"Yes. I would like to visit the old cemetery again and wondered if you would come along with me?"

"To the Abbey Graveyard?"

Henrietta stroked her brown suede gloves as if removing wrinkles, "Yes, that's what I mean. I do not know how to explain it. I am a long way from home, but have been thinking a lot about my mother and people of my family who have passed on. Next Monday is November 1st, All Souls' Day, and I would like to go back to the Abbey Graveyard."

"I don't see why not, I'm off work as it's a public holiday," Lily felt it was important to Henrietta. "Genie and Branly can come too."

"It will be good for all of us to connect with the past." Henrietta fixed her scarf, "It is freezing – do put on a coat, Lily."

****

Lily groaned – there was a pressure on her stomach and a purring sound. She turned on her side, then opened an eye, "Messy – what do you want?"

Messy raised her tail and miaowed.

"You want to go into Genie's room, is that it?"

Lily decided to accommodate the cat and got up; the next day was All Souls' Day, and a chance to sleep in. A happy Messy followed her. It was cold – there was a breeze from somewhere. She looked for an open window, but didn't find any – and finally put her ear to Genie's door. The draught was coming from inside her room, but Lily did not want to disturb her.

Lily gave the cat a biscuit and rearranged the cushions in its basket, "Now, Messy, that's your bed."

Messy rubbed against her leg.

Lily accepted defeat, took the cat in her arms and went back to bed. She chuckled, maybe Messy was disturbed by the fairies; it was Halloween after all, a night for witches and ghosts.

Henrietta had been curious about Halloween and Lily, having revised her knowledge while helping the girls with their homework, explained that nowadays it was very commercialised but originally it was a Celtic pagan feast, Christianised by the Early Church and renamed All Hallows' Eve, dedicated to All Saints' Day, October 31st. In Medieval Ireland, and during oppression by the English through the Penal Laws, Catholics were forbidden to practise their faith and resorted to old pagan celebrations. It was thus that the feast day resurfaced as the Festival of Samhain (Summer Festival). It marked the end of summer with rituals to protect families, land and livestock from sickness, bad luck and the darker days of winter. It was also a time when souls were believed to visit graves and that explained why people used to light candles in graveyards.

When Lily was a child, the night of Halloween was the time to try to frighten people, tell ghost stories, make predictions and play games. Children played Snap Apple, which involved attaching strings to the apple stalks and hanging them from the ceiling, rafters, clothes line… The goal was to try to take a bite out with one's hands behind their back. Others played a similar game by putting an apple or a coin in a basin of water. Her favourite memory was making the traditional brack for tea, called the Barmbrack. The yeast bread was sweeter than sandwich, but not as sweet as cake, and with raisins and sultanas. The brack was still popular and sold by supermarkets and bakeries. In a burst of nostalgia, Lily had baked a brack for the girls that afternoon. Following tradition, she had put little predictive tokens wrapped in greaseproof paper in the cake mixture. The fun was to see if a token turned up in your slice: a pea symbolised you would not marry the following year, and a ring that you would; a small coin predicted you would be wealthy. Lily had deliberately excluded the piece of cloth symbolising a life of poverty, and the stick representing violence; she didn't want Branly unluckily getting one of those and encouraging more of her morbid thoughts. However, when Lily herself, much to the glee of Branly and Genie, got the ring in her slice, she was not so amused.

"What's wrong with that girl today, she's like a wet rag?" Lily discussed with herself over the sink the next morning. "My daughter and the cat are lifeless lumps on the bed – sleeping innocence." She had woken with a slight headache herself. The night had been very disturbed by turbulent dreams about the blackmailer's threats; there had also been bumps, cars and banging windows.

"Genie," she called, "it's eleven o'clock. I'm going downstairs for a minute. Do you hear me at all?"

"Uh, hum."

"After lunch, we're going to the graveyard to clean up the graves. It's the feast of All Souls, the day we honour our dead."

"Do I have to, Mum?"

Lily put her head in the bedroom door, "I thought you wanted to.

What's brought on this change of mind?"

"Sheila O'Connell mightn't like us on her property."

"The devil take her – what's it to her? That graveyard, like the new one, is open to everyone. It belongs to the church of Killdoe and to all the community. Our people are buried there and we'll visit them whenever we want."

Genie clambered out of bed and limped.

"What's the matter?"

"A football injury."

"Let me see."

"It's nothing," Genie scurried into the shower.

Lily's suspicions heightened as she noticed a puddle on the floor. She opened the window and remembered the draught she felt last night outside Genie's door. She looked out and saw wooden pallets piled high descending into the yard below. Lily realised a fit girl could climb easily in and out the window at any time. She would not confront Genie yet until she was certain about what was going on. Maybe I am over-thinking, Lily thought.

Lily nipped downstairs and into Mack's, pausing for a moment in front of one of the supermarket mirrors. She hardly recognised her own reflection. Since returning to Killdoe she was taking better care of herself. She was cutting and styling her hair more often and paying attention to how she looked. She had lost some weight. It was no wonder, Lily thought, always looking over her shoulder or waiting anxiously for Genie to get in from school or football practice.

Lily took a trolley and went in search of gardening gloves to do some cleaning up around the graves. Though it was a public holiday, there was a flow of people into the supermarket. Lily groaned to herself as she saw Maura approach her. She had too much on her mind and was in no humour to socialise.

"You're out and about, Lily?"

"Like yourself."

"We're never done, if it isn't one trolley we're pushing, it's another. Do you know who was up at Malt Hill yesterday?"

"No."

"Sheamie Fitzgerald."

"Was he?"

"He was then."

"It's a big hill, Maura."

"He was up at the old farmhouse."

"I'm sure he has his reasons." Lily tapped her shopping trolley, "I won't be delaying you, Maura."

Maura didn't need a second hint, "Good luck to you so."

What was Sheamie up to now, Lily wondered – what would carry him out to Malt Hill?

✳✳✳✳✳✳✳✳✳✳✳✳✳✳✳✳✳✳✳✳✳✳✳✳✳✳

Lily lingered at the graveyard gate on River Road letting Henrietta and the girls go in first. She began to meander through the sea of gravestones across rough grass and bumpy ground. Here and there, plastic holy water bottles, flowers and pictures had been placed. Some were discoloured and faded. Something glinted on the ground. It was a soggy, glittery scarf, like something Branly would wear; in fact it looked exactly like Branly's. Lily picked the scarf up and put it in her pocket. Branly looked more washed out and tired than usual today. Had she been to bed at all? Both girls had been acting oddly. Genie had gone through the graveyard like a thief – head stuck in the collar of her coat and looking around as if she were avoiding someone. Branly was talking a lot of nonsense about the dead, saying little prayers and not making much sense.

"May the souls that shed their blood to save our lands be blessed and those who betrayed us and took the side of our foes burn in hell."

"That's an awfully strange prayer you have, Branly. It doesn't sound much like the novenas I learned growing up," Lily commented.

Branly blessed herself, "It's better in the day time. Last night – "

"Mum," Genie interrupted, "they say that ghosts and spirits live around graveyards – have you ever seen one?"

So they had been up to some Halloween tricks, Lily thought, now connecting the draught in Genie's room and the puddle on the floor. No wonder Genie was being evasive and snarly with her. "A graveyard is quiet, some say peaceful, but in the middle of the night it can be active."

Genie and Branly huddled closer together.

"When you think about it," Lily continued, "there must be more dead creatures than living ones. So you could say that we, the living, are the minority. The dead are everywhere in one form or another: ash, dirt, burnt and buried. No wonder we say prayers for the dead in the hope that they don't remain attached to places like this, but instead are clapped off to another world: good, bad and indifferent. It's hardly surprising that some prefer to think that there are no spirits and no life after death."

"Just ash and dirt," Branly said.

"What a macabre conversation," Henrietta joined them. "You will frighten the girls, Lily."

"Well, I hope I put some fear in both of them," Lily walked on to a grave, went on her knees and began to pull at tufts of grass. She took out a cloth from her bag to wipe the marble stone. Suddenly, noticing some fresh scratches, she stopped, "I don't believe this – who would do this?"

"What's the matter, Lily?" Henrietta stood behind here. "Oh, of course, your family's grave."

"That's right, this is Caseys'." Lily polished the marble with determination. "I was thinking about my conversation just now with the girls and about our prayers and rituals to appease the spirits. But I might ask what would happen if we did the opposite."

"I'm not sure I follow you, Lily, I'm not an expert."

"None of us are. But that O'Connell woman thinks she is with her constant preaching and playing God. That woman can keep well away from Caseys' grave, and McCarthys' too."

"You are upset, Lily. It was my idea to come here, but perhaps it is too hard for you." Henrietta traced a finger over some of the inscription, "Jenny is a nice name."

"I've always liked it myself. She was given the grand name Eugenia at birth, but people just called her Jenny and that's what they put on the tomb, 'Jenny Casey-nee McCarthy'. I am upset because of what some vandal did here," Lily dropped the cloth.

Henrietta put on her glasses, "Are those fresh scratches, Lily – did someone deliberately try to scratch out her maiden name? What's written below it? Oh, an Irish word maybe – 'IFREANN'."

"Shush, I don't want the girls to notice. Irish is one subject that I was good at, at school, and 'IFREANN' means 'HELL'."

"Are you going to report this?"

"It won't do any good. Even if I have my own idea, I can't prove who did it and I don't want the Gardaí in my personal business."

The girls' chatter echoed from the other end of the graveyard.

"Branly is behaving in a peculiar way today," Henrietta said.

Lily explained to Henrietta her suspicions about the girls visiting the graveyard during the night.

Branly's voice was very high, "My mother can't remember me when I'm alive, who will remember me when I'm dead?"

"Oh, Branly, don't talk that way, you won't be dying for a long time," Genie said.

Henrietta addressed Branly, "You have forgotten something very important – you have a good friend here in Genie. Many go through life and never have one good friend."

Branly cheered up and linked arms with Genie, "I have the best friend in the world. I can tell her everything and anything, she knows my deepest thoughts. We've sworn to be forever loyal to each other and never to reveal each other's secrets."

Lily's eyes met Henrietta's, "We're talking too much about death and in the wrong way. We're all alive and have many more things to do, and what we're going to do next is, get out of here. We've done our duty for All Souls' Day. We have done enough remembering for one day."

"Now we will indulge in cake and ice-cream at the hotel," Henrietta added.

Lily worried as she felt the damp scarf in her pocket. Somebody was playing with Branly's mind. A dog barked from the top of the graveyard; Sheila O'Connell's wolfhound was prowling around the abbey ruins. Lily marched out letting the gate bang behind her.

"Hi folks." Sheamie drew up his car beside them, "Can I offer you pretty ladies a lift some place?"

"We're going for tea to your hotel," Lily said, "to boost your profits. We're well able to walk there." She was mad at him. Huh, she thought – what was he doing up at Malt Hill?

"Sheamie, I need to talk to you," Henrietta began.

"I know and that's why I'm here. I was scouting out for you. I've got everything you were asking for back at the hotel. So, sit in and take the weight off your legs, and I'll drive you there."

Sitting in the front was too close, almost intimate, so Lily urged Henrietta to sit up front with Sheamie instead.

"It's cold, but what a clear sky," Sheamie said, "why not go up that height to admire the view."

The girls didn't care much about views, but being driven around in a big Mercedes was a thrill for them. Still, Lily was happy to see Genie's animated face. She should be more upset that Genie sneaked out the window, but at least it meant her daughter was forgetting about the blackmailer's threats. But now, Lily wondered what Sheamie was up to. Could she trust him?

"We have a great view of Malt Hill as well from here," Sheamie remarked.

Lily leaned forward, "I haven't been out there for years. Are there many changes to the place?"

He adjusted the mirror, "I can't remember when I was out there last myself. If I had time it would be nice to cruise around the countryside."

Lily scratched her head. If what Maura had told her about Sheamie being seen on Malt Hill was true, then why was he lying?

14

Henrietta sat up in bed in her hotel room and examined each document. Sheamie had gone into a lot of detail; there were pages and pages of material, official stamps and certifications. She took off her glasses and laid them on the small bedside locker. She would send the file by express post to the detective in the morning. It was his job to check the authenticity of the facts, figures and dates, and she had every confidence in his professionalism. It was hard to believe that Jean, Thibault and Sheamie had not already collected and put together similar information. How could accomplished business men who brokered big deals and negotiations fail to apply the same rigor to their personal affairs?

Henrietta fixed the pillow behind her head and switched off the light. Another night begins, she thought. She never used to count them and was playing with the little time granted her, trying to fool herself into believing that there was a lifetime in front of her. Getting attached to people in Killdoe was not wise.

Standing in the Abbey Graveyard today was more turbulent than she'd expected. The name 'Jenny' had kept coming into her head, vibrating from every stone, again and again.

Jenny, you are not where you should be – Jenny, come home.'

The presence of her own sister's spirit by her side had also been very strong all day. If Jenny was not buried in the right place, then neither was Francoise. It turned and turned in her mind. All her life, she had shut out the past, not realising that she had shut Francoise out too. It wasn't just the ghost of Jenny that was calling to her, but her sister, Francoise, as well.

Henrietta could not forget, either, seeing Branly looking lost among the gravestones searching for her past and not finding it. Francoise had been condemned before having a chance to grow up and become the person she might have been. But Branly too was condemned and struggling to find some threads to hold on to, something of her past and present, and hope for the future.

Suddenly, Henrietta had a vivid mental picture of the vandalised headstone. She put a hand to her chest and lifted her body up in the bed. It wasn't her first time suffering from shortness of breath. She propped her back with a second and third pillow. Sheila O'Connell's influence was suffocating her. All the time she and Lily and the girls had been in the cemetery that evil woman's shadow was hovering, watching from the stained glass window of her chapel. What was it about Lily's past that angered that woman? What demons were driving her? If those demons were confined to her thoughts and mind, they would destroy only her. But if they got out, who knew what she was capable of doing.

Henrietta skipped breakfast at the hotel and decided instead to go directly to the public library.

Thirty minutes later, sensing a pair of eyes drilling through her, Henrietta raised her head from the large and engrossing research volume she had been reading. On each visit to Killdoe Library, Sheila O'Connell was either there before her or came in after her. Today her acknowledgement had been ice cold and she had stared hard at the book on Henrietta's desk. Ellen O'Brien, Chief Librarian, had gone to a lot of trouble to fetch the thesis from the basement archives. Henrietta had asked for material from the early part of the twentieth century. The thesis bearing the title, *Priests and People in North Kerry during the Irish War of Independence*, had been the doctoral research of Ellen O'Brien's own son. Henrietta read the sections that mentioned Killdoe. One captured her attention:

'On the night of March 16th, 1920, a small convey of British soldiers, consisting of RIC, Black and Tans and Auxiliaries, was on its way to

Listowel Garrison, when it was ambushed on Keale Bridge outside the town of Killdoe. Irish rebels operating under the name of the Irish Republican Army and captained by Patrick Connell attempted to blow up Keale Bridge. The explosion only partly succeeded and a group of British soldiers arrived on the scene in support of their comrades. There followed a bloody shoot-out between the rebels and British forces. In the confusion that ensued, Patrick Connell was shot dead, together with Daniel Healy and Michael Forde. Other rebels escaped to Malt Hill Forest and were hunted by the British forces. However, due to the density of the forest and lack of knowledge of the local terrain, they failed to capture the remaining Irish rebels…'

The writer explained that it was later established that 20 British soldiers had died in the botched explosion and subsequent shoot-out. The British soldiers who came in support of their colleagues had probably been tipped off by an informer. Orders came from Dublin to crack down on any sign of rebellion and to watch certain households in Killdoe and the surrounding area, including McCarthys. James McCarthy's forge was suspected to be a den of conspiracy and where the ambush had been planned.

Henrietta understood from the foreword that very little original documented evidence survived from those years. The period known as the Irish War of Independence, 1919-1921, was followed by the signing of the Treaty and the Irish Civil War. From her husband's readings of history, she knew that during the Irish Civil War, 1922-1923, people who had fought side by side for Independence became enemies. Families, friends, and neighbours were divided and horrific killing and brutality followed. As most of the documented evidence was burnt in a fire in Dublin Castle in 1941, the facts about the horrors were lost forever. Many happenings would have remained part of the hidden past and gotten passed on or not through oral history and folklore in various forms of truth and invention. The document quoted by the researcher about the ambush was one of the few papers that had survived.

Feeling eyes on her, Henrietta looked up in time to catch the dagger stare of Sheila O'Connell. Henrietta sighed, sure that Sheila must have her own version of the ambush and how her grandfather had died.

15

Michael McGrath was not around lately. Lily didn't know why or where McGrath had gone to, but she pushed her trolley more easily on the corridors.

She peered over Maura's shoulder to see what she was reading on the notice board. It was a poster advertising a Christmas Draw at The Treasure Chest. Customers had to just enter a draw for chocolates. Cheap boxes of chocolates, Maura agreed. It was hard to imagine how Sheila made her living out of such a shop; and Lily concurred that she must have other sources of income coming in as the shop couldn't possibly pay the bills.

The crackling of a walkie-talkie distracted them both. A security man came and stood at the end of the corridor. Lily had seen him a few times behind the desk. There was something about him that reminded her of someone; it was his tall stance and way of walking.

"Did you find out his name, Maura?"

"I heard somebody call him Pat. He's temporary and covering for Rory Flynn who broke his leg. There are a lot of temporary workers, I hope we'll hold onto our own jobs."

"Are you alright for money, Maura?"

"We're managing better since Joe got the work from Sheamie. That's thanks to you, Lily."

"Don't thank me. I only mentioned to Sheamie that Joe was looking."

"Sure Sheamie's besotted with you, Lily, he'd do anything for you."

"Don't be talking foolish," Lily didn't want to hear.

"Hmm," Maura took out her duster, "I was foolish about the money, but I know love when I see it."

Lily didn't want to encourage Maura on the love front. Could she trust a man who she noticed was lying about his visit to Malt Hill? She thought about Sheamie a lot; whatever about him being besotted with her, he was often cajoling her to take up one of his job offers. He had scores of job opportunities for her that entailed working with the public. For Lily those jobs brought trouble, because people were trouble.

Lily was still thinking about Sheamie when she came home later that day to find her daughter drenched in sweat and excitedly wanting to tell her about her day at Malt Hill.

Lily sat down, upset that Genie had not waited for them to go together, "You went out to Malt Hill without telling me first!"

"You said we would go to Malt Hill ages ago," Genie argued.

"Did you wear your helmet?"

"I did, but Branly has none. It was fun cycling past the trees, fields, cows and farms."

Lily recalled fondly cycling to and from Killdoe many times. In her memories, it was always summer and sunny… Along the road, the hedges were adorned with beautiful yellow furze bushes and drooping blood red and vivid purple fuchsia shrubs. Malt Hill was a wonderful sight showing off a multitude of greens, and the forest was home to oaks, hazel, ash, elm, beech, Scots pine, conifers, and spruce… She liked to remember a childhood of picking bluebells and looking for mushrooms. At the top of the hill, she would get off her bicycle and look down into the rich valley of fields and meadows. In spring time, the fields were tinged with purple clover, but in late summer freshly harvested meadows reminded her of a green and yellow chequered table cloth. The wynds of hay dotted the land in shades of gold, left to season and mature in the August sunshine before finally being brought home to barn sheds for winter cattle fodder.

"Did you meet anyone?"

"A farmer was there in the yard where the old house is and – Mum, are you mad?

"I'm not mad, Genie. I have no problem with you and Branly cycling out a bit, but you should have told me beforehand." She didn't want to say that her real worry had more to do with the stranger showing up again to threaten Genie.

Lily stood up to make tea. "I got a second-hand car. It's parked outside."

"The black Clio? Cool."

Lily was forced to recognise that it had been once again thanks to Sheamie. He'd introduced her to a reliable car dealer who had the perfect car for her. Sheamie's thoughtfulness gave her a warm feeling. It was another point in his favour, she thought. That was the snag, he was building up his credit and she hated owing people.

****

Lily gripped the steering wheel, driving straight on towards Malt Hill. She was fighting the fear in her stomach, but was not turning back now. She had come home to Killdoe, but for the first time was returning home to Malt Hill. She turned on the wipers to fend off the drizzle.

It all passed through her mind as she drove towards Malt Hill: growing up on the farm, why she left the first time twenty-five years ago… She'd returned fleetingly for the funerals – her father's first, then her mother's.

Lily remembered when time had stood still. After her brother's death, the house became a tombstone and the farm a graveyard. The farm was passed onto her brother, Frank, though he hadn't wanted it. Frank wanted to travel and wasn't a farmer by nature.

He had been speeding home that day, hurrying back to milk the cows. Her father and Shep, the dog, waited at the crossroads for him. Frank, the son, was the only one her father saw.

'Your parents and grandparents fought for this, made this for you,' her father would chastise Frank when he was late or complained about tending to cows or fields.

A few years after Frank's death her parents sold the farm to a cousin, Ben Casey. Lily was never informed of their intention or the financial details of the arrangement. But after both her parents passed on, she discovered that Ben had taken advantage of them and bought the farm way below the market price. Her parents finished out their days in the old farm house, but let it go to wrack and ruin. There wasn't enough money left to pay for her mother's funeral and Lily covered the funeral costs herself. By then, her cousin had sold off most of the farm piece by piece to support his drink problem.

When Lily stood in the graveyard the day of her mother's funeral, she had wanted to shout out, 'I was there too and could have taken over the farm.'

Hadn't she, their daughter, counted or mattered to them? But her brother's death had clouded all, it had opened her eyes and broken something definitely with her. She would never matter to them and there was nothing to tie her to Malt Hill or Killdoe anymore.

There never had been bad words exchanged between Lily and her parents. The problem was – there never had been any words between them, not even during that tragic time.

After Frank's funeral, her parents closed their door on life. Lily couldn't blame them for mourning and had been shattered herself, but she had blamed them for not wanting to live again. They'd given up and wouldn't try, not even for her. She'd felt useless and empty. Day after day, she would think, 'I am your daughter, am I not reason enough to want to go on? I want to live – have to live'.

In the end, she couldn't stay decaying with them and had to get out of that farm, out of Killdoe and as far away as she could.

Sheamie was her comfort and a shoulder to lean on during that time. He listened and consoled. How much she'd told him, walking along Ballybunion beach, talking and talking. He'd shared his plans for the future and she her disillusionment and hunger to leave and move on. She wondered if her words still had a place in his memories. Sheamie had known exactly what he wanted. He had wanted to marry Lily and to make a family with her.

Lily liked Sheamie a lot, but couldn't have stayed with him back then. He'd been her first, but yet it hadn't been enough for her. In her mind it would have been using him, living a lie. She hadn't been ready to give him a family life and wanted to leave Killdoe. She didn't want to watch her parents slowly die, or see a house and farm decay. She'd have moulted and moulded and Sheamie would have paid the price. How she must have hurt him anyway, Lily realised now as she drove steadily in the drizzle.

She had gotten out, that was for sure. Years later, she found love again over in London when she met Jimmy Cronin. Jimmy was originally from Dublin, but they'd both been fish out of water, trying to survive in a foreign city. When she got pregnant and Genie was born, Jimmy was nothing but trouble. The last straw was the evening, when once more, he came home drunk, smashing everything on the kitchen table. She'd kicked him out. He came back begging and looking for help, but she kept her door closed. Lily and Genie, who was then two years old, had a better chance of a life without him.

Jimmy died in a crash just a few hundred metres from the flat.

Lily had gone on with her life without Jimmy and without anybody's help.

Lily parked the car and held her breath as she got out slowly and took tentative steps, stealing up on the old farm. She heard voices in the distance coming from a new house built a little farther up the passage. Whistling came from an out-house. The yard was sloped and the mud made the concrete slippery and slimy. A strong smell of manure drifted in the air.

There in front of her eyes she saw the old homestead. The walls, black and grey in places, were partially covered in a green moss. The windows and doors were boarded up. The front door was padlocked with a heavy chain. The chimney stack was still towering and dominant. She tried to look through one unboarded window that was caked in mud and could just make out the big open fireplace. It was still easy to imagine people sitting round it. She looked to the upper window to the room where she was born.

She wanted to cry for all of them and for the lost moments. But although the tears welled up, the pain was less than she expected; it was a dull ache. The emotion didn't drown her, but instead, just leaked through. Maybe, there no longer was any anger or bitterness. There was nothing festering there, only regret and willingness to move on.

Lily had decided to come on her own, fearful of what might possess her, thinking it would be better to see for herself, before talking to Genie or showing her the old farm. Things hadn't happened in that order. She would come back again with Genie, sure that while there was and would always be sadness, that part of her life had truly ended. They all could live with the past and move on. People talked about closure – there was none to make, at least not that way.

Then why was that dread still inside her – an apprehension that all was not over?

She walked away, turning once for a last look at the house. Nobody would ever live in the family home again. She was glad the new house was built and happy to hear the sound of children playing. This place was made for a young family now who would enjoy working the land. That's how things should be.

Lily drove towards Killdoe, unhurriedly deciding to detour back through the forest. Branly and Genie had come this way, they told her; she didn't like it, it was too isolated and didn't appear safe. She would have a word with the girls about the dangers of the forest. She parked in a clearing, got out and stood for a long time. Nana had brought her here as a little girl. They'd had picnics in the forest, but in her memories it had been warmer and brighter. She was surprised how dark and ominous it was.

Suddenly something felt different in her body. It was a strange sensation as if she were in another time. She could feel Nana's hand in hers guiding her somewhere.

"Where are you taking me, Nana? Do you want to show me something here?"

She heard laughter and a couple appeared – like wisps of smoke in the haze before her eyes. They were embracing and there was much passion in the air around them.

She heard Nana humming and sensed her pointing to a songbird gliding through the air, singing in chorus with her.

Nana's hand slipped away. Her spirit walked ahead, floating through the trees, then paused, looked back and beckoned at Lily to follow.

Lily couldn't resist and walked deeper through the pines following the trickling sound of running water. She saw a stooped man leaning on a stick near a small waterfall. He touched the leaves of a little briar bush.

Lily called to him, "Granda, what are you telling me? Why are you so sad? What do you want me to do?"

Then the answer came to her – it wasn't the spirits of her parents or brother that needed closure, it was her grandparents. There was something unfinished on Malt Hill; now she understood that Nana and Granda weren't at peace. She put her hand to her breast and felt a deep hurt.

A car engine sounded, bringing Lily back to reality momentarily and reminding her that she'd forgotten to lock the Clio. But her eyes stayed fixed on the vision of her grandfather who was pointing with his stick.

"What's there, Granda? What's the matter?" Lily ran towards him, but the vision disappeared.

Lily looked around disorientated. Had she really seen the ghostly figures of Granda and Nana?

Rain was now falling heavily. Lily pulled her cardigan over her head and hurried back to the car. The car door was swung open. She was sure she had closed the door. Her chest tightened as she saw a brown envelope on the driver's seat. She dreaded envelopes and notes. Lily opened the envelope and quickly unfolded the note inside. It was blank. The warning was clear to Lily – 'We are watching you and don't forget it'.

16

When Lily bumped into her in Mack's supermarket, Henrietta sensed that it was no accident. Something was upsetting Lily and that's why she accepted her invitation to pop upstairs for a cup of tea. It was her first time entering the flat and the vibes in the place were good; it was homely with enough disorder to relax in. Lily removed some books from the sofa and Henrietta assured her that the cat, called Messy, was welcome to curl up near her.

She sipped tea from a pretty cup, while her host stood and sat several times to fetch the milk, a spoon, open the window and close it again. It was obvious to Henrietta that Lily was on edge but not yet ready to tell her why. So Henrietta asked many questions about Sheila O'Connell and her family. Lily told her about a sister, Bernie, in the nuns and remembered she had some relatives in Cork. Sheila herself had not featured in Lily's life very much growing up in Killdoe.

"But Sheila's ancestors played a big part in Killdoe's history. I was reading earlier today in the library that in 1920 there was an ambush near Killdoe during the Irish War of Independence."

Lily grimaced, "That was long before my time."

"A man called Patrick Connell was killed in that ambush. Was he Sheila O'Connell's grandfather?"

"He was indeed. But if you were going by her, he was the only one killed. The Caseys were involved too, so were the McCarthys and many others."

"Did your grandparents talk about it when you were growing up?"

"No, and they never spoke about the Irish Civil War either."

"You mentioned your grandfather saying that the Caseys and O'Connells fought on different sides, it must have happened afterwards in the Irish Civil War."

"God only knows who was on what side in whatever war. You're becoming a great expert on Irish history, Henrietta."

"I am not, but I am trying to understand Sheila's dislike of you and why she looks at you oddly all the time."

"The way she looks at me! She looks at everyone with that evil eye. That woman isn't normal. The last time I passed her on Ash Road with her dog, she called me 'a Casey land grabber' to my face – and I took it all from her, didn't say boo."

"Land grabber – what does that mean exactly?"

"Land grabbers were people who grabbed other people's land during The Famine, 1845. They took advantage of the poor who were often dying of hunger and unable to pay rent to landlords. Those misfortunate and poor people were evicted and others who could afford to pay even higher rent stepped into land that way."

"Then it was a terrible slur for Sheila O'Connell to say that about your family."

"Yes, what does she or anyone know about what really went on during those times? It's all nonsense in her head; between that and religion the woman's demented."

Lily poured Henrietta another cup of tea and asked of her return to Paris. Henrietta explained that her plan was to make it back to Killdoe for one brief visit before Christmas and to return once again in the New Year to finish renovations in The Old Forge.

"Will you visit Normandy while you are in France this time?"

Henrietta studied her cup, "I would like to."

"Have you ever known people who gave up on life?"

It was an odd question but Henrietta took it in her stride, "A few, yes."

"It's terrible to be alive and to have stopped living – that's what my parents did. Do you remember the story I told you on the bus the first day we met?"

Henrietta's face filled with compassion, "You were speaking about your brother and father, weren't you?"

"Yes, losing my brother, Frank, was hard. But it was harder watching my parents give up and being the invisible daughter."

Henrietta nodded.

Lily straightened her cardigan, "Enough on that, it's all behind me."

"Dear Lily, talking is sometimes good. I cannot pretend to know how you felt, but it must have been awful for you. I am sorry they did not see what a beautiful, strong and courageous daughter they had in you."

"I went to Malt Hill today," Lily blurted.

"And?" At last Lily was getting around to explaining her agitated state and why she entered the supermarket looking like she had seen a ghost.

"It was very odd. Some of it I expected, like resentment about being excluded and regret over my parents. The farm was to be Frank's, but my parents sold it after he died. I felt shut out because they did not give it to me or at least involve me in their decision. It will always spoil my memories, but I was prepared for that and can live with it. However, I wasn't prepared for the force and pull of my grandparents. You know, while I was in Kinsale it was Granda's voice that I heard again calling me home. Believe me, home was the last place I wanted to go. Killdoe wasn't in my plans. But I trusted it was Granda's spirit guiding and protecting Genie and me from danger in Kinsale."

Henrietta put down her cup, "Lily, you are going to have to face up to what happened in Kinsale. If you cannot tell me or someone else, then at least listen to the voice of your granda."

"But that's the damper, Henrietta, I don't know what he is telling me and I don't know how much is real or coming from my own imaginings. Besides, if I talk to anyone, Genie's life will be in danger." Lily stood up abruptly and went to the window. "I got a blackmail note –"

Henrietta waited.

Finally, Lily turned to look at her and shook her head, "I can't involve you – it's my trouble."

"You already have involved me. You told me some of it, Lily, now tell me all."

Henrietta listened in astonishment as Lily spoke in breathless sentences

– needing to tell, but struggling against it. As Lily poured out the words, she realised this was major trouble: blackmail, knives, threats, and possibly murder.

Lily plopped on onto the sofa, put her head in her hands and sobbed.

"Lily?" Henrietta touched her shoulder lightly, "Thank you for telling me. You do not need to carry this burden all by yourself. You must ask for help."

Lily shook her head, "It was Sheamie I wanted to tell first, but couldn't."

Henrietta stiffened at the mention of Sheamie. Lily needed help and this was quite a conundrum.

Lily fussed around the kitchen making another cup of tea.

Henrietta explained to Lily about her investigations into the racehorse affair, without pointing blame or reproach directly at Sheamie. She revealed hiring a private detective and wanting to find out more about the deal with Sheamie.

Hope came into Lily's eyes as the possibilities dawned on her, "Do you think your private detective could help me?"

"His name is Denis Curran and he is very discreet." Henrietta reflected on the best way to handle it while also saving Lily's pride. Such services were expensive. The safest way for now was for Lily to allow Henrietta herself to mediate the initial stages and transfer the information back to her. Mr. Curran could widen his scope for her. If the police were already looking into the overdose in Kinsale, then it would have forced the blackmailer to keep a low profile. Lily's unexpected decision to come home seemed to have heightened the danger. Did the blackmailer have a base in Killdoe or did he follow Lily and Genie here? Lily was adamant neither of them had spoken to anyone, but Henrietta was beginning to wonder about the girls' friendship and their secrets?

"Let me make some inquiries firstly with the detective and we will take it from there," Henrietta resolutely stated.

"But you must tell me how much it would cost."

"Only after he has begun to provide evidence." Henrietta could see the doubt return to Lily's eyes, but persuaded her that in the interest of all, it was better that way.

****

Henrietta walked to The Old Forge, relishing the sensation of a crispy bed of frost under her boots as she ambled along Sméar-dhubh Lane. The bushes were bare of blackberries but ice glistened everywhere. A magpie perched on the slate roof of The Old Forge; it would have been thatched in the old days, thought Henrietta.

She sighed, it was difficult to concentrate her mind, all this trouble with Lily and Genie had taken over. Her discussion with the detective had not been as satisfactory as expected. Checking the credentials of people connected to a horse deal was one thing, pursuing criminals who might be guilty of killing was a whole other affair, Mr. Curran had told her. He pointed out to her that maybe it was a job for a special task police force. She used all her powers of persuasion to convince him to at least make some preliminary inquiries on her behalf.

A shadow eclipsed Henrietta's light for a second as the tall, straight-backed woman holding her wolfhound on a long leash passed her near the cottage gate.

Although she had come face to face several times with Sheila since the cemetery visit, barely a word had been exchanged. Long conversation which was normal for the locality did not seem possible with that woman. Everybody in Killdoe indulged in an abundance of wordy sentences.

Given Lily's current dilemma and her own encounters with the ghosts of The Old Forge, she was beginning to wonder where it was all leading to and if she were missing some vital connections. The documented information in the thesis and the fact that several people had died in that ambush still stuck in her mind. Sheila O'Connell's grandfather had been shot dead in 1920 and obviously the details of what happened would have been passed down in her family. It explained Sheila's grudge against the English and her obsession with keeping out foreigners like herself. But Sheila's resentment against Lily and her family went deeper, and it seemed that she really believed that Lily's people had not only grabbed O'Connells' land during The Famine but had betrayed them during the Irish War of Independence. It was frightening to imagine that Sheila was carrying a grudge from so long ago.

She shook her head, a few short months before, all these people had been strangers to her – now they were part of her life. Everything was tangled up. She wanted to deal with one thing at a time, but it was not going to be that way.

Henrietta went to the garden and took up a set of chiming bells Genie had given her as a gift for The Old Forge, a trinket probably bought at The Treasure Chest. Genie had been so proud to offer it and they had ceremoniously hung it near the bird grave. It was just a trinket, but the clinking sound stoked up a memory. The 'tintelles' had rung like that in her childhood; in villages in France, they had been used to call labourers for the milking of the cows. She shut her eyes and heard the language of music calling her back home to her Normandy village. Lily had faced Malt Hill; maybe now it was time for her to face the home she left at the age of fourteen. It was time for her to face her own ghosts from the past.

17

"Lily, it's the perfect job for you."

"I'm no manager, Sheamie, so there's no way in the world I could run a dry-cleaning business for charity. I'd end up ruining you financially. When dealing with money and people, charity or not, a person has to be tough and not allow their heart to rule their head."

"You'd manage, Lily, you'd run it with your heart and your head. I trust you," Sheamie put a hand on her shoulder and looked into her eyes.

Lily moved away, glancing round her; gestures like that wouldn't go unnoticed when they happened to be standing in front of Mack's on Abbey Street. "You trust me?" Embarrassment made her speak harshly, "What do you know about me? You know nothing about what I've done with my life since leaving here."

"No, Lily, I don't, and you know little of mine."

There was sadness in Sheamie's eyes and it made her angry that it should make her soften a little towards him in her heart. "What about Golden Girl?" It hadn't been her intention to bring it up just then, but it had popped out. "What sort of foolishness is that?"

Sheamie's colour heightened and Lily immediately regretted her words. They stood facing each other in an awkward silence. Cars passed down the street, people came and went in and out of the supermarket, but neither paid any attention.

Finally, Sheamie spoke, "What do you mean, Lily?"

"I – mean, I mean nothing, Sheamie, nothing at all."

"You mean something, Lily, so spit it out."

"Sheamie, I can't wheel and deal in business like you do – and make a profit like that," Lily clicked her fingers.

"But making a profit wouldn't be the first aim of this charity business. The idea is to do good for the community and just break even."

"I appreciate your trust – I really do, but I can't accept. There are too many things going on in my head and my life and – "

This time, Sheamie gripped her arm, "What, Lily? What is wrong? You've been behaving like a frightened rabbit since you moved to Killdoe – "

Lily freed her arm and pulled out her car keys, shaking them, "Frightened rabbit? Is that what you think of me? I've had enough, I have to go; I promised Genie I would pick her up from football practice."

"I don't want to discuss here either, Lily, but you are so complicated. Every time I try to have a word, you make some excuse to leave."

"Look at who's talking? That's exactly what Henrietta says about you."

Lily rolled her eyes, Sheamie Fitzgerald calling her complicated. Was wishing a quiet life for she and Genie too much to ask for? Until the Kinsale incident, being a cleaning woman had been the easiest job to do. But in this town, being a cleaner made her complicated in the eyes of people. She put her hands on her hips and looked towards The Treasure Chest. On top of it, that blasted O'Connell woman was snaking all over the place and keeping her on edge.

"Lily? Have I upset you?" Sheamie drew closer.

"No, not at all." Lily checked her mobile, "Genie will be waiting for me."

Sheamie was reluctant to move, "I've seen her on the Raleigh, I think she's really enjoying it a lot."

"Yes she is."

"I noticed that Genie and Branly Hartigan are still friends; you are very good to Branly," Sheamie remarked.

"Sheamie, you have a lot of influence around the town – isn't there something you can do for Branly's family?"

"My influence doesn't reach into family affairs. That's a very delicate situation and that's why the social workers are handling it."

"I know, but I heard that Lena Hartigan has money problems and there are rumours of drugs – you could help out with that."

Sheamie took out his cigar, contemplated it, put it back in his top pocket. "How friendly are the girls with Sykes and his gang?"

"Branly more than Genie, but I don't know all their secrets anymore."

"There is a lot of trouble with drugs here in Killdoe. The Gardaí are onto it, but they have to catch them red-handed." Sheamie held her look, "The problem with all these rumours is that there is no real evidence for the Gardaí. Everybody is talking about what they heard, but when the Gardaí question people, they close up and refuse to give any information."

Lily shuffled her keys, "It's dark already. The lighting is very bad on this street, you should get on to the County Council and do something about that."

"Huh, that's something I can influence and will do."

****

Lily walked up Main Street and yawned. Oh if only it were possible to go back to bed and sleep soundly. But at least, at this time of the morning she didn't have to talk to too many people. That was one advantage about doing the early morning cleaning shift. However, that gave her a lot of time for thinking which wasn't always good. Sheamie's latest job offer had been turning in her head all night. The idea of a charity cleaning business tempted her. Sheamie understood at last what she might agree to do and Lily hated admitting he had eventually won this battle with her.

But Lily had so much on her plate right now that it was difficult to think clearly. Branly was getting harder and harder to take care of. Lily could tell that the responsibility of being Branly's friend was weighing heavily on her Genie. Sometimes, Genie's calls and messages to Branly weren't returned. At times, Branly would come knocking at the door, planning and talking about new excursions. Lily tried to explain to Genie that Branly gave what she could and she was not responsible for carrying Branly's burdens and troubles.

The best thing for Branly, Lily believed, was to keep her busy. Branly liked sewing and had helped Genie make the curtains for the flat. Henrietta had suggested that Branly make curtains for her own bedroom. But Branly hadn't been motivated, explaining that coming in on other people's projects was fun, but starting something and doing it for herself was too hard.

'Oh that's nice', Lily thought as she stopped in front of NATHALIE'S BOUTIQUE to study the woollen jacket on that mannequin on the window. It was grey with large red squares which brightened it up and made it much dressier than the rain jackets hanging in her wardrobe.

Genie too, Lily noticed, had started paying a lot more attention to clothes. Genie's way of walking had an added swing and her interest in high heels suddenly developed. Genie was now a teenager and was becoming aware of boys and her attractiveness as a female. Henrietta's love of couture, fashion and style was impacting Genie as well. She had come to recognise Henrietta's 'Tut – tut – tut' and her comments on fashion mistakes wisely reserved for those who had spent a lot of money on something that was badly cut and designed. There were many arguments especially with Genie; the most recent about her purchase of a denim jacket and jeans. Henrietta had mentioned that the jacket rode up the back and Genie had retorted that it was the shape of the back. Henrietta had demonstrated with hand movements that the beauty of learning to re-cut was to camouflage such flaws and enhance the body; clothes should float or fit, but not fall between.

Branly had been quick to defend Genie, saying that it took a lot of money to be fashionable. But Henrietta had reminded them that while it took a lot of money to be a slave to fashion, one did not need much money to be fashionable. When poor and obliged to knock on doors for work, she hadn't had the money to buy pretty blouses or tops and had taken scraps from workshops to make pretend blouses. By sewing a collar or cuffs to the inside of her jacket, she was able to fool people into believing she was wearing a new outfit each day.

Branly said that it was a gift.

"Maybe," Henrietta had replied, "but imagination is plentiful and free."

They could make up their own story out of scraps. No two scraps were the same and simply by sewing one on their jeans, they could add a personal touch, or even by sketching something with a special pen on the patches.

Henrietta confided in Lily that she had stolen her first pair of shoes to model one of her creations, only to discover on returning to her room that they were two left shoes. The wooden war clogs were not totally to blame for her damaged feet.

"Nobody is perfect," Henrietta had explained to the girls; "we have one shoulder too high and another too low, a long torso or a short one, a narrow waist or no waist, legs to show or not… There is so much to flatter, tease and disappoint." Then she had admitted that her own sewing skills were only adequate; being a good seamstress, even a very good one, but never a great one. Her talent had been as a creator and designer. Sewing and designing were related, but not the same. The difference was the stitch along the material and the material around the body.

Lily herself had learned a lot about clothing and fashion from Henrietta's way of teaching. Henrietta's advice was to watch people and see how they walked and carried themselves. One could depict pride, humility, arrogance… It was the same with the animals; one could study how a cat on the prowl moved. It was no secret that animals too had tricks to camouflage. Likewise with clothes, one could hide or show oneself, radiate sexuality or sensuality, confidence or lack of it. Clothes could be the extension of the best or the worst.

Huh, thought Lily, she was no expert on fashion, but could see that Sheila O'Connell always wore black and that her walk was heavy like a man.

Lily went through the gates of the Business Park and counted three cars parked there. She took out her badge and entered her part of the building. The security lodge was empty.

"Lily, Lily," Maura came racing in after her, "I forgot my badge at home and was hoping to catch up with you."

Lily held the door for her, "You could almost climb over the barriers here and security wouldn't notice you."

"Oh, they have their routine and we have ours." Maura got into the lift with Lily and pressed the basement button, "Saw you talking to Sheamie Fitzgerald the other day. You were engrossed. I was afraid to break into your conversation, it looked very personal."

"Well, you could have broken in, it wouldn't have bothered me in the least."

"Oh now, Lily, I wouldn't be interfering in affairs of the heart," Maura winked.

"You're beating up the wrong track there." People thinking that she and Sheamie were an item was the last thing Lily needed. "Maura – about that money lender, are you sure Joe doesn't know his name? Do you think he could be the same fellow that's bringing in the drugs?"

"I don't know – don't know – we've tried to put it behind us. Those people are vicious."

"That's alright, Maura," Lily saw the distress on her face and was sorry for asking. She passed her badge over an electronic lock and pushed opened the cleaning room door.

"What's the French woman like? Maura asked.

"She's wonderful –"

SLAM!

Lily jumped. "Maura, someone is following us! Hurry up and lock the door."

Maura looked at her, "Lock the door? Are you mad?" She walked out into the corridor.

Lily heard Maura talk to someone.

"Just security," Maura came back. "He's checking fire exits. You frighten for nothing, Lily. Now tell me about the cottage." Maura had heard that Sheila O'Connell wanted to buy it and couldn't understand why or where she would have gotten the money. The rumour was that someone else with money was behind her and that it may be her cousin who had done well in England.

Lily told Maura that Killdoe was lucky that Henrietta's family had bought The Old Forge and she was happy to describe the great work done there. It struck her that while she and Henrietta had shared secrets, they didn't know a lot of personal details about each other. Yet a natural understanding and respect had been kindled between them. She couldn't even begin to imagine what Henrietta's childhood growing up in World War II had been like; it was so far removed from her own childhood on Malt Hill. Henrietta's hands weren't those of someone who'd been brought up with a silver spoon; they showed the marks and scars of working hands. Henrietta could have been her mother, but she reminded her of Nana. There was something of an old soul about her with that quiet strength and forgiving non-judgemental nature.

Henrietta was ill-at-ease about Sheila O'Connell. Lily had no qualms about admitting her dislike of that Treasure Chest woman, although she knew it was wrong to harbour spiteful feelings like that. But Henrietta appeared to be more disturbed about Sheila O'Connell's influence over the children. As far as Lily could see, Branly was influenced by everyone and everything; her trips to The Treasure Chest couldn't be blamed on Sheila O'Connell.

"Is that a newspaper in your coat pocket, Lily?" Maura asked.

"It is, but it's yesterday evening's."

"Can I have a look at it?"

"Of course you can, it's the *Evening Echo*."

"The *Echo*! It's time for you to stop reading those Cork papers, you're living in Kerry now."

"I like to keep up."

18

The idea of making a quilt for Branly's birthday had come from Genie. Branly always complained about being cold at home and making a very big cosy quilt was the ideal solution. Her birthday was the day after Christmas and Branly believed that she'd missed her star, but Genie thought that to compensate they could put stars on her quilt, just like the patches on their jeans.

Henrietta and Lily had greeted the idea with equal enthusiasm and agreed that Branly should participate in her own project. It would make the present all the more valuable.

Henrietta laughed at the girls' astonishment when she entrusted them with the keys of The Old Forge. "Make your quilt here, it is easier. You will have to find lots and lots of scraps – so get hunting. I will help you begin it, and after, you are on your own. I will be back to see the result in December and we can celebrate Christmas early."

"The quilt will be like the rainbow," Branly formed an arch with her arms.

"That is a nice idea," Henrietta agreed. "Make up colours and invent your own illusion. You can create movement." If Branly cannot find her focus, Henrietta thought, she will find it here.

"Movement?" Genie made a face, "What movement is there in a blanket or quilt?"

"Oh, Genie, I suffer to make you understand," Henrietta said. "There is movement everywhere. That is how people see things: dots, lines and waves. Branly's bed can be an ocean, if she wants. She can float in her quilt or tread on soft grass and feathers. She can be tucked into the down of a bird soaring across the sky."

"Yeah," Branly flapped her arms, and for a second, her face was like a child. It was full of innocence and flecked with cinders of hope.

"Branly will dream in it, maybe travel to exotic lands or to the glistening snow of the Arctic," Henrietta joined in Branly's fantasy. "It will be full of motion, and you will make it with colours and patches of different shapes. Let yourselves go."

"What if she wants to be still and not move?" Genie persisted.

"We are never still, Genie, quieter yes, but still no. We are alive and therefore breathe. In sleep, our bodies rise and fall, the heart pumps and the blood flows. In death, our flesh and blood change and come together with the natural elements. Things never stop moving."

"Well, okay," Genie wasn't convinced.

"Do not just throw in the colours for the sake of using up space," Henrietta cautioned; "think about what you want. You have a great choice, from white through to blue –"

"Oh yes," Branly added, "I will have greens, reds, oranges, purples, pinks and –"

"Remember the fictional colours," Henrietta said, "chocolate, corn, cream, raspberry and whatever you want. It can be mint green, electric lime, hot pink, or desert sand."

The girls stared at her for a moment, the possibilities dawning on them.

Henrietta turned to Branly, "What would you like? What can you imagine?"

Branly closed her eyes and concentrated, "I see green apples on the ground ready for gathering. There are blackberries mashed with blackcurrants. I see the foam of the sea dashed on cliff rocks. I see ice of powdered soot and cornflakes swimming in milk. There are lots of raspberries covered in dollops of cream, topped off with crystal icing sugar. We are pouring everything into a copper bath. Genie is stirring it round and round, faster and faster – and I can't wait to open my eyes and see the final result." Branly opened her eyes, her smile broad and laughter coming up, "Can we make that?"

"We can try," Henrietta said. "You are a little poet."

"Making up poems is like making the quilt," Branly said, "I put pieces together from things I've heard or read. But it doesn't work much in real school. I'm bad at history. We are doing the Irish War of Independence and Civil War in school and it's hard to follow."

"I agree with you," Henrietta said.

"Sheila O'Connell tells me that I know nothing. She tries to teach me, but I'm bad at learning."

"What does she try to teach you exactly?"

"Both of us," Genie qualified. "Sheila said that the English soldiers were ex-convicts. They had black and tan uniforms because they didn't have enough money to buy the right uniform. When they were in Ireland, they terrorised people around the countryside."

"Sheila's grandfather was killed by the Black and Tan soldiers," Branly explained. "They shot him in cold blood, even though he wasn't armed. Her grandma was left to raise her family alone."

"He was betrayed by a traitor," Genie said. "The same traitor was an enemy of the O'Connell family during the Irish Civil War."

A window suddenly burst open and a gust of wind blew into the kitchen, sweeping some markers on to the floor.

"Oh la la," Henrietta exclaimed, "I have to repair that window catch." She felt that it was Genie's use of the word 'traitor' that had upset the spirit of Jenny McCarthy.

"Weird how that should happen just now," Genie said as she picked up the markers and put them back on the table.

"Does that mean we shouldn't use black or tan colours in the quilt?" Branly scratched her head.

Still so young, how their minds wandered, "You will choose what you like." Henrietta took up a yellow and black marker, "It could be lemons and olives. That is enough on the subject of war. When the quilt is finished and you put it around you, I wonder what it will feel like?"

"It would be like wearing air on my skin to make me dream, or warm water spraying on top of me." Branly, encouraged in her poetry, looked for images, then whispered the name Mikie in Genie's ear.

Henrietta saw Genie blush. "Of course when you are old enough, much older than what you are today, you can take your imagination further," she said, dryly.

The girls were left to their whims and the mood was elevated. Their laughter lifted the cottage and filled it with warmth and much needed joy, a joy probably not heard in years.

The veil lifted once more and spirits showed themselves. Henrietta saw the ghosts of the past sitting by the open fire. There was music, song and raised fists of rebellion. Jenny McCarthy was there serving food and drink to the guests and rovers. But Henrietta could see that Jenny did not dance and behind her false smile was sorrow and hurt.

Why does Jenny mourn? Henrietta wondered and tried to see the images more clearly. Then she understood – the young woman was carrying a secret, but a secret that would soon be revealed. A tall man stood in the background watching Jenny. There was love and admiration in his eyes, but also sadness –

Henrietta let the vision fade and looked at Genie who was drawing with the markers, unaware of the presence of the ghosts. Henrietta noticed that Genie looked very like Jenny McCarthy, and felt that Jenny watched over and protected her.

It was not the same for Branly, thought Henrietta.

Branly came towards her and spontaneously hugged her, "Thanks, Henrietta, thanks for the wonderful quilt. It's invisible still, but I can see it. It will soon be real and that makes me feel special."

Henrietta tucked bleached locks behind the girl's ears, and said to herself, 'And we will do what we can for you, Branly. But will it be enough?'

Henrietta tidied up the girls' work and reflected on the ghosts she had seen. Henrietta understood the cottage was re-telling her its history, revealing the secrets of Lily's ancestors. All families had secrets and maybe it was best if some of them remained so. Lily had enough on her plate and did not need to be informed of her visions. The sooner they sorted the Kinsale problem the better, but progress was painfully slow.

She picked up several scraps of material and held them to her face. A quilt, Henrietta whispered, "You made one especially for me, Francoise. Do you know that I have kept it? When I open it out, I imagine your perfume there. But it is the stitches that remind me most of you; I see your hand in each one. I press it to my skin and feel your love. I know you are here guiding me. I am old now and soon it will be my time to go. But it is not Branly's time and she needs you more right now. I see no light around Branly – have her angels deserted her? We need your aid, Francoise, because you know her despair. We will fill her hands with creative work; it will help her to hang on and give reason to stay on at this side of the veil. Let the quilt be her light – fill it with angels to protect and watch over her."

****

Henrietta couldn't rest. No matter how hard she tried, sleep evaded her and butterflies of foreboding stirred. There were voices in her head shouting, 'Go to hell, go to hell, to hell with them'. She was thinking about all the darker things too much. She finally decided to get up, get out and grab some fresh air before breakfast.

The doorman saluted, "Have a nice walk, Mrs. Bontemps."

"Thank you, Bill, I will."

Brrr, the breeze had an edge and a grey, freezing fog mantled everything. It was still dark and the street lamps flared through the gloom. Killdoe was like a slumbering, tired beast. Henrietta pulled on her gloves and let her feet take her. She crossed into Abbey Street and branched off at the bottom, before turning onto River Road.

She knew it was not wise to be wandering alone at dawn. However, her feet were steadier today; she had come this far and would keep going. A pale light came through as the sky slowly opened its shutters. Henrietta's eyes adjusted to the tarmac pathway which was bordered by a low hedge and followed the meandering narrow river. It took her past the sports grounds, a small park and into the countryside – square, rectangular and triangular fields of different shades of green: emerald, fern, moss, pine… There were some hedgerows of sleeping foliage which promised delights in spring. The Keale waters flowed freely. The river was beautiful and melancholy, telling its tales. It had centuries of them. By leaning in to fill just a single cup, one could write volumes.

The rust-coated animal startled her at first; it had been years since seeing one like that. It stood watchful and wary. What damage had that fox done tonight? It was always disquieting to see a wild animal unexpectedly like that. We are never alone in nature, she thought. How many more creatures were out there?

Henrietta was homesick, but not for her French home, it was another feeling that seemed to permanently follow her this past year. Her body was tiring more easily and still there were so many things to put in order. Renovations were creating a strain on her. Time was precious; it had always been, but never more than now. Yet, she couldn't help delaying over it and drawing out the moments. With a stronger will the cottage could have been finished sooner. It would have been better to do so, to go back to France and manage her other affairs. Instead, here she was, walking a river bank at dawn, sharing time with a fox, wondering about a place and people that would get by very well without her. She should have stayed outside like the fox, stayed on the margins, instead of getting in the middle of lives and events she did not fully understand: Lily's problem in Kinsale, Sheamie, the girls… They were all in there somewhere, just like Lily called it – magnets flying around. She could simply ask Jean and Thibault to put The Old Forge up for sale and then she would disappear out of their lives. The river would keep flowing, never judging.

She had allowed herself to be taken in by her family's enthusiasm and to do something that only the rich could afford, the luxury of making mistakes, of buying a place they did not need. And it was all to please her husband and son. Of course, they worked hard to earn their money and the right to spend it, though sometimes their ambitions were too heavy for her to carry. She had followed, eyes wide open, knowing it might be a mistake. But it was done and she would stick with it to the end. 'If only I had more strength. I am certainly no magician and cannot make things right for everybody. It does not work that way; I am not even able to make them right for myself.' Henrietta stood for a long moment looking into the water, searching for answers, wishing for them, before reluctantly turning back.

At the graveyard she went to the gate to look through the rails. Henrietta could see how a young girl might be overwhelmed by such a place.

All of a sudden, she heard a strange voice and saw Sheila O'Connell's dark form moving around the graves. Her wolfhound sat nearby. What on earth was the woman doing? Henrietta withdrew to the sides and stayed quiet as a mouse, watching. A shadow was cast over different headstones as Sheila once more spewed her curses in Irish. A string of words sliced the air and needed no translating. The venom was in the sounds of scourge, hardship, pain, grief, sickness, trials, thorns, crosses, and on and on.

Abruptly, Sheila O'Connell broke into English, "Damn them all, the traitors. The wind is blowing in my direction and the Almighty has had a hand in it. Pádraig Óg has told me all. He is a good man using his time to give out the Holy Bible and pass on the word of God to others. I am proud of him; my own flesh and blood bears a good name. Nothing can be done about the land, but one day, maybe. Oh ochón, ochón a Daideo, Mamó told us of her grief the day they lowered your coffin. The black widow's veil was with you to the end of your days, Mamó. A Casey grabbed the land that was ours and a Casey protected the devil who took Daideo's life."

Henrietta shrunk further into the shadows, mesmerised as Sheila O'Connell splashed holy water around and shouted, "I am here, I live and will do what has to be done. If it's the last thing I do, the black veil will cover another woman's face."

The torrent of words dried up and there was silence, at last. Sheila O'Connell stood looking across her sacred ground and then turned back up the path, "Come, Faelen, it's time to go inside."

Henrietta did not move for several minutes. Was it possible to be so deluded and taken over by lunacy and do what that woman was doing? Chanting over graves of people that she did not like or hated was not going to have much effect on anyone, except drive her completely crazy and to her own contorted destiny. Was that her morning ritual of spitefulness? It was sad to be living in such hate and to build one's life on that.

Henrietta approached the gate again and thought of an old proverb – 'Like a fluttering sparrow or a darting swallow, an undeserved curse does not come to rest'. Being more of a doer, most of her life she had not been given to praying. However, she bent her head now and spoke a few words asking for good to replace evil and to wash away the curse. Her words may not have a lot of power, she thought, but doing it made her feel better. In a certain way, she now had an answer to some of her questions and was no longer in any doubt about seeing things through to the end.

It was good to return to the warmth and welcoming atmosphere of the hotel breakfast room. It was uplifting to share the energy of everyday people moving around – normal conversation, normality. Sheamie was sitting at a table, reading a newspaper.

"Henrietta, you're an early bird."

"I did not know you took breakfast here."

"We just haven't run into each other."

"But of course, you are spoilt for choice."

"Will Jean be joining you again soon?"

"Maybe, a flying visit. He has an age advantage over me and I cannot keep up with him. They say, never marry a younger man."

Sheamie dropped several lumps of sugar into his coffee, "If Jean is younger, you hide your years very well. He's devoted to you."

"We are never too old to be flattered and you know how to do it very well, Sheamie. I think Jean will wait until the New Year to return and for some of the racing trials."

Sheamie folded his newspaper, "That's right. You got the documents and can see that every transaction has been accounted for."

"So it seems."

"What do you mean – seems?"

She took the opportunity to press further, "Are you sure you have done a thorough check of everything?"

Sheamie put down his napkin, "What are you getting at, Henrietta? Golden Girl is a good horse. Naturally, we can never be fully sure until we see how it runs. We'll have to judge its performance in real competitions. In the unlikely case of it being a dud, we'll cut our losses and get out."

"A dud?"

"A poor horse, a bad investment. It's too soon to say. Anyway, that's the risk one takes and that's the excitement of it."

Henrietta pursed her lips.

"Now, now, Henrietta, don't say it, I get enough of that from Lily – that sermon about men behaving like children with their wild plans and ideas. We're not all careless or heartless and we know how to balance the risks."

She made a clicking sound with her tongue, "Can you afford to lose your investment?"

"Yes of course. I wouldn't have invested in it if that weren't the case."

Henrietta let it go – if Sheamie could afford to lose the money, there was no need to worry for him. She wanted to have a proper face to face discussion with Jean and Thibault before closing the case, then leave it to Jean to talk to Sheamie, man to man.

With some skill, Sheamie guided the conversation in a different direction, "You know, Henrietta, meeting Jean and Thibault at a race meeting of all places was just pure chance. I hit it off immediately with both of them. And all that brought you to Killdoe – and then you meeting Lily like that. It's amazing how things happen."

She smiled, "If I follow that, I would say that you are a good business man. We could have bought a house anywhere."

"No, no, coming here was your choice. I just facilitated in helping you find the place." He lowered his voice and concentrated on the sugar bowl, "Henrietta, I have a favour to ask you – it's about Lily."

"You mean about Lily and you."

Sheamie flushed, the directness of her statement catching him unawares.

"Were you lovers in the past?"

He looked down at his plate, "That was a long time ago and we've both changed a lot. I'm not trying to go back to the past."

"No, but you have feelings for Lily."

"Oh, I've always had feelings for her, but you know how difficult she is – one of the most difficult women I've ever known. It's hard to pin down what she wants or thinks, and even more difficult to get her to let me do one or two simple things to help her out. And that's my real question, it's not about Lily and me, it's about getting Lily to accept to work on this project I have. You know how stubborn she can get and if you could – "

Henrietta interrupted him, "One moment here, Sheamie, I am all for helping you, but do not ask me to try to influence Lily. I will not do it. I have too much experience of life to know that we cannot do that. People make and take their own decisions."

Sheamie leaned across the table. There was nothing he liked better than a good negotiation; he'd done business with Henrietta about the cottage and knew she drove a hard bargain, and rightfully so. "No, Henrietta, I'm not asking you to influence Lily. For the moment, I'm just asking you to listen to me. After, you can tell me what you think."

When he had finished, she could only admire his tenacity. "Sheamie, you are persuasive, but I am not sure I can help you."

He wasn't to be dissuaded, "But she might discuss it with you and you could encourage her in the right direction."

"I will do no such thing. I will listen to her as I did to you and let things take their natural course." Even as the words came out, Henrietta was shaking her head, knowing that by virtue of being the ear of both, she was once more being drawn in.

Henrietta tried to be objective about Sheamie. He came across as a good man, but she would, for Lily's sake, say her piece. "I can tell you that you are wrong when you say it is not about you and Lily, it is all about you two. If you want her to consider you as more than a friend again, you have to stop trying to change her and her way of being. I think she is afraid of that more than anything else. Lily has still to settle after relocating from Kinsale."

"That's another thing, Henrietta, Lily's so damn secretive about Kinsale, she's just – oh, let me alone about Lily Casey," Sheamie fell silent.

Henrietta put down her piece of toast, "Listen to me. You are a certain age, but I am a lot older and give me credit for seeing some things. You and Lily could do well together, you go back a long way. But give her time to rediscover her feminine side again. Make her feel like a woman. I think Lily has already started to see that she had shut down a part of herself and is trying to open it up again. She is an intelligent lady and will do the right thing in her own time."

"Oh, I know that, just having her here in Killdoe has given me some insights. Lily makes me laugh. She challenges me as no woman has ever done. I just wish I were a young man again, but I'm old and fat and middle aged."

"Do you think that Lily does not feel the same about herself? Being a certain age does not mean that you stop paying attention to some details. In fact, you should be paying even more attention to the same things."

"What?"

"Expensive suits are not enough, you have to know how to choose them, and middle age is no excuse for not keeping in shape."

Sheamie looked down at his paunch and sucked it in with discomfort, "I try, but it's hard."

"Well, try harder, if only for your health as much as anything else. If that is not motivation enough, you can try also for Lily – she is a wonderful woman."

"That she is."

"And as I am being direct, Sheamie, it is fine to have breakfast in your own hotel, but maybe a little less butter and sugar and a little more fruit would be a good idea."

He grunted something unintelligible and reached for the coffee pot.

Her point had been made and they finished breakfast in a relaxed atmosphere. No more questions were asked and no more answers needed. She asked him about Sheila O'Connell's family. He was adamant that the woman never had any children, although a cousin sometimes visited. Henrietta wondered – why had Sheila been ranting about her 'own flesh and blood' and someone called Padraig? Perhaps it had another meaning.

Henrietta learned that Sheamie was a cultured man and, although rooted in Killdoe, his knowledge was wide ranging. He was open minded and interested in many things and places in the world. She could understand the attraction between Sheamie and Lily; one of them generous, logical and structured, the other so less structured but equally generous. Henrietta finished her coffee. Maybe they were better that way, a couple without really being a couple.

She stood up, "Well, Sheamie, I'll be on my way or something like that. Everybody here uses that expression."

Sheamie stood up too, "Thanks for the most interesting breakfast I've had in a long time. I could make a habit of having breakfast every day with a charming woman such as you."

"Sheamie, the charm is all yours."

"You'll think about what I said to you, Henrietta?"

"I will and you think about what I said to you," she gave him a little pat on the tummy.

He looked rueful, "I'll do my best to make more of an effort."

Henrietta hoped it would work out for Sheamie and Lily and that they might have a second chance of love.

19

Lily loved Christmas; it was a time for giving and forgiving. But this year, it wasn't easy to get into the spirit of things. Her choice would have been to lock her door and hide away from the world. Though, it was nice to know that Sheamie, despite all her doubts, shared her wish to help people in need. Some good ideas had come straight from her and she was proud when he had accepted her proposal to give out low-priced meals from the hotel for the holiday season.

Lily was less qualified when it came to advice about how to give Killdoe a festive make-over. But even she, who wasn't usually much given to considering the aesthetics of things, had to admit that Killdoe still had its share of mavericks. Main Street resembled rows of gypsy caravans – each home and business uniquely decorated with its own blend of colours and design rather than seeking cohesion.

Sheamie studied the street, looking out at the Christmas lighting from the hotel entrance, and muttered, "All the time and effort for that."

"It's not so bad, is it?" Lily asked.

"I don't know, Lily, I try to do my best. I wanted to get the town to go greener this Christmas. But apart from my own premises and Maggie's Bar in The Square, it's mishmash, and every man to his own design."

"But fair dues, you've managed to push the energy-saving bulbs and

LED lighting in at least a third of the shops." Lily was afraid that Sheamie, as the principal business man around town, would have to bear the brunt for the Christmas Lift sponsorship.

Sheamie stroked his jaw, "It's not good enough. Overall, the Christmas look is irregular, that final finish isn't there."

"Do we want it to be? Whatever you do to the town, it will always look at bit odd. Look at us, we're never going to have the Parisian chic. We don't have that sophistication or polish. There'll always be a raggedy end here and there, something unfinished, sticking out, in the wrong place and hanging down when it should be up."

"That's Killdoe, it beguiles in a slovenly way," laughed Sheamie.

"That's a good thing and it shows that there's a lot of the rebel spirit left in Killdoe and its surrounds. Maybe, it doesn't compare to other places, but this is the area I knew growing up and what has moulded me. Standardise things if you like, Sheamie, but please don't overdo it or you will take away the spirit of what keeps us mavericks. What is it now?"

He was looking at her in a special way, "You know, Lily, I love the way you see and put things. You've changed your hair, I notice," he put his hand out to touch it.

She drew back, "Just spruced it up a little."

"Well, it suits you."

"Oh, it's just shorter."

He touched it again, "No, no, it suits you, it brings out your lovely hazel eyes."

Her face grew hot, "It's more for Genie than for me. She's at the age of being a tad over-critical and beginning to get particular about things, especially the things I wear."

Sheamie frowned, "Teenagers are like that. Genie's a lot like you, Lily."

"Anyway," Lily continued brusquely, "I want her to be at ease with who she is and, yes, to be proud of her mother and not go round with a chip on her shoulder – " Lily stopped, seeing compassion in Sheamie's eyes. "Of course, if there are side effects from my new look, then that's alright too."

Sheamie laid his arm tentatively on her shoulders, "Lily, I have to talk to you."

"Aren't we talking?"

"No, I mean really talk to you about a lot of things."

"Oh, don't, Sheamie, we can't go back," Lily moved out of his reach.

"It's not just that, there's some trouble brewing."

Lily grabbed his jacket sleeve, "It's that grey-suited McGrath, isn't it? Is it the inspection?"

"Look – amm – it's linked – all sorts of things are being audited. You know how it's a pot of stew here, so it's taking a lot of my time. I'll be able to throw more light on it early next year."

"Are you in trouble, Sheamie?"

"No, not at all," he denied quickly. "I'm not worrying for myself, it's other people that give me worries."

Sheamie looked down at her and it suddenly struck Lily that he was waiting for her to speak, that somewhere in his vague words he'd been talking about her. Was she giving him worries? Was Lily Casey tangled in this famous inspection, and was all this leading back to Kinsale? She looked up at the street decorations and right then they didn't seem as delightful or quaint as a few minutes before.

"I can't say or advise anything, Sheamie, until you come out with it straight. But I'll be here to listen when you are ready to talk about whatever it is."

Sheamie took her hand in a warm gesture, "Promise me one thing, Lily – if you need help for anything, ask me and don't go borrowing from others."

Not sure if she felt offended or touched, Lily yanked her hand free, "I'll catch up with you later – have a few things to do."

****

Lily gave it a week before going to The Old Forge to see how the quilt was progressing. Henrietta had started the girls off and there had been some tremendous industry and progress for a while. She had been pleased to see that the girls had enjoyed spending days gathering and collecting patches and scraps. Lots of material had come tumbling in and it had piled up. But as Lily suspected, with the passage of time and without Henrietta there had been a notable slackening off.

Henrietta had explained to them that it wouldn't exactly be a patchwork quilt, but rather a quilt with patches on it. They didn't have time to create the real thing, nonetheless, they could also make pillow cases, throws and other fancy accessories.

What Lily found were two stranded girls. They'd clearly lost direction along the way, or more like it, had never found it. She knew her own daughter well enough to detect panic in the air. Genie was sitting in the middle of the unfinished mountain and doing her best to straighten things out. Branly was sitting on a stool, supposedly advising. Lily saw the box of cigarettes on the table, but decided to say nothing about it. The place smelt fresh, so it seemed Branly was at least doing her smoking outside. If there was any evidence of smoking inside, she'd take the keys of the cottage back from the girls.

"Oh, Mum," Genie was relieved to see her mother and readily transferred the burden of the problem, "we just don't know how to pull it together. It was easier when Henrietta was here and explained."

Branly held up an end for Lily to see, "We are stumped. It's frightful hard and I can't make head or tail of the pattern."

Lily studied a badly sewn part. What stood out was every sign of her daughter's gartering – rough and approximate stitches. Other parts were more than passable, but the patches so small you would need a magnifying glass to see them. There was neither shape nor form to the quilt. Someone was going to have to take the project in hand and organise the work. She wasn't much of a seamstress herself, but could guide them along. The girls would have to start from scratch again and work at top speed to be ready for Henrietta's return.

"Okay girls, we've plenty work to do and there's no time like the present."

She noted how quickly Branly understood and made her fingers follow. Poor Genie understood but couldn't make her fingers obey. It was obvious where their problem had come from; Branly had the sewing skill and Genie the work ethic, but there had been no boss. Lily shook her head, she'd been such a rebel against authority in her life, and yet leadership was so necessary to complete such a project. It was her fault, Lily admitted, for not having supervised sooner.

The girls looked up simultaneously and smiled at her and Lily realised that she had been talking out loud.

Branly put down her needle. There, the girl's concentration had gone. Dark roots showed through tinted hair, there were bags under her eyes and the acne had worsened. Rumours persisted about the girl turning up in late night spots with the motorbike gang.

Rubbing her arms up and down, Branly claimed her fingers sometimes were numb and turned blue just like some of the corpses at wakes she'd attended in Bridge Street Funeral Parlour.

Seeing Genie looking upset, Lily felt Branly's fingers, "They are only cold. Swing your arms around to bring the circulation back. Soon, you will have the quilt to keep you fine and warm."

Branly rolled around in the material, "It's so soft, if I could just lie here and sleep forever and never wake up."

Oh Lord, Lily thought, Branly needs a lot of love and care.

After several days, the quilt began to take shape. In the end, it surprised Lily that they'd produced something decent. The girls were excited about Henrietta's return. They were going to celebrate Christmas before Christmas; to have two shots at the day was cool. Branly thought it even cooler that her quilt should be put away and she would be receiving it as an early present to herself.

"I can't wait to sleep and dream in it. I'll think of all the good friends that made it. I'm lucky to have friends."

"That couldn't be truer," Lily said, "and remember, good friends are like quilts – they age with you and never lose their warmth."

****

"Lily Casey!"

Lily had gone several paces past the door of The Treasure Chest. "Did you call my name?" She took a few steps back – the woman's eyes sunken in her grey face were flashing fury.

"YES – YOU!"

Lily looked at her phone. It was cold – oh she longed for her snug and cosy flat. She had a bad feeling about this encounter.

"What can I do for you?" Lily asked with artificial politeness.

"I am missing books from my place," the words were spat out.

"I'm sorry to hear that, but what's it to do with me?"

"They were stolen from my prayer room – two Holy Bibles."

"What are you saying?"

"Your daughter and the Hartigan girl were in that room."

"Are you accusing them of stealing?" Lily's throat contracted.

"Those books were put to safe keeping and they are now missing. Some of them have precious relics, very precious relics," Sheila O'Connell cracked the knuckles of her thick fingers.

"Did you see the girls take them? Have you asked them?"

"They are liars and deny all. But I know that they did it. They are nothing more than dirty thieves – and where else would they be got?"

Lily was close to snapping, but kept her voice very low, "Stop name calling, I will not stand for it."

"I already caught them stealing into my graveyard in the middle of the night; Faelen soon put the fear of God in them. I could have reported them for breaking into my property."

"Your property! That graveyard is public property."

"You – you –" Sheila O'Connell pointed her finger in Lily's face, "I want those Bibles back."

"I am not putting up with one more word from you," Lily held back from slinging the shopping bag at the woman and stormed across the street.

20

Lily had been determined to meet Henrietta at Shannon Airport. As they drove homewards negotiating the heavy traffic of Limerick city and suburbs before finally getting onto the North Kerry main road, Henrietta realised that while Lily was a good driver she was a fast one too.

"So, Lily, is Killdoe ready for Christmas?"

"In a manner of speaking, you could say that, we're all set anyway. The girls are bursting with expectation," Lily swung the car around a sharp bend.

"Is Branly's mother still going to the special meetings?"

Lily took another turn, swinging left, "By all accounts, and Branly has missed fewer days in school, but still looks very pale and drawn in the face."

"I received a lot of emails from both of them and I have done my best to reply. They have even got me on their Facebook pages – sent me documents and said, 'Just copy and paste it'. I sit in front of the screen and I think, copy and paste? Do they know how difficult technology is for me? I find it easier to write my messages with a needle and thread. Give me a pair of scissors and a swath of cloth and I will make my own fibre world faster than you can say cyber space or whatever they call it."

Lily drummed the steering wheel, "It's called keeping up with the times,

Henrietta. But sometimes, I think that it's a blinkered world."

"Lily," Henrietta began, "I know you are anxious and –"

The car swerved slightly and Lily's hands tightened on the wheel.

Henrietta had not planned to discuss the other business until safely in Killdoe, but realised she should discuss it sooner rather than later and asked Lily to pull over to the side of the road.

"It's bad, isn't it? Lily took her eyes off the road for a second, "You've been hinting about some shady dealings around this horse business. You told me that you opened an investigation, but you haven't told me what you really found out. I'm thinking that if you haven't told me it's because Sheamie –"

"Lily –" Henrietta tried again.

Lily parked at the next garage and switched off the engine, "He's swindled you over the horse, hasn't he?"

"Lily, calm down. Sheamie did not swindle Jean and Thibault. I am now quite certain about that. However, the three of them were swindled by someone else."

"The fools!" Lily put her hand to her mouth; "I'm only talking about Sheamie."

"Do not apologise, because they were all very foolish. The private detective, Mr. Curran, says that the papers certifying the horse are forged. It is taking him time to identify the real culprit. Police have to figure out false names and fictitious companies, some in England. Apparently the horse deal was linked to a racket of illegal gambling unbeknownst to our men."

Lily turned in her seat, "Gambling? You mean betting! Sheamie has a Turf Accountants –"

"The bets were placed in many betting offices, including Cork and Kinsale."

"But Sheamie could be involved."

"The detective assures me, no. I think, Lily, if Sheamie is not forthcoming, it is because he is embarrassed and knows he has been duped. Jean, Thibault and Sheamie have lost a lot of money on that horse and I do not think they will ever recover it."

Lily told her that Sheamie had dropped hints about carrying out his own inquiries, but was not sure if it were related. It was time to talk directly to him about it, though it would have to wait as he was spending a week with his daughter in Dublin.

Henrietta proceeded to fill Lily in on the rest of Mr. Curran's findings, mainly the link he had made between the money lending and the gambling. All of them were victims directly or indirectly of the same man.

"Then could he be the man who threatened me in Kinsale, warned Genie here in Killdoe and left the blackmail notes?" Lily jumped up in her seat.

"That is a possibility, but we do not have a name yet and nobody can describe what he really looks like."

Henrietta explained that Mr. Curran thought the criminal was operating alone and very cunning. Of course there was a network of sorts, but he was difficult to pin down. However, the woman's death would have forced him to pull out of Kinsale, at least temporarily. While Genie was apparently the sole witness who might identify him – had that been his only motivation to come and hang around Killdoe, a small town? Surely it would have been sufficient to have threatened them and to have disappeared out of the picture? Lily's decision to return to Killdoe with Genie and her ties with Sheamie could not have been foreseen by the criminal. But maybe if he had other links to the place it might explain his need to continue warning them. If Sheamie himself had begun investigating the Turf Accountants, that might have tipped off the criminal that the police were on to him. Mr. Curran had told Henrietta that it was no ordinary drug and crime investigative work and that he would have to open his inquiry and involve a specialised police force. She had not wanted to give the okay to Mr. Curran without consulting Lily first.

"So it might be dangerous for me to say anything to Sheamie yet?"

"You will have to make up your mind on that, Lily, but I feel it is wiser to keep our silence for a little longer. I wish I could tell you more right now."

Henrietta hoped for the sakes of Lily and Genie that the criminal's threats had been just that and given their continued silence, he would be satisfied to leave them alone. But if he got even the slightest hint that someone was on his track, there was no telling how he might react. Lily was naturally intent on Genie leading a normal life in Killdoe and minimising events. Balancing what she now knew with carrying on as usual was not going to be easy.

Henrietta held back from reminding Lily what they both already knew

– that the girls were vulnerable. Exactly what Genie might have confided to her friend was not clear, but Branly's erratic behaviour and association with gangs and drugs were exactly what they did not need.

****

It was the week before Christmas Day and Henrietta decided to make her first visit to Killdoe Church. For years, Henrietta had kept away from such places of worship; but she would go today as Lily told her the girls would be there for Christmas choir practice. Henrietta timed her visit just a few minutes after the practice should have finished.

The church was a simple low-roofed brick and mortar building. On entering, Henrietta was abruptly overtaken by a vision. She hung on to the door for support and pressed a hand to her stomach as the memory rose painfully and overpowered her, taking her back to that day…

- Henrietta is a child again in her Normandy village, running across the cobbled yard of the Presbytery.
- The bombs are falling round them and the noise is ear splitting.
- The main church building has been evacuated, but screams rise to her ears. She runs in the direction of the screams calling out, "Francoise, Francoise –"

Henrietta reaches the stables and bursts through the stable doors. A click of metal brings her to a stop. Before her, Francoise's stained prayer book lays open on the straw; a pressed rose from her father's funeral grave slides out from between the pages.

A man looking like a wild creature is staring at Henrietta – his white collar stands out from a black robe. In one hand he holds a gun, and his other hand smothers over the mouth of her sister. Henrietta sees horror and pain on Francoise's face.

Henrietta does not stop, but rushes to where Francoise lays. "Leave my sister alone," she flings herself at the man and digs her nails into his face.

He roars out loud, slinging her sister back against the wall and points the gun at her – his finger moves on the trigger.

Suddenly, boots resound on the cobble stones outside and the stable doors are flung open. A German soldier stands there.

- Deafening shots ring out – the priest falls to the ground, bleeding.

The soldier in enemy uniform bleeds from the thigh. He lifts Francoise to her feet and then leads them both outside.

"Run," he shouts, "run to the forest – you will be protected there. You are free – the war is over."

They flee, running until their lungs pain them. The sky is ablaze with red and amber flames and the air thick and black with burning lead.

They hide in the shelter of the trees until the waves of bombs and gunfire subside at sundown…

Their lives were saved, but Henrietta saw despair on the face of Francoise. Hers wasn't a wound that would heal. Francoise would never recover. The German soldier had not gotten very far either – the Allies captured him.

Henrietta's head was throbbing now, but the memories persisted. She recalled again how Francoise was dragged before the local court as the community sought its own retribution. It was not a real court, but set up by the people considered to have authority: the priest, the doctor, the teacher and the Mayor. The facts were presented coldly by the Mayor:

'Fr. Renard accuses Francoise Morney of fornicating with the German in the stables. She has betrayed her country by sleeping with the invader. Let her head be shaved so that all may know of her shame. The stain on her family will remind us of what dishonour is and of whom our enemies are.

Her sister, Henrietta Morney, discovered them,' the Mayor's voice continues. 'The German raised his gun to shoot the little child. At the peril of his life, Fr. Renard entered the stables and fired at the enemy soldier. His courageous action saved Henrietta and her sister. He sustained a bullet to his arm defending the girls. And now the possessed young woman, Francoise Morney, wants to blacken Fr. Renard.'

'Lies, it is all lies,' her mother cries out. Henrietta sees her mother's stark face and watches as her sister shakes her head in shock, her face white as snow. Her mother whispers, 'They will not believe Francoise, what is her word against the white collar.'

'The child, Henrietta, knows the truth. Let the child speak,' the teacher's voice of reason calls for justice.

Henrietta is led to the top of the Justice Hall. Dozens of hateful faces stare at her. They were once all friends and neighbours of her mother: farmers, labourers and shopkeepers. Walking to the top, she keeps her head down, rather than see that white collar.

'Tell us what you saw, child,' the teacher speaks solemnly.

Henrietta opens her mouth – but no words come out. She tries again and again to say something, but still no distinct sound comes. Her speech has splintered into an unrecognisable stutter. Shattered syllables tangle in her throat and stick to her tongue. She is incapable of uttering one word. She sees Francoise's despairing eyes and tries again and again to speak, but fails.

'Leave the child alone,' her mother cries out, taking her by the hand. 'My daughter, Francoise, is innocent, but whatever I or her sister, Henrietta, may say will not change your minds…'

In 1945 the Allies had freed France, but people in her village and villages and towns all over France were imprisoned in hate.

As a child, Henrietta couldn't understand why her family were made to suffer. Her sister was innocent, yet why had she been lined up as a traitor and her head shaved? Why had the captured soldier who had saved them been shot without mercy?

Henrietta rested her hand on the church door and squeezed her eyes tightly. She remembered some weeks after the village trial, August 29th, 1945, sitting in their farmhouse kitchen. Night had fallen and Francoise was late returning from the fields where she had driven the cows to pasture. Her mother was about to go in search of her when somebody knocked. A servant woman from a neighbouring farm entered and told them that Francoise was dead – she had taken her own life. They had found her hanging from a tree. Francoise would have been fifteen years old the next day, August 30th.

Her mother went with the servant and brought Francoise's body from the forest.

A note was found in her pocket.

'My dear Mother and sister, Henrietta, it is the only way to restore honour to the family. I cannot bear to live or bring into the world what is not mine. God will be my witness and 'Le Pere Renard' will reap punishment for his actions on Judgement Day. Do not weep for me. Know that when you read this, I will be happy with my maker.'

Night fell permanently on their home. The villagers were pitiless. In taking her own life, Francoise had defied God's will and would not be buried in a consecrated graveyard.

The sun dulled when she learned about her father's death. But Henrietta lost the moon and stars the night she learned that Francoise had taken her own life. While the war had taken many things from Henrietta, she feared that the white collar had taken God from her.

Six years later, at the age of fourteen, Henrietta left her Normandy village to find work in Paris. Shortly after, her mother sold the farm and moved to another village in Normandy where she finished her days. Henrietta got employment in the clothing workshops on Rue du Temple, Paris, where she toiled by night. By day, she attended Parsons School of Design, Rue Saint-Roch, and earned her diplomas and qualifications. She then slowly climbed the ladder of the rag trade, establishing her own successful business and reputation as a fashion designer. Light resurfaced again for Henrietta through her creativity with clothes. However, Henrietta Bontemps had never made her peace and never returned to the Normandy village where she grew up. And now, on her second day back in this Irish town, the simple action of entering the grounds of a small church had forced the old memories to resurface. Killdoe was making her face her fears and her childhood past in Normandy all those years ago.

A door shut –

Startled, Henrietta looked up at a man in a black suit and white collar.

"Hello," he smiled and held out his hand.

She stared at him too surprised for a moment to speak or move.

He smiled again, "I'm Father Sheehan."

She shook his hand, "I am Henrietta Bontemps."

"You're the new owner of The Old Forge, aren't you?"

"I am."

"Welcome to Killdoe Parish." His face was kind and his eyes were honest.

"Thank you, Father."

He bowed his head slightly and walked slowly towards the sacristy.

His was a quiet presence and there was healing there. Henrietta dipped her fingers in a font and blessed herself, making the sign of the cross. Old habits died hard, she thought. She walked around, trying to distract herself with the pastoral surroundings and to soothe the painful memories. The church was as unremarkable in its interior architecture and décor as its exterior. It was too new to catch the grandeur of medieval and too outdated to offer anything to modernity. There were no pews and it was just large enough to have one main central aisle. There was a baptismal font at the back and two confessional boxes. The altar was made of pink marble and there was a stained glass window depicting Mary and Christ.

Murmured prayers rose from the front row bench, freezing Henrietta to the marrow. Sheila O'Connell was doing her religious duty and had taken the direction to the candle stand. I will light one too, Henrietta thought; it will be for old time's sake.

They faced each other across the stand. Although the heat coming from the flames was strong, Henrietta felt the wall of ice around the other woman and sensed that Sheila O'Connell was cursing her. The wall had become a scalding furnace, but Henrietta held her ground and looked directly back at Sheila O'Connell's dark and empty eyes.

Dear God, that woman really thinks I am the evil one, bringing bad, thought Henrietta. Henrietta felt nauseated but continued dropping coins in a slot and lit a candle for the protection of all her new friends. Sheila O'Connell turned her back brusquely and returned to her seat.

Henrietta left the alcove and saw Branly's bowed head farther down the aisle. She wondered about that kind of binding control Sheila O'Connell seemed to have over such a young person. It should not be like that. Branly was just a pawn in O'Connell's madness.

Where was Branly's friend, Genie? The shield must be there somewhere. Just then she saw Genie sitting on a bench at the back, waiting for Branly. Henrietta walked down the aisle and sat with her.

They both looked on as Branly continued to pray in her feverish fashion for a while longer, before moving to the front of the altar and standing for a long moment. When Branly finally finished, she paused in front of Sheila O'Connell. Some words were exchanged and she came reverently back down the aisle.

Something had changed in Branly, Henrietta thought. At times, the girl seemed so solemn and grave, though slivers of her old self still came through. She had not stopped dressing up and dollying up, but was thinner – too thin, just a painted shell. Branly was not okay. Even if her mother was no longer drinking, something was eating her up and they were losing her. Henrietta could not let things go on that way; maybe Killdoe's Parish Priest could be trusted to help.

She went outside with the girls and asked them to tell her more about their Christmas plans.

They were talking nineteen to the dozen and it took a while to get back into their rhythm of speech and to key into their accents. She had missed them, really missed their dispersed chirping and prattling.

"We're going to make money on The Wren. We've got two tunes for it," Genie said.

Branly did a version of a tap dance and a batter on the pavement, "And maybe a dance. It was Genie's idea. On my birthday, Stephen's Day, December 26th, we'll go from house to house, play a tune and get money."

Henrietta had heard about The Wren; she'd been given long explanations by mail and plenty attachments on the subject. She understood that it was a tradition whereby locals formed groups, wore Christmas-themed fancy-dress and went from house to house and pub to pub, playing music and collecting money. The money collected was used to hold parties or for charity. Fortunately, the custom of carrying a dead wren on a stick had disappeared decades before. As with all traditions, children and teenagers liked to get on board if there was any chance of making money.

She took Branly's cold hands and massaged them, "You have to keep the blood flowing into your fingers. It will be difficult to play music if you cannot feel your finger tips."

"I can't keep the blood in them, I told Genie's mum that I have dead fingers."

"No you do not. You should wear warm gloves."

Branly wasn't listening, "Genie has worked out a travel route for Saint Stephen's Day."

"That's right," Genie said. "The main thing is to strike the houses where we're likely to get the most money."

"That is a good motivation, I think," Henrietta said.

Branly started playing her tin whistle again and then explained that it was a song she was composing in honour of the birds of the forest.

Henrietta wrapped her scarf higher to cover her mouth from the cold air. "Genie, Branly, you must be like frozen icebergs in those jackets. Do you not feel the cold? I mean, the jackets are pretty and I appreciate that you made the effort to dress up for me, but at least wear a scarf. Nobody said that fashion should kill you."

The girls seemed immune to the freezing temperature. They were wearing similar jackets, but in different colours; Genie was in classic blue denim and Branly was in a pink version. They both had very tight jeans and were a little offended when she pointed out that there were too tight. They said tight jeans were back in fashion.

"Do you compromise you or fashion?" Henrietta challenged them.

"That's being conservative," Genie said.

"Depends, conservative is hiding your individuality. If the fashion says you must wear a very short skirt and if you do not have the legs, do you still wear very short? Or do you find a creative solution around it and still look good in it? You must always adapt fashion to what suits your body type. You both have nice figures, but in those jeans you appear flat at the back. With one or two little alterations, you can adjust it to keep the look and also flatter your figures."

"Can you show us?" Branly asked.

"Yes," Henrietta realised that Sheila O'Connell had been standing in the vestibule of the church listening to their conversation and wished the woman would mind her own business. Henrietta stared at her until Sheila was obliged to exit and cross the church yard. Although only four in the afternoon, it was beginning to get dark and Killdoe's Christmas lights and street lamps came on. Henrietta tapped each girl on the shoulder, "Come with me back to the cottage and I will show you how to adjust those jeans and flatter your figures."

21

Lily looked at her watch for the fifth time. The evening shifts seemed harder and longer, especially when Maura was off. Thankfully, her work was almost done for today. It would be good to get home and see how Genie was doing.

Genie hadn't been herself in the morning, had been very out of sorts, but wouldn't tell her what was wrong. She'd admitted to crying and pretended that it was because her team had lost the football match. Her daughter never cried before over lost football matches. She got angry or complained, yes, but had never cried tears like that. Once Lily was assured that nobody had approached her with threats, she decided it probably had something to do with Branly.

She had wanted to broach the subject of the stolen Bibles and Sheila O'Connell's accusations, but had changed her mind. Why take that evil woman's side and grill her girl? She'd also deliberately not mentioned anything to Henrietta on the Bible subject. She felt sorry for Henrietta with all she was dealing with: the damage to her cottage, the shop-lifting incident in Tralee, the horse swindle deal, and the blackmailer and all that nasty business tied up with Kinsale. She must be having regrets she ever came to Killdoe. If stories of stolen Bibles were added, it might be the last straw. It would be for her, Lily thought.

And as for Sheamie – it had been a relief to get assurances about his innocence, but she was still angry at him. It was stupid of him to squander so much money. Still, she trusted the investigation of Henrietta's detective and was relieved to be finally getting answers.

Lily wheeled her trolley slowly to the end of the corridor.

CLACK CLACK – Suddenly everything went dark –

Damn, what a bother, all the lights had gone out. It was unusual that the emergency lighting hadn't come on like it should. It was impossible to see a thing. Lily gripped the trolley and listened. What was that thudding – footsteps? Who was it? The thuds got closer and her heart thumped hard – a sweaty odour reached her nostrils and her ears picked up the heavy breathing of someone. She screamed, shoved the trolley back towards the person. She heard a grunt, but Lily didn't turn and instead ran straight ahead as fast as possible while bumping off the wall several times.

"Lily, Lily Casey?"

She recognised the voice and stopped running.

The lights came back up – a young dark-haired man was standing there.

"Lily Casey!"

"Matt, what happened?" But it couldn't have been Matt who'd been back there in the dark.

"I don't know." Matt ruffled his thick head of hair, "The lights have never gone out like that before. The cold weather must be interfering with the circuits."

"You're probably right."

"Oh look, your trolley has gone rolling off by itself," Matt ran after it. He swung it round and brought it back to her.

"Thanks, Matt. Are you on duty alone tonight?"

"I am – Pat went off duty an hour ago. Have a good evening," he gave her a boyish smile.

"The same to you."

His cologne lingered after him. It was definitely not Matt back there in the dark. She was not imagining it – somebody had been prowling the corridors. But why? Was this Kinsale all over again?

****

In Lily's own words, the pre-Christmas celebration would be done French style, Henrietta's way, but with a lot of Killdoe chaos thrown in for good measure. However, nobody would labour over a stove; it was easier to invest the money and get other people to make what they wanted. Henrietta said that sometimes one should let money do the work and it was one of the luxuries of being old and rich.

The idea was simple: Henrietta, Lily and the girls would share a Christmas meal at The Old Forge. Afterwards, the girls would have the additional treat of being the first to officially sleepover in the cottage and have a French breakfast with Henrietta the next morning. France would come to Killdoe, Lily thought as she happily planned the event for the girls.

Everything arrived in boxes of all sizes. Lily helped to fancy up the table, adding candles, colourful napkins and Christmas crackers. The choice of music was diverse, from carols to classical and the girls' current favourites – in Lily's opinion, grating electronic noise. They got a real fire going in the open fireplace and the presents were placed near the mantel. The quilt took central pride of place among the gifts, waiting to be unveiled by Branly in all its glory.

The table was laden with finger food, what Henrietta called, 'Amuse-bouche'. The plan was that it should be light, fun, and just exotic enough to appeal to the girls. There was every sort of toast and canapé, goose and duck foie gras, smoked salmon, quiches, pâté, savoury buns, cheese and olive cakes, blue cheese walnuts and bresaola roll-ups. There were lamb and pistachio kebabs and simple chicken wings and drumsticks. And to round it up – a Christmas ice-cream log. Henrietta followed Lily's advice on keeping the drinks as healthy as possible and had made a special fruit cocktail that Branly had described as being fresh as a spring shower.

With great ceremony, Branly was presented with her patchwork quilt, her present to herself. She tore off the wrapping in theatrical style, "There's a piece of all the people I love in this."

Lily and Henrietta praised it, noticed all the detail and creativity in the quilt and wrapped it around Branly. If there were little botched parts here and there, they didn't point it out, instead focusing on the better crafted pieces.

"Look at the stars," Branly cried.

"They are beautiful," Genie held part of the quilt to the light, "and they shimmer."

"Did you sew those, Henrietta?" Branly asked.

"I did and hope you do not mind. It was meant to surprise you."

"It has, it has," Branly began to sing 'Twinkle Twinkle Little Star' and Genie joined in.

Henrietta touched several stars with her finger tips and whispered a wish.

"What did you say?" Lily asked.

"I said – may the stars guide and protect you."

Lily and Henrietta encouraged the girls to open the other presents: vanity cases and books from Lily, and Henrietta had added gift vouchers from the music store in Tralee.

Lily too allowed herself to stay in their French Christmas bubble for the evening. She savoured looking around at the little group soaked in love, peace, and joy emanating from the girls.

By the end of the evening, it was clear that Henrietta was exhausted, but was making a big effort to go the distance. It was worth it because the girls were never happier together. It would be wonderful if they could keep this moment somewhere in their memories – a landmark, signalling a new rite of passage into adolescence. Both Genie and Branly practically were now thirteen-year-old teenagers and it would be a long time again before a simple meal celebration would catch their imaginations. If only this time could have been captured and preserved forever.

Lily gathered some of the torn gift-paper, recalling that of all the things she might have expected when coming back to Killdoe, it hadn't been this. What an unusual jumble of people and scraps of lives now intertwined with hers. What coincidence or destiny had brought them all together – odds and ends, patches and friends?

It had been some time since a man had called for her, even if it was only Sheamie and nothing was as ordinary as their friendship. He had just returned from Dublin and insisted on picking her up from The Old Forge after the Christmas meal.

However, Lily felt uncomfortable being under everybody's scrutiny. "You be good now," she waved her finger at the girls in order to distract attention from her own grand departure.

"And you too – be good," Henrietta gave her a little peck, "Happy Christmas, Lily. And happy Christmas, Sheamie," he was bestowed a bigger kiss.

Sheamie gave Henrietta a warm hug.

"We'll be going so, Sheamie," Lily skidalled hoping nobody noticed the blush washing over her face.

Keeping her mind focused on his disastrous horse deal would be a good way of staying mad at him and of not falling for his charm.

Sheamie took his time turning the car, "You had a good evening?"

"We had a great evening, it couldn't have gone better."

"Do you like Christmas, Lily?"

"You know I do, always have. It wasn't all sad days on Malt Hill; we had good times too." He wasn't in a hurry anyway, Lily thought, anyone would have walked Main Street faster than Sheamie was driving it. "And you – do you still like it?"

"I like it when Noelene, my daughter, is there to share it with me. Lately, I've found it a lonesome time, so I try not to think about it and keep myself busy. But this year, knowing you're around changes things."

Lily decided to let that one sit.

Sheamie coughed, "Amm – Lily, would you ever see yourself going back up to Malt Hill, buying a site and building there?"

"I haven't thought about it."

"Could you see yourself as a farmer?"

"No, it was never about the farm, it was about being considered not worthy to take over the farm or at least being involved in decisions about it."

"Dan Foley has put up a new cow house there."

"When did he build that?"

"It was a while back," Sheamie fixed the cushion at his back, "quite a while."

Why did Sheamie kept hiding the fact from her that he'd been driving around Malt Hill recently?

"Do you remember the evening – " Sheamie began.

"That was a long time ago," Lily was thankful that the night hid her face.

Sheamie said nothing more and parked in front of Lily's apartment. The engine fan hummed in the background.

"Well then," said Lily.

"Lily," his hand was light on her cheek.

He was too close and her defences were already off guard. Lily wanted to lean on Sheamie and cry on his shoulder. It would feel good to unburden all her troubles and worries on him. It had been too long since someone had touched her like that.

"No, Sheamie," she pulled back.

"Lily?"

"Sorry, Sheamie, sorry." It wasn't the moment to give in to her weakness. Letting herself go with her old friend would only add further complication to her troubles. It hadn't been enough before, why should it be different now?

Sheamie stayed still, his hands resting on his thighs.

"I'll be off, Sheamie. Good luck and thanks," she got out.

"Good night, Lily," he said flatly.

His disappointment was clear and it made her feel guilty. She had to stop feeling sorry for him.

Only when Lily had reached the door did Sheamie restart the car engine and drive slowly away. Damn, she thought, damn – she shouldn't have left it happen like that. How tempting it had been, how nice it would have been to go into Sheamie's arms.

She had wanted to talk to him about the horse and some of the investigation, but everything had felt wrong.

It took forever to get the key in the lock. The lighting was indeed poor on Abbey Street, but the lights were on upstairs at The Treasure Chest. Lily hoped McGrath wasn't back; that was all she needed. Although the blinds were drawn there were some shadows moving inside, one like Sheila O'Connell and the other clearly a taller man. She hadn't remembered McGrath to be that tall, but at night-time everything was deformed and blurred. The man's shadow was very still, while Sheila O'Connell's seemed agitated. She kept waving her hands and her silhouette moved forward and backwards. At one moment, Lily saw the man grab her arm, as if to calm her. No, it wasn't McGrath. This man was much much bigger. Lily shivered, for a second it seemed like the man was going to hit Sheila O'Connell. She had no love for that evil woman, but didn't wish bad on her either. He appeared to be holding both her arms and forcing her to stop marching around. His action must have had some effect because Sheila stopped moving and gesticulating, and was listening to whatever he was telling her.

'I'm worse than a peeping Tom,' Lily told herself, shutting the door after her. 'I've sent Sheamie home and would prefer to gape at that woman.' It would be another night of disturbed sleep, she thought. At least the girls were going to have nice dreams in The Old Forge. But she couldn't resist looking across the street again from the safe vantage point of her own living room window. The Treasure Chest was now in darkness. Could it be possible that Sheila O'Connell had a boyfriend? Lily puffed, that was difficult to believe. That woman could be categorised as an out and out spinster, with her own version of puritanical to the point of believing herself a saint. 'Look who's talking,' Lily chastised herself, 'you could put yourself in the same box.'

Ah, now there was something happening. She could see somebody had opened the door of The Treasure Chest. She looked hard and saw it was the man carrying a large box to a car. He loaded the boot. It was definitely not McGrath. But who was he? She could not see him clearly; the collar of his coat was high and he was wearing a cap on his head. Sheila O'Connell was holding open the door for him. He might have just been carrying some stock from the shop; yet, there was something in the way they behaved with each other that suggested it wasn't a usual business relationship. It might be her cousin. Lily slapped her leg – that was probably it. That man was an O'Connell; he was tall and hefty like all the O'Connells.

'Did Sheila just kiss him on the cheek?' Lily was afraid to go closer to the window in case they looked in her direction. After a short verbal exchange the man got into the car and drove off. 'Well that's a wonderful night's entertainment,' Lily plugged the kettle in. It had certainly taken her mind off Sheamie for a while.

22

Henrietta rose very early, comforted by the soft snoring from the girls' room. She said hello to the morning and the garden before returning to the kitchen and quietly preparing breakfast.

The girls were two big sleepy heads and slumbered until after ten o'clock. Genie was the first to stir, yawing her way to the breakfast table, still trying to walk with more poise for Henrietta's sake. Most of the new found etiquette would wash off, but a little would remain. Though resembling her mother in some aspects of her personality and ways of speaking, Genie was physically long and willowy and this must have come from her father's side.

"I think my father was no good," Genie mused as if reading Henrietta's thoughts.

Henrietta poured slowly from a jug of freshly squeezed orange juice. Where had Genie gleaned that from?

"Now, why do you say that?"

"That's why my mother left him. Do you think if your father was no good, you'd have half a chance to be no good either?"

"Where ever did you get that idea from?"

"It's my own." Genie's chin had that intractable angle, "It's logical."

"It might be logical, but fortunately human nature does not follow logic. It is not because you put A and B together that you come up with a little of A and B. You come up with C maybe, or D, or something else."

"Maybe four or five," Branly made her entrance. "My father wasn't much good either and my mother isn't much better."

"My mother is sound," Genie said with conviction, "she can be partly your mother too, Branly."

"They told me my father died in an accident," Branly said, "but it was really from drink."

"My father died from drink too," Genie finished.

"How do you know that – is that what your mothers told you?"

"Nah," Genie said, "I overheard people say that."

"That does not make them bad men, we all make mistakes."

"But it does make them no good, if you see what I mean," Genie insisted. "Your father died in the war, died in honour. I'd have preferred if mine had gotten shot like yours."

"Yes," Branly agreed. "When a man dies in action, you can talk about it, but if he dies from drink, you have to shut up."

"Look girls, I do not know about your fathers, but I do know that you are responsible for your own lives. If your fathers were the best in the world or the worst in the world, it has nothing to do with you. You are responsible for yourselves and your actions. It is in your hands and your hands only, and that is what matters."

"I'm frightened of the night, Henrietta," Branly deviated in another direction. "But last night when I saw the colours of the quilt I had no attack of fear like I normally do."

"I am glad."

"It lights up too, the stars are luminous when I shine the torch on them. Genie's mum said that a bed without a quilt is like a sky without stars. Now I have the stars in my bed. When I reach out and touch the material, I remember the hours Genie and I spent doing it and redoing it, and how her mum had to help us and the stars you put on it." Branly yawned loudly and stretched, the chiffon sleeves glided down her arms. She dropped them again quickly. But Henrietta had already seen it – another mark.

She took Branly's arm gently and rolled up the sleeve. The scratch wasn't very deep, but looked like it was intended to be a cross.

"Tell me about this, Branly."

"It was an accident."

"No Branly, it was not. Tell me the truth. Why did you cut your arm?"

"I didn't cut it – tell her I didn't cut it, Genie."

Genie did not lift her head.

Both girls went dumb.

Henrietta fought back her urge to ask another question. 'How unwise you are,' she told herself, 'have you learnt nothing from your childhood?'

"I do not know about you, girls, but I am still hungry," she got up and took out a tray with some pain au chocolat from the oven.

"It was sort of an accident," Branly picked at a flake of pastry.

"What were you doing?" Henrietta passed the plate to Genie.

"I was fooling around with Mikie's pocket knife. He has a tattoo on his arm and I was just messing, telling him that I would get my own tattoo. The blade was a lot sharper than I thought."

"I'll wash the dishes," Genie stood up.

"We will all do it together," Henrietta went to the sink. Branly had a story for everything and it was hard for her to discern.

"Here's Mum," Genie jumped excitedly.

Branly ran to open the door, "We had a great night."

"Did you indeed." Lily looked over Branly's head to Henrietta, "Were they good?"

"They were angels," said Henrietta.

Lily had not slept well, Henrietta thought. Glasses were a good camouflage, but they did not hide the dark circles under her eyes. As the girls wandered into the garden, Henrietta took the opportunity to inquire about Sheamie.

"Oh, Henrietta, I didn't get the chance to talk to him about anything last night and there wasn't sight or sound of him this morning, nowhere to be found."

"It is probably for the best." She had been thinking about the risks for Lily and Genie. Jean had promised to talk to Sheamie about the horse. For the rest they would have to be patient. Sheamie's feelings for Lily might get in the way if he knew the true situation. They couldn't risk Sheamie over-reacting.

****

The transition to staying nights in The Old Forge had been an easy one for

Henrietta to make. She appreciated experiencing that before returning to France for Christmas proper and New Year. She stood at her favourite spot by the kitchen window and admired how the Christmas lights illuminated Killdoe, adding more colour than usual, but in the background, Malt Hill's dark and moody forest commanded her attention.

The room temperature suddenly dropped and her body felt lighter. Henrietta was not afraid, had almost been expecting it. The air grew smokier and through the clouds the ghostly form of Jenny McCarthy appeared before her like a vapour image. She could sense the loneliness and heartache emanating from the ghostly figure and concentrated to try to understand the words Jenny was communicating –

'My love is gone and he will never know. My love will never hold his baby in his arms.'

Henrietta found herself being drawn slowly and completely into the world of the vision…

The air is drenched with merriment and celebration; it is a festive evening in The Old Forge. A big table is laden with food and drink. Men are leaning against the walls, sitting in corners and by the open half-door, smoking and talking. Old women are sitting around the chimney, smoking pipes and taking snuff. Others are at the table drinking tea and eating.

Several musicians play their instruments: violins, accordions and strange whistles. Four strong men move the big table from the centre of the floor and soon couples begin to dance, pounding the flag stones to lively Irish melodies.

Jenny is among them, but remains in the background watching the musicians and dancers.

Somebody calls out her name, "Jenny – sing us a song, sing 'Carraigdhoun'."

Jenny declines many times, but finally relents. She places a hand to her heart and begins to sing the very sad ballad.

A tall man stands apart from the others, listening attentively as Jenny sings. He whispers – Jenny McCarthy – your voice is sweeter than the song of the thrush. You have snared my heart.'

The song tails off to great applause and Jenny withdraws into the garden. The tall man goes after Jenny and walks quietly towards her. He speaks for a long time, but his words are not audible. However, Jenny's face is clear and her changing expressions vivid. At first, her eyes show disbelief, then sadness. The man reaches out and catches a stray tear trickling down her cheek. His hands appear rough, but his eyes are full of compassion. He stands strong and proud – and Henrietta can perceive that he is very much in love with Jenny.

His name forms on Jenny's lips, 'Daniel', and there is hope in her voice…

Disorientated, Henrietta swayed for several seconds and looked around in confusion. She was in the garden and staring at the now vacant space where the ghosts had been. They had vanished before her eyes. She walked to where the couple had stood, near where the girls had buried the thrush. The wild bramble that grew there had spread and was sheltering the grave, but there was not a trace or a footstep on the soil. Henrietta was sure that the vision she just saw had been Lily's grandparents, Jenny and Daniel. She was struck again by how much Genie resembled the woman and admired the sensitivity of Daniel. She looked once more at the skyline and the forest of Malt Hill. These spirits were trying to communicate with her, but Henrietta wished she could fully understand the message.

23

Lily stood inside the changing room of The Munster Department Store in Tralee, a pair of jeans in her hand. It wasn't difficult to figure out that Henrietta was annoyed. Lily had only made an offer to clean the cottage; it was the least she could do given all the trouble Henrietta had been going to with Genie and Branly.

"Lily, I do not want you cleaning The Old Forge. I know you are a professional cleaner, but you do not work for me. I consider you a friend and will not remind you again."

"I heard that the French are very fussy about things and am now inclined to believe it," Lily could say that much from behind the curtains. She felt hunted. It was Henrietta who'd followed her around the department store and put the pair of jeans into her hands. Lily struggled into the jeans, afraid to look at the mirror. They said shopping took one's mind off of things and Lily was beginning to understand why. When shopping with Henrietta, it was never truer. She realised that it was Henrietta's clever way of getting her to change her mind and to focus on something else until they had more news from the detective.

"You can be inclined whatever way you want, that is your liberty. Come out here and let me see you in those jeans."

"I hate shopping and hate clothes shopping above all," Lily peeped through the curtain of the fitting room.

"Come out," Henrietta ordered.

Lily emerged, shyly.

"Oh," Henrietta gave a gleeful squeak, "Lily in jeans. How different you look. They take years off of you."

"Well, I don't know," Lily looked in the mirror dubiously.

Henrietta inspected her model, "But those are not exactly the right ones for you." Before Lily knew it, Henrietta had her trying on pair after pair. 'Haut Couture Henrietta' had taken over the place, finding different cuts and designs. She had even asked for pins from the assistant and was pulling and tugging at the material, sticking the pins in here and there.

"At last we have it, that is the cut for you," Henrietta stood up to admire her temporary handy work.

Lily was pleased when she saw her reflection in the mirror, "I used to wear jeans, years ago, but got out of the habit, thought I was too fat for them. There's nothing worse than seeing people going around swelling out of the front and back of their jeans, or any trousers, for that matter."

Henrietta turned her round, "You are not swelling out of them, or swimming in them either. I would say, if anything, you are sexy in them."

"What are you talking about, at my age?"

"You do not see yourself in the right way. It is all a question of how you wear them. What are you going to match them with? What about shoes and a nice casual blouse or top? Let's keep going, I have not finished with you yet."

Lily's mouth open and closed several times, 'Oh, what was the use in arguing.'

Tops were added, blouses, skirts, and a cool evening dress.

Lily surrendered, "It's for Genie really that I'm doing this."

"Really." Henrietta chuckled and gave the jacket Lily was trying a hard tug, "I hope it is not only for Genie, because that is the wrong reason. Be honest with yourself, Lily."

"I don't mind being honest with myself, but don't like verbalising it," Lily was hanging on to her last shred of defence.

"Sheamie will not get any of the credit?" Henrietta teased.

"No, well, I'll never be twenty-one again, but there is a bit of a stretch to my real old days and I don't want to give up like my parents either. As the saying goes: it's better to wear out than rust out."

"So you will use Sheamie as anti-rust – that is until your real old days, as you call them."

"I'm not saying that, but he's someone I could get comfortable with."

"So, he is okay because you can be comfortable with him."

"Henrietta," Lily warned, "don't pick everything I say to death. I'm trying my best and it's Killdoe we're talking about here and not Dublin or Paris."

"Of course, so let's see what else we can find."

Lily was slowly shedding her old skin and stubbornness. For so long, layering herself with long skirts and frumpy blouses and cardigans had seemed right; she'd let her hair go, let everything go. But Lily Casey just didn't seem to fit that look anymore. How prudish she'd become and how far the older woman had strayed from the wild Lily of her youth.

She valued the time Henrietta was giving her. It was probably much more tiring for her.

"Henrietta, about cleaning the cottage, you have to be fair and let people do what pleases them. Dressing people is what you're good at and – well, I get pleasure out of cleaning things. I like shining them until they're like brand new. When I see a gleam off a window or a floor, it does it for me."

Henrietta kept going through the rails of clothes, "You really do like cleaning, don't you?"

"Well yes! Why else would I keep doing it? I'd never keep doing something if I didn't like it, not even for the money. I'd find a way out."

"I see," Henrietta carried on foraging through yet another rack of clothes.

"To others," Lily explained, "it's just long, winding corridors, dozens of open spaces and desk after desk – a space that must be cleaned morning and evening. To me, the cleaning space takes on its own personality."

"Go on."

"I walk into a huge, enormous space and everything seems impersonal. But while going from cubby hole to cubby hole, I catch the personality and character of the employee, bits and pieces of people's lives filter through. I've the feeling of putting something right in people's lives, for a while. One by one, the workers arrive and I've touched their world. Then, like the fairies, I'm gone, my work unseen, and they start untidying the place up again."

"People do spend a great part of their lives turning around and between desks. We are creatures of habit and like to put our stamp on things. The way you explain it makes a lot of sense. You are creative in your own way, Lily."

"I don't know about that. But even here in Killdoe, I pick up things about people and I see a whole other side. How the chair is used can tell you how someone has been sitting; I'll say to myself, he'll have back problems –" Lily stopped. "Henrietta, am I boring you?"

"Not at all. We are very alike, Lily."

Lily stroked the denim, "When I feel this fabric, it takes me back, makes me feel young and joyful. I never imagined it could bring up such emotion." She felt her eyes tear up, "Oh God, I'm sorry, I don't know why that happens. Since I returned to Killdoe, it happens more often, I get all teary for nothing."

Henrietta gave her an affectionate hug, "It is perfectly normal. You have been turning over stones from your past and you cannot expect to do that without feeling it."

"This must seem strange to you, Henrietta."

"What?"

"Here. I mean, you could have chosen anywhere in the world, why Killdoe? What are you going to do around here with your husband?"

"Maybe that was the attraction, an ordinary place where we could live ordinary lives for a few weeks at a time, which is what we intend to do – I think."

"You think?"

"I thought – that is a better word. The Old Forge has a soul, Lily, and I do not know if it is mine to possess. Now that I have started staying there at night, I feel the energy of the cottage even more strongly. The past calls out to me and it is all tied up with your people."

"You've lost me there, Henrietta." Lily was beginning to get light-headed; all this shopping couldn't be good for one.

"You have mentioned your grandparents several times. You even said it was the voice of your grandfather that brought you back to Killdoe. You are open to believing in ghosts – or spirits, if you prefer, are you not?"

"Yes, in a manner of speaking – I've had some psychic experiences that cannot be explained easily."

"Did you ever hear your grandmother sing, Lily?"

Lily's face lit up, "Nana was a beautiful singer; when she sang everybody in the room stopped what they were doing to listen. Granda would often ask her to sing a favourite of his, 'The Lament of the Irish Maiden'; I still get teary eyed every time I hear it sung today. Nana always sang it in Irish, 'Carraigdhoun'."

Henrietta nodded, "The Old Forge is filled with the past, your grandparents' past, Jenny and Daniel. They are talking to me and want me to know something about that time in their lives. I have the impression that there are unresolved issues which are important."

"I don't know," Lily said. "I remember them as two people who loved each other. They both had strong characters."

"Did they have many children?"

"Only my father, Danny Casey. They doted on my brother Frank and me. If I was thankful for one thing, it was that they had passed away before Frank's death."

"Only one child, are you sure?"

"Of course I'm sure. But Nana had many miscarriages which was normal for those times."

"They were hard times."

"Is there something else, Henrietta? I mean, was it just about the past, these – these ghosts, or was there something linking them to the here and now?"

"I don't know," Henrietta removed a stray thread from Lily's jacket, "I'm not sure."

****

Sheamie had avoided Lily since the embarrassment in the car. But he seemed to have gotten over it and today practically hugged her off the street, insisting on her coming into the hotel for a cup of tea.

Lily recalled their innocence and youth; Sheamie full of big ideas, telling her what he wanted, what he was going to do, the money he was going to make – and her thinking, 'Sheamie, I can't go with you on that.'

The young Lily had been adrift and hadn't known what she wanted. There had been too much churning inside her. It had been so vague for her in those days but so absolutely clear for Sheamie.

That Sheamie would ever seek her advice surprised her, because she couldn't recollect ever saying anything of great significance or intelligence that could have helped him. When the chubby teenager had told her he was going to open a fish and chip shop, she was struck that he had something so concrete in his mind and admired his vision. Sure, she'd given him a hand with the shop, which in the beginning was no more than a little kitchen with a counter and a few tables. She had given her support when he was short-staffed. It was disconcerting to think about it, because if Lily admitted it, there were more memories built around those days with Sheamie than she'd realised.

They had been a first for each other. If she let the gates open, it poured in: the sand, the salt and the sea, and the bubble that had surrounded them that night. It had meant a lot. But back then, it had meant so much more to Sheamie. He had dreams of running his empire with her by his side. It had frightened her and she hadn't been able to see herself in it, or to picture Lily Casey as the local benevolent patron's wife, not to mind imagining raising children and being the dutiful housewife. She'd specialised in underachievement and was still doing it.

He'd dreamed of having a large family, running a big estate and a successful business; and she'd longed to leave.

Lily had escaped, leaving Malt Hill and Killdoe behind her. Sheamie had married a few years later and had settled for one daughter. The rumour was that the divorce had been difficult. However, his daughter had turned out well and was studying to become a doctor. He was very proud of her and rightly so.

Lily had lasted less than a year in university herself and had wandered here and there getting involved in causes. There had been so many.

Almost twenty-five years had passed and Sheamie's world frightened her much less, but it didn't interest her much more. It was in this very hotel that Lily had broken off their relationship. He'd taken it hard at the time. She had been too young, unsure and lacking belief in her own self to see how hard the break up had been on him. It was difficult for her to explain to him that she didn't love him enough and couldn't share his dream as she had no dream of her own back then.

Lily couldn't forget the disappointment and hurt in Sheamie's eyes that day she had refused his hand in marriage. It would have helped if he'd been more vicious, but no. He'd been too kind. How fast the wheels had turned. Here Lily Casey was, a mother who was a little too old-fashioned for her thirteen-year-old daughter and still without dreams for herself.

There was Sheamie, still on about his projects and dreams, still believing and giving. She was older – yes, wiser – maybe. But being wiser didn't make her feel any different. Older did – it slowed her down, restricted and constrained. Being wise couldn't save her ageing body from that. Age indeed was beginning to force her to select and choose where to spend her energy. Age and maturing shifted her focus to placing limits, paying bills and satisfying outside demands, rather than focusing on her inner dreams.

"Sheamie, why are you so kind – why don't you hate me? Why don't you just let me be? I'm no good for you and wasn't any sort of friend to you."

He was searching her face for something. There was a look in his eyes that made her feel happy and sad at the same time.

"Is that what you truly think, Lily? Don't you see that you're always giving? I've never known you not give. Maybe the person you don't give enough to is yourself. You have courage, the courage of your conviction."

"What conviction, Sheamie, the conviction not to commit to anything, except to keep running?"

"The conviction not to be dragged down by material traps. You've never given in to that. And you've never run from a situation."

Lily squirmed, if he only knew. "Sheamie, I think you've an idealistic view of me."

"No, you squared up to your parents and never pretended that you would be different, even to me. You lived your life and took responsibility for it. You never came back crying to anyone. That's honest, Lily, and if other people built ideas around you or put hopes on you, that was their doing, not yours." He put his hand across the table and placed it on hers. She left it there and looked at him, trying to see, looking – looking for what? She didn't know, except that, whatever else, they could be friends.

His name had been linked to a number of women. True or not, it was his life and she wanted him happy. But men could be foolish and all the intelligence ran out of their minds as soon as they got a scent of a female. Sheamie was old enough now to know the difference and handle the consequences of fortune hunters; for that's what most of them were. Some said he was an easy touch, too soft when he felt affection for someone. He was already telling her not to worry about Genie's education. She would never accept his money, but that wouldn't stop him from trying to sway grants and subsidies in her direction.

Lily wanted Sheamie to tell the truth and for him to own up about losing money on the horse. She wanted no more beating around the bush. Everyone had heard of businessmen and tycoons who'd lost everything, empires collapsing, turning out to be no more than shams. It wasn't because he had a string of businesses that he was immune to financially sinking like others. He'd a lot on his shoulders, what with staff depending on him and expenses to be paid. In a small place like Killdoe, he wouldn't or couldn't lay-off workers just like that. He would only fire an employee for a valid reason. It wouldn't be his way to subcontract business to an outsider. He was a local and gave local employment – he was bound ethically and committed to this business ethos. It must weigh heavily on him, Lily realised, and her heart felt pain for him.

"You've overstretched yourself, haven't you, Sheamie? Tell me the truth, have you gotten in too deep?"

He looked confused at first and then laughed. "Lily, you're a devil, always trying to call my bluff. I'm not in trouble, nor overstretched, except around my belt. Look, I work hard, building my business and challenging my entrepreneurial spirit. I like to tend to my businesses like mushrooms –"

"Mushrooms, that's some image."

"Well, it's true. Businesses are no more than that – they can grow fast, but wither just as fast. I keep tending to my mushrooms, trying to keep them fresh. I need my pleasures too and a little craziness on Golden Girl is not going to break me financially."

Finally, he was half admitting his foolishness, Lily thought to herself and softened her heart.

"I was thinking Goldilocks as a name, but thought you'd never forgive me."

Lily went a deep red and put her hand to her hair, "Sheamie, it's a long time since my locks looked golden."

Bringing up his old nickname for her was both sweet and embarrassing to her. How could she respond to that? She felt like a tongue-tied teenager.

"But it was gold, that's how I still see you. You'd a beautiful head of golden hair, and you never liked the name."

"No, because the name is from a fairytale. 'Goldilocks and the Three Bears' is not exactly, well you know –"

Sheamie shrugged, "It was my fairytale and not yours, so I'm not asking your opinion on it."

"Sheamie, my hair is silver and yellow now, like a bale of hay in a wet summer."

"That's up to you, Lily. You talk yourself down and dress yourself down. But you know, whatever your intention is, it's having the opposite effect on me," he smiled with assurance.

Lily tightened her fists, "I have no intention, none at all."

"Right and while we're being straight with each other, can you tell me why you really left Kinsale?"

Oh, he was a clever one, moving the conversation right along from his financial situation to her. She looked away. It was ridiculous, she wouldn't lie to him, but couldn't tell him, "I can't talk about that now, not yet."

"What's the big secret, Lily?"

"It's not a secret, Sheamie, not exactly. It's just that I have my good reasons."

"It's to do with money, isn't it? You're in trouble with a money lender, is that it? I heard that some members of staff up in Kinsale with Blarney & Lee were caught up with a lender and that there was gambling and all kinds of things going on."

Lily gaped at him, "What do you know about Blarney & Lee? What's that company got to do with you, and what do you know about my life in Kinsale or before?"

"Don't take my words where they were never intended, Lily."

"And if you're talking about money lenders and racketeering, it might be under your own nose too. I'm inclined to think that you've lost the run of your affairs – everyone could be pulling the wool over your eyes and you wouldn't see it."

Lily knew from his intake of breath that he was controlling his anger. It gave her some satisfaction because she was tired of the nice, understanding Sheamie. But she regretted it immediately; he didn't deserve her dumping her frustration on him.

"I won't answer that, Lily. I'm concerned for you and know how hard it must be making ends meet and taking care of Genie."

"Don't be worried for me, I'll manage fine. Being a cleaning lady mightn't seem much, but it gets me where I want to go and –"

"You just love to do that, don't you? You love to drop that one in, to put yourself at the bottom of the pile. Don't play that game."

"I'm not playing at anything. Maybe the cleaning lady bit bothers you, but it's the truth – that's my professional limit and what I aspire to."

"God damn it, Lily, it's not about being a cleaning lady, it's about using it to annoy people. Just tell me why you left Kinsale?"

"Fine then. Genie was starting secondary school, we didn't have roots in Kinsale, but I had here and wanted her to find hers in Killdoe. I wanted to finish with the past and the best way of doing that was to come back, face it and go on living. I'm no different to you or anyone in wanting to come home. People like me, even at the bottom rung of the ladder –"

Sheamie put down his cup –

"Even at the bottom rung of the ladder," she ploughed on, "people like me need to open our own closets. We must air them out and sort the junk from the valuables. I love my work, Sheamie. My grandmother was a blacksmith's daughter and I'm a farmer's daughter at heart; cleaning, washing things, and working with my hands aren't any different than working iron or the soil."

Sheamie's eyes never left hers, "And that's all, that's the whole of it?"

Lily didn't have it in her to be dishonest, "No, Sheamie, that's not all, but that's all I'm going to say now." She got up, "And I'm paying for my own tea, even if you own the hotel, I'm paying for my tea."

24

Their screams raised the roof.

"You are growing up so fast that I was not sure, but I took the risk," Henrietta held out leather jackets in front of two bewitched girls.

"Oh, my God." Branly was close to tears, "Versace, a real Italian designer jacket. Are they really ours, Henrietta?"

"Yes, if you will accept them and –" she did not have the time to say more as they were all over her with kisses and thank yous.

"We've been dressing up all our internet models with Italian designs," Genie put out a hand to feel the jacket.

Henrietta laughed, seeing the delight on their faces. She had crossed fingers that they would be the right size and that they would have no adjustments to make.

"Don't go spoiling them," Lily admonished, "we don't want them believing that if it isn't designer, it isn't good."

"I think after the effort with the quilt and the work they have put into their own clothes, there will be no risk of that. They know the value of things and that is no small thanks to you, Lily." Henrietta ushered them into the spacious master bedroom and let them open out the doors of the main wardrobe which were lined with mirrors, "Fit them on and we will see if we need to do a little reworking."

"If there's reworking," added Lily, "and I know full well there will be with your critical eye, Henrietta, the girls must do it and every bit of it."

"Of course. I got them at a bargain price, Lily."

"Well, I hope so. Look at them making shapes in front of your mirror, Genie looks so feminine and Branly so, so –"

"So chic and classy. She has it in her; it just takes the right combinations and set of brushes to bring it out in her. And Genie is not just feminine – she is a stunner. But that is to be expected, you are a very good looking woman yourself."

"Oh, now, well –"

"Lily, I – oh no –"

"What is it? Oh –"

They looked recent, Henrietta thought, all those scratches on her lower back. 'Branly will deny if I ask, but she is letting us see them.'

Branly had taken off her pullover and was hugging the jacket to her, "It's so nice close to my skin. I'll try it with nothing under first and then add on tops and bottoms, piece by piece."

"It is a good system and quite practical." Henrietta approached, "What's the story about those scratches this time, Branly?"

"I was experimenting with something, but I gave up on it. It was a bad idea."

Lily turned Branly around so that her back was reflected in the mirror, "Were you trying to copy something or someone?"

"I read in books that martyrs wore chains and sharp things to experience pain. It was their way of absolving their sins and the sins of others," Branly pulled away, "but like I said, I gave up on that. Genie gave me some cream and my back is fine now."

Lily turned to her daughter. But Genie kept her eyes averted.

This was too much and too often, thought Henrietta. Branly needed help and professional counselling; it was beyond her competence and that of Lily's.

"It happened in a hallucination," Branly seemed to think that explained all.

"Did you take something?" Lily asked.

"I was out fooling around in the forest of Malt Hill and I hallucinated."

Henrietta glanced at Lily and made up her mind that a visit to Malt Hill Forest was necessary. There was a chance that by going there, Branly might reveal more. There was no time like the present.

Lily nodded, following her cue. Even though the day was threatening rain, the forest would provide ample shelter.

The girls were quick to agree.

****

Branly ran the pathway through the trees and Genie tried to keep up with her. Henrietta took Lily's arm. The scent of damp pine and woodland was striking. It reminded her so much of the forest in Normandy where she and Francoise had played and gone for walks – and where Francoise had committed suicide.

It was full of sounds. Genie called it sticky noise, like the earth was alive under their feet. Branly thought it like the 'snap, crackle and pop' of the breakfast rice cereal before it got too soggy.

They followed a way through the trees that ascended gently until the music of flowing water reached their ears. They climbed a little farther until finally they could see the water cascading down a stairway of rocks – the fall turned into a rapid stream flowing several meters before disappearing underground.

A happy smile lit Branly's face and she started singing. Then cupping her hands and capturing some drops from the fall, she shouted out, "Look up there – there are some wild roses."

"That's just a bush, Branly, there aren't any roses," Lily dismissed.

"Yes, there are, or there will be," Branly kept climbing. "And look, see the thrush. It's our thrush, Genie, the one we buried in Henrietta's garden. Listen to it singing."

"Our bird is dead," Genie said.

Henrietta did not see any rose or hear the bird, but believed that Branly sincerely thought they were there.

"My bird will be happy here," Branly opened her arms wide. The freshness of the outdoors and forest energy temporarily erased the grey pallor from her glittery face. She took a rolled up paper from her pocket and began to open it out.

"What is that?" Henrietta was curious, but not unduly, having gotten used to Branly's capers. "Oh, it is the cage with the bird."

"Yes it is – it will be able to breathe here. I've left the cage door half open, so the bird has the choice. If it's afraid, it can stay inside and if it wants to be free, it can fly away. I'm hoping it flies off and then I'll be released too."

Henrietta did not look at Lily but could guess her thoughts.

"What's its name?" Genie asked.

"I think it's a she. Her name is just 'Bird' because if she's to leave the cage and be free, she must have no name. She will be called Bird of the Forest."

They watched as Branly took several thumbtacks from another pocket and affixed the picture to a tree trunk.

"Where is the den?" Henrietta took a corner of the flimsy paper between her fingers.

Branly pointed to a narrower and steeper pathway that appeared to wind up and up, "That's where Mikie and Peter and the gang go. There are other dens farther up."

Lily prompted Branly to explain more, while Genie hung back and picked at the bark of an elm.

Branly denied that she had ever been up there herself, and besides, her friends were more interested in doing stunts on their bikes. Peter had a strict code of behaviour: no messing with alcohol or other substances while driving. His rules weren't always respected though and there were often fights. Sometimes there were major disputes with other gangs who were into hard drugs. A supplier often came, but she had never seen him. She had heard him referred to as The Bishop.

At the mention of the name, Lily turned ashen.

Henrietta tried to extract more information but Branly had raced to an oak and hugged it, "It's less cold here. I feel the heat coming up from the earth and it's just like the sensation in my quilt."

Henrietta could sense Lily's frustration and Genie's confusion. "I think it's time to go home," she suggested.

"Can't we keep going into the forest?" Branly asked.

"We will not," Lily was firm, "it gets denser and darker. It's easy to get lost especially on a day like today. Even as a child, I stayed on the main paths."

"It's time to go home," Henrietta reaffirmed.

****

The trip to the forest gave them lots to think about. On returning to the cottage, Henrietta contacted the detective, Mr. Curran. Unfortunately, the information Branly had given in the forest added nothing new to the identity of this man they called The Bishop, although it did tie in with what had been pieced together from Kinsale. But they were no wiser than before about his real identity. Their only consolation was that nobody had threatened Lily or Genie for over three months. Hopefully he was assured that they had been frightened into silence. Perhaps they could let it to the professionals and go on with their lives.

25

Sheila O'Connell stood in the middle of the footpath. Lily nodded and tried to side step past, but Sheila with her wolfhound on leash moved back into her path.

"Excuse me," Lily said, "this is a public right-of-way."

The dog growled as Lily tried once more to edge around them. "Will you take your dog out of my way, this is not your footpath."

"Where are they?" Sheila O'Connell hissed, making no effort to control her dog.

"What are you talking about?" Lily held on to her temper and kept her voice low. It was evening and Abbey Street was quietening down, but she didn't want a public display.

"I want those Bibles back."

"I don't have them." Lily wasn't in the mood to be conciliatory, "I've never seen them and stop your harassment this very minute; I have no time to listen to this."

"Those girls will burn in hell!" Sheila O'Connell shouted.

"Enough of that rubbish about burning in hell. And what's more – what nonsense are you trying to fill their heads with?" Lily kept an eye on the dog.

"I teach the truth and the word of God," Sheila O'Connell blessed herself.

"You can teach it to someone else. Branly and Genie have been forbidden from going to your shop."

"You are not Hartigan's mother." Sheila O'Connell gave a high cackle, "Don't care if I never see those thieves again."

Lily forgot about the dog and raised her finger, "Stop calling them insulting names. If you don't stop with your accusations, I'll bring the Gardaí to sort it out."

Sheila O'Connell cackled higher, "Listen to her, listen to Lily Casey. Bring whoever you want. It's not you or that foreigner in that cottage in Sméar-dhubh who will be believed."

"Are you referring to Mrs. Bontemps – the owner of The Old Forge?" Lily couldn't believe the words coming out of Sheila's mouth.

"I am talking about the foreigner who has occupied the blacksmith's cottage."

Lily had to get off the footpath to let a woman with two shopping bags go by, "My great-grandfather, you mean. That cottage belonged to my family."

"Oh the shame, the shame," Sheila O'Connell marched towards her door.

"What are you implying?" Right then, Lily didn't care if the whole of Killdoe watched, she was ready to box sense into her.

"You can keep your girls. Like I said, it's not that foreigner who is going to save them. And you can go back to Kinsale or wherever you came from. You can't hide away in Killdoe," Sheila O'Connell stood at her doorway.

"What do you mean?" Lily talked bravely, but that last comment stuck in her like a dagger. She made an attempt to follow Sheila O'Connell inside the shop, but backed off as the wolfhound barked and the door of The Treasure Chest was slammed in her face.

Lily wanted to kick it down again. She was furious, but especially angry with herself for getting into a verbal match with a mad woman. She crossed the street almost causing a collision with a car pulling out from in front of the supermarket. She pounded furiously up the stairs to her flat.

THUMP-THUMP-THUMP – An even louder noise resounded back at her.

Now, what was going on? Somebody was pounding inside the flat. What was Genie up to?

She threw open the door. Genie was standing near the sofa. There were books scattered all over the floor and the flower vase had tumbled over. Messy was nowhere in sight.

Lily paused, "Is everything alright, Genie?"

"Yup." Genie began picking up some of the books and magazines, "I was – it was an accident with the football."

Lily put together what she imagined had taken place. There was enough contrition in Genie's body language to explain the rest. Was it another teenage outburst or was her girl punishing herself? Lily said no more, but noticed the telltale marking on the wall near where a picture of boats on a harbour was hanging crooked. It bore all the signs of being used as target practice.

With the excuse of getting butter from Mack's, Lily hurried out again. After her run in with Sheila O'Connell, calming down time was needed.

She delayed a good fifteen minutes in the supermarket, before returning upstairs, having come to the decision to be vigilant with her daughter's behaviour in the future. However, if the marks were wiped off and the place tidied up, that would be the end of discussion this time as far as Lily was concerned.

Lily glanced around. The place had been put back in order. Messy had reappeared and was prancing in front of the fridge where Genie held a carton of butter in her hand accusingly.

Lily pointed to the zero fat label on the carton she'd just bought, "It's time for me to lose a few pounds."

Genie shook dry cat food into Messy's dish, "Mum, I'm bad, all that bad stuff is coming out of me."

Lily petted Messy and let Genie have her say – and she did have a lot to say.

"That's why I'm throwing things. It's like I'm possessed. Branly was told, and I heard it too, that some people inherited evil and were evil? They take on all the sins and badness of their family. They are the carriers and conductors."

"Is that the rubbish Sheila O'Connell tells you? You and Branly must stop going there."

"I don't want to go there anyway. But Branly thinks it's because she isn't good that her father died and her mother is sick. I think it is her mother who is a bad woman."

Lily put on the kettle to boil. "Genie, listen to me, I don't know where you're getting all these ideas about being bad or good. Of course, bad and good exist, but bad is certainly not what you and Branly are, or for that matter what Branly's mother is."

"If her mum isn't bad, why doesn't she help Branly?"

"Lena Hartigan's sick and absent, she makes promises and then forgets. We must try not to judge people."

Well, now, that was some fine talk, Lily thought. Wasn't she the first one to have her judgement about Sheila O'Connell? It was difficult to live up to our own standards. But that comment from Sheila O'Connell about her hiding in Killdoe had stuck with her.

****

Lily sat opposite Sheamie at Les Saveurs Des Oliviers, trying not to think of how long it had been since she had last accepted a dinner invitation from a man. But Sheamie's persuasion as usual won out and she couldn't stay mad at him for long. His invitation to the French-style restaurant in Dingle Bay had been well timed to coincide with Genie's first weekend away from home. Her daughter had been very excited to join the football training camp, which meant they were considering her for the first team. Lily had put her hands together and praised God for that. Going with the club for a weekend was normal and what young teenagers did. More importantly, it would give Genie a break from Branly and that Treasure Chest.

Lily folded and refolded her napkin and looked around her. The restaurant was small, friendly and intimate. Sheamie knew too grand a place wouldn't impress her. Sheamie told her that the food was reputed to be very good, though neither of them appeared to be sampling much of it. She had managed to eat a few bites of the Mediterranean Salad, but was making poor roads into the Poulet Basquaise. Finally she gave up any pretence of having an appetite and sipped the red wine. Sheamie had only done marginally better with his Green Bean Salad and was taking his time with his Steak Au Poivre.

Finally the waiter removed her barely touched chicken and Lily took several minutes to assure him that it was lovely, but that she hadn't been very hungry.

The dinner conversation between Sheamie and herself was stilted. They were working hard at it and yet it didn't feel right. When dessert arrived, it was a relief to dig into a sticky chocolate pudding.

Lily was self-conscious and she knew that made her awkward. She felt like a teenager out on her first date.

Sheamie wasn't much better – talking for the sake of it and forcing the mood too much.

Neither of them was dressed right either. He was too business-like in his suit and she already regretted her own clothing choice – it wasn't the most seductive thing ever worn by a woman. She planned to wear one of her new purchases, but in the end hadn't been brave and had gone for the trusty sensible skirt and blouse. It was something that would have been more suited to the old Lily Casey.

What's wrong with us? Lily thought. The atmosphere had never been sterile like that between them before.

The drive home from Dingle felt very long and she began to feel really down. By the time Sheamie pulled up in front of the hotel, Lily was feeling totally deflated.

Sheamie turned to her, "Will you come in for a night cap?"

"I will." He might have been asking her if she took milk with her tea.

Sheamie unlocked the residents' bar. Everyone had gone to bed. Lily looked at the hotel clock – midnight! Her aggravation was growing by the second.

She sat at the counter staring at her dry white Martini, but not touching it.

Sheamie stayed standing, sipping a Cognac, "Lily?"

"Yes."

"Remember when I asked you to marry me and – "

Lily wobbled off the stool, losing patience with herself, him and just about everything. She cut through to the bone, "Look Sheamie, I'll go a certain distance with you." She put her hand to her mouth, mortified. Bloody hell, where had that come from? That certainly killed off any romantic mood.

"Huh – who – what?" Sheamie stammered. "What are you saying? Lily, I'm no fly by night."

She'd taken the lead and he wasn't pleased – and Lily, being Lily, couldn't leave the situation rest.

"Oh, Sheamie, a lot of people sleep together, that's no big deal anymore. It's not as if we haven't already."

"Lily, Lily, you've got me all wrong here –"

"I'm going too fast for you, is that it? Look, years ago we –"

"Yes, years ago, and it meant something. You were just a slip of a thing–"

"Are you saying I'm more of a handful now?"

"Ah, I didn't intend it that way."

"No, so in what way?"

"I mean we were hardly aware of what we were doing."

"Is that so? Well I certainly knew. Losing our virginity to one another was a big deal. How did you know that I wouldn't end up pregnant?"

"We were careful."

"Were we? Oh I don't know – we took chances."

"I would have married you. This is getting ridiculous, Lily."

"You're right," she swallowed her drink in one gulp.

Sheamie brought her a second and that also went down too fast. Coming back to Sheamie's hotel wasn't the brightest idea he'd ever had. But neither of them had seemed terribly inspired. It was a let down. Lily had been waiting for that extra something – a special feeling that would tell her she could yield to him. But it hadn't come. And now she was clumsily cobbling things together, no thanks to alcohol either, like it was her duty to force it to its conclusion one way or another. If they weren't meant to be, they might as well get one night of sex out of it.

"Look, do you want to sleep with me or not?" It wasn't wise to drink that fast.

"Yes, no – not like this, in this hotel, this is my business place. Do you have to be so direct," he was annoyed – half angry.

Lily pushed the stool aside.

"Where are you going?"

"Home, Sheamie, the night's over," she walked a straight line to the door.

"Lily, wait. I mean, look, at least let me accompany you home."

"That won't be necessary. It's not like somebody is going to jump on me – at my age I'm at no risk. I'd prefer to walk home alone."

"Damn it, Lily –"

Lily didn't give Sheamie a chance and stormed out the door and onto the street.

Lily was fit to be tied she was so irate with herself. Instead of keeping her big mouth shut, she'd behaved like a child. "Sheamie, the years haven't improved our finesse," she said out loud. It was her first free weekend; there was nothing to clean and no teenager hanging out around the place – and she'd blown it. She'd made 'a balls' of everything. 'Lily Casey, you're one simpleton.'

Lily stood on the street, fuming and feeling like a fool. The Sapphire night club was emptying out. A bobbing, tinted head drew her attention. Was that Branly? She wiped her glasses to try to see better. Whatever about her eyesight, her sense of smell was fine and those weren't ordinary cigarettes she whiffed. The girl had put on her helmet and was getting on the back of a bike.

"Branly," Lily called, but her voice was lost in the rumpus. Some bikes sped away, followed by half a dozen more, drowning out all other sounds. There were still some bikers left hanging around. They must be a different gang, Lily decided, because they seemed older, tougher and meaner. What was bringing them to Killdoe? The town was getting very rough and it would be wise to get off the streets.

Lily took a short cut through Abbey Lane. The lane was narrow and bordering people's back yards.

'Miaow – miaow – miaow.'

Messy? How had that rascal gotten out? Somebody must have left a window open.

"Here kitty, kitty, kitty; come here, Messy."

'Miaow – miaow.'

"Messy, come here – "

A car door banged and a man was coming in her direction. He was tall and wearing a cap. The lower part of his face was covered by a scarf. He held something in his hand – it looked like a large bag.

He stood still and waited for her to come closer. Lily just managed to utter, "Good night."

"Night," he walked on.

Lily scurried away. There was something unreal about it all; it wasn't the big city, but she'd been alone in the lane with a strange man. She felt unsafe and decided to leave Messy to her own devices and get off the street.

Once home, Lily worked herself into a temper thinking about the evening. What a blasted waste of an evening. Feeling like she was no better than Genie with her tantrums, she huffed off to bed.

She woke up a few hours later from a bad dream in which a man had been running after her down Abbey Lane. She thought about the man in the lane. He could have been coming from The Treasure Chest – the back entrance was on Abbey Lane.

Lily tried to sleep again, but kept seeing Sheila O'Connell's dark face and hearing her shout about her precious Bibles.

Lily's foul humour hadn't lifted by late morning. Messy danced on the bed, obliging her to move.

"So you decided to come home did you, little sprite. Did you sneak back in the window? Now, you want me to get up and feed you."

Lily tickled the cat, "You are cute though. Oh no, Messy, what's this? Are you getting fat, or are you bringing trouble in the door to us?"

There was no doubt about it, the cat was expecting kittens. How were they going to manage those? Oh, that was the least of her problems.

Lily got out of bed cursing her hangover. She felt depressed which was an unusual emotion for her. Her problem was that she'd been too long without a real man in her life.

There was only one cure for it – work. Lily threw herself into it and cleaned everything: pots, pans, floors and windows. She then dived into another bout of cleaning in the afternoon. The place wasn't big enough for her nervous energy. She thought about tidying Genie's room, but changed her mind. It was important to respect her daughter's privacy. Maybe it would be alright to just tidy up her clothes – but a quick cup of tea was in order first.

Lily stood at the window and let herself dream for a moment. The next instance, she saw Sheamie parking across the street. At the sight of him something warmed up inside, and even Sheila O'Connell looking out from inside the shop window couldn't dampen her rising spirits. 'Oh, Sheamie, you're too good for me,' she thought.

Lily opened the door at the first ring.

"Come on, Lily, we're going driving." Sheamie was looking handsome, dressed in his best casual outfit.

Lily smiled, "All right." They were old enough to give each other second chances and third – or more if needed. They would just forget about the night before.

"Do you want to come in because I'm going to be a few minutes?"

"No, Lily, I'll wait for you downstairs. Take your time, I'm going nowhere."

Lily put on her jeans and a simple top. She applied the Henrietta touch and felt like she was eighteen again.

It was in his eyes when she walked out. Sheamie was looking at her like she was the sexiest woman in the world. She strutted in her faded, re-cut and redesigned jeans by 'Haute Couture Henrietta'. Gone was Lily the cleaner and the mother, and back was the younger Lily on a day out with Sheamie.

This time, Lily followed his lead. They weren't driving that far; it took just over an hour to get to the little town of Ballybunion where the sea air was gusty, but invigorating. They walked along the cliffs – directionless, taking their time. Their arms naturally found each other. She let him talk and he let her talk. They learned nothing new, just ordinary details, but rediscovered that it was good to be together like this in the open air. This was natural and unstaged. Sheamie took her hand and led her down the path to the beach. Dusk was falling and the tide was way out. It was cold, but she loved being with him. It was their old spot and they were alone.

His lips touched her cheek gently and then just as tenderly her mouth. She closed her eyes, shed the years, and let herself travel with him. She became once again that crazy creature who would go with the wind and rediscovered that girl who somehow knew that Sheamie would be the first and that one day she'd come back to him. When he took her in his arms, Lily could tell that he was as nervous as she was, and that relaxed her. He led her inside a cave opening.

"Lily –"

"Shush, don't say a word, Sheamie." She let her fingers run down the front of his shirt and smiled to herself. As she'd suspected he'd been getting into shape. He'd lost weight and there was muscle definition on his chest and arms. A giggle rose in her throat – she knew it would be all right. When his hands moved over her skin, Lily shivered. There was something about his touch, the place and the moment. It was daring and exciting.

He lowered her onto his coat, telling her that she was beautiful and his whispered words made her feel beautiful. Lily drew him fully into her and they forgot everything, letting themselves go with the ebbing tide. In the end, she felt nothing else except what he gave. They clung to each other, abandoning themselves to passion and sensation.

It was damp, cold and in the middle of winter. Weather conditions couldn't have been more wrong, but it was all right. It was wonderful. It had always worked between them, but she never remembered it being this good.

Lily realised she had been wrong and that, yes, the years had improved their finesse. Perhaps their initial moves were awkward, but for the rest, they had matured and knew what pleased them both.

They lay where they had many years before and the ocean swept them back washing away lost time.

"Lily," he gathered her to him, "I hadn't planned it like this."

"I'm glad you didn't – it's better this way. But I think we should leave. Before we freeze to death, we'll drown."

"As long as you are with me, I don't mind."

It was lovely to hear words like that and to fantasise that nothing else mattered.

They laughed together, dusting off sand and scrambling around to find their clothes. They left the cave to discover that they would have to paddle through pools. The moon was their torch, lighting their way back to the steps and up the cliff walk.

"Wow, we got out just in time," Sheamie said as they gazed out to sea. "We were like foolish children," he didn't sound a bit sorry.

Lily felt happy and light and he took her back in his arms.

Only when a shower became more persistent rain did they return to the car. Sheamie switched on the wipers and the lights came up. They both looked slightly dishevelled and grinned foolishly at each other.

"Lily, I want to show you my house."

The house was one mile outside Killdoe on a little hill called Killdoe Upper. It didn't look new, but neither did it have the character of an old homestead. It was simply unfinished and lonely. There were numerous rooms and lots of furniture, but it seemed empty of life. Lily had always lived in small rented places and thought if she owned something as big she would have made the effort to make it homely and lived in. She felt the house had never quite become a home. Maybe it had been better at the very beginning when his wife and daughter were with him, but it was difficult to detect even signs of happier times.

"It's very large, Sheamie, there was – is – it must take a lot of work keeping it in order."

"We had a cleaner," he gave a rueful grin. "A woman came in a few times a week." He told her his ex-wife, Delia, didn't like doing domestic chores. "I still pay someone to come in from time to time, but it mostly gathers dust now. I can't decide whether to sell it or live in it and so I have someone clean it up occasionally while deciding."

"The world needs cleaners, always will. I'm not insulted that – " Lily saw the concern in his eyes. "It's one of the best jobs in the world," she finished off quickly, and for once, had nothing else to add.

He reached for a tendril of her hair.

"It's full of sand, Sheamie."

"It's golden and rare."

"Where are you taking me now?"

He opened a door to a smaller room, a cosy bedroom. It smelt fresh and inviting. He lit little candles – there were flowers and pretty ornaments decorating the place. She picked up one of the candles and saw that her name was printed on it.

"Oh Sheamie –" It was just a silly candle, but imagining Sheamie going to that trouble won her heart in a way no one had ever done.

"I did this myself," his voice was thick with emotion. "No cleaning woman had a hand in this. This is what I'd planned."

Lily kissed him, "This wasn't a bad plan and it will work perfectly for stage two."

"Stage two?"

"Well, you're not planning to take me home now, are you?"

She woke in his arms and thought how nice it would be to stay there forever and never have to think or worry again. That would be heaven.

"Sheamie?"

"Yes, Lily," his hand lay possessively on her thigh.

"I appreciate the effort you made to lose weight."

"It was hard work."

"You just need to lose a few more kilos and it will be perfect."

"What?"

She punched him, "Knew it – I could always make you run."

"Sheamie, what are you doing?" Lily squealed.

"Still ticklish. That's your downfall, always was."

****

Lily was on cloud nine for the rest of the week and didn't want to let go of that feeling of exhilaration. Inevitably, euphoria would wear off, but she was staying up there as long as possible.

Sheamie's words came back to her, 'You're a beautiful woman, Lily.' What was he doing calling her beautiful, she'd almost forgotten what her body looked like. She drew closer to the mirror and studied herself. It didn't displease her, especially in the soft light when the lines and tresses of her face were less visible. With a little makeup, her high cheekbones could be highlighted more and her whole look enhanced. More regular trips to the hairdresser might keep her hair from turning into a wild bush and the grey roots from showing up. The door gently closed – Genie had come in like a thief. Lily jumped back from the mirror, like someone caught in an illegal act.

Lily's concentration deserted her totally at work. It was so much nicer to day dream her way through hours of dusting and cleaning. Maura surprised her several times in the middle of a reverie. Unfortunately, Lily also seemed to have picked up a cold and she used that as an excuse to avoid Maura. Maura was quick to jump to conclusions about Lily's elevated mood and quicker to air them, and did so that very morning.

"That's a bad cold you're after catching and you're hoarse. Here, try these lozenges," Maura took a packet from a pocket of her overalls.

"Thanks, it's a light cold. I'll soon shake it off."

"Sheamie Fitzgerald has a touch of the same thing," Maura said deviously.

"Oh, these things go around," Lily replied, ignoring Maura's innuendo.

"A truer word was never said," Maura's skit let her know she wasn't being fooled by Lily.

Maura could guess away, Lily didn't intend telling anyone what was going on between herself and Sheamie.

26

Henrietta could accept that Lily did not want to go too deeply into the past. Lily had built a very positive image in her mind about Jenny and Daniel Casey; they were her heroes and that admiration of her grandparents had been passed on to Genie. Lily's parents had let her down in one way, but in time she would rebalance and rewrite her memories of that part of her life. The happier days would shine through. But respect and adoration of her grandparents was essential to who Lily was. In her eyes, they formed a couple that had been very much in love. And the grandparents Lily knew had been exactly that.

Henrietta's ghostly visions continued to reveal to her that Jenny McCarthy had suffered for love and had been lucky in love. She was already with child when Daniel Casey had declared his affections for her at The Old Forge. Henrietta deduced that it was the English soldier's baby she was carrying. Jenny had been genuinely in love with the soldier. But of course in those days, having a lover, not to mention someone coming from the wrong side of war, would have been a huge scandal. Her own sister, Francoise, had taken her life, but she had been raped and publicly humiliated. Had Daniel been aware, she wondered, that it was the soldier's baby Jenny had been expecting? In the scene Henrietta watched when Daniel had declared his intentions, what Jenny actually told him had not been clear. Henrietta recalled that in the versions that Lily and Genie gave her of Jenny McCarthy, she was supposed to have nursed the English soldier back to health and had been condemned by locals for that, and that Daniel Casey had defended her. But in Henrietta's visions, the ramblers singing and dancing in the cottage seemed unaware of Jenny's dilemma.

They probably would never know the whole truth, so what good would it serve to tell Lily about her visions? What business was it of Henrietta Bontemps to rewrite or indeed pry into Lily Casey's past, based on patchy visions and scraps of times long gone? How could she be sure that those visions had not been made up? Our minds played many tricks and games with us.

Sheila O'Connell had called Lily's ancestors traitors and many other names. She had said that Jenny Casey betrayed her own family. Henrietta had read the historical document explaining about the ambush outside Killdoe and how it was partially foiled because of a tip off from an informer. People died in the fight that had followed, including Sheila O'Connell's grandfather. But how would knowing any of this change today? There must have been many families with secrets; war brought confusion to everyone. It might be impossible and unnecessary to try to collage together a story especially when she was unable to verify the truth.

For her part, Henrietta knew that delving into The Old Forge's past helped her revisit her own memories of Francoise because it had been something she had lived, not part of somebody else's past. But Lily had started life in totally different times to those of her grandparents. Whatever had been their start as a married couple, Jenny McCarthy had evidently grown to love Daniel Casey deeply. Lily had stored that love in her memories. Was that not enough for everyone? Why did anyone really need to know the truth about the past? Did it even matter?

But apparently it did matter to Sheila O'Connell. Sheila was feeding on her version of the past to serve her anger. Her whole life was built around honouring the O'Connell family and festering on the wrongs she believed were inflicted on them. She succeeded in brainwashing Branly with some of her twisted ideas and even Genie a little. Henrietta fully supported Lily's decision to ban the girls from going to The Treasure Chest. But while Genie was more likely to obey, Branly would do her own thing.

Lily was better placed to deal with the practical end of parenting the girls and even assumed the unofficial role of foster mother to Branly.

Henrietta tried to help in other ways. She had taken it upon herself to visit Father Sheehan and learnt that he was a new Parish Priest and had been in Killdoe for a shorter period than her. They had spoken about her fears with respect to Sheila O'Connell and in particular her association with the Abbey Graveyard and ruins. He had listened carefully and had taken her words seriously, promising to follow it up as he made his rounds and got to know his parishioners. He had already made one important change – the River Road entrance to the cemetery was to remain open during the day. A second entrance, independent of The Treasure Chest shop, would be created the following summer from Abbey Street. It was a small victory over Sheila O'Connell.

Henrietta thought to herself, 'How audacious of me to interfere behind the scenes. I am a foreigner who knows nothing of the ways of the place.'

While at best a light sleeper, this time Henrietta woke up feeling a really bad sensation. She sensed the presence of somebody outside the bedroom window. She got out of bed and reached for her dressing gown. She decided to leave the lights off, thus taking longer to make her way to the kitchen and the still shutterless windows. She found it difficult to see anything outside in the dark. Telephoning for help crossed her mind, but suddenly she noticed a torch light moving from left to right and could discern very recognisable shadows. Resolved and fearless, Henrietta marched to the door, pulled the bolt and swung the door wide open, while at the same time flicking the outdoor light switch.

"Who is there?" she called out.

Everything was quiet.

She stepped out into the garden, anger overcoming fear. "I know it's you, Sheila O'Connell, and your dog. I am not afraid of you or your curses."

Her voice echoed back.

Henrietta waited another minute before returning inside and banging the door closed. She went to the armchair near the fire, warming herself by the last fading cinders. She knew getting back to sleep would be impossible, so she concentrated on building a wall of positive energy around her. She decided not to tell Lily of the incident and alarm her unnecessarily. There was no point either in reporting the prowler to the Gardaí. She was determined, however, to find her own way of coping with the menace of

Sheila O'Connell. Whether she stayed in The Old Forge for a brief or long period, others would live here, and she feared that The Treasure Chest woman would not give up until she had in some way destroyed the cottage or used it to damage Jenny McCarthy's memory.

'I have to go to The Treasure Chest once more,' Henrietta decided. The only way was to face that woman again and try to provoke something – anything that would help make her abandon these threatening behaviours. She had to try.

✳✳✳✳✳✳✳✳✳✳✳✳✳✳✳✳✳✳✳✳✳✳✳✳✳✳✳✳

Henrietta looked at the sky; it would be another wet, grey day. It was a good excuse to carry a long umbrella. She tried not to think about the fact that the umbrella had other practical uses if necessary.

On arriving at the shop, her welcome was a closed door. Henrietta did not know if her feeling was relief or disappointment, but decided to follow up her second choice and return to the Abbey Graveyard.

She knew almost by heart the way to the headstone of Jenny and Daniel Casey. It was immediately apparent that something was wrong. 'Oh no – not again.' The potted plants that Lily had placed on the grave on All Souls' Day had been smashed to bits. 'Oh God,' Henrietta bent down and picked a shard. It was clear that the damage could not have been caused by the wind; the pots were smashed by a person.

"You!"

Henrietta turned slowly to find Sheila O'Connell and her wolfhound towering over her. "Hello Mrs. O'Connell," Henrietta replied haltingly trying to control her anger and contempt.

"You." Sheila O'Connell repeated. "What are you doing here?"

Henrietta opened her palm to reveal a shard, "That is obvious, is it not? Besides, this cemetery is open to everybody, I am sure Father Sheehan will have told you that."

Sheila O'Connell stood even closer to Henrietta, "Why do you keep coming back here?"

"I like it."

"You are French, this graveyard holds nothing for you. What do you want from here?"

Henrietta did not reply immediately and then chose her words carefully,

"I was born in a place like Killdoe where our traditions and customs were and are not so different. My family farmed land and we worked hard."

"That gives you no right to interfere here," Sheila O'Connell tugged at the leash of her wolfhound.

"What exactly is your problem?"

"Foreigners cannot understand."

"We have cemeteries also in France. I was brought up with your religion and honouring the same God."

"And?"

"That God does not ask us to damage graves and to curse people. He does not ask us to trespass on private property."

"You would accuse me," Sheila O'Connell tugged harder at the leash – the wolfhound growled.

"That God," Henrietta continued, "does not ask us to manipulate innocent girls or encourage them to inflict pain on themselves."

Sheila O'Connell prodded Henrietta's shoulder with a forefinger, "You are a foreigner who knows nothing of the ways of Killdoe. I am the innocent one and I do God's will. Those girls are thieves and the Caseys traitors."

"I do not know on what grounds you accuse the girls. What you think Lily Casey's ancestors were or did has nothing to do with Lily, her daughter, and certainly not Branly Hartigan."

The other's voice came out like her wolfhound's growl, "They are thieves and traitors, all of them. They bring bad to Killdoe."

Henrietta could not take her eyes from Sheila's fingers twisting round the dog's leash.

The wolfhound's warm breath was too close to her leg and forced Henrietta to step back. The dog barked loudly and Sheila O'Connell began to laugh. It was a piercing screech, "You think your silly fantasies and nonsense can help the girls. Return to your country, foreigner, Killdoe is not a place for you." She snatched the leash, pulled the dog away and strode up the cemetery through the abbey ruins towards the door of her chapel.

She is insane, Henrietta thought. Unfortunately, nobody, certainly not the Gardaí, would believe her or take action until Sheila did something illegal or hurtful.

Sheila O'Connell continued walking to the top of the cemetery to where a man stood at the chapel doorway, waiting. Family? Perhaps he was just a supplier making a delivery to the shop. However, if he had entered the cemetery from the shop, he must know Sheila O'Connell very well.

Henrietta found a plastic bag in her pocket and gathered the broken flower pots into it.

****

Lily came to the cottage door with some fresh eggs, explaining that she had got a dozen from Maura and would not be able to use all of them. Henrietta invited her in, noting that Lily seemed different, lighter – happier than before the weekend.

On seeing the needle and thread in Henrietta's hand, Lily wondered what she could possibly be making now and was surprised when Henrietta explained that it was curtains for the garden shed. Her hope was that the shed might also be used as a spare room.

Henrietta made a few stitches and listened while Lily told her of one of her run-ins with Sheila O'Connell and of trying to keep the girls away from the shop. She confirmed that Sheila lived alone, but had been known to take in lodgers. Henrietta informed her about the tall man she had noticed on a few occasions with Sheila. Lily had also seen someone like that and thought it might be a cousin that was known to visit occasionally.

"If one of her relatives is still visiting, it might be worth inquiring about him to see if he is more reasonably minded," Henrietta said.

"That's true for you, I could ask Sheamie. But if you had a cousin off her rocker, wouldn't you know it already?"

"You should, that is if you are not 'off your rocker' too," Henrietta tried out Lily's expression. It would have been funny if she was not convinced that Sheila O'Connell was dangerously demented.

Henrietta would have pursued the subject but clearly Lily had more pleasant thoughts on her mind.

"Where is Sheamie?"

"He's gone to Dublin to visit his daughter."

"Did you not go out to dinner Friday evening?"

"Hmm."

"I am sure that those bright eyes and nice rosy complexion of yours did not come from your cleaning at the Business Park," Henrietta chided.

"Don't ask questions; I will just say that it was a long weekend and the day's shopping in Tralee for my new outfit wasn't wasted."

"I am glad that the jeans were the undoing of you."

Lily's cheeks burned. "I don't know about that," she coughed and popped a lozenge.

"That is a nasty cold you have got."

"I – it's getting better – fast."

Henrietta nodded, "Passion is a great healer."

Lily tried to settle more comfortably on the stool.

Henrietta's eyes twinkled, "Are you officially going out together?"

"Officially? Ah – no – " Lily almost lost her balance.

Henrietta realised that Lily had not even begun to consider her new relationship with Sheamie in those terms, "Forgive me if I seem nosy."

"You are, but I don't mind. I haven't said anything to Genie."

"I am sure Genie has put two and two together."

"Damn it – why can't we just go with the flow and enjoy things as they are? Why do we have to think about troublesome details, such as official or not?"

"You do not have to think about those details yet – but you do realise that your life will become more public once people know you are with Sheamie?"

"I suppose, oh no –"

"Couples share secrets, Lily."

Lily put a hand to her mouth, "I've been stupid."

Henrietta assured her, no. But it meant that it was time to tell Sheamie all, because even if Lily told him nothing, the blackmailer would in any case assume she had. And with Sheamie involved, they might be able to pressure faster answers.

Henrietta led a troubled Lily to the cottage gate and watched her walk towards the town until out of sight. She then went inside and telephoned the detective, Mr. Curran. It may or may not help, but if he were to make any progress, he had to have all the details. It was time to find out more about Sheila O'Connell's cousin; it might be a false trail, but they had to know. Branly was going to that shop even more often than they realised. Henrietta knew that it was easier to make her talk when she was in a depressive mood. Who knew what the girl might unwittingly reveal; Sheila O'Connell could have gleaned a lot of information from her.

27

Lily pushed her cleaning trolley. She wasn't superstitious, but the March rain dragged everything down. They were subjected to two full days of cold lashing rain; winter hadn't had the last word.

She felt something uneasy in the air and already regretted her impulsiveness with Sheamie. What had she been thinking of – exposing Genie to more danger? But at least once she told him all, he would understand the need to keep their relationship under wraps. As soon as the shift was finished, she would find him. He should have come back from Dublin that afternoon. Henrietta was right when she said that it might help all round if Sheamie was aware and could put his influence behind the investigation.

Footsteps clipped on the corridor, "Mrs. Casey?"

Lily gripped the trolley handle – McGrath was back!

"Mrs. Casey?" he called her again.

She pushed forward, pretending deafness, ashamed of her cowardice.

"Mrs. Casey?" he raised his tone. There was no mistaking it, McGrath was addressing her.

"If you have a minute, I'd like to have a word with you," he stood by his office door in his grey suit waiting for her.

Resigned, she stopped and parked her trolley, then walked slowly in his direction.

McGrath gave her a peculiar look and opened the door wider to let her pass. Lily braced herself for the worst and walked in.

Lily emerged shortly after, completely baffled. What to make of such a request? Of all the things she had been expecting, it certainly hadn't been to do some cleaning work for his cousin. For various reasons that he didn't elaborate on, McGrath had moved out of the flat over The Treasure Chest. He'd spent a few days in Sheamie's hotel, but his stay in Killdoe was longer than expected and he had moved in with his cousin near Malt Hill. As his cousin was a very busy woman with children, he thought of helping her out with the cleaning.

"Lily, where were you?" Maura came down the corridor.

"I just had a small bit of business to attend to." Lily peered over the top of her glasses, "Maura, did you move my trolley – I left it right here?"

"Why would I do something like that? Are you sure that you left it here?"

"Of course I'm sure, why would – " Lily tried to get a hold of herself. There was no reason to get narky with Maura.

"What's that poking out of the toilets?" Maura didn't try to hide her amusement.

"How did it get there?"

"I don't know, Lily, but I think something has gone to your head. You've been working too hard, that's all. It happens the best of us, especially when we're burning the midnight oil."

Lily didn't think so, but didn't say so. She concentrated instead on steering her trolley back out. Someone must have shoved it in there as a prank.

"Maura, what I need is a strong shot of coffee or tea or –" her voice faltered "– or whatever that distributor has."

The brown envelope with her name printed on it was sticking out from under one of her dusters. She snatched it before Maura had a chance to notice and stuffed it in her overalls pocket.

"Maura, I'm just going to spend a penny, my bladder is about to burst," her voice sounded unnaturally calm.

"All right, dearie."

Lily closed the WC door firmly after her. She awkwardly opened the envelope and took out the small square piece of paper. The words were different to the first time –

'RETURN WHAT DOES NOT BELONG TO YOU – THEN KEEP YOUR MOUTH SHUT OR YOUR DAUGHTER WILL PAY THE PRICE'

Lily slipped out of the toilets and bolted down the corridor.

"For goodness sake, where are you off to?" Maura called after her.

"I think I forgot to switch off the cooker back at the flat; at least, I can't remember if I switched it off. Genie's at football practice, I can't take the risk." How easy lying came to her when she had to.

"Your head is gone altogether from you today, Lily. Go on with you so. We don't want you burning down your place. Love birds," Maura started lilting a tune.

Lily ran down the street. It was happening again; it had been bad enough getting the first, then the blank one, and now this one. It was her wake-up call. Too much time had been lost blundering with detectives these past six months.

Where was Genie? Her daughter wasn't answering her phone, and Branly wasn't answering either.

Lily raced to the flat panting and gasping. She rang Genie again, but in vain. Genie never did that, she always answered. There had been football practice after school, but that should be well over by now. Her daughter never lied to her. Lily thought about it – never lied, but had deceived her a few times. Deceived was a strong word, but she had to admit that certain things had been hidden and most of them were to do with Branly. That's why Lily hadn't pried; she'd have done it herself at her age to protect a friend and indeed had done so many times.

Her head was spinning making it impossible to think straight. The right thing would be to go to the Gardaí and forget all this detective nonsense.

Why had the note been put in her trolley again? Did the blackmailer know about the investigation? What did it mean, 'RETURN WHAT DOES NOT BELONG TO YOU'?

Lily felt her legs turning to jelly and her throat was so dry that she couldn't swallow. Courage, Lily told herself, you need Nana's courage.

Something had frightened him; desperation led people to do desperate things

Messy rose and padded to the door. 'Oh thank God, Genie was home,' Messy was never wrong. Lily tried to stop shaking and waited.

Genie slammed the door.

Something was the matter, "Genie, where were you?"

"At football," Genie ruffled Messy's fur.

"You weren't," it came out too quickly.

"I was at football, Mum."

"You didn't answer your phone, I was anxious. And where is Branly?"

"I was at football. They selected the team for the championship match and I'm not on it. They said I wasn't fit enough. But it was because my period came and nothing went right and I couldn't tell them that. And I don't know where Branly is."

It got through to Lily. She could almost laugh; that was it, her period. She could handle that. They had already had talks about menstruation and Lily reassured her daughter that girls didn't lose talent because of periods, she'd make the team the next time.

Lily went to the window and looked across at The Treasure Chest shop. Her fingers grasped the note – Genie had to be protected, first and foremost. Messy jumped onto the window ledge beside her and gazed onto the street. She needed to have a word with Henrietta, that was the safest bet. But shouldn't she talk to Sheamie first or go to the Gardaí right away?

✲✲✲✲✲✲✲✲✲✲✲✲✲✲✲✲✲✲✲✲✲✲✲✲✲✲

Sheamie got off his office chair and towered over Lily, "Lily, how could you be so, so – "

Lily raised a finger, "Sheamie, don't even say it. If you're going to lambaste me and give me a bollocking, do it another time, this just isn't the moment for it."

"You're not staying on your own. You and Genie will move into my house – and – and you're stopping work up at that building. In fact, you're stopping work everywhere. You will stay with me and that's final."

"Well, that's intelligent; if I do that, they or he or whoever will know for sure that I've reported the thing. Then we'll all be in more danger. I mustn't change my routine."

Sheamie scratched his head, "We have to inform the Gardaí. Does Henrietta know about this?"

"Yes, she was following her own investigation and the two things got mixed up together."

"Her own investigation?"

"Oh, come on, Sheamie, don't play the innocent with me. You know very well that you were badly swindled and – "

"Badly swindled!" he interrupted her – "What in God's name! Lily, how could you not say something?" Sheamie was purple and puffed up to the gills and his ruddy complexion only added to the high colour.

"There is no need for you to get a heart attack over it. How can I tell you anything, if you are going to explode like that? It's no wonder I keep secrets to myself."

Sheamie reined himself in, "We're going first to report to the Gardaí and we're going to tell them everything."

"But that's too obvious."

"I'll drive around, ring them, we'll meet them somewhere out of the way. We won't go near the Garda Station."

Lily could see that Sheamie was beside himself with worry, not sure whether to sit or stand – shake her or hug her. "Now, Sheamie, maybe we'd better talk to Henrietta first and get her slant on things. Then we can get onto her detective and have our story right before talking to the Gardaí. Oh, Sheamie –"

He tightened his arm around her shoulders, "I might be angry, but only because you didn't trust me enough to tell me. We have to find out who wrote the note and how he managed to plant it in your cleaning trolley."

Lily allowed herself to relax in his arms for a second. It felt good to let down her defences a little and to lean on someone.

"I don't know – Maura was there with me as usual and I'd gone in to McGrath's office because he wanted a word with me about a cleaning job for a family on Malt Hill."

"He asked you that! I didn't authorise him to talk to you."

She stepped out of his arms, "What do you mean?"

"Nothing at all."

"McGrath's working for you, isn't he?"

"In a manner of speaking."

"You told me he was an inspector, but now it appears he's on your pay roll. Sheamie Fitzgerald, what's going on? Did you send him to Kinsale, has he been following me?"

"No," Sheamie fidgeted with his phone, "just keeping an eye."

"Bloody hell, Sheamie, he's a detective."

"Not in the way you think."

"Explain yourself."

"Look Lily, that isn't the issue right now. The safety of you and Genie is my main concern."

"Explain yourself or we're not leaving here."

"Oh, very well then. I suspected a betting scam; it was small scale and there were a few unusual bets placed in my shop. I had a tip off from a friend in Kinsale; I didn't want to draw attention to the thing, so I hired McGrath to look into the matter discretely."

"And," Lily folded her arms, "what did he find out?"

"His enquiries led to Blarney & Lee in Kinsale and also to the Business Park here – "

"You suspected me, didn't you?"

"I did not, Lily – will you let me finish. It led there, but he couldn't make the link with anyone. However, he discovered a big mess in Kinsale, a racket of money lending, drugs and what not. And I understand, though I'd be waiting forever for you to tell me, that you reported something to the Gardaí. I was anxious for you and I asked McGrath to look out for you."

"I see," Lily said, "I reported everything to the Gardaí. But did they do anything? No. Henrietta got her detective to look into things and he hasn't come up with much more than you. Everything is muddled in my head. I even thought in the beginning that you'd swindled Henrietta's husband and son over the horse deal."

"You what! Had you so little faith in me?"

"Look, Sheamie – are we or aren't we going to the Garda Station?"

"We're going to the Garda Station, but I'm getting McGrath to get extra protection for you and Genie. And you are not going out there cleaning for that family on Malt Hill."

Lily got irate, "I already said I couldn't and I suggested Maura as a substitute. Moreover, Maura lives in that neck of the woods. Now, can we go?" she angrily marched out in front of Sheamie.

28

Henrietta switched off her phone. People of all ages resorted to throwing things, shouting, and many other energetic exercises to demonstrate and evacuate anger and frustration, but she had learned to keep emotions under tight control. It had never been her way to shout and scream. When life had served up bad and worse, patience and perseverance had been her best friends. Nonetheless, there were times when it might have felt good to let things fly. The cottage gate banged. Lily would not be very happy to learn the latest news.

"Much good authorities are." Lily sighed as she paced around The Old Forge, "I'm telling you, Henrietta, we'd have been as well off reporting nothing. We're no wiser now than when we set out."

Henrietta took off her sewing glasses, "You have to give the Gardaí time."

"Time, don't talk to me about time."

Henrietta heard the quaver in Lily's voice and pointed out that there was some Garda protection, and though Genie had not been told, a Garda had been assigned to keep watch. To take their minds off things she invited Lily outside to inspect the new garden suite.

Lily sat and tested some of the furniture, "They're grand chairs."

"They appear to be, but I am sending one of them back."

"What's wrong with it?"

"It was slightly damaged in transit. The paint work is scratched, so I cannot accept such a chair." Henrietta let her eyes follow a movement on the wall.

"Henrietta?"

"Yes."

"You've spaced out on me and gone to the moon."

"I am right here; I was watching the light and shadow playing together. Look at the designs they are making on the walls and footpath. Would you not love to paint that?"

"If one were an artist, yes. I don't think I see exactly what you do, Henrietta. What I do see is that there is a rim of something marking your wall."

"So there is, it will come off easily with water."

Lily got up, "I'll sort that out."

"Lily, sit down, I will do it myself or ask one of the girls to do it."

"It's a strange circle."

"A circle is just a circle." Henrietta knew it was different, or intended to be, but did not want Lily worrying about that. It had been made with a piece of charcoal like the first time, and the same curse wishing her soul to the devil had been scrawled inside the circumference. She had already washed most of it off and was not going to lose energy over a deranged act.

"Lily, I said sit down."

Lily sat and tapped her feet on the ground.

Henrietta thought that it would be calming to encourage the conversation towards the girls' school projects. Lily proceeded to explain that Genie had chosen to work on The Emergency, which was how the Second World War had been described in Ireland. Genie wanted to compare the daily life of an average individual in Ireland with one in France. Henrietta told Lily that she would be happy to help out by telling some of her war time stories. That Branly should have chosen The Great Famine did not surprise her.

"She wants to explore the fields overlooking the River Keale," Lily said. "According to local historians, there were hundreds of mud cabins with families living there before The Famine. They say that most of those had died or had emigrated by 1850."

"Those are incredible statistics and I understand why Branly would want to walk the fields."

Lily wasn't convinced that Branly would follow the research through to the end, "Her mother –"

"Her mother cannot do the job, that is all," Henrietta words came out more harshly than intended.

The hard tone of Henrietta's voice surprised Lily, "Are you angry about something, Henrietta?"

Henrietta did a double stitch and put down her needle, "You remember Golden Girl?"

"How could I forget – is it still a problem?"

Henrietta shook her head; "I have tried to put that loss behind me. I am angry because I discovered that, despite all, Jean and Thibault are scheming to invest in another horse."

"Sheamie too?"

"I am afraid, yes."

"What! Sheamie has been picking around in my affairs and getting so mad that I hadn't told him sooner about the threats and the blackmail – and look at himself."

"Shush, Lily, I do not want to turn you against Sheamie or any man."

"You're older than I am, Henrietta, you should know that men are all the same. They are all promises and sweet words, but still children in a playroom. You'd think they'd learn. And we women are worse for going along with it."

Henrietta laughed, glad to have got Lily annoyed enough to forget her troubles momentarily. "I am sorry to upset you and did not intend to start a war between the sexes. We go along with it, Lily, because we enjoy their sweet words and appreciate their compliments, even if we do not believe them. We need our dreams. Where would we be without them?"

"A lot better off maybe."

"We might be in despair. Oh, there she is," Henrietta turned her head.

"Sheila O'Connell?"

"Yes, it is her time to walk the dog. O'Connell is a fine Irish name."

"There are many fine Irish names," Lily said, "and that woman is very proud of hers. We used to just call the family the Connells, but they or she nailed that 'O' back on. The mother and father were called Connell. Cousin married cousin – that can't be healthy."

Henrietta retraced the circumference of the circle with her eye, "It is chilly – shall we go back inside?"

"Yes, but here are the girls now," Lily buckled her coat belt, "I'm going to leave them with you, Henrietta, while I go and search Sheamie out. I have a bone to pick with him, that's for sure."

"French or sewing?"

"It's history," Genie said, "but you can tell us in French and we can improve on both."

"It's a deal and I have something here that needs finishing."

"Oh, no," Branly grumbled, "more sewing."

"God," Genie groaned, "we're never done."

Henrietta reminded them of how the skill would serve in the future when and if they had their own places.

"If I had a husband and kids and if I lived in a place like here, I'd be the happiest girl in the world," said Branly. "Mikie and I could settle down for ever."

Henrietta followed the needle that Branly let hang from the thread. It swung like a pendulum, before finally finding its level. 'Oh Branly, Branly, what have you done? What has happened; do you even know?' Henrietta wondered.

"Is Mikie still your boyfriend?" she asked carefully.

"Sort of."

"Sort of?"

"We're too young to marry."

"You certainly are." Henrietta pointed to the cover on the table, "Girls, let's get down to work."

She then obliged and told them many stories and tales about the war, reinventing her own version and painting the picture she wanted the girls to remember.

When they had their fill of those stories, Henrietta broached what had become her new concern – their motorbike friends.

"Peter's a blow-in, no roots in Killdoe," Genie said.

"He has so," Branly defended, "he's been here a few years."

"That's true, I suppose," Genie agreed, "he's been living here long enough, longer than me."

"But your mother came from here and that makes you from here," Branly said. "You're more of the place than I am, Genie. My parents came to live here and I don't fit fully in the place, even if I have lived all my life here."

"Is that how you really feel?" Henrietta asked.

Branly did not reply, only hummed, and took the pair of scissors in her hand, pretending to examine it.

"One day, Branly will become a beautician and people will come from all around to her salon," Genie said.

"Why not," Henrietta supported Genie's efforts at cheering Branly up. "Would you like that, Branly?"

"Yeah, if Genie helped me, it would be better. I'm no good at doing things on my own."

"Sheamie is trying to get Mum to go into business with him," Genie said.

"What sort of business?" Henrietta feigned surprise.

"I don't know, she gets mad every time I mention it."

"It's nice to have people to get mad at," Branly picked idly at the material in Henrietta's hand.

Henrietta stroked a finger lightly across the young girl's forehead, "Branly, remember when you are lonely and feeling wretched, real human contact is warmer and stronger than anything else."

Branly lowered her eyes, "I'll remember, Henrietta. When I'm under my quilt, I feel the warmth of all the people who made it."

"Do not forget that ever."

29

Lily had been furious before at Sheamie, but never more than now. The hotel was abuzz with customers as it was lunchtime. She looked over her shoulder. If there was some detective shadowing her, he was well hidden. Sheamie was apparently elsewhere, much to her disappointment, because she wanted to stay furious.

Lily left the hotel and went to Abbey Street. She popped into the Turf Accountants and hopped up the stairs two steps at the time, before knocking hard on the office door.

"Come in," Sheamie answered in a preoccupied voice.

Lily didn't care if it was the good time or not to disturb him. Sheamie was always busy and there was never a right time. He'd told her before to disturb him whenever and wherever.

"Look here," she began, "oh –" Michael McGrath and Sheamie were both sitting in front of the computer, glued to the screen.

Sheamie looked up appearing hot and bothered, "Yes, Lily? Where's Genie?"

"At The Old Forge with Branly." He'd disarmed her again. It was clear Sheamie was in the middle of some serious matter and his first question had been for Genie's safety. He'd taken the wind right out of her sails immediately. She felt calmer and no longer in the mood to fight.

Lily changed tactics, "We'll talk about it another time. I can see you're busy. If you'll excuse me – oh and Mr. McGrath, in case I forget it, Maura is okay to go out to Malt Hill for you."

"That's great, Mrs. Casey."

"Lily will do, just call me Lily."

Later on that evening, Sheamie rang Lily to check if she were free to talk. As Genie and Branly were having supper at The Old Forge with Henrietta, it was the perfect opportunity to discuss. But Lily preferred not to invite Sheamie to her flat; it was too cosy and intimate and she might end up in his arms rather than giving him a good telling off. Instead she returned to his office at the Turf Accountants.

"So?" Lily stood at the doorway and folded her arms.

"So, you wanted to see me earlier today? Was there an emergency or did you miss me so much that you couldn't wait to get your hands on me?" Sheamie came towards her.

But Lily raised those very hands, "Don't try on that sweet talk with me. It won't work, at least not until you tell me everything about that racehorse."

"I was going to tell you, but Henrietta got there before me. As you know, we were unfortunate with Golden Girl, but discovered the worst of it in time, before any of our names were sullied," Sheamie swelled himself up.

"I see, you were so smart with the first horse that you have now decided, with your vast experience, to invest in another."

"Oh well –"

"Is it true?"

Sheamie drew up his shoulders, "It's possible that Golden Girl didn't have the pedigree, but we're sure about White Lightning and –"

"Oh boy," Lily looked at the ceiling, "I can't believe I'm even listening to this."

"Anyway, we might recover some money from Golden Girl and –"

"And you'd still like to have your kicks and lose more money on another horse. I don't blame Henrietta for being angry. What's wrong with the whole lot of you men is that you have too much money."

"I was naive with the first deal – that's all. I didn't approach it the same way I would have with my businesses. But I have learnt and don't repeat mistakes."

Lily didn't want to hear anymore and didn't want to risk staying longer in case she said something hurtful. The disappointment and disillusionment were too much for her. She had temporarily put Sheamie on a pedestal and now he was sliding off. How could she be with someone if she did not have faith in him? If Sheamie was unable to admit his foolish business deal she could not trust him enough. She didn't doubt his honesty and sincerity and he was clearly capable in the other areas of his business, but Lily knew herself and how hard it would be to hold her tongue and avoid being sarcastic or firing off insults from time to time. Everything was turning sour for her.

Sheamie saw the change in her and realised that Lily was emotionally withdrawing from him.

"Listen, Lily – where are you going now?"

"Nowhere, just out. I have things to do."

"Lily, come back, don't just go, letting the situation like this. I can be an ass about things, but I prefer you laughing at me, or angry at me, rather than looking like that."

"Like what?"

"Like, giving up on me."

"I'm not the person for –" Lily didn't know what to say, it was too difficult. Why take it so seriously? After all, if she was looking for character flaws, Lily Casey had many more of her own.

"Lily, this isn't the right moment," he trapped her face between his hands, "and I wanted to ask you in a special place –"

She tried to move away, "Don't, Sheamie, don't."

"Are you going to refuse me? Is it because of the horses? My timing's all wrong, I can't help it. I am like a kid in front of you because I love you."

"No," Lily shook her head, "it isn't just the horses." She didn't know anymore if it was or wasn't – "I can't, Sheamie."

"Why can't you give us a chance of happiness together, what's wrong with that – do you want to make me suffer all my life?"

"Sheamie, I am happy with you. We are happy together, at least we have been this past while. Why change that?" Lily thought dejectedly, I should have walked away. How did she get from a horse to this, from being angry to being guilty?

"Because that's the way I am. I want you by my side for the rest of our lives. For me that means really married. I don't want to be 'good old Sheamie' or even 'silly old Sheamie', but to be Sheamie your husband. I can't be straighter with you – why can't you just give me a yes?"

Lily couldn't give him a reason he'd understand and just stood there.

"It's because you don't love me – that's why, isn't it?"

"Sheamie, I do – I do love you and would do anything for you – you must know that. But you must know too that I've never been convinced by tying things up in neat packages, wedding rings and bonds."

He looked so wretched and she felt so mean.

"Don't look like that, Sheamie, please, don't be sorry. Marriage doesn't prove love – it just gets in the way. My feelings for you are special and they will be with me all my life. That is the measure of my love for you. But I need my space."

"I won't take over your space, Lily. Marriage doesn't have to do that, you could still go on doing all the things you do now."

"You don't see, do you? We'd be under the same roof day and night. Situations like this bring it out in me; I don't want to be that nasty old nag with you."

He looked even more downcast, "I guess my feelings for you are much more than what you have for me."

"It's not about feelings. Can't you see that being married and living together in the same house wouldn't give us more time together than we have now. It would only tear us apart, lead to resentment and regret."

"Just excuses, Lily. We have to take chances and risks, and loving someone means that."

There was no point, Lily thought and stared out at the bleak sky. She'd hurt him again, that's all she ever did to Sheamie, hurt him. Who was she to judge what he did with his life? If he threw money on ten horses and each one a failure, that was his business and shouldn't make him any less of a man to her. She wanted him to have his pleasure and get into whatever scheme grabbed him. Getting involved in new deals was part of what made him Sheamie. If she married him, Lily was afraid of not accepting that about Sheamie and they would only argue about it all the time.

The question was what did she want – what were her future dreams for herself? Genie would grow up very fast and live her own life. Lily didn't fear that and looked forward to it. Being alone didn't trouble her. Sure, it wasn't going to be a bed of roses growing older, and marriage wasn't going to make it any easier, she knew. She hated that feeling of being sucked into somebody else's world. It would be so much easier to be his friend than his wife, but Lily knew Sheamie didn't want it that way.

"Will you at least consider the other thing?" Sheamie was changing strategy, trying to salvage something.

"What? Oh, yes, the Charity Cleaning Business. It's a good idea, interesting and a generous way for you to give something back to the town. I will consider it, Sheamie." She might finally retire her mop and bucket to do that work. Working with young people and helping old people was something she valued. It opened up many opportunities. Why, they could even open a charity laundry service, or get into the business of cleaning people's homes, and not the home help variety, but helping out mothers with big families. The possibilities were endless.

He forced a smile, "I can see that offer appeals to you, that's something anyway."

30

Sheamie did a fifth tour of The Old Forge kitchen. His coffee untouched, now lukewarm, sat on the kitchen counter.

Henrietta put down her sewing and leaned back on the lazy armchair by the fireplace. She felt for him, "Do not be hard on Lily – give it time, Sheamie."

"Time! How long – another twenty five years?"

"Do not try to hasten things, let her get started with the Charity Cleaning Business and go on with your own life. You are a busy man, there is not a lot of space in there for someone else."

"I can make space."

"You can if you let go of some business commitments, but I do not think Lily would want that or that you would be happy doing it either. Perhaps in time – you are only fifty, in the prime of your life."

"Exactly. Why is she so dead set against marriage?"

"To understand that is to understand an important part of Lily. You have to see it from where she is standing, and when you do, you will be even closer and your friendship stronger."

"Friendship?"

"Yes – I think Lily knows and accepts you more than you do her."

"But you married, Henrietta."

"I did and so did you once before."

"Mine was – well – you're happy, you never regretted it."

"I married a very good man who is also a very good friend. But I would have been happy too without the ring. Times are different today and you cannot draw similarities between us. I had a different life back then."

Sheamie rested his hands on the window sill and looked out at the garden, "The worst is feeling Lily doesn't trust me and prefers to carry all that fear and worry alone."

"But you did not trust Lily either, Sheamie."

"I only held back to protect her."

"And to protect yourself," Henrietta qualified. "Protecting is what she is doing for you. Do not forget that Lily was threatened and has been blackmailed. Her daughter's life is at risk."

"How could I forget it?"

"Oh I know you have people watching and keeping guard over Genie and Lily. But you cannot guarantee their total safety. On top of that, she feels we are all at risk now because of her. Lily is tired of waiting, Sheamie, nobody has been arrested yet."

"I know, I know. They'll nail our man, they have to."

"Yes, but they haven't so far."

Sheamie put his face closer to the window, "I think it's going to snow, the sky has one more gift to bestow upon us before it lets spring in the door. Be careful with your plants and shrubs, Henrietta. Don't let the frost get at them."

"That is good advice, Sheamie, but I have no idea what is growing out there. Gardening is not my strong side, I do not have green fingers so I pay a gardener for that. And when the garden is finished, it will be something simple. However, I discovered a little jewel pushing up. Let me show you."

Henrietta led him outside and showed him the bells that Genie had given her, and that they had hung over the bird grave. Next to the grave was what she had thought an ordinary bush, but now was obviously a rose bush. A few buds had appeared on it. Jack Riordan thought it was a very old bush, but swore it had not flowered for the thirty years he had been coming to The Old Forge.

Sheamie looked at it, "Yes, it would be unusual if it flowered in March. I doubt if it was planted in Lily's Nana's time. Then again, they say Lily's great-grandfather, the blacksmith, was a real rebel and held Secret Society meetings here plotting the enemy's downfall. Maybe, the bush has some of the blacksmith's iron spirit in it."

"I do not know, but if you look closely, you can just see white and red colours coming through."

"This hard freeze we're having will probably kill it off. Don't build up your hopes."

"Do not be defeatist, Sheamie."

Lily came knocking at The Old Forge less than an hour after Sheamie had left. She immediately proceeded to pace up and down as Sheamie had done.

"See that," Lily pointed in exasperation as she looked out the kitchen window.

"What is one supposed to see?" Henrietta wondered how many more visitors were going to turn up at her door today. Lily, just like Sheamie, was so nervous that Henrietta expected her to go through the window pane any second.

"It's pounding hail."

"Thanks for the information, I can hear it on the roof."

"If you get that every day, will your family still be happy to spend time in Killdoe?"

"I would, I would, Lily."

"What do you mean, 'would'?"

"It is difficult to hear you above the noise."

"Din."

"Din?"

"Noise that's even noisier than noise."

"Okay, above the din then. Weather like this makes people spend more time together."

"For a few hours maybe, but they'd soon get fed up of each other," Lily wasn't inclined to see the bright side of things.

"What happened between you and Sheamie – you are not in a bad mood just because of the weather?"

"I think you know," Lily sighed.

"Yes, he wants marriage and you, no."

"Would you say I'm selfish?"

"No, but I do not want to get in the middle of this."

"You're already involved, you can't get out of it now."

"I can listen, but cannot do more."

"I'm sorry, Henrietta, that Killdoe has been so much trouble for you. You came for a quiet life and walked into our muddle."

"Do not be sorry, I am not. I have changed; Killdoe has changed me in ways I would never have imagined. And you, Lily – are you still the cleaning lady you used to be?"

"A cleaning lady is what I am and what I'll always be."

"Ah, but you are much more than that. You will continue to deny it, but you are a lady of character. Furthermore, you are also the right-hand woman of Sheamie – and his lover."

"Huh – you make me sound like a dangerous mistress or something."

"Mistresses do not get marriage offers. You are his girlfriend."

"Girlfriend sounds worse, so dated for people of our age."

"Forget the social codes, you do not have to put a label on your relationship."

"So you agree that it isn't necessary to get married."

"We are not talking about what I think here, Lily, but what you want."

"I think that Sheamie would be a wonderful step-father for Genie."

"The last thing Genie needs is for you to get married for her sake; it would be the worst reason. Do not punish yourself too much, take your time and make up your mind when you are ready to."

"I've had so many things in the balance these past few months and now he springs marriage on me."

"His offer is hardly unexpected."

"I can't think now – I keep imagining the blackmailer's eyes everywhere. Sheamie has undercover police guarding us, but it does not make me feel safer. I am suspicious of everyone, even Maura. The poor woman can't make me out, I'm jumpy and cranky."

"You have weathered it well, I do not know how you have lived with it."

"I have this constant fear inside me, it's horrible. There's no better friend than Sheamie, but I don't want to lay all my troubles at his door because then for sure I'd really feel guilty. It would compromise our relationship and I would agree to marry him out of a sort of duty."

Henrietta shifted on her chair, "Enough of that, you are making your life very complicated. Whatever you do or decide, it will be mixed up with

Sheamie. The two of you are destined for each other, as friends or lovers. Sometimes, it is better not to analyse."

Lily sat down, "What are you doing with my coat?"

"Looking at it. Where did you get it?"

"I bought it at Nathalie's on Main Street. You don't like it?"

"I did not say that. It is a little large on the shoulders for you. Let me do something with it."

"It's just to take me through the last of the winter."

"That is good, but let me just do something with the shoulders. Why not make us both a cup of tea and I might get it finished before you go home?"

"Oh, all right then, if you insist, because until you do it, I won't be able to wear it in front of you without the feeling that the shoulders don't fit properly."

Nightfall slowly descended and the fire in the grate warmed the hearth as they sat together like old friends talking as if they had known each other all their lives. Some people just go well together, Henrietta thought, tailor-made for each other.

Lily brought in the cups of tea on a tray, remarking that she had taken Genie to magic shows a few times and that Henrietta reminded her of a magician. She used needles and scissors like a wand, doing zigzags, dips and tucks, taking everything apart and putting it back together again like a magical illusion.

"It's fascinating watching you work, Henrietta, twisting, turning and manipulating my coat. There's a lot of ripping, cutting and sewing going on for an alteration.

"That is my trade."

They heard a dog barking from the lane. Henrietta recognised Sheila O'Connell's wolfhound. She wished she had real magic to make that woman disappear. She had not drawn Lily's attention to it, but Sheila O'Connell had walked past the cottage several times in the past two hours. The woman was more and more agitated. Henrietta could sense a shower of curses falling on The Old Forge each time Sheila crossed in front of the gate.

Lily tried on the coat one more time, "It's perfect, Henrietta. I can see the difference fully now, I don't feel or look half as bulky."

Henrietta studied it back and front, "It is much improved. Why look fifty when we can look forty?"

Lily stared out at the darkness, "Do you want to leave the curtains open – doesn't it bother you that people can look in?"

"It does, pull them." Henrietta went to the back window, "Did I tell you about the wild rose bush? It has buds and one of them is beginning to open, can you imagine in this climate. The colour appears to be a mix of red and white."

"From the same bud, I have to see that, a Tudor rose in the old cottage."

"What sort of rose is that?"

"It's not a real flower; just the colours red and white together make the English Tudor emblem. But you are probably mistaken about it being a rose, it must be some sort of shrub."

Henrietta smiled, "We will see."

****

Henrietta had never minded being alone and during her life had often sought out moments of solitariness and isolation. But since Lily left that night, the uneasiness had grown within her. Adding a block of wood to the fire and stoking it to make the flames waltz was not enough to cheer her.

Her solution was to return to her work table. But the purpose was slipping away. The thread wiggled out through the eye of the needle and her fingers were too feeble to catch it before it was gone. She took up her sewing bag. How had all that got knotted – Genie's handy work?

The needle swung from the end of the thread. There were all kinds of tricks, magnetism and energies drawn from the elements: earth, fire, air and water. People used the stars, witches, mediums and wizards of every variety. Her son would be a father soon. She had a premonition on her last trip back to Paris and had seen the baby coming, but had waited for them to tell her in their own time. They would be good parents and do their best for their baby, her grandchild. Life was so precious, we had to value every second.

The needle dangled, swinging one way and then the other. The last time

Branly had come to the cottage, Henrietta sensed from the energy of the needle that Branly was pregnant. In the past, people pretended they could tell the sex of the unborn baby using a needle and thread like a fortune teller's pendulum. Sophisticated sonograms did that now. But there was no technology on Earth that could foretell the personality of that baby. What sort of mind would it have? Maybe the needle had a better chance of divining that, of knowing if the child would become a kind person or not, a star or a pauper...

'My poor Branly,' Henrietta thought to herself, 'who will take care of you? You are forgotten and ignored. Is there nobody there for you?' Henrietta had so wanted to share her fears about Branly being pregnant with Lily this evening. But Lily had too many other worries on her mind that Henrietta decided to say nothing yet.

"Francoise," Henrietta spoke out loud, "how can people of this world help Branly? For neither I nor Lily, nor her trusted friend, Genie, can save her. We cannot do it by ourselves. You were alone, Francoise, but it does not have to be so for Branly."

Henrietta continued to watch the needle swinging back and forth wishing that her years gave greater insight and more clairvoyance.

Here she was sitting and sewing out the days in a place called Killdoe. Had it all been a mistake? The horse deal certainly was a mistake. But what was coming now? When her intuition and feelings did not come up with the answers, duty and practicalities spurred her on. There were so many loose ends of her own making and of others to tie up. She felt like a bird of Branly's design, caught in a storm and forced to make an emergency landing in a temporary resting place. They needed deliverance.

'Deliverance – Deliverance,' Henrietta thought. Being liberated by the Allies on D Day was so long ago. She remembered the first time some American soldiers stood in the yard of her Normandy farm. Through the eyes of an eight-year-old, they appeared smiling and friendly. The soldiers offered her some chocolate and spoke in English. The English words sounded welcoming compared to the harsh German language she had been used to hearing. It opened up an outside world to her that gave her a desire to see beyond her Normandy village. She remembered also the white teeth smiling out from faces so dark. The child, Henrietta, had not known skin could be so dark except in pictures she had seen in books. A black American soldier had taken a cup of creamy, frothy milk offered by her mother from the milking bucket. He was one of their saviours. The smell of burning and death was around them, and there was destruction everywhere, but they had been saved.

There had been great joy, but that joy had turned to pain. When the smiling was over, there was retribution and bitterness. Hearts had been slow to forgive and a price had to be paid. Once more Henrietta heard the voices accusing her sister, Francoise, of betrayal. But when she pushed those accusing voices from her childhood out of her mind with more ease than a few months earlier, they were replaced by the ghostly voices of The Old Forge. As Henrietta slipped into a trance, The Old Forge's voices grew louder and louder…

Jenny McCarthy, what have you done!' a woman's hard voice accuses. 'Shame, shame on you – trollop, sleeping with an English soldier and bringing disgrace to the house. '

'Mother, you do not understand – don't condemn me without hearing me – '

'You are a traitor. We spilt our blood fighting for freedom and you turn your coat to sleep with the enemy,' the cold words of a man echo.

'I am no traitor. Please hear me out – I beg you, father. He is not the enemy. He has laid down his arms, he will fight no more.'

'You have dishonoured God and your family. You carry his baby, his English blood in you. BE GONE!' her mother orders.

'I beg you!'

'GO TRAITOR,' both mother and father command…

The voices faded and Henrietta rose from her chair and went for her coat; fresh air would clear her mind.

But the room immediately seemed to spin round and Henrietta could no longer resist as a veil enveloped the cottage…

Jenny's ghost is wearing a long skirt, a shawl, low booties, and carrying a small bag. Her head is bowed.

There is the sound of Jenny's sobs and of a door opening.

'Leave here Jenny McCarthy. The forge is no longer your place and McCarthy is no longer your name,' the voice of the father is pitiless.

'Don't ever come back, striopach. You are nothing but a whore,' the voice of the mother shouts. 'You've betrayed and dishonoured us. You will bear that child alone.

Don't ever darken our door, your name is blackened forever.'

A door bangs and the ghost of Jenny walks away – alone. A swirling fog swallows her as her ghostly image goes out the cottage gate.

Daniel is standing near the gate, waiting. 'I will give you a home, Jenny,' he speaks gently.

'You mock me,' Jenny says. 'You have a large farm on Malt Hill and can have your choice of wife. I am unworthy and stained.'

'Not in my eyes.'

'But I do not love you, Daniel.'

'I will wait for you to love me. It will come. Until then, I have love enough for both of us.'

'Do you know I'm with child and who the father is?'

'I know Jenny. Your soldier was brave. Your father is brave too, but he isn't able to understand. Your family reject you now, but time will be a friend to us. Your child will be strong and good. Your child will be my child. I have love enough for all of us.'

'But if that cannot be, if I cannot love you?'

Daniel holds out a rose slipping, 'Jenny, do you remember the wild rose bush I gave you and that you planted in the garden?'

'Yes.'

'I stole this slipping from it. It is not mine to keep, for it is wild. I will plant it in Malt Hill Forest to remind you that I will never bind you. You will always be free...'

Henrietta watched the ghostly images fade away. What had Lily or Genie got to do with Daniel and Jenny? Surely the passage of time was meant to dilute pain, clear the past away and sprinkle it with change.

Her time in Killdoe helped her understand so much and to forgive so much more about her own childhood and past. But why, Henrietta asked herself once again, was the ghost of Jenny McCarthy revealing herself to her and what was she supposed to understand and do with this knowledge?

31

The end of March teased their senses with its temperamental weather; there were days when the cold temperatures and freezing rain reminded Lily that they still had not escaped the claws of winter; on other days the lighter, warmer breeze was an encouraging sign that spring was on the way. But for everybody, the extra daylight was condusive to long walks in the evening.

Lily, Henrietta and the girls decided to explore some of the fields that local historians said had been heavily populated before the Irish Famine. Lily also thought that it might encourage Branly in her school project. She got permission to enter the property of John Crowley, one of the farmers whose land would have been concerned.

Lily walked slowly for Henrietta and let the girls lead the way through the gentle sloping fields that overlooked the River Keale. Today, the early grass and slate-coloured water of the river seemed far away from those times in the 1840s when the area would have been covered with mud cabins filled with families of fifteen or more children, many of whom perished from starvation. It was heartbreaking to think that others had gone off to workhouses or done public works, like breaking stones to make roads, earning barely enough for food. It was chilling to realise that millions had emigrated and many had died on those coffin ships to America.

They caught up with the girls in time to hear Branly launch into one of her usual eulogies, advising them to pray for all who had died of hunger. She informed them that not only English landlords but middlemen caused the Famine, and not every middleman was Protestant, some were Catholic.

Genie explained to Henrietta that middlemen had emerged due to absentee landlords and the subletting of the land again and again. The potato was the best food to feed many mouths from tiny land plots. But when the potato crop failed due to blight, those at the bottom of the system suffered the most.

Branly thought that everyone who survived during that time was responsible for the Famine, and whomever's ancestors were alive today must in one way or another have taken advantage of those who died. Some even changed religion to survive as it was one of the conditions set by the Protestant churches that gave charity. She pulled some grass and held it up, "The sins of the past have to be paid for by those of us alive today."

Lily detected a wild and glazy expression in Branly's eyes.

Henrietta waved a hand in front of her, "Branly, Branly – are you alright?"

Branly came to and spoke as if nothing had happened, "Can you imagine all the people wandering here, hungry, eating the grass and dying from want of food, all because of greedy landlords and middlemen?"

Lily tried to find a way of settling the discussion and told them that everyone must have had relatives who were land owners at one time or another. Some had been decent and others not so good. Nobody could totally account for what our ancestors had done in the past, but she knew her parents and grandparents and was sure they had done the best they could. Things were never black and white, she explained. The girls should keep their minds wide open and avoid overzealous judgements.

Branly wasn't satisfied with Lily's explanation and wanted to know where all the pain, suffering and feelings from the past went.

Lily let Henrietta handle that metaphysical question.

Henrietta obliged, explaining that painful energies filtered through the generations and got passed on via stories, writing, music and song. Feelings and energies were captured in the paintings, architecture, the ways of people, and the habits and customs we could see today.

"But we still can't know what really happened," Genie said, "it's frustrating."

Henrietta smiled at her, "There is a truth somewhere, or at least we think there is. However, we can never have the full version of anything and we have to accept that. We can accumulate different versions, try to see things from as many angles as possible and build the layers. But when we put everything together, it is still never the whole truth."

"Never!" Genie cried in disbelief.

"Never through mortal senses," Henrietta emphasised. "See how your memory can mislead you. What you see, hear and feel starts to change the moment you try to remember it. That is why it is good to have competing versions of everything. Beware of anyone who gives you one definitive version."

Lily felt that Henrietta had said it well, but wasn't sure that the girls understood what she had wanted them to understand. Experience would teach them.

"Do you know what," Branly said, "I think that finding out the truth is a bit like my quilt, with its bits and scraps, different shapes and colours. We're only stitching and piecing it together – patching the past so that we can put it around us to keep warm and comfy. That way, we can imagine, dream and be who we want to be."

"Exactly," Henrietta said, "patching time and making it rhyme."

"That's a good way of putting it," Lily agreed.

Genie kicked her football, "Nana went out with a Black and Tan English soldier – "

Nobody spoke for several seconds.

Lily felt someone had thrown a boulder at her. "Who told you that?" she tried to keep her voice steady.

Genie refused to look at her.

"Who, Genie, who told you that? Nana saved the life of a dying man."

Genie stamped the ground defiantly, "Nana went out with him and had his baby."

Lily gripped her daughter's arm. "Where are you getting that from?"

Genie jerked her arm away.

"Sheila O'Connell," Branly volunteered.

"What right has she –" Lily tried to suppress her fury, "just what right has Sheila O'Connell to decide the history of our family?"

Henrietta laid a restraining hand on her shoulder.

"Sheila O'Connell's right, isn't she, Mum – Nana wasn't a hero? How could she have gone with the enemy?

"What else did Sheila O'Connell tell you?" Lily had to know.

"That my family is bad," Branly said.

"Branly," Henrietta tried and failed to take her hand.

"That Nana married Granda Casey through trickery," Genie said, "by making him believe she was carrying his baby."

"That's not true, Genie. He married her out of love."

"Sheila O'Connell said Nana was a traitor and that Daniel Casey was not my great-grandfather at all. She said all the Caseys were land grabbers."

"That's enough, Genie, you've said enough," Lily warned.

But Genie didn't seem able to stop herself, "Sheila said that her own grandfather was killed by Nana's Black and Tan lover. She said that he shot him in cold blood and that Nana informed on an ambush that had been planned against the Black and Tans. Nana did it to save her lover's life."

Lily took her daughter by the shoulders and shook her, "That's enough, Genie, enough of lies and slander."

"Let me go, Mum, let me go, you're hurting me."

Lily dropped her arms, distraught.

Genie ran through the field. Branly followed, calling after her.

Henrietta looked to the sky for inspiration, "Lily, are you okay?"

"Oh, Henrietta, I made a mess of that. There we were talking about truth and the past, and there was I preaching about honour, and that's what Genie was thinking."

"And what do you really think?"

"I can only draw from what I heard and put together myself. Nana saved the life of the dying soldier. Sometime after, they fell in love. Such was the soldier's gratitude for her act that he switched sides. He deserted the English army, but his life was put in danger because of that. His only choice was to go into hiding. If not he would have ended up being killed by his own comrades or by the Irish rebels. Nana knew they could never be together and couldn't risk their lives or those close to them. I believe that Nana urged him to return to England and to forget her and that she never told him she was with child."

"So they parted?"

"Yes, they agreed never to meet again and said their goodbyes in Malt Hill Forest. I have seen the ghosts of that memory."

"You must tell Genie your story," Henrietta advised. "I believe it and also that your grandfather knew Jenny was carrying another man's child before he married her. His love was such that he was prepared to love her and the baby."

"Is that true, do you really believe that?"

"I have seen and felt the past also, Lily. The Old Forge reveals the past to me in ghosts and images too, it has from the beginning."

Henrietta shared her ghostly visions with Lily and watched the burden of the past lift from Lily's eyes and shoulders.

"I've never doubted that, but hearing someone else say it helps me a lot," said Lily. "I don't believe that the soldier killed Sheila O'Connell's grandfather either. It might have been a Black and Tan, but it wasn't Nana's soldier."

"That soldier was your father's father, and so your grandfather."

"Yes, my God, when you put it like that, it's strange."

"Strange, but true. And you told me that your grandparents had no other child?"

"No – my father was their first and the only child that survived."

"I believe the visions tell us that your grandparents were honourable people."

"Thank you, Henrietta, thank you for sharing what you saw and not thinking me crazy to believe in ghosts and visions."

Henrietta hugged her, "If you are crazy, then I must be crazy too."

Lily returned to the flat. Genie had gone to her room and was talking on the phone. From the conversation it was clear she was making some arrangements with Branly. Lily waited for the call to end and then called out to her daughter.

There was silence.

Lily spoke, irrespective. She talked of everything, of how Nana had saved the soldier, of how he'd risked his life out of love for her, how Nana had let him go out of love. She spoke of Granda and of how his love had been unconditional. There was no shame. The shame was for a community so turned in on itself that it hadn't been prepared to understand or to accept the truth. She explained that Nana couldn't have informed on the ambush to save the English soldier since he had already deserted the army by then and couldn't have been with the other soldiers. Why would she risk the life of her own father?

Lily stood at her daughter's bedroom door. Genie was holding the old photograph of Nana and Granda.

"As sure as God is my witness, that is the truth as I know it, Genie. It was never clear in my mind until now. I never sought to deceive you about it. You have helped me to put the pieces in place."

Genie kissed the photo and put it back in the box.

'Miaow, miaow,' Genie picked up the cat, but put her down again. "Messy's getting very heavy and awkward to carry."

"Messy's expecting kittens."

"Kittens! Will we keep them?"

"For a short while, but then we'll find good homes for them."

Lily brushed back her daughter's hair, "Do you have any more questions? I promise you I'll answer them as best I can."

"Did the farm on Malt Hill belong to the O'Connells at one time?"

Lily felt her blood pressure rise, Sheila – bloody – O'Connell. "I was told that the farm came to our ancestors before the Famine and that the Caseys were highly respected. I'm not saying that's all of it, but there are archives and records and maybe you and I can research it. Will that do you, Genie?"

"Yes." Genie stroked Messy, "It's amazing to imagine kittens inside.

"Life is full of miracles."

32

Henrietta's head fell on the pillow and she drifted into a dreamlike state…

…She floated down Main Street, her feet barely touching the ground. A voice was crying, 'Henrietta – Henrietta, help, help us, please.' It was Branly's cry. 'Henrietta – Henrietta,' her cries grew louder and louder. There was another voice singing, then weeping. She recognised Francoise's voice – 'Henrietta, Henrietta, she is calling you. Go to her.'

Henrietta found herself in front of The Treasure Chest. She hammered at the door and shouted Branly's name.

A strong wind blew up sweeping her away to the cemetery gates on River Road. Black smoke billowed and spread over the grounds. Branly was among the graves and tombs, dragging her quilt. The bright stars Henrietta had sewn on it sparkled through the smoke.

Henrietta attempted to call out again, but had no words. She tried to bang the bars of the iron gate but her hands just floated through soundlessly. Only the stars on the quilt and the occasional star in the sky glistened. Suddenly a grotesque giant black bird swooped into the cemetery. Branly was on her knees waiting for it.

The giant bird perched and its head transformed into Sheila O'Connell. A wolfhound leapt from the abbey ruins and crouched beside the bird.

The hideous bird then tried to pull the quilt from Branly, 'Burn it, burn it.'

'No, I must keep my quilt here,' Branly's timid voice pleaded. 'If I am to make the ultimate sacrifice, I want all the people I love near me.'

The giant bird screeched, 'Death to that devil of a foreigner in the cottage who made the quilt. Throw the quilt away, there is no good in it.'

The wolfhound snarled and tore the quilt from Branly's hands, then brought it to the giant bird who flung it far.

Henrietta tried desperately to call out again and to go through the gates, but still no words came and her body felt paralysed.

A tall man stood where the quilt had landed and the wolfhound bounded around him.

The giant bird pointed its black wing, 'There is a man of God. Bring back the holy books to him and bring Casey. He will help you make the final sacrifice.'

'No, no,' Branly wailed.

The bird-like creature roared and hooked its talons around her.

Suddenly Francoise's image appeared, passed through the bars of the gate and floated across the cemetery towards the bird creature and Branly.

'Francoise – why have you come?' Henrietta asked as she put her hand towards the gate.

Her hand struck something –

Henrietta woke with a start. She was in her own bed in The Old Forge and had just struck her hand off the bedside table. She glanced at her phone, it was three o'clock in the morning. Had it all really just been a dream? There was a strange sensation in her body. Henrietta tried to feel her legs, but they had gone dead. Pins and needles broke out all over her and wave after wave of breathlessness came. Breathing brought acute pain. 'I have to move, the best thing is to move.' She tried to put her feet on the ground, but swayed and wobbled and only managed to sit on the edge of the bed. There was tightness in her chest and her breath came in gasps. 'I must not panic,' Henrietta lay down on top of the blankets, resting her head on the pillow, trying to relax her body.

After several minutes, the panic had subsided and she attempted once more to stand up, putting one foot tentatively on the floor and then the second. Holding on to the bedside table and the headrest, Henrietta managed this time to stand upright. Feeling better, she went to the kitchen and boiled water for herbal tea.

Henrietta thought about everything that she had dreamt, going to The Treasure Chest and the cemetery. Her own anxieties had led to that nightmare. And yet it had felt so real, almost like a premonition.

Henrietta was too tired and drained by her disturbed night and nightmare to sew. Instead she spent the day doing light dusting and cleaning around the cottage. At five o'clock in the afternoon she heard a timid knock and found Branly in her leather jacket and alone. Henrietta was relieved to see her there. After the terrible nightmare, she had been battling with a haunting feeling about the girl's safety all day.

Branly went on a walking tour all over cottage, looking at this, examining that, and asking a host of questions.

So far away and distracted and strange, thought Henrietta. I have about five percent of her attention. The girl finally alighted on a stool at the work table.

"What's on your mind, Branly?"

Branly swung her legs and hummed. "I love my quilt and I love this cottage. Everything is right here."

Her face was very pale and her skin looked sore and painful from acne. Henrietta took a lotion and some cotton wool from the bathroom cabinet and dabbed her face.

"That feels much better." Branly looked in the mirror, "My skin depresses me."

"It will go away as you get older."

"Genie doesn't have that problem. She complains about being too tall, like a bean pole. I think Genie is beautiful, don't you?"

"You are both beautiful. You have a lovely heart-shaped face."

"Do I really?"

"You do and just take a look at those honey eyes and cute little nose."

Branly grinned and tried to catch her face at different angles between the mirrors. "I'm not a good person, Henrietta, I do bad things and bring bad on people. Genie and her mum and you would be better off away from me. You are too good to me and I don't deserve it. Mikie is afraid of me. He says I'm crazy."

"I do not mind that you talk that way, Branly, but you are not going to convince me of your badness. If the feelings behind your words are the same, then you must try to change them. If Lily and Genie are there for you and if I want to see you, it is because we like you for who you are. You can talk about all the bad that is in you, but it does not put me off, because I know it is not true. Love is deeper than that."

Branly stared at Henrietta and then ran into her arms, "If I could stay here forever."

33

Lily was reluctant to lay more of her troubles on Sheamie and tried to hide her upset when she related to him the events that took place during her walk in the fields with Henrietta and the girls. But Lily could see from the compassion in his eyes that Sheamie immediately understood how deeply the stories about her grandparents affected her. He sat on the sofa of her flat, listening intently as she gave him all the details.

When Lily finished speaking, Sheamie stood up and held open his arms, "Lily come here, you've had a shock and need time to put it all together."

"Oh, I'm alright, Sheamie, I'll get over it; we have more important things to worry about than stories of my grandparents."

"Come here, Lily," Sheamie opened his arms wider.

She walked into them and he hugged her tightly. Lily let a tear fall, "How poor Nana must have suffered, carrying a child out of wedlock in those times. They must have given her the road. She'd have been abandoned and disgraced. Granda was a great man."

"Did she make it up with her own family after?"

"She must have, because there was never a word of it when I was growing up. There must have been reconciliation later. It was money from Malt Hill that helped raise and educate her brothers and sisters and the rest of the McCarthys. The blacksmith was poor and couldn't have done it. Still, relations with that side of the family were distant. I never knew my great-grandparents from Nana's side. The cottage was eventually sold off and that was the end of it."

"Don't cry, Lily, it all worked out for the best in the end. Lily, darling, don't cry."

"But, Sheamie – how is it that it took Genie's stubbornness to make me see? It kills me that she heard it from Sheila O'Connell first."

"We all have information inside us that we don't know we have. You said yourself that you'd no curiosity about the past. You're a woman of the present and you like to take the here and now. Genie's different and has her own character."

"Genie needs to know about the past. That's because she didn't know her father and –"

"Don't blame yourself, I'm proud of you."

"Proud of me, after the shambles I made of everything?"

"You've made a shambles of nothing and only tried to do the right thing. Genie is a wonderful girl and you are a wonderful mother."

"You're too kind, Sheamie."

"I'm not kind. I love you, Lily Casey, always have and always will," he brought her hand to his lips.

"Even if I won't marry you?"

"Even if you won't marry me."

"Oh, Sheamie, you know that I love you, I truly do."

"Lily, you've never said it like that before – do you really mean it?"

"Yes."

He enveloped her tightly in his arms. Lily forgot everything; that it was in the middle of a Saturday afternoon, that she was in her own little living room and that Messy had made a messy escape from the sofa. All rational thoughts left her mind. She'd never let her heart go so wild with anyone else. With Sheamie it was effortless to let go of the tension, anxiety and worries. It was just sensation and his voice murmuring her name. Her thoughts were of nothing else, only him.

"I love you, Sheamie."

"Lily, my only love."

Their love-making was hungry and passionate until finally release came and they crumbled together helplessly.

Lily heard nothing but his beating heart – no, that was hers – it was both. And what was the other noise – a dripping tap? She should get up and shut it properly, but was incapable of taking any reasonable action right then.

"Are you – are you alright?" He was bent over her.

Lily lay in a rumpled heap, half on and half off the sofa. She must look ridiculous, he looked ridiculous, they were both ridiculous.

Sheamie kissed her on the cheek, "I was too –"

"Say nothing, Sheamie, you were perfect." She put her hand in his, locking their fingers together, "We're like a couple of lovers called Lily and Sheamie. I hope we stay that way forever."

'Miaow, miaow,' Messy came back for her dose of attention.

Sheamie shifted slightly to let Lily sit up.

Lily read his watch and jumped up, "Jesus, is that the time – I'm late! I promised to call at The Old Forge and you're supposed to pick the girls up from dancing."

****

"I got delayed, Henrietta."

Henrietta cast an eye over her, "I'm glad you did and that Sheamie had a part in it. Come outside and see my Tudor rose."

"Put on your coat, Henrietta, it's bitter outside."

"Oui, Madame. It must be my age, I do not feel it, my thermometer is out of order," Henrietta draped a Cashmere shawl over her shoulders.

"It's unbelievable," Lily marvelled, "we've had frost, snow, hail and the worst month of March ever, and those buds are beginning to show signs of flowering."

"They're little miracles. I call them my angels. Your grandmother, Jenny, planted that bush and her spirit comes back to cherish and protect it. My vision showed me that your grandfather, Daniel, gave the bush as a gift to Jenny. Jenny did not know that Daniel would be the man she would love then, but he never doubted his love for her. Later, he took a slipping from here and planted it in the forest."

"It's a beautiful gift."

"It is more than that."

"And you, Henrietta, how do you remember your family? Does the thought of those who have passed on comfort you?"

"There was a time when it was too painful to remember. It might be hard to believe that I would have to reach the age of eighty before learning to live with the past."

"Come inside, Henrietta, you're freezing. I'll make some tea."

Lily listened as Henrietta recounted the horrors of her childhood. It was impossible to stop the tears on hearing about the horrific attack on her sister and the accusations against her. Henrietta's stammer increased while explaining how Francoise had taken her own life.

"It must have broken your heart," Lily took a handkerchief to dry her eyes.

Henrietta nodded, "They refused to bury her in the Catholic cemetery. But I returned for the first time this year and I requested for her body to be laid next to our mother's."

"After all these years?"

"I had shut the pain out. I did not believe anymore in God or life hereafter. Since coming to Killdoe, I have felt Francoise's spirit here beside me, guiding me and taking the burden of the past from my shoulders. She has never been far away, but I was not open to receiving her spirit. I had to forgive Henrietta, the child. My burden of guilt kept a wall between us. But finally the veil started coming down."

"She's your angel then?"

"Yes."

****

Lily immersed herself in her cleaning work at the Business Park; it was the only way to stop mulling over everything she'd learnt about her grandparents in the past week, or worrying about Genie and the blackmailer. But from the moment Maura arrived this morning, Lily could see that she was bursting to tell her something.

"What is it, Maura?"

"I don't know if I can tell you."

"You can and you have to. Is it money again?"

"It's the cursed money lender," Maura put her finger to her lips. "I heard that his car was outside Lena Hartigan's house the other evening and that he's doing several other houses there."

"I know, Maura, but I think the Gardaí are watching all that."

"It's worse than that. I also heard that more of the youngsters are doing drugs up there in the estate and that he might be in that business too. I know that's not news to anyone, but you see, Lily, this time I heard it from someone I trust and the worst of –"

"Maura," Lily put the brakes on her trolley, "this is too serious – we're going to have to report it. We can't let that go on any longer."

"But, Lily –"

"We have to, Maura; we can do it without mentioning your troubles –"

"But Lily –"

"Maura –"

"You don't understand, Lily – somebody saw Branly go up to his car."

"When was that?"

"Yesterday evening."

"Are you sure?"

"As sure as I can be. Branly Hartigan is in to all sorts of bad things with the bikers – Genie might be going down the same road."

Lily spotted the security man in the lodge, "Maura, keep your voice down."

"They made him permanent," Maura said.

"Who?"

"That security fellow. I don't like him at all, not one bit. I'm happier when Matt is on duty, but that fellow –"

"Forget about him and tell me exactly what you heard."

"I can't say for certain, Lily, but was told by someone reliable. If they told me, it was because they knew I'd pass it on. Branly was seen out of her mind in Malt Hill Forest too and Genie was with her."

"What do you mean!" Lily didn't know if she wanted to hear more.

"Branly was seen wandering half crazy around the forest, not a coat or a jacket on her, singing to the birds. Genie was trying to bring her home. It's sad, that's what drugs do to you."

Lily took off her overalls, "Maura, I have to go, can you –"

"Say no more, dearie, I'll finish up here. You go off now. Some things are more important than cleaning."

Lily thought about the best approach to take as things had gotten too serious and there should be no more secrets between them.

People were chatting inside the flat. Lily had totally forgotten that Genie had invited Henrietta for afternoon tea. Forgetting about it was indicative of where her mind was these days.

From Henrietta's speculative look as Lily walked in, it was evident that she wasn't doing a good job of hiding her anxiety. It might be wise to wait, but Lily was beyond being careful.

"Hello all," she threw her bag on the sofa. Then it came straight out, "Genie, has Branly been getting drugs from someone?"

"I know nothing, Mum," Genie said shortly.

Lily was determined to get to the bottom of things. "If Branly is in trouble, you have to let us know. It might seem like telling tales on your friend, but it will be for her own good."

"Lily –" Henrietta tried to speak.

Lily turned to the kitchen sink but read the message on Henrietta's face warning her not to force Genie to tell tales on her friend. Henrietta was right, if Genie had to tell secrets, things would never be the same with Branly again. It wouldn't be wise to make Genie talk against her will or to denounce her friend. Forcing wasn't the solution and would end up making Genie angry and herself angrier into the bargain.

Lily filled the kettle, "I need tea, lots and lots of it – Henrietta?"

"I will join you for another cup. Genie," Henrietta spoke softly, "what about you?"

"No, thanks," Genie went off to her room.

They drank tea in silence, knowing that anything discussed in the kitchen would reach the bedroom.

Suddenly, Genie's exclamations and Messy's miaows got their attention.

"Genie," Lily called, "what's going on?"

"Something's the matter with Messy. Come quick."

Lily rushed in. Genie was on her knees in front of the wardrobe. "Oh, look at that! Messy's having her kittens, and right there in your wardrobe. Isn't that a fine place to pick?"

"What a clever cat," Henrietta said. "How many kittens are there?"

Genie counted, "Three so far. It's amazing, I've never seen anything like that."

"Messy won't like us to move her, but it's best for all of them if I do. I'll get that big old basket that I was going to throw out," Lily said.

She brought in the wicker basket and lined it with torn pieces of a bed sheet that had been cut up for dusters. "When Messy has had the last one, we'll put the entire family in here."

There were five kittens in all. Genie put a complaining Messy carefully in the basket, then took and placed each kitten with their mother as if handling porcelain.

"That is a big family," Henrietta stroked Messy cautiously.

"Luckily," Lily said, "I've already been looking for homes. I'll have to clean out the bottom of your wardrobe, Genie."

"No," Genie stepped in front of her.

"No?" Lily queried.

"I mean – I'll do it myself, Mum."

"I will remove your new family to the kitchen, Lily." Henrietta lifted the basket, "It will give you more space."

Lily put on some gloves and began to extract the soiled pullover from the wardrobe.

"No, Mum," Genie tugged at her mother.

Lily had already lifted the bag Messy had been lying on. There before her eyes were two large books, each with a white hard cover and the title, *AN BÍOBLA NAOFA*', printed in gold. "Genie," Lily had difficulty to speak – "what – what are those?"

Genie just stared.

"Answer me, you're not running away from this."

Henrietta came back, "Are you – oh – Bibles – the holy book."

Lily felt like she'd been struck by lightning. Everything flashed before her at the same time: the man with the bag in Abbey Lane, Maura's words and Sheila O'Connell's accusations. "Where did you get them?"

Genie shook her head.

Lily took one and opened it, "Did you buy these books or did someone give them to you – or did you steal them?"

Genie continued to shake her head in bewilderment.

Lily put one of the Bibles on the bed and turned the pages. Hadn't that woman said something about the books being precious because there were relics inside?

Genie found her voice, "What are you looking for?"

"You won't tell me, so I have to find out for myself." Lily began tearing the lining from the cover. "Oh," some sachets filled with white powder spilled out – she dropped it as if burnt.

"Drugs," Henrietta said.

"I trusted you, Genie – is this what you've done with my trust?" Lily demanded.

Genie flapped her hands, "I never imagined that there was something hidden inside – I never did, Mum, you have to believe me."

"This is serious," Henrietta said.

"Yes." Lily reached for her phone, "We'll call the Gardaí. They'll question you Genie, I hope you have good answers."

"No, Mum – no. Don't call anyone, they aren't mine. I didn't take them – didn't know anything about what was inside the covers."

"Did you and Branly steal them from Sheila O'Connell?"

Genie kicked the leg of the bed.

"None of that behaviour – you must have taken them, admit it."

"No, I didn't take them."

"You are lying. They were in your wardrobe, they didn't walk there."

Genie wiped some tears, but remained mute and stubborn.

Lily searched her daughter's immobile face, "Very well, you leave me with no choice. Where is Branly?"

"I don't know, she hasn't answered her phone all day."

Henrietta stood at the doorway, looking wretched for both of them.

Genie picked up a sachet, "Is it cocaine?"

"What do you think?" Lily asked. "Are you going to own up to bringing those books in here or not? Ring Branly again."

Something in Genie snapped. She pushed the Bibles off the bed and kicked a chair several times until it tumbled over onto the floor; "Fuck – fuck – fuck – nobody ever believes me – I'm fuckin' fed up of being blamed –"

"You won't speak like that under my roof!"

"I'm fuckin' sick of everything."

Lily slapped her. It wasn't hard, but it shocked Genie into silence.

Genie put her hand to her cheek.

Lily was shaking. This was too much, Genie had gone too far, but slapping a teenager wasn't the solution. Anger and sorrow struggled inside her. She had never ever hit her daughter.

Genie turned her back and stood at the window.

Lily picked up the Bibles, "You stay in your room and only come out of it when you're ready to give us the truth. You must explain; this is very serious."

Lily went back to the kitchen and took her mobile phone out of her bag. Henrietta followed her, at a loss to intervene. That was worse than anything, Lily thought, I humiliated Genie in front of Henrietta. My daughter will never forgive me for that.

"Are you calling the Gardaí?" Henrietta asked.

"No," Lily whispered, "we need Genie's and Branly's side of the story first. I'm calling Sheamie. He'll know what to do."

Sheamie was in the middle of a business meeting in Galway. He suggested informing Mr. Curran and McGrath and getting advice on the matter. The advice came twenty minutes later: they were not to call the Gardaí directly. If they wanted to catch the drug dealer, they should wait. They would find out where Sheila O'Connell had originally gotten those Bibles, but they would have to avoid alerting whoever was behind it all. They had to find a way of snaring the drug dealer. The Bibles should be put in a bag and passed on to McGrath. It would be better if Henrietta delivered them to him that evening. McGrath would pick them up from her cottage and he would liaise with Curran and the Gardaí. Apart from that, they were to carry on as usual.

"That's a fine answer," Lily threw her phone on the sofa. "It's months that we have been carrying on as usual. Look where it's gotten us."

Henrietta had tried Branly's number several times without success. Finally, she took the bag with the Bibles, "We will do as we are told. I will pass these on. Maybe Branly will turn up at the cottage."

Lily felt miserable, and recalling the shock on Genie's face when she slapped her made her more remorseful. She looked from her window at the dark sky. Would the sun ever come? Lights came on inside The Treasure Chest shop. Could Sheila O'Connell be a drug dealer? Was that possible? But what about that cousin of hers? Henrietta told her that she'd asked the detective to check that angle out. McGrath also told them that when he was staying above The Treasure Chest, he suspected that someone had been rummaging in his affairs and that had been his reason for moving out. In light of the new evidence, it all made sense. Sheila or her cousin had many opportunities to uncover information.

There was that Sheila again and she was definitely out of sorts. One minute, the 'Closed' sign was up, and the next, the 'On a break' sign had replaced it. Didn't Sheila O'Connell have some good works to do, something to keep her busy? Apparently not, for now she was walking out with that big hound. Lily watched them and something caught her attention. What did that walk remind her of? It stirred in her memory but wouldn't come to her. It was so frustrating not to be able to put her finger on it.

Sheamie rang to tell her that he would be leaving Galway within the hour. She urged him to wait until morning as the roads were frosty and icy and the last thing they wanted was him taking risks. But he promised to be careful.

Lily made supper and cooked Genie's favourite dish, Spaghetti Bolognese.

"Genie," she called, "it's alright. Come down for your dinner."

There was no answer. Lily pushed the door. Genie was stretched on the bed, face turned into the pillow. She laid the tray on the chair beside her.

When Lily returned an hour later, nothing had been touched and Genie was asleep. She drew a blanket over her. It would be better in the morning for all of them.

Messy got a double share of affection instead.

34

Henrietta walked around her garden following pathways outlined by newly installed stainless steel solar-powered lanterns. It must be almost midnight, but sleep would not come. It had been a long winter and it was not over yet. It would be nice to come back in late spring or early summer to see how the garden might look. How lovely it would be to bathe in the colours and fragrances.

She thought about their discovery of the drugs hidden in the Bibles in Genie's wardrobe earlier this evening and tried to convince herself that the Gardaí had all the evidence they needed and would very soon catch the criminal. It did not take a lot of detective skills to work out that Branly had stolen the Bibles and that Genie was protecting her. But to what extent was Sheila O'Connell involved? Henrietta was prepared to believe that Sheila was so set on getting some twisted revenge on Lily's family that nothing was beyond her.

But the investigation no longer dominated her thoughts. In a certain way, Henrietta felt detached from all that. It was the strange foreboding in her gut that consumed her. She had wanted to discuss her suspicions of Branly's pregnancy with Lily, but so many things had come to a head that it had gotten pushed aside.

The garden listened and she listened back. The rose bush stood timidly under the glow of one lamp. 'I see you, Francoise, in every flower and leaf. You loved roses. One day, you said you would make me a patchwork quilt of multi-coloured roses.'

Was that another bud? What a sturdy bush. She opened her hands and captured a snow flake. Snow in late March was not a first, but the rose buds would never survive that. The flower was out of step with nature. Would it ever bloom or find its full splendour? Why give birth to a child and offer it little chance of survival? Would the buds return again in summer and flower?

Henrietta caressed the leaves and the thorns grazed her skin. Nature was intelligent; thorns would never turn in on the flower and pierce its heart. But no one asked humans to place a crown of thorns upon our heads, and yet we did it to ourselves.

Would Branly reach the summer of her life? Genie needed Branly even more than anyone realised. And Branly, what had she to learn – peace and acceptance?

All at once a melancholy keening rose and spread over the garden and a lonesome voice called out to her.

She listened hard but could not comprehend. 'I wish I understood your language, Jenny McCarthy,' Henrietta sighed.

Although the snow had begun to fall thickly and heavily, Henrietta saw the luminous spirit form of Jenny and her caring and kind face. Her eyes showed distress as she uttered the word *'Girls'*.

"Are they in danger? Can you take me to them?" Henrietta asked the spirit form.

But the ghostly form disappeared and another image came in its place. This time, Henrietta was shown Branly and Genie. There were dazzling lights everywhere. Branly was swaying and dancing. She was holding a drink and offering one to Genie. Then, Branly was hugging Genie as if saying goodbye, like they would never meet again. There were many people dancing around them. But standing in the shadows watching them was a tall man. In the vision, his eyes grew larger and larger and his intention was obvious to her. The vision faded.

I have to go to them, thought Henrietta. The girls are in grave danger. I do not care if everybody calls me crazy, but that man is not just a drug dealer and blackmailer – he is a killer.

Henrietta looked at her mobile phone in vain as no one answered. Where was Lily?

She rang 999 and attempted to explain to Gardaí. Henrietta stammered and knew she was incoherent. The line went dead. Had they understood her message or dismissed her as a crank or a drunk caller?

Henrietta grabbed her bag, pulled on her coat and ran down the lane into town, not stopping until she reached The Sapphire on Main Street. She wished she had younger and nimbler legs as time was of the essence.

In her vision the girls had been in the nightclub. The bouncer and staff at the ticket office looked at her askance as if she were insane. Henrietta ignored the bouncer's glare and paid to get inside. For several seconds, it was impossible for her to see or hear anything – her senses were stunned by the flashing glare of lights and hundreds of blinking mobiles. The atmosphere was charged with an electric-human mix creating a piercing, metallic sound. The girls were nowhere in sight.

Henrietta rebuked herself, 'Listen to the voice, listen –'

She heard it again, *'Go to The Treasure Chest. Hurry! Hurry!'*

She went back outside and ran to Abbey Street. Lily's apartment was in darkness. Henrietta tried telephoning again, but realised she'd forgotten her glasses. After several attempts, she gave up fumbling for the number.

She went to Lily's building and tried ringing Lily's intercom, but nobody picked it up and then she remembered that Lily disconnected the bell in her flat at night to stop pranksters from ringing it and disturbing them.

Too much time had been lost. Henrietta crossed the street and hammered at The Treasure Chest door until her knuckles were raw. But again nobody answered.

'Henrietta, you are going mad. Quieten your mind and listen to the voices. Do not try to reason or think, just follow where you are led.'

Another vision came showing her a freezing mist and a blanket of darkness. The mist whirled and through it came the voice of someone singing. It was Branly walking ahead. Henrietta followed until the form disappeared. However, Branly's direction in the vision was clear; she was heading to the Abbey Graveyard.

Close to the entrance, Henrietta stumbled and almost fell over something on the road. It was a flimsy shoe – Branly's –

The gate was locked, but Branly was tiny and could easily have squeezed through the bars. The night was still. Henrietta sensed that Branly had been here but a long time ago. Was it too late? How could she have had that vision of Branly walking? Did that mean Branly was dead? Had that been her ghost? Where did Branly go – and where was Genie?

Henrietta went into the hedging and hid as she heard someone coming. People were speaking in low voices. The cemetery gate creaked. Somebody was unlocking it. A man came through, carrying a cumbersome bundle in his arms. Sheila O'Connell was with him. The gate was shut again and they walked to a car. The man appeared to be putting the bundle in the boot. The snow made it difficult for Henrietta to see clearly, but she deduced from the banging of the car doors that they both got in. The engine revved up and the car drove away.

Henrietta came out of the hedge and tried ringing her phone again, but it would not even switch on. "Awful – stupid technology," she muttered.

A voice screamed in her ears. Henrietta called out, "Somebody help me please, help me. Tell me where the girls are, help me to find them."

'The forest – they are in the forest.'

Where had those words come from? Were they of her own making? She was no longer sure of what to do, but decided to listen to the voice and to go to Malt Hill Forest.

The roads were treacherous for motorists because of the ice and snow and only two cars passed by as Henrietta walked on. She thought of waving the second car down and asking for help, but her mind was numb and her reactions very slow – it was too late and the car had already gone. After an hour, the snowflakes fell more lightly and the white blanket on the road helped show her the way. She prayed that Lily or Sheamie had gotten her message and the Gardaí were looking for the girls.

Henrietta walked for another half hour before smelling the perfume of the conifers – Malt Hill Forest, at last. It had none of the charm of daytime; the crackling sounds, squeaks and cries of nature were more distinct. The loudest noise was coming from her chest. Her knee bumped against something hard. It was a car bumper; she felt the metal bonnet and got a faint smell of fumes.

Henrietta took the main path into the forest. But it was too dark and it was easier to use the trees to guide her way. Faltering from trunk to trunk, she went deeper inside, propelling herself towards the den that Branly often spoke about.

She listened for human noises or voices, but only heard some wood pigeons cooing.

Then the snap of a bramble alerted her, bringing her to a halt. She stayed still for a long moment and decided there was nothing. She began to walk again –

Suddenly a hand gripped her, muffling her scream. She saw the trees spin around her and everything blacked out.

Henrietta came to, confused, groggy and unable to move. Her arms and legs were tied. She saw her attackers, nearby – watching her. She tried to scream, but nothing came.

"Stupid French woman. What are you going to do with her, Pádraig Óg?" Sheila O'Connell's voice boomed.

"We will deal with Casey first and then we will dump the French woman somewhere. Old ladies die easily of heart attacks," the man replied.

"Ho, ho, of course. Nobody will care about a foreigner."

"We didn't bring her here. That damned woman came herself after the girl." The man spat on the ground near Henrietta, "But it complicates everything and I will have to leave Killdoe until the fuss is over. And you will have to keep your mouth shut. I have removed all the other Bibles from the storage room."

"Is it time to deal with Casey?"

"It is. I will get her from the car boot."

"We will have no more trouble from Hartigan. The girl was out of her mind in the graveyard."

"Hartigan served her purpose by drawing Casey to The Sapphire. I only needed one opportunity. She was too doped to even see me take Casey. It was easy to spike their drinks. Casey is the one I want. She saw me in Ryan's yard in Kinsale?"

"Ryan's yard? I don't understand you half the time, Pádraig Óg. But the Caseys are traitors and evil and they deserve what is coming to them. It is God's will."

The man grunted, "What did you do with Hartigan?"

"I cleared her from the graveyard. She wanted her blasted quilt that

I dumped in the ruins to shut her up over a week ago. She pestered me to put it there saying that the holiness of the abbey would soak into it. I forced the miserable creature to take it back and set Faelen after her. Hartigan wanted to sacrifice her life to God and said she had everything with her to kill herself."

"Then she has saved us the trouble of killing her ourselves."

"Yes, we will have no more trouble from Hartigan. We have Casey now and she's the only one I ever wanted."

Henrietta was sick to the stomach. Her face was on fire and her lungs were exploding.

The man walked away as Sheila O'Connell began reciting prayers and words in Irish. A few minutes later, he returned, carrying Genie in his arms.

"She's coming around. I haven't given her enough," he said.

"How are you going to kill her, Pádraig Óg?" Sheila O'Connell asked.

"I'm going to give her an overdose."

"Oh my beloved Lord, I give praise to God almighty. The moment of revenge has come at last. You don't know, Pádraig Óg, you cannot know how I've waited. It will be a life for a life and Daideo will be finally avenged. It is here that Jenny McCarthy carried out her treachery. The moment has come for the debt to be repaid."

"Calm yourself – calm yourself! Give me the needle. I have to do it carefully – it has to appear like an overdose."

"Here you are," Sheila O'Connell rasped.

"Switch on the torch and hold it steady. We have no time to lose – she's waking up."

In the light of the torch, Henrietta could see Genie's head turning and the face of a crazed woman looking down at her. Sheila O'Connell's eyes were devouring Genie and her mouth was foaming.

Henrietta tried to shout to Genie, but still no sounds came out.

Genie began to make spasmodic movements.

A needle glistened in the light.

Henrietta feverishly tried to stand up but rolled over.

The man held Genie down and brought the needle closer. "There's only one way to be sure of silence. If your friend hadn't stolen those damned Bibles, it might have been avoided. But they're hunting me and I won't be trapped because of you."

"Do it now, Pádraig Óg – do it now – Daideo is waiting. God is with us," Sheila O'Connell began praying.

The man turned angrily, "Will you step back, woman. This has to look like the girl did it herself."

Henrietta heard Genie cry, "Nana! Nana!"

Sheila O'Connell shouted, "To hell with the Caseys. No traitor is going to save you."

"Hold her down. The bitch is kicking."

Henrietta saw a knife flashing.

"Don't you dare try to move again, bitch!"

"Do it now, Pádraig Óg. Do it." Sheila O'Connell laughed hysterically, "This is the moment."

Henrietta shouted, "Genie, run, run." This time her vocal cords worked and her voice hollered.

Another light appeared and glowed brighter until it dazzled. Then a strong wind swept through the trees. 'We are not alone, thank God.' Henrietta prayed. 'Help has come, help Genie, please.'

"PÁDRAIG ÓG!" Sheila O'Connell wailed.

"What is it now?"

"They are here! They are angry – I see them. Can't you see them! Daniel Casey and Jenny McCarthy are here." Sheila O'Connell screamed again, "They are strangling me. Help!"

"Quiet, woman – I see nothing."

Something rumbled.

"What is that?" Pádraig Óg dropped Genie's body. "What's that noise? Run," he roared at Sheila O'Connell. "Run – be gone – get out of here. Do you hear me, run."

The sounds of brakes and engines broke the silence.

Henrietta tried to roll in the direction of Genie.

"Shit, fuckin' bikers," the man growled.

"What's going on here? Get away from her, you bastard."

There was scuffling, punching and shouts.

"Get him, mates – get him –"

For several minutes, the scuffling continued –

"We have him – take the bastard up to the den and keep watch."

There were voices, engines revving – and again silence.

Henrietta heard squelching and treading on brambles. There was a soft tread –

"Genie?"

An English voice – Peter.

"Genie, can you get up? Take my arm."

"Can't move," Genie whimpered.

Thank God, thank God, Henrietta wept – she knew Genie was safe.

"Here, let me help you up," Peter was calm.

Genie started muttering, "Nana fought off the Black and Tans and drove them off Malt Hill. She chased all of them, except for one that she saved."

"Huh, what the hell are you raving about? Blimey, you have a big mouth on you. You must be drugged."

"My Nana – Henrietta's here – God," Genie started vomiting.

"Bleedin' hell, you're not alright. It's better to puke it up now."

"I have a strong headache."

"Here, take these – here are some hankies. Let's get you home. What did you say – Henrietta is here?"

"I am here," Henrietta said feebly.

"Henrietta," Genie stumbled to her.

"Bleedin' hell," Peter went on his knees and with his pocket knife cut the ropes that bound her.

"Henrietta," Genie sobbed, hugging her.

Genie's hands were bruised and bloody and her leather jacket torn.

"I am fine," Henrietta said, "do not worry about me. You had a harder time than I had – and – we'll leave explanations for later. If that young man would help me to my feet."

As Peter lifted her up, the pain in her limbs subsided and the circulation returned. She gritted her teeth while the blood flowed back slowly. The sun was now rising and the trees visible.

She found the energy to ask, "Peter, what have you done with that man and where is Sheila O'Connell?"

"Do not worry about that man," Peter folded his arms, "we tied him up and will deal with it from here."

"Sheila O'Connell?" Henrietta repeated.

Peter looked puzzled," Was she here – I only saw the man? What exactly happened, Genie?"

"My drink –"

"Your drink was spiked. What were you doing in the club, you're a child? Peter scolded Genie like he was her older brother.

"I'm thirteen."

"You're lucky, very lucky, Genie Casey," Peter said.

Henrietta had only one thought, "Where is Branly?"

Peter was more baffled, "Didn't Branly go home from The Sapphire?"

"I don't know," Genie pushed back her matted hair. "She must be at home. Peter, ring her brother. Can we go to Ash Road, please?"

"Both of you go," Henrietta urged. "But call the Gardaí first and tell them – and ring your mum, Genie. I will wait here."

Peter looked at his phone, "I have a message from Branly's brother, Greg. He says that Branly didn't come home last night."

35

Lily was dreaming of miaows. A dog was chasing the cat and she was running after them – miaow, miaow, miaow… Genie was crying and Sheila O'Connell was striding in front of the shop. The tall security man was walking the corridor. He had the same walk and the same gait as Sheila. They were from the same family. He held a Bible towards her and Genie was running away with the Bible. Messy was calling her…

Lily woke up to the sound of banging.

"Messy, what are you doing, what a commotion?" Lily jumped out of bed to see what was causing the disturbance coming from Genie's room.

"Oh my God," Lily screamed when she saw the empty bed and window wide open –

****

Sheamie put down the phone in the hotel lobby, his eyes grave, "They haven't found them yet."

"We can't wait," Lily had enough of non-action.

"The Gardaí are looking," Sheamie said, "but they're too slow, everything's too slow. They said they had a confused call from a French woman and now they don't know where Henrietta is."

"Henrietta tried to ring me too, but I had put my phone on silent and missed her calls. Then I discovered Genie's disappearance. When I tried to call Henrietta back, she didn't answer her phone. Oh, Sheamie, we can't sit waiting here."

Sheamie took her hand.

The tick-tock of the hotel's old clock wound the minutes forward to five o'clock in the morning.

Sheamie's mobile rang. "That's the Gardaí, they might have news."

Lily put her hands together in prayer.

Sheamie stayed on the phone for what seemed like a long time. From his solemn face it was clear the Gardaí had not found the girls or Henrietta.

Finally, Sheamie hung up, "Nothing, but they tell me that they just had a report from some lads in a Jeep. "They were driving home from The Sapphire when they saw something strange."

"What?"

"Well, the driver almost crashed into an obstacle on the road. They said it was a bundle of lights."

"A bundle of lights?"

"Yes. If it hadn't been illuminated, the driver would have gone straight into it. It was right in the middle of the road."

"Were the lads drunk?"

"Apparently not. They drove on, but after a few miles, decided to turn around and come back to where they had seen the bundle. They had some doubts and thought that it might have been somebody wrapped in a blanket."

"Did they find the bundle?"

"No. They searched everywhere, but it was no longer there."

"And that's it, that's all the Gardaí have to say?"

"They are talking to other people who saw the girls in The Sapphire. There is a report that an elderly French woman was in The Sapphire too."

Lily put her head in her hands and tried to think. "Sheamie – listen to me. They might have gone to Malt Hill Forest where the gangs go. The girls could have hooked up with the motorbike gang in The Sapphire. Have the Gardaí gone there?"

"They will. They are preparing to search the forest and the river as soon as it's bright enough."

"The river!" Lily couldn't bear the thought. "We'll drive to Malt Hill

Forest right now," she ran for the door.

Sheamie took a set of keys, "My Land Rover's outside; it's better than my car for driving in these weather conditions. Let's go, we have nothing to lose; I'll ring the Gardaí on the way."

As Sheamie screeched to a halt twenty minutes later, Lily leapt out of the Land Rover and saw Peter walking through the pines, an arm protectively around Genie. Henrietta was standing farther off, her back resting against a tree.

"My God," Lily cried. They were almost unrecognisable, all muddied and dirty, clothes torn and blood everywhere...

"Mum! We are looking for Branly. Is she okay, is Branly alright? She's pregnant, she's –"

"Genie's okay," Lily had difficulty to speak. "Genie, oh Genie – oh my baby – Sheamie – my baby's safe – " she burst into tears.

Lily ran with Sheamie, half climbing and falling up the path – slipping and sliding. Her girl was okay.

"Are you hurt?" Lily held her daughter in her arms.

"No," Genie said, "I'm just bruised."

"Henrietta, are you – what happened?" Sheamie asked.

"Henrietta, you don't look well," Lily was startled by her pallor.

"I am okay," Henrietta tried to smile, putting a hand to her forehead to wipe the perspiration.

"You are not okay," Lily said. "Call a doctor, Sheamie."

"I have called everyone." Sheamie waved his phone, "Ambulance, Gardaí… Peter, I want to talk to you a second."

"Where is Branly?" Henrietta asked, turning to walk back through the trees.

"Henrietta," Lily called.

Henrietta didn't stop.

Lily caught up with her, "Henrietta, what is it?"

Henrietta's face was grey. "Do you see those?" she pointed towards the waterfall.

"I see nothing," said Lily. "What do you see?"

"I see Jenny McCarthy in that cloud of mist."

Lily saw nothing. It was like Henrietta was in a trance and talking from somewhere else, far off.

"Young Jenny is with the English soldier. I feel the love and courage of both. The couple is dissolving into the haze. And the older Jenny is here. She is holding the hand of a man. It is Daniel Casey. He is stooped and carrying a stick. There is an immense sadness in his eyes. They are both looking at the waterfall."

"Henrietta?" Lily took her arm, "I know their spirits are around here."

Henrietta didn't heed Lily and walked on towards the waterfall. She looked over her shoulder, "We did not believe her, but Branly is right – there is a rose bush near here. It looks just like the Tudor rose in The Old Forge garden?"

Lily noticed a piece of paper stuck on a broken branch. She picked it off and held it out to Henrietta. It was almost completely washed off, but they recognised Branly's sketch of her Bird of the Forest.

Henrietta said, "Get Sheamie and the others back here."

"Why, Henrietta, what is it?" Lily thought that Henrietta was going to collapse.

"Branly is – is here somewhere – we have to look –"

They searched everywhere in thickets and brambles. It started to sleet on top of them, but they continued to search more and more desperately.

"Damn, the Gardaí should be here – the ambulance should be here," Sheamie said. "What's keeping them?"

"Peter, you're hurt," Lily saw a trickle of blood on his hand. "Go back to the car and wait for the ambulance."

Peter just shrugged and continued to search.

Sheamie's phone buzzed and he gave several hurried instructions.

"The ambulance team got lost," he spoke to them. "They took the wrong entrance to the forest. The Gardaí are up at the den with your boys, Peter. You and your gang did well to tie him up and lock him in there."

"The quilt!" Genie shrieked, "Mum, Henrietta – that's Branly's quilt over there."

The quilt was coated in mud and torn, but some purples and blues were visible, and a few yellow stars twinkled.

Henrietta knelt and pulled back the material. Branly was inside, rolled into a little ball.

"Henrietta – is she alive – please tell me she's alive?" Genie stroked Branly's face.

Henrietta felt the pulse.

"Oh hell," Peter said, "she's gone, Branly's gone."

Lily looked at Henrietta.

"I do not know." Henrietta moved her fingers, "I feel nothing –"

"Henrietta, is Branly okay? Lily – is she –" Sheamie's voice trailed off.

Lily raised a stricken face and shook her head.

Sheamie looked to Henrietta. Her fingers were on Branly's wrist.

Genie took Branly's hand and tried to rub life into it. "Do something, Henrietta, please, do something. Her fingers are hard." Genie rubbed them furiously, "They aren't supposed to be hard – hard means –"

The bitter sleet fell mercilessly on them.

Henrietta looked towards the Tudor rose and touched a star on the quilt.

A hand clasped hers. 'Francoise – you are here. Help me. If there is a God, then let this child live.'

Suddenly Henrietta felt a feeble pulse flutter under her finger tips. Though faint it was beating like the wings of a butterfly.

"She is alive," Henrietta shouted out, "Branly is alive."

Sirens sounded loudly.

"At last, and about bloody time," Sheamie's voice cracked.

The medics wasted no time in getting Branly on a stretcher into the ambulance to begin immediate treatment. Genie begged to stay with Branly.

Lily picked up the quilt. It had been her last protection; but for the quilt, Branly would have perished long before from hypothermia.

"She is here, Lily."

"Who? What are you talking about now, Henrietta?" Lily asked.

"Your grandmother was never buried in the Abbey Graveyard. Jenny is buried right here. That's why your grandfather could not rest and why there was never any closure for her, for him, or for you."

"But how – how do you know, Henrietta?" It was too much for Lily to comprehend.

"Lily, I feel it. I'm sure Jenny McCarthy was buried right here. Perhaps, somebody moved her body here a long time ago."

"Oh, Lord God," Lily said, "it's crazy, but I believe you."

Henrietta prised open the damp, crumpled paper and looked at Branly's bird. "Jenny was never free. I felt it in The Old Forge and you felt something yourself."

Lily took Henrietta's arm, "Do you see that?"

Henrietta looked back into the trees, "Oh mon Dieu!"

A rope hung limply from a branch.

"Lily, Henrietta," Sheamie came towards them, "they're all gone in the second ambulance. We'll follow them in my car. What's that? Branly didn't try —

"She had planned the act," Henrietta could not take her eyes from the rope. "Something or somebody changed her mind or prevented her from hanging herself."

"Oh Lord," Lily blessed herself, "God was on our side."

36

Scarcely thirty-six hours had passed since the traumatic events in the forest, but to Lily it felt like a lifetime. So much had happened. Fortunately, both Genie and Branly appeared to be recovering fast, at least from the physical injuries.

Sheamie put his phone in his pocket and joined Lily and Henrietta at the sewing table of The Old Forge. "You were right. His name is none other than, Pádraig Óg – Patrick O'Connell. To think that he was acting as security guard in Ash Road and in Kinsale, all this time – he could have done anything to Lily."

"I knew he was strange," Lily said, "just couldn't put my finger on it. It was the walk too – he had Sheila's way of walking."

"Why did it take so long to identify a relative, even if he was a master of disguise?" Henrietta asked.

"He's not just a relative, but Sheila's son."

"No!" Lily exclaimed. "How did they keep it a secret?"

Sheamie reminded her of the story circulating about Sheila joining the nuns with her sister. In reality, Sheila was pregnant. More than forty years ago, it would still have been a terrible shame, especially in a family like hers. The father was never named. Sheila was sent away to the Poor Clares convent and kept there until the baby was born. Patrick was given up to a distant childless relative in Cork to be raised and he went off to England after he turned eighteen. Abroad he became involved in crime. The relative who raised him died two years ago, triggering Pádraig's return to Ireland. He knew who his real mother was and saw the opportunity to get into her life again and use her in his crime spree.

"How clever this Pádraig Óg was." Henrietta sat down, "He used Sheila's grudge against Lily's ancestors to get her to play along with him. It was so easy to harness her hate and let madness do the rest. He re-invented himself under many guises: money lender, security man, and giving out his sugar Bibles."

"Oh, the Bibles were a great cover," Lily said. "Stashing his drugs inside and keeping them in The Treasure Chest was clever. When I heard Branly and Genie explain about the prayer room, I couldn't believe it. Imagine that demon of a woman having her own personal chapel!"

"Where God will have his church, the devil will have his chapel," Henrietta cited.

Sheamie took out a handkerchief to mop his face and hands, "I can't bear to think of how close Lily and the girls came to –"

"Death," Henrietta finished.

Lily squeezed Henrietta's hand, "Thank God for your clairvoyance. Without it, we'd have been waiting for Curran, McGrath and the Gardaí to solve the murder."

"Peter and his gang saved Genie," Henrietta reminded them, "they were the real knights in shining armour. I hope the Gardaí will be lenient on their other activities."

"I think they will," Sheamie said. "Peter's a good lad and they weren't into hard drugs. They didn't do deals with Pádraig Óg."

"What about Kinsale – why did he overdose the cleaning woman, Mary Sheehan, in Ryan's yard?" Lily asked.

"McGrath told me that it's a complicated story," Sheamie said. "They were lovers and Mary Sheehan had a lot of things over him. She was threatening to expose him."

"Oh Lord above, it's a sad story whatever way you look at it. He killed her and we will never know her side of the story. What would have happened to our Genie if Peter hadn't saved her?" Lily dried more tears.

"Genie has borne a lot," Henrietta said, "she was also carrying the knowledge of Branly's troubles."

Sheamie pressed Lily to his chest, "We'll be there for both of them. We almost lost Branly. I don't know what you did, Henrietta, but we'll be forever grateful to you."

"I thought Branly was gone, I was sure of it." Lily looked at Henrietta, "You saved her, didn't you, you did something – worked a miracle?"

"Miracle! Do not try to put a halo over my head. I did very little. God protected her. The irony is that if Branly had not been drugged in The Sapphire, she probably would not have lost consciousness and may have gone ahead and hung herself. You know, when I came here first I thought that buying The Old Forge was a mistake and I might have sold it sooner were it not for you and the girls. I stayed for you. Destiny had its way."

"This Old Forge needed you," Sheamie said.

"We needed you," Lily qualified. "And what of that devil, Sheila O'Connell? She was there helping her son to kill Genie! Look how she messed with Branly."

"The Gardaí are out looking for her. The girls were drugged heavily and their stories are still confused," Sheamie said. "Sheila hasn't come back to her shop. They're sure that she's in the forest and they are looking for her there."

"That's not good enough," Lily said, "they have to catch her and put an end to her demon ways."

Sheamie kissed Lily on the forehead, "She can't run far, the Gardaí will get her. It's just a matter of hours."

"And Sheamie, my – Nana – " Lily began –

"I know, Lily. I might be the man around town, but things move slowly. We have to follow procedure with the law and with the Catholic Church. But I'm working on it. Fr. Sheehan has taken a shine to Henrietta and has promised to ask his hierarchy in the Church to grant permission to exhume the body, if they find it, and to bury Jenny in the Abbey Graveyard next to your grandfather."

"Do not be in too much of a hurry," Henrietta advised, "the truth will come in time."

Lily began pacing, "Did Sheamie tell you that we'll be fostering Branly?"

"I had hints about it," Henrietta smiled. Then her face grew serious, "She will need you to help her heal, and to deal with the miscarriage – "

Lily's forehead lined with worry, "I blame myself for not spotting that she was pregnant. But I was so anxious about everything."

"Don't torment yourself," Sheamie said, "I don't know anyone who would have managed better in the circumstances."

"Sheamie is right," Henrietta said. "Will you do it together – I mean foster her as a couple?"

"No," Lily said quickly, "we'll have separate roles in helping her, but she will live with me."

"That's right," Sheamie's voice was strained.

Henrietta inclined her head, "Branly is very much shaken, but she will be stronger with your love brushing off of her."

"Your love too," Sheamie said.

"True." Lily went towards her, "Henrietta, when you said buying the cottage was a mistake, what did you mean?"

Henrietta nodded to Sheamie, "Lily, I have to talk to you about something. Come into the garden with me."

Sheamie left and Lily followed Henrietta outside. She then listened in astonishment as Henrietta explained her plans to give The Old Forge to Lily and the girls and her own wish to return very soon to France. When Lily tried to protest and question these decisions, Henrietta simply waved her words away and drew her attention to what was growing in the garden.

"See my rose bush, there is a tiny flower poking its way out. A wild flower will always survive because it grows where it chooses."

"They say roses are never really wild," the grief was too strong for Lily to hide.

"Lily, I am not planning to bow out yet – just returning to France. I want you to remember me at my best. I am an old woman, but have my pride. I will telephone and write to you and the girls often, but may not be able to come back."

"Yes, I know it's the best way, Henrietta. It's just hard," Lily tried to be brave.

Henrietta laughed, "You are so like Genie." She touched the fragile rose again, "It is wild, Lily. When we plant or make a home for something, somewhere, we decide for it, we tame it. However, it does not continue to stay and grow if it does not want to, not if it is wild. Either it dies or it goes and grows its own way, finding what is best for it instinctively. People can do that too, but we have blunted our instincts and our senses. We should know where we are coming from and going to, but things get in our way. Wild flora and fauna know and remember better than we do."

Lily looked at it again. There was no mistaking that this time a flower had formed. It was tiny, white with a bashful tint of cherry red. "It's a sort of accidental shrub."

"It is wild and it is a rose. That is how I see it with my eyes and that is how I have chosen to remember it."

"Well then," Lily blew her nose, "if that's the case, then that's how I'll remember it too. What's that in the garden shed?"

"It is Branly's quilt. I have washed it, but wanted to let it drip dry. It is covered in her lucky stars. I will mend some parts of it and you will make sure she gets it back."

"It has served her well." Lily walked into the wooden hut and handled the material, "It's still damp – do you want me to have it dry cleaned?"

"Leave it for now, you can see to that after."

"This place is cosy and warm."

"I have come here often, just to watch the garden."

The gate rattled, "Henrietta, the girls are here now."

"All right."

****

Lily hurried to the hotel to find Sheamie.

"You knew," she accused.

He shook his head, "Not for very long. Henrietta spoke to me and asked me to organise about the cottage and to sort it out with her family that way."

"But," Lily wiped her eyes, "but, Sheamie, it's her family's place, it should go to them."

"Maybe, but they agree to Henrietta's wishes and there is no law against selling it cheaply."

"At that price?"

"It's all legal. The cottage will be yours, Lily – for you and the girls."

"Isn't there something to be done for her heart condition? I can't see why she's giving into it like that – with all the progress in medicine."

"Henrietta's not giving into it and can continue for some time to come. But she's very tired and needs the energy to do what has to be done back in France. Don't forget her age, Lily. She's almost eighty-one."

"But some people live up to a hundred and longer, lots of people have heart problems," Lily knew she was talking like a child, but couldn't seem to find another way of handling it.

"Oh, Lily, I don't know better than you do. I think Henrietta's been going on borrowed time, patching her body up, and it's time to rest now."

"She said there were no goodbyes, but Sheamie, if there are no goodbyes, why does her leaving hurt so much?"

37

Henrietta let them go. She never had them, but had been granted time with them. That is how it was meant to be. She smiled and shook her head, recalling that despite all the emotion and her efforts to comfort them, she had still noticed that one leg of Genie's trousers was dragging on the ground. Her fingers were damp from their tears – she looked at the creased skin and laughed as a little of Branly's glitter winked back at her.

Henrietta shivered and added a few more logs to the fire. She let her heavy lids finally drop and she went into a deep sleep.

…A terrifying howl rises from the belly of the earth. It is a diabolical sound of terror coming through the dark ages of time. All of nature shrinks. Sheila O'Connell is running, crying wildly and shouting, pouring her bile everywhere. 'He has let me down, Pádraig Óg has failed me.' Sheila tears at grass and brambles until her fingers bleed. 'It isn't possible, this isn't supposed to happen. The O'Connells have lost this battle. But it isn't over; I will take revenge myself alone. Daideo,' her cry slices through the hoary dawn, 'Daideo, I'll make her pay…'

Henrietta woke wondering if her dream were another premonition or her mind's way of working its way through the nightmarish events of the last day. Was it ever going to end? Action was the best way to wipe the horrible images from her mind. Jean would be arriving the next day and she needed to start her packing now.

It was getting dusk and she went to the garden shed for her suitcases. Henrietta hated the business of packing, but it was not going to happen without her. The weather had softened. Was winter finally over? Was this touch of spring Killdoe's goodbye kiss?

She heard a creature moving around the garden.

Henrietta walked slowly across the grass. A big dog was crouched by the rose bush. "Where is your Mistress?"

The wolfhound did not move as she approached cautiously – then it snarled –

"YOU!"

The dark figure of Sheila O'Connell faced her.

"So you have come."

Sheila O'Connell did not reply.

"What do you want?" Henrietta tried to engage Sheila O'Connell in conversation while slowly backing away in the hope of making a run for it.

"You will pay," Sheila shouted.

Henrietta turned to run, but it was too late. She did not have a chance as Sheila O'Connell's fingers twisted round her neck. Henrietta saw the woman's eyes were insane and completely possessed.

Henrietta struggled and fought against her.

Sheila's foot got caught in the rose bush, tripping her, and for a second her hands loosened their grip.

It was enough and Henrietta managed to tear herself away.

The wolfhound bounded to its feet, causing Henrietta to stumble backwards and fall towards the shed. She scrambled inside and pulled the door bolt.

Her breath was coming in gasps. She touched her throbbing throat. It was not over. They were still out there – waiting.

Henrietta listened carefully and could hear Shelia O'Connell moving around outside. Then there was a flash and a blaze of light. Realising that Shelia had set fire to the roof, Henrietta fell on her knees and covered her head with her arms. The shed was a death trap and would explode into flames. Panic assailed her. Where was the door? Her chest was hurting. Pieces of the roof fell down and her body was consumed by fits of coughing.

Sheila O'Connell stood outside watching, "That you may burn in hell, foreigner. No Casey will save you from that. Where is Jenny McCarthy's power now? The blacksmith's forge will burn down in dishonour. Hurray for the O'Connells!"

"Henrietta, Henrietta," Branly raced to the shed.

"Stupid girl. Run as fast as you will," Sheila O'Connell screamed, "it's too late. Come, Faelen," her laughter soared. She strode towards the cottage splattering petrol everywhere, "May it all burn down."

Henrietta crawled in circles. The heat was unbearable. She was in a furnace and would not survive. Smoke engulfed her. "Help," she sobbed, "this is not how I want to go, get me to the door."

Suddenly, two stars shone brighter than the inferno of flames. Henrietta moved towards them, no longer thinking, focused only on those lights. She stretched her arms until something cool touched her skin. It was if a mist had sprinkled the air and dampened the flames. The quilt had fallen over her, providing a protective layer against the fumes. She rolled in the soft fabric, inch by inch by inch, having no idea of her direction, but miraculously making it to the door. A scorching pain seared her fingers as she pulled the bolt.

Henrietta grasped at hands – Branly's – pulling her – they both fell to the ground –

Branly called to her and voices shouted over the deafening sirens –

****

Henrietta's hands were swathed in bandages, but she had survived this time. The hospital room was cool, calm and safe. They were all there around the bed.

"Will you be able to sew again?" Genie asked, putting a hand tentatively towards Henrietta, afraid to touch, in case of hurting her.

"Of course I will. The doctors tell me I will. If a hem needs mending, I will manage."

"And if you can't," Branly said, "we'll do it for you."

"Come here." She kissed them both, "Now do not cry. I am a tough lady. They are letting me out of here tomorrow."

"Girls," Lily called them, "go downstairs and watch out for the French man, Jean Bontemps. When he arrives, show him up here."

"And get yourselves something from the food machine," Sheamie gave them some change.

The girls left the room.

"Adult talk," Genie whispered.

"I know," Branly said, 'I'm not hungry, but I am curious to see Jean. Come on, we can practise our French on him."

Lily looked at the frail woman in the bed, "I washed the quilt. It isn't in great shape. It's badly singed, but a few of the stars are still shining."

"I always knew it was special," Henrietta said. She dug deep for energy and pulled herself to a sitting position, "I am still here – Sheila O'Connell did not get me."

"The Gardaí have put that crazy woman away," Sheamie said. "They caught her in the Abbey Graveyard screaming and cursing. Sheila set the dog on them, but they overpowered both of them."

"My only satisfaction," Henrietta said, "is that the damage to the cottage is minimal. Those old stones did not go up in flames. Branly had the wits to call the Fire Brigade immediately. Now we can all rest in peace."

"She's the closest to a demon that I've ever seen," Lily's voice trembled.

Henrietta pictured the eyes of Sheila O'Connell again – driven by evil – darkness seeping through the pupils. She shuddered and whispered, "May all the forces of good protect us from her wickedness."

38

"Summer holidays, at last." Branly dropped her bag, "I thought school would never end – and then making us recite that stupid prayer for fine weather. I ask you, as if that's going to order the sun to shine all summer."

"Yeah, I know. What a long day, it nearly killed me to stay sitting. Did you see the article about – you know?" Genie gave the *Evening Echo* newspaper to Branly.

They looked at the headline – MAN CHARGED WITH KINSALE MURDER—

They both read it in silence. The article explained how Pádraig Óg (Patrick) O' Connell had been charged with the murder of Mary Sheehan…

"Mum said that Sheamie and Michael McGrath put pressure on the papers not to print all the other details about us, Henrietta, Nana and the rest of it."

"I want to forget about it," Branly said.

"Me too."

They lapsed into silence again.

"What are you thinking, Genie?"

"Not thinking, but wishing. If I'd one wish, it would be that Henrietta came back to spend summer with us – you know, to see the new garden shed and new curtains hanging, go to Tralee, or to the seaside."

"Henrietta said she'll always be here. We just have to look in our minds for her and we are sure to find her. I dream of her often and see her in her beautiful blue dress."

"Henrietta never wore a blue dress, that's your imagination."

"That isn't true," Branly said, "she had a blue dress. You're not very observant, you never were."

Genie shrugged, "Mum said that her family might visit this summer and bring her granddaughter, Francoise, with them."

"That's nice, but if I ever have a baby girl, I will call her Henrietta," Branly said.

"I don't want to have any baby, not for a long, long time," said Genie.

Neither spoke for a while as different memories settled in their minds.

"You know," Branly said, "I don't think I want to be a beautician after all. I want to travel first."

"Me too. I want to go all over the world. I'll always come back home to Killdoe of course to visit Mum and Sheamie." Genie turned towards the bike roaring up Main Street and raised her hand to salute.

"He has the hots for you."

"Oh," Genie said, "Peter's okay, for a local boy, but I'm going to concentrate on study."

"Yeah, Mikie's okay too, for a local boy."

Genie elbowed her, "He still likes you. You shouldn't lead him on if you're not interested."

"He's very kind with me, but I don't love him. Love isn't free. I don't dish it out for nothing. We'll just be friends from now on."

"Sure. You heard that we all have to go to the ceremony on Sunday for the burial of Nana. It's weird to be re-buried years after."

"It's way out," Branly said, "wish I had a nana like that."

"She's yours too. You're sort of my sister now. Our nana –"

"Great-grandnana –"

"Yes, our great-grandnana was probably the most courageous and heroic woman in all these parts. Only Henrietta could equal her courage."

"Definitely," Branly said, "and Henrietta is our nana too."

"Yes – and always will be."

"We will make Henrietta proud of us," said Branly, waving her hands in the air.

They both looked up to the stone-washed sky. It was light blue with a dusting of clouds. If they squinted, the blue got deeper until it was almost black. It seemed like someone had taken the colour out and the sky had become a dark canvas decorated with white shapes and forms. It was like a photograph of bygone days.

"Where's your mum?" Branly picked up her bag.

"She's down at the bottom of the street with Sheamie. They are starting the renovations to that vacant old shop for her cleaning business."

"Charity Cleaning Business," Branly pronounced the words with pride.

****

Lily and Sheamie stood in the middle of dug up floors and stripped down walls, discussing the progress of the renovation. The former confectionary and sweet shop on Main Street would soon be converted into the hub of Lily's Charity Cleaning Business.

"Sheamie, out with it, no more secrets."

"What, Lily, what is it?"

"Maura told me you were up at Malt Hill, at the farm?"

"Is that so?"

"What's going on, out with it?"

"Look, Lily, I bought a piece of land there."

"In heaven's name – what did you do that for?"

"For you – your heritage; it's just a field and – "

"No, Sheamie, that's over – "

"What do you mean?"

"I've said it before – land is there to be passed on, farmed, shared, but not hoarded. I've let go of all of that."

"But – Genie?"

"Genie doesn't need land. She has family and that's enough." Lily suppressed a laugh – Sheamie's face looked so disappointed.

"This Charity Cleaning Business will take up a lot of time, that's enough for me."

"Are you sure?"

"Tell me, have you signed for this land?"

He nodded, "I just wanted –"

"Can't you turn it over to the community of Killdoe?"

"For what?"

"The old football field below is rough and people are always complaining about it."

"Are you suggesting we make a sports field on Malt Hill?"

"You could, couldn't you?"

"Yes, but —"

"There'd be more parking spaces."

"True."

"It could be used for soccer and Gaelic football and hurling. Isn't that the way to move forward? You could call it after the Caseys."

"Caseys' Stadium?"

"That's a grand word, but along those lines," Lily wasn't for hanging on to the past, but allowed herself some leeway.

"You'd like that?"

"Nana and Granda would, and Frank and my parents would be proud too."

"It might work."

"I can see that you need someone to keep an eye on you. If not, you're likely to get into all sorts of risky ventures."

"What do you mean?" he stood back and prepared to argue with her.

"You can't be left out of my sight. I'm going to have to keep a close eye on you, a very close one —"

"Lily, that's not fair, you —" Sheamie suddenly picked up the meaning behind her words and his face spread into a delighted grin. "You'll have to marry me so."

"Suppose I'll have to. Careful, Sheamie, we're in the middle of a building site — the tradesmen will hear us — and you're too old to be lifting me —"

Sheamie wasn't listening, he didn't care, "Is that a yes, Lily, my love?"

"Yes, Sheamie, yes I will marry you," she went into his arms.

BIOGRAPHY

KATHLEEN CURTIN Was born in Ireland in 1964. She grew up on a small farm in County Limerick. Later she attended University College Cork, where she graduated with a Ph.D in Geography.

At the age of twenty-three, having been awarded a scholarship by the National University of Ireland, she went to Paris to continue her studies at the Sorbonne. Paris has become her adopted home. Writing is her passion and she cannot imagine a day without putting words to work.

Email: kurtin@orange.fr
Twitter: kathleen curtin@kitybern
Facebook: Patching Time-Kathleen Curtin

Previous publications: Madame Lune (Thriller novel published 2015 by Open Books Publications)

www.ingramcontent.com/pod-product-compliance
Lightning Source LLC
Chambersburg PA
CBHW031249160726

47993CB00001B/83